FIRE LIGHT

TRINITY OF MIND

BOOK 1

WRITTEN BY
J. ABRAM BARNECK

Second Edition, Version 3.0 (June 14, 2026)

ISBNs
  Paperback: 978-0-9898109-4-4
  Hardback: 978-0-9898109-6-8
    Ebook: 978-0-9898109-1-3

This book has met the rigorous quality standards needed to earn the Certificate of Quality Publishing in 2026, originally 2013.

These Quality Publishing Standards are intended to raise the quality of small press and independent works.

For more information see this site:

http://scififantasyreaders.com/services/certificate-of-quality

DEDICATION

For my wife who goes crazy when I'm in front of my computer.

For Jentri who is still with us and Justine who is not.

CHAPTERS

OTHER WRITING

TRINITY OF MIND

Fire Light	Book 1
Breaking Glass	Book 2
Torched Heart	Book 3
† *Forthcoming*	Book 4

CONTEMPORARY SCI-FI

Technically Magic

SHORT STORIES & NOVELLAS

† V.I.T. (Alaina Valentine)
Drindél the Winged One
Winged Ones
* Future 7, Inc
* Mud in the Gutter

POETRY

* Post-millennial Sonnets
* Fantasy Poems
* Free-verse Poems

† Release forthcoming
* Available at: https://jabrambarneck.com/writing

A FEW MONTHS AGO . . .

I dreaded the moment Luiz dropped me off at my house just after midnight. I fiddled in my pocket for the key to my front door and minimized the noise as I unlocked it and slipped inside.

My house wasn't exactly big. With just the light from the single lamp next to the couch, I could see the kitchen, family room, and upstairs hallway, all from the front door. I walked over to the couch, expecting to find my mother sleeping on it. Yeah, she was there. It was her halfhearted attempt to wait up for me. I would turn eighteen in several months, so I didn't think she needed to fake trying anymore.

I didn't want to wake her. I knew how she'd react. Still, it was a house rule to tell her when I got home, so I shook her shoulder.

I hovered over her, waiting for her to wake on her own, but she didn't. The dim lamp cast knifelike shadows over her face like she was a creature that was only wearing my mom's body. I shook her shoulder again. She took a deep breath and turned her head. Her eyes blinked open and settled on me. Then her eyes widened, and her face trembled. She jumped to a sitting position and recoiled from me, frantically scrambling backward to the far end of the couch.

"Aaahhhheee!" she screamed, covering her face. Her breath escaped in short, quick gasps. Even her chin quivered.

"Mom. It's me," I breathed loudly. "It's just me, Jake."

She peeked between her fingers with one eye. She cursed under her breath. "Jacob. I'm sorry . . . I was dreaming about . . . and you look just like him now." She lowered her hands and looked at me with both eyes until the weight of the emotions she saw on my face forced her eyes to drop to the arm of the couch.

I swallowed the lump in my throat, burying it deep.

I heard a door open and saw the light turn on in the upstairs hallway. My stepdad, John, whom I thankfully did *not* look like, stumbled to the edge of the stairs. The image of his portly figure in boxers made me want to scream and scramble back as my mother had just done. He surveyed the situation. His droopy eyes came to life, and his eyebrows pulled together, forming a vertical wrinkle between them.

"What the hell are ya screaming for?" he shouted. "I was trying to sleep." He turned on one heel, rotating his globe-like torso, then stomped back to his room with an irritated grunt.

I turned back to my mother. Her chin still trembled on her colorless face.

I stepped to the stairs and clenched the cheap wood railing in my left hand and squeezed till my palm hurt.

"I'm going to bed." I glanced back over my shoulder, then turned and went upstairs.

I could feel Mom's ashamed eyes on me until I closed my bedroom door.

I couldn't control who I looked like.

AIM, FEEL, FIRE

Charles set his long gun case down and unlatched it. As a sniper, he'd never targeted anyone under eighteen.

Why had Caradoc dropped everything to focus on this young man? Charles didn't know, but he trusted his wise leader. When Caradoc had disappeared, Charles began following the teen. Caradoc's blood was special, and Caradoc had wanted to inject the boy with it. That duty now fell to Charles. But Charles was being watched. If he got near the young man, *they*'d sense it. How could he inject Caradoc's blood into the boy if he couldn't get near him?

The hospital would do it for him. The idea was brilliant.

He meticulously assembled his M2010 Enhanced Sniper Rifle. He took special care with the optic.

Once assembled, he set it on a table. He'd raised the table on wood blocks so it sat just higher than the windowsill. He was just under a thousand meters from West Jordan High School.

Charles took his time aiming the rifle at the entrance doors, setting the crosshairs at thigh level. He didn't want to kill the young man. He only needed him to lose enough blood for the doctors to order a transfusion. He didn't need to worry whether they'd use Caradoc's blood. He'd already taken care of that.

The young man always left school with his friend. The tracking software on the friend's new phone showed they were still inside. He'd know when they approached the door.

Charles waited for nearly an hour, the rifle tight to his shoulder, before the tracking software showed his friend moving toward the locker room. Any minute now. An hour wasn't long for a sniper. He'd waited longer in real combat.

Charles picked up his burner phone and dialed 911. When the operator answered, he said, "A boy's just been shot at West Jordan High. Send an ambulance." He hung up.

At this distance, the odds of hitting a thigh were slim, even for an expert. But Charles wasn't *only* an expert sniper. The energy flowed around him. He felt his aim like a breeze passing over freshly cut hair. Some called his accuracy *magic*.

The instant Jacob Stevens stepped outside, Charles fired.

CHAPTER 1
BULLIES

There was something about seeing a helpless geek getting pushed around that I couldn't stand. Some indescribable desire to protect him bored its way inside of me and grew until it was ready to explode out of my chest like a little baby alien. The right kind of setting could enhance this desire and the back side of the high school near the dumpster during summer vacation sure was the right setting. If I hadn't happened by, only the dumpster would have witnessed their atrocities against . . . uh . . . who was this kid again? Honestly, I couldn't even remember his name, so maybe I was just as bad as the three bullies looming over their trembling target.

They had their backs to me so I stepped toward them, careful not to make noise as my shoes touched the pavement. I recognized the poor, picked-on boy as a member of the band. What instrument did he play? He was little, even for a sophomore. He reminded me of myself a few years ago. He had brown hair like mine and the same thin and frail-looking body I had had until just before my freshman year. I wasn't frail anymore.

The redheaded bully grabbed at him, trying to pick him up. They weren't content to let the dumpster witness their attack. They planned to include it in their evil ways, and the dirty rust bucket seemed more than happy to oblige. It had one side open and seemed to be begging the bullies to feed it the pathetic little music maker for its meager meal.

Two of the bullies had thick bodies, and I was pretty sure I knew them well, but the alien desire to protect the kid allowed me to ignore that knowledge for now. One bully was taller than thick, and he stayed back. I watched the other heavyset bully step forward and try to assist the redhead in grabbing the little band kid who thrashed and pulled away, leaving his hair sticking up awkwardly.

I hadn't been forced into a fight for over a year. I hated fighting. Mostly, I hated taking punches, and there was a good chance I was going to take a few before this was over.

I found myself near enough to grab the tall bully that was hanging back when the poor kid's brown eyes turned toward me and blinked. Sure, he was already scared, but when he saw me, his eyes quivered, and his fear increased until it dripped down to his trembling frown. He expected me to join in on tormenting him.

The tall boy turned to see what the kid was looking at. Unfortunately for him, he was the bully I reached first. He'd turned just in time to see my fist flying mercilessly at his face. He didn't have time to dodge before my knuckle connected just under his right eye. His head whipped back, and he made a grunting sound before collapsing to the ground. The skin on my knuckle split open, and instantly, I felt wet blood dripping into the thin ravine between my middle and ring fingers.

I wondered whether I would have let my fist fly so freely if I had really taken time to see who I had aimed it at. The answer to that was yes. Deep down I'd known who I was punching all along even though this alien growth of an emotion inside me that demanded I protect this poor kid tried to keep their names from my conscious mind.

Jason's eyes widened in surprise to see Mike crumple to the pavement in front of the dumpster. Being a left tackle on the football team, it was in his nature to protect Mike at all costs. Even if it meant defending him from me, the star running back. Jason dropped his shoulders and lumbered his overweight figure into my chest.

Unfortunately for Jason, he was also a wrestler and must not have grasped the concept that this was not a wrestling match. There were no referees around to blow the whistle and deduct points from me for raising my knee while shoving his head down. Knee, meet face. Jason's nose cracked. The left tackle let go of me and twisted away, reaching for his face. I helped him along, shoving him to the blacktop with both hands.

Then I felt the fist crash against my temple. My head jerked to the side, and two lightning streaks of pain shot into me: one into my brain and one down my neck. I raised my forearm to block the redhead's second swing. Gunther played center. He was big, and my right arm nearly gave out under his. During football games, Gunther often drew a yellow flag from the ref for blocking with his fists. I'd wondered what it would feel like to be on the wrong end of his illegal fist blocks. Now I knew. Good thing he was on my team and usually blocking *for* me.

I jumped back, anxious to never experience one of Gunther's fists again.

Gunther stepped toward me but stopped. Mike had stood and put his hand out. His eyes spread wide as if in fear, but the way his upper lip lifted slightly indicated disgust. He glanced at the band kid who now looked at me with rhythmic blinking. Then Mike's cheeks relaxed, and his mouth dropped. Shame reflected in his eyes. Guilty conscience? Did I mention Mike went to church with me? He'd been taught better. He hadn't even realized until this very moment that he was actually bullying the poor brown-haired, stick figure sophomore.

"Sorry, Jacob." Mike's hand reached up and touched his right cheek.

"Maybe you should skip weightlifting today." My voice came out as a growl through my clenched teeth. "Take the weekend off if you want," I added. "But you better be here Monday morning." I swallowed, more for the need to clear the fluid in my mouth than for any real emotion.

Jason stood up, holding his nose. The blood flowed freely between his fingers.

"Help Jason," I ordered Mike. Then I turned my back on the three of them and walked over to the band kid. The need to protect the kid vanished as abruptly as it had arrived. The only difference between my unnatural desire to protect and *The Alien* was that this emotion didn't *actually* rip a hole in my chest on the way out. That and Sigourney Weaver wouldn't have to track it down and kill it.

A pair of glasses lay on the ground. I picked them up and handed them to the boy. I put my hand on the boy's shoulder and he stiffened, then relaxed.

"You're going to be fine," I encouraged. "There's nothing to worry about now. They won't try again."

"What about you? Will you be fine?"

"Me?" I asked hesitantly. "Why wouldn't I be fine?"

"You just punched our star quarterback."

Smart kid. I ruffled his hair.

CHAPTER 2
WATCHED

"And ten," Luiz said as he grabbed the bench press bar I was holding and guided it to the rack. "Wow! Three sets of ten at two-twenty-five. Jake, your muscles must be on Miracle-Gro," Luiz declared. "If you don't feel sore *mañana*, then you're not normal. Some government agency is going to lock you up for some pokin' and proddin'."

I never should've told Luiz that I didn't get sore after working out. Luiz didn't realize it, but normality was my holy grail. His comment about pokin' and proddin' had pushed me further from it.

I sat up and brushed my sweaty brown hair out of my eyes. I glanced around at the high school weight room. Other than Coach Ferguson, we were the only boys left. Coach slipped his keys out of his football jacket and spun them on one finger. Coach usually had a relaxed face under his baseball cap, but today he clenched his jaw impatiently. Keeping him here late wasn't the best way to say thank you for opening the weight room for us every afternoon. Luiz and I had finished working out anyway. We yelled a thank you and hurried to the locker room.

Some of the other boys must have showered because the locker room air felt damp and sticky. It smelled like old socks, too.

I stripped off my sweaty tank top, and Luiz smacked me in the chest.

"Why you always gotta show off your muscles?"

Luiz was my best friend. I was young when Luiz's family moved from Mexico to the Salt Lake Valley and eventually settled right here in West Jordan. I barely remember when he and I first met. He'd always lived just around the corner.

"Hey, you want to play Xbox at my house?"

"No, I gotta work," Luiz reminded me. He worked at the Taco Time down the road—the one just past Ninetieth South.

My shoulders sank in disappointment. Luiz cracked a grin. "You mock my pain!"

He forced a fake frown and tapped a fist to his heart. "*¡Pobrecito!*" His fake frown made him look older, like his dad. Luiz was about five-ten, three inches shorter than me. He was thin and wiry—though his muscles had started to take shape over the last year. He had his dad's long nose and kept his black hair cut short for summer.

"You were supposed to say, 'Life is pain!'" I replied, giving him a friendly shove.

"Oh, I missed that reference," he laughed.

I slipped a T-shirt over my head. It stretched over my chest and felt a little tighter than before. I'd been putting on muscle fast this summer. Freakishly fast, actually.

"I can't believe you punched Mike." Luiz shook his head. "Do you think you broke Jason's nose?"

"They'll be fine," I shrugged. Had I gone too far defending the band kid?

"You want a ride? I have my mom's car. I'm going to shower here." He grabbed a towel from his bag.

"No, I'll walk. See ya."

"*¡Luego!*" he called to my back.

Once he was gone, I glanced around to make sure I was alone. I stepped on the scale that stood against the wall. I slid the weights further right until they balanced. 202 pounds. I stared at it.

As I walked through the high school halls, I shoved some earbuds in and turned on some music. I was surprised Dylan hadn't been part of the trio torturing the band kid earlier, but come to think of it, he hadn't been as obnoxious the past two years.

I stepped outside the high school doors. *Ouch. What the . . . ?* I rubbed at the skin on my chest. It felt like something had hooked my skin there and tugged. I scratched at it with my nails, but when I peered down inside my shirt, nothing was there. Still, the tugging on my skin wouldn't stop. I had no idea what it was. I tried to ignore it and started walking south down the sidewalk toward home. It stayed with me for about a block before going away.

A minute later, I'd forgotten all about it.

CHAPTER 3
HOME

Thirty minutes later, I was home, standing in front of the blue door to my house. The newer brick homes made the tan siding and the peeling shutters on my house look worse than they really were. We had the best tree in the neighborhood, an apricot tree, but that was because it had twenty-five years on the trees in other yards. Too bad the apricots choked the grass, leaving it thin under the tree.

I hesitated to open the front door as my mind attacked me with all the reasons that suggested I should find somewhere else to go. If only Grandma were still alive.

I took a breath and opened the front door and stepped inside. I could smell steamed rice. Mom busied herself in the kitchen, already cooking dinner. I'd forgotten it was Friday. She didn't work Fridays.

Mom had her light brown hair pulled back into a ponytail. She wasn't exactly overweight, but she often complained that her short height made extra pounds harder to hide. The built-in fan above the stove blared loudly, which was why she hadn't heard me come in. Mom glanced up, not expecting to see me standing there, and flinched.

Yes, she flinched.

She recovered with a smile. I loved my mom's smile. Except lately, her smiles were fake to cover up her flinching. It wasn't me that scared her. It was who I reminded of.

I forced a smile back, "Hey, Mom. What's for dinner?"

"I'm making chicken and rice casserole," she replied.

We chatted a bit like nothing was wrong, and maybe nothing was wrong. Maybe Mom could push her memories to the side. I wasn't sure, and I didn't want to ask.

As we ate, the awkwardness between Mom and John was distracting. They must have had another fight today because they didn't say a word to each other. John kept his eyes on his plate, and the only sounds came from scraping forks and chewing. Mom glanced at John with a pained expression. John never looked up, not even while getting himself a second helping. My mom was near tears when John left the table. A simple thank you would have made her day.

I finished off the rest of the casserole, which was another three helpings. I could eat more than anyone I knew—a lot more.

Mom never noticed my split knuckle, or if she did, she didn't say anything.

Except for my shower, the evening didn't get better after dinner. My mom went off to read a self-help book. I have never seen much improvement in her after reading one, so I've never read one myself. Reading a chapter or two must have motivated her to try to talk to John, which resulted in an hour-long yelling match in his den. I drowned it out by playing Xbox with the over-the-ears headset on.

Two hours later, I begrudgingly put the game console away and pulled out my laptop to watch film of last year's football games. I normally shied away from attention, which is why I played running back instead of quarterback. I wouldn't even have played running back if I'd known how much attention it would bring me. I would've quit, but the idea of getting a full ride out of here was too tempting to pass up—especially since a couple colleges started recruiting me last season.

As I watched the game film, I analyzed the defensive scheme and determined where the running hole would most likely open up before unpausing and watching the play. It was a total jeek— part jock, part geek—way of analyzing a football game.

When the scholarship did come my way, I planned to make sure I never really played. I could imagine the news article: *Shocking Story of Star Running Back's Conception.* No way I'd let anyone find out about that! I'd slide by on the bench and disappear into a normal life. I wouldn't even feel guilty about taking a scholarship from some Rudy out there who really wanted to play. OK, I'd feel a little guilty.

After a while, I got sick of watching game film, so I grabbed the remote and turned on the TV. The History Channel came on with somber music. A voice spoke solemnly from the speakers. "Last year on July twenty-fourth, over one thousand people all over the world left their homes for work—many of them well-known political and business leaders—not knowing they would never return home again." The incident had dominated the news for the past year. The president's face flashed on the screen. "The Day of a Thousand

Deaths is the worst act of terrorism since Nine-Eleven." I'd seen that speech live at Luiz's house. I watched a few minutes of the documentary, mildly interested, before changing the channel.

Just before midnight, I started watching a college chemistry class that a BYU professor had shared on his YouTube channel. No, I wasn't enrolled in college. Watching this before my senior year started was my trick to an easy A in AP Chemistry.

If football doesn't get me out of here, my brain will, I thought.

About halfway through learning about the nucleus of atoms, Justine came home from her Friday night date. Sis was short, blonde, and thin—which was perfect since she danced for the drill team. She knocked before entering my room. She rolled her eyes at my streaming choice, then picked up my to-do list of game-film to watch and shook her head as she read the label.

"You're such a jeek," she said, laughing.

"Yeah, I am," I conceded. "How was the date with Austin?"

Her grin switched to a grimace, and she ran her fingers through her straight blonde hair.

"Come on, Jake. It was Nathan," she complained. "You know Austin and I ended things after the Fourth."

Actually, I hadn't known that, but I played along.

"Oh, yeah! Nothing like fireworks to end a relationship. Was it *sooo* romantic you just couldn't take it?"

She scowled at me.

"Or maybe you were too hot for him to control himself. You didn't let him past first base, did you?" I teased, laughing.

She didn't laugh. Her face froze for a second. *Oops.* I had joked my way to the truth. She was going to try to play it off, but I didn't let it go.

"What move did he make on you?"

She didn't want to tell me, but we were pretty close. The secrets between us were few. She spilled. "We were making out, and he slid his hand up my shirt." The dimple on her right cheek showed up, which only happened when she was embarrassed.

"Oh . . . he had a solid base hit. He tried to steal second . . ."

"But I threw him out!" she finished for me, grinning slightly.

It was too bad. She had liked Austin. My sister wasn't that type of girl though. She went to church every Sunday, dragging me along whenever she could. She was the type who was going to wait till marriage. Austin supposedly shared her beliefs, but his hormones must have trumped his belief system that night.

"Sorry, Sis," I said and meant it.

"For what he did or for you being insensitive about it?"

"Both."

She smiled at me and shrugged.

"He's lucky he doesn't play football," I added. I didn't like the idea of him messing with Sis. "So how about this Nathan guy?" I asked, changing the subject.

"He was fun but . . ." she paused. "I don't know. Nothing there with him, I guess."

"Was the dinner at least good?" I asked.

"Oh, heck, yeah! We went to Ruby River."

"Loaded, huh?" I asked.

"No, he used a fifty-dollar gift card his dad got from work. Nathan only pitched in a few bucks."

"Ah," I nodded.

She went to the kitchen, which wasn't exactly a separate room.

"You want to pause that and watch a movie?" she asked, pointing out my bedroom door to the family room. "I'll make popcorn."

I followed her out to the family room and pulled up Netflix while she microwaved popcorn.

"You pick something," I suggested.

She brought the popcorn back and reached for the remote. Her eyes fixated on the split in my knuckle, and her hand switched targets from the remote to my hand.

"What's this?" she asked, pulling my split knuckle in for a closer look.

"Mike, Jason, and Gunther," I said their names as if that explained everything.

She raised her eyebrows. "They were picking on you?"

"No. Some skinny band kid."

"And of course, you felt an overwhelming desire to protect him. That hasn't happened in a while."

I nodded.

Sis dropped the subject and grabbed the remote. She picked a romantic comedy—the latest with Taylor Lautner. OK, it wasn't really a comedy, but it made *me* laugh. She fell asleep about twenty minutes in, her head on my leg. I kept watching until it ended, which was about two in the morning. OK, maybe I did like it more than I let on. I slipped my leg out from under my sister's head and threw a blanket over her.

I love my sister. She was the only part of my home life that didn't suck.

I went upstairs to bed.

I had that same dream again. My biological father, who looked exactly like me, stood before me. I couldn't see anything around him, just him. He wore a simple button-up white shirt and jeans.

"You've turned out like me," he grinned. "A freak!" His face had smile lines like mine but deeper, only his grin corrupted his features.

I watched him, unable to pull my eyes away.

"Can you do this yet?" he asked. He held his hand up, whispered some words I didn't understand, and flame flickered up from his palm.

I stepped back, surprised, yet knowing from previous dreams what was coming.

He lifted the fire to his lips, and as if blowing me a kiss, he blew the flame toward me. The fire burst out from his palm, engulfing my body.

CHAPTER 4
SCRIMMAGE

Saturday I woke up from the dream just after 6:00 A.M., so wide awake I couldn't stand to be in bed anymore. Yes, I only slept from two to six—that was the norm these days. I once told my sister about my new sleep habits, but she had shrugged it off. I haven't brought it up again.

In most places, the further east you live, the sooner the sun hits your house in the mornings. In the Salt Lake Valley, the tall Wasatch Mountains shade the east side—the rich side—until after eight. So, opposite the rest of the world, the further west in the valley you live, the sooner the sun hits your house. I don't live on the rich east side. I live in West Jordan. So even this early in the morning my room was nice and bright.

I threw on my gym shorts, a tank top, and running shoes. I stopped in the kitchen to grab a bit of cereal and a Gatorade before setting off on foot toward the high school football field. Yes, on foot. A few years back, some drunk in a company delivery van rear-ended my stepdad. Even though he has money from his settlement, he made it clear that Sis and I would never get a dime of it for a car. Mom gets some from him for Sis and me, though. Enough to cover my date money. She couldn't swing a car, which was fine with me. I liked the exercise.

My knuckle wasn't so split anymore. After a single night, it had scabbed over, and the scab was loose, about to fall off. I tried not to dwell on the fact that none of my friends healed as fast as me. I shoved some earbuds in and started running toward our high school while listening to some Chris Daughtry.

Unfortunately, it was Saturday, so the turnout for our unofficial football practice sucked. Mike actually showed up, black eye and all. I nodded at him as if I hadn't smashed my fist into his face yesterday. Jason and Gunther were no-shows. Even with Mike playing quarterback for both teams, we barely had enough for five-on-five, so we didn't have running backs. That forced me to play receiver. Luiz showed up, but the other jeeks didn't. They must have stayed up gaming all night. Luiz was on the other team. He was a pretty good receiver, but a better cornerback. He did a good job of keeping the ball out of my hands all morning. The jerk.

"Next touchdown wins," Luiz called because it was almost time to go.

It was fourth down and my team's ball. I stepped to the line of scrimmage. I could smell the wet grass and feel victory in the air. "Hike," Mike yelled. I sprinted ten yards downfield and cut inside. Mike threw the pass my way, and I reached for it, but . . .

"*¡Bloqueada!*" Luiz waved his finger at me after batting down the pass. "It's our turn now!"

On the other team's first down, I stepped to the line, guarding Dylan, a fast, defensive player who was also filling in as a receiver. Dylan was a pretty good middle linebacker, but he lacked drive to play at the next level—and lacked the brains to be a jeek. I followed him uselessly down the field and watched the pass go the other way to Luiz. He caught it and spun around his defender, a nice juke move, allowing him to run the rest of the way to the end zone.

"Goooooooooaaaall!" he shouted, acting like it was soccer and sliding on his knees while stripping his shirt off. I went ahead and yelled and clapped for him. His team tossed some high fives his way, and a minute later, we were all on the sidelines taking off our cleats and getting drinks. As I untied my shoes, Dylan and a couple of his friends were talking about going wakeboarding later.

It was strange to think Dylan wasn't bigger than me anymore. He was still thicker than me, but I had him by two inches. Back when Luiz and I were in junior high, before we turned our geekdom into jeekdom, Dylan used to make fun of us. Now he was always trying to hang out with us. We jeeks started calling kids like that *barnacles*, because they cling. Dylan used to be the worst of them and the primary inspiration for the term. I didn't want to start hanging out with him now, but wakeboarding was too tempting to pass up.

I sat back on the grass with my arms behind me and let the morning sun hit my face. "I love wakeboarding," I called over.

"You want to come, Jake?" Dylan asked.

"I don't know," I said. "I want to come, but I was going to hang with Luiz. It's his day off."

"Luiz can come too," Dylan called back.

Wow, that worked?

"You in?" I turned and asked Luiz.

"I'll come, but I'll drive separate. I'm on call for the evening shift tonight. They might call me in for some emergency taco making," Luiz laughed.

"Tell us where to meet you," I told Dylan.

Dylan put one hand through his sandy brown hair. His eyebrows lowered and pulled together. Was he disappointed that I wouldn't be riding with him?

"We're going to Jordanelle Reservoir. Come around noon and call me when you get close so I can tell you which beach we're at."

Neither Luiz nor I had a cell phone, but my sister got one a few months back when she turned sixteen and started dating. I was definitely bringing her. No way would I let her suffer an entire Saturday alone with Mom and John. Besides, nobody ever complains about an extra girl—especially since my sister was what the other guys called DDG: Drop-Dead Gorgeous.

Ouch! What the . . . ? I grabbed my chest as something tugged painfully at my skin. I looked inside my tank top, but again, I found nothing there but sweaty skin. I should know what this feeling meant. It seemed like . . .

Am I being watched?

I had no clue why the tug made me feel watched, but it had. I looked around and didn't see anyone until I caught sight of an old, white Chevy truck parked across the street. Coach Ferguson sat in it. He wasn't allowed to coach us until August—state high school rules—but nobody could stop him from watching us. We'd been practicing all summer long, and I hadn't seen him before. Had he been watching us every day and I never realized?

"Hey, Luiz," I said, nodding toward the truck. "Coach saw your touchdown." Everyone looked and waved.

He made a hand gesture. At this distance, he either flipped us off or gave us a thumbs up. It must have been the latter.

I should have noticed that the tugging on my chest remained well after Coach drove away.

CHAPTER 5
WAKEBOARDING

Wakeboarding was awesome! I wished I could pull off X Games-like stunts, but I've only wakeboarded a few times. I did get a little crazy and tried to do a flip, which my sister caught with the camera on her phone.

Sis shivered as she wrapped her towel around her shoulders. The slight breeze wasn't strong, but it was cool enough that with her hair and swimsuit wet, she had goosebumps. The sun would be up for a few more hours. It would warm her up soon enough.

The Jordanelle Reservoir sat in the middle of some tall, rolling hills so there wasn't much beach. However, Dylan's family had chosen a nice, sandy area that wasn't too steep. The reservoir was big enough that the breeze created some small waves that splashed rhythmically against the hills. Dylan's mom stood under a pop-up canopy, making sandwiches for all of us while his dad took out a few of the kids who'd been waiting their turn.

Sis sat down on the beach blanket, let the towel fall around her waist, and held up her phone with a paused video of me on the screen. "Check this out," she called.

All of us crowded around behind her to watch me on the phone's tiny screen. I practiced little jumps over the wake, then took an aggressive approach and kicked off the rising water with a jump and a twist. Except halfway through my rotation, I landed headfirst into the water. My feet and the wakeboard flung forward and splashed a wave of water into the air.

Everyone responded with a mix of cheers and laughs. I had sucked in a mouthful of water, too, but that wasn't evident in the video.

"That crash was wicked cool," Dylan commented.

"Glad you liked it," I flashed him a grin.

Sis shed her towel and started reapplying sunscreen. I wrinkled my nose at the chemical smell. I've never used sunscreen, and not just because I don't like the smell. My skin tanned almost as dark as Luiz's—in the summer at least. I don't remember ever really being sunburned.

I thought Dylan would bug Luiz and me all day. Instead, he spent the day treating Sis like gold. He'd offered her a water bottle on several occasions, and he'd helped her both on and off the boat. After Sis wakeboarded, Dylan had a towel ready for her to wrap up in after I lifted her out of the water. Now that we were back on the beach, he was sticking to her like Velcro. Surprisingly, I didn't mind—which was partly because Sis didn't mind either. As long as he treated her better than Austin, I wouldn't have to knock him around during football practice.

"So what books do you like to read?" Dylan asked Sis.

"I don't know. I am trying to read all of Jane Austen lately," Justine replied. She brushed her wet hair behind her ears and lifted her face to the sun, trying to warm it.

"What are you reading now?" Dylan shifted on the blanket, moving a few inches closer.

"*Persuasion.*"

"Really? Did you know that Jane Austen never once described what Anne Elliot looks like?"

Whoa! Since when could Dylan speak Jane Austen? I may have been wrong about Dylan being too dumb to be a jeek.

Dylan's mom paused making sandwiches. "You've read Jane Austen?" she asked.

"Yeah, uh . . ." Dylan stammered, "I was forced to read it in English class last year."

Liar! I had English with Dylan last year, and that book was not part of it. He'd read it on his own. I didn't adopt Dylan into the jeek club or anything, but I wouldn't ever see him as a clingy barnacle again.

It took Dylan a couple more attempts at conversation before he finally got up the courage to ask my sister out.

"There's a youth fireside tomorrow about six. You want to come with me?" Dylan asked my sister.

"Yes, I want to go," Sis beamed.

Once Dylan looked away, she nudged me with a wide smile that reached her green eyes.

Go, Sis.

Luiz tapped my shoulder and quietly asked, "Is a fireside a church thing?"

"Yeah," I responded.

He nodded.

"Sandwiches are ready," Dylan's mom called from under the pop-up canopy, and we all grabbed a sandwich.

As I took my first bite, I felt a trembling below my skin. I'd never really felt it before, but I knew something was wrong.

"Excuse me," a gruff voice rumbled into the canopy. We all looked up and noticed a park ranger, green uniform and all, stepping toward us. The ranger had a wicked scar cutting vertically above and below his right eye. Despite the scar, his eye was perfectly intact.

"What is this about?" Dylan's mom stepped between the ranger and us teenagers as if her motherly instincts also detected something was wrong, and she planned to protect us.

"We've received reports of a creepy old man in the area." He pulled out a picture that had a close-up of an old guy with a full head of white hair.

"Have you seen this old man?"

"No," Dylan's mom replied.

"What about you kids?" the man asked, holding up the picture for us all to see.

We all shook our heads.

The ranger gave a smile, which only made the strange sensation I was feeling under my skin worse.

"Well, if you see him, give us a call." He handed Dylan's mom a card, then turned and left. The weird sensation under my skin faded as the man walked away.

We stayed at the lake until dusk approached. It took us an hour to dock the boat, wipe it down, and pack everything up, and then another hour for Luiz to drive us home. When Justine and I walked in our front door, the lights were off and Mom was clearly in bed already. The door to the den was closed, but light seeped out the cracks. Was John hiding inside looking at porn? Sis and I crinkled our noses at each other.

Sis went straight to bed and crashed right away. I watched the second half of the chemistry class. I couldn't bring myself to study any film of past football games, so I played Xbox with headphones until two, then I crawled under my covers.

CHAPTER 6
CHESS

On Sunday, my split knuckle itched. I rubbed my wound and found no scab, just a pink scar. I tried not to think about how quickly it had healed.

Mom and I grudgingly agreed to head to church with Sis. Justine could be pretty persuasive, especially when the other option was to stay home with John. I used to go about once a month, but lately, I went more and more because it was another excuse to get out of the house.

The three hours of church came and went painfully. I was relieved to step out of church and breathe in the outside air—at least until I felt something tug on my chest.

Ouch. I rubbed at my chest through my white church shirt. *Who's watching me now?* Everyone was leaving church, and there were too many people to pick out one pair of eyes in the crowd. A mom was running after her little boy, shouting at him to stay out of the parking lot. I could hear the chatter of people talking and cars starting. I tensed, wanting to get out of there fast, but the only place to go was home, and I would trade going home for being watched any day.

The tugging on my chest snapped as we drove the half-mile to my house. I wished the drive were longer than a half-mile, but churches in Salt Lake are like gas stations; there's one on almost every corner.

As we walked into the house, John was watching golf in the front room. I'd been hoping he would be hiding away in his den when we got home. That left me without the Xbox or the DVR. I swore under my breath.

"Hey," Sis said, smacking me on the arm.

"What?" I responded. "Isn't golf a swearing sport?" I laughed.

Mom witnessed our interaction and glanced at John. She took a breath, then asked, "John, could you watch that in your den?"

He glanced back at Mom, his eyebrows pulled low. "The hell I will," John shouted.

"Don't swear at me!" Mom shouted back.

Uh oh. This was going to be another yelling match.

My sister and I hurried upstairs. I wanted out of my shirt, slacks, and tie as soon as possible anyway. Mom and John shouted back and forth for about an hour before John shut himself in his den. Not for the first time, I wished John wasn't in our lives. We'd make do without his settlement money.

I pulled off my church clothes and put on some shorts and a tank top. Sis knocked. I let her in. She'd put on her comfy, pink pants. Her white camisole was the same one she'd worn under her dress to church. I shut the door behind her because I could hear Mom and John still yelling at each other.

Sis and I watched a movie in my room on my laptop. I let her pick the film again. She chose an old Eighties chick flick called *Some Kind of Wonderful*. Sis caught me smiling when the main character Keith gave Watts the earrings.

Sis had her date with Dylan that evening, and I was unwilling to venture into the war zone downstairs, not even to play Xbox, so I went over to Luiz's and played chess against him and Mr. Espinoza, his dad. I tried really hard to win; I really did. They took turns playing me, and they each checkmated me twice.

"The trick, Jacob," Mr. Espinoza offered, "is to always have a second way to attack." He spoke with a Spanish accent, saying *ees* instead of *is*. Mr. Espinoza was thirty pounds overweight and had the same black hair as Luiz, but Luiz, at five-foot-ten, had outgrown his dad by a couple inches.

"Always have a second wave of attack planned," he continued. "If your first wave is blocked, use your second. Then always have a last resort. Three waves." This suggestion went beyond chess and blended into the challenges of life.

"I can barely mount a good *first* wave of attack," I laughed. Honestly, I wasn't that bad. I could hold my own against anyone else on the school chess team except Luiz. "I want to see you play each other," I told them.

"*¡Por supuesto!*" Luiz answered, and they started a game. Luiz still hadn't beaten his dad—ever—but their chess match was taking longer than all four of mine put together. Decades ago, Luiz's dad supposedly beat the number one ranked chess player in the world. I paid attention and learned a few moves for next time.

After they'd traded a few pieces, Mr. Espinoza started coughing hard, and Mrs. Espinoza came in and helped him up. She was a short round woman with black hair and soft, motherly eyes.

"*Discúlpanos*," Mrs. Espinoza said, excusing them both as she helped her husband to the kitchen. I glanced at Luiz, but he didn't say anything. He concentrated on his next move.

"Is everything OK?" I asked when they returned.

"Fine," all three of them answered at the same time. But Mr. Espinoza didn't look fine. His face looked pale, and his eyes were droopy.

"Why don't you play for me, Jacob?" Mr. Espinoza suggested, and he and his wife headed to bed.

"Is your dad OK?" I asked Luiz again.

He looked away from me as he spoke. "Yeah, he has *la gripe*." That meant the flu. "Take over for my dad." Luiz pointed to the chess set. "You might win."

"I'll try."

I survived longer with Mr. Espinoza's setup until, "You're forked!" Luiz laughed, using the chess version of the F-word. He took my queen with his knight. I hadn't seen it coming. It went downhill after that. Luiz wiped my pieces one by one. "Checkmate!" he grinned at me.

We hung out for another hour chatting about football and girls and our upcoming senior year before I headed home. I played video games on my laptop till 2:00 A.M. before checking if Sis got home from her date with Dylan. She was already asleep, so I went to sleep, too, and happily did not dream of my biological father.

CHAPTER 7
EVIL

Monday morning started at the football field. Official practices were only a couple weeks away, so the turnout was improving. We had full teams—eleven-on-eleven plus some subs. It felt like someone was watching me the whole time even though Coach's truck never showed. The constant pulling on my chest distracted me, and I didn't play well. It was a frustrating morning.

Luiz dropped me at home afterward. We made plans to find some trouble to get into later with the other jeeks, and he took off. I walked into the house and knew something was wrong. If my muscles had slightly trembled Saturday at the Jordanelle Reservoir, they were downright crawling now.

Am I sensing . . . evil?

As I walked upstairs, I could hear my mom's muffled curses at John over the hum of running water in the background. The water came from the bathroom in the hall, not the master. Sis must be awake and showering. Mom and John fight all the time, but it seemed different today. John wasn't really fighting back, which was way out of character. Also, my mom should have been at work.

"Keep your dirty mind in your den, you filthy—" my mom continued cursing at him viciously but keeping her hissing voice low. "I spill coffee on my shirt," Mom continued in a low growl, "and I come home to this. If I ever catch you looking through that hole again, I'll report you, and we both know that between my call and what's on your computer, you'll go to jail."

Looking through what *hole?* I wondered.

I heard the shower turn off, and Mom stopped talking abruptly. Normally, I fled from their yelling matches, but this one drew me in. My mom started talking again even more softly, but her voice still hissed at John, making it just loud enough that I could hear her outside their bedroom door.

"If anyone ever found out the kind of filthy Peeping Tom you are—" She rattled off a few more expletives, all directed at John. Then there was another two seconds of silence before she spoke again. "We won't tell anyone," she snapped. "It never happened."

Oh!

John had been caught looking through a hole in the wall—from the master bathroom to ours—while my sister showered.

I froze in place.

At that moment, Mom and John both stepped out of the master bathroom and into view of the hallway where I stood like a statue staring into their bedroom. Mom flinched when she saw me, and she stopped breathing, her mouth hanging open. She composed herself, walked to the closet, and pulled a shirt from a hanger. Then she started walking toward me.

"Don't you mention a word of this to Justine," Mom growled through clenched teeth and pointed at my nose. "I have to get to work," she spit the words out as she slid out the doorway past me. I listened to her walk downstairs and go outside. The car started and drove away. I turned back to John. His upper lip twitched up in disgust—whether disgusted at what he'd done or at getting caught, I'd never know.

"Listen to your mother." He frowned all the way down to his double chin as he walked past me. I listened to his heavy footsteps as he headed downstairs. Then I heard a door close. He'd locked himself in his den.

My mom was going to bury this. She wanted to pretend it never happened—like my unwanted conception. She should know by now that bad things don't just *un*happen. I was her proof of that. Every muscle tensed up inside me, fueled by hate toward John for what he had done and anger toward my mom for wanting to bury it. Too late, my fists clenched. I should have punched John. Instead, I stood frozen like a coward. I didn't move for several minutes. The hum of Sis blow-drying her hair pulled me out of my daze. I finally went to the bathroom door and knocked.

"Jake, is that you?" Sis yelled over the blow dryer.

"Yeah," I managed.

The blow dryer turned off, and she opened the door—a pink towel wrapped around her. Only a small section of her blonde hair was dry. Images of John watching her forced their way into my mind—my muscles crawled under my skin again. My sister was completely unaware of what had just transpired. I should have told her, but my mouth remained shut. She smiled at me.

The smile made me feel even guiltier for not punching him—or telling her what he'd done.

"I'll blow dry in my room," she offered, crinkling her nose at me. My grass-stained tank top clung to my still-sweaty chest. I'd just returned from football and needed a shower, but I was too distracted to think about that. I opened my mouth to tell her what had happened. I wanted to tell her she had been violated, that this house was not a safe place for her anymore. My mouth opened, then closed.

"Thanks," it was all I could say.

She unplugged her blow dryer and grabbed a few things and carried them to her room.

My stomach turned like I was about to throw up, but it didn't happen. That was the closest I'd ever come to throwing up since . . . well, I couldn't remember ever throwing up. I stood inside the bathroom door for some time before I finally moved to the shower.

I immediately investigated the state of disrepair the bathroom wall was in. Besides cracked paint and moldy corners, the drywall had a couple of fist-sized holes that had been there as long as I could remember. I had a vague memory of John trying to fix a pipe back when I was just a kid. But the holes were only in the sheetrock on our side of the wall. I didn't remember being able to see all the way through to Mom and John's bathroom or surely we would have patched them by now. I examined the holes closely. There were holes on the other side but they were small, nail-sized holes. We'd made a pinhole camera in science class a few years back. Just like a pinhole camera, nobody could see through the tiny holes unless they were in Mom and John's bathroom and put an eye right up next to one. How long had the nail holes been there?

Oh, no! How likely was it that Mom caught John on his first offense? The muscles under my skin crawled even more.

As I showered, a numbness took over and swelled up from somewhere inside me, pushing away the crawling under my skin. I finished up and went to my room and dressed. The need to protect my sister took control of me. I thought about running away with her, but I had nowhere to go, and she was barely sixteen. Maybe if she were turning eighteen soon like me then that would work.

I could fix the wall.

I latched onto that thought. I grabbed my backpack, walked out the door, jumped on my bicycle, and rode for three miles until I reached the nearest home improvement store. I spent every spare dollar I had on stuff to mud and paint the bathroom. I fit most everything into my backpack—except the paint can. Riding back with a heavy paint can hanging from one handlebar was awkward. It fell to the ground twice and dented before I finally made it home.

The house was eerily silent. My sister had gone to her friend Kendra's house, and John was hiding in the den, so I didn't have to explain the paint to anyone. Without waiting, I got started. I wasn't very good at patching the drywall. I couldn't get the mud to smooth out, but I didn't care. I just slapped more on. The mud was supposed to dry for over twenty-four hours, but I didn't want to wait until tomorrow, so I went to my sister's room and retrieved her hair dryer and rigged it to blow on the splotches of mud, then I moved everything I could out of the bathroom. The waiting was killing me, so I went to the master bathroom and patched similar holes.

It took me a couple of hours to get everything that wasn't supposed to be painted taped up and protected. I didn't have enough plastic, so I used some trash bags to finish covering some edges. Another hour later, I gave up waiting for the mud to dry and painted the first coat in our bathroom. After that, I painted the first coat in my parents' master bathroom.

One coat looked crappy, but I didn't have any more paint or any more money. I don't know where I got the courage, but I walked into John's den without knocking. He was at his computer, and he quickly minimized whatever had been on his screen. His desk was a pile of papers and junk food wrappers that he hadn't thrown away. I had to step over a few things to approach him.

"I need two hundred dollars." I impressed myself by not allowing my voice to waver in the slightest.

He swiveled in his computer chair and gave me the eye like he was going to tell me where I could shove my request. But his eyes shifted from my face, and he took in the splotches of white paint all over me. It was hard to tell with his double chin, but I think he gulped. Maybe he was nervous I'd turn him in.

He turned back to his desk and opened the top left drawer. He rifled through it before pulling out a checkbook and a pen. He wrote me a check right then and there. The creep didn't say a word. He handed me the check and swiveled his chair, turning his back to me. I should have asked for more.

A little over an hour later, I was back home with enough paint for two more coats. I immediately put the second coat on. I didn't want to wait hours for the paint to dry, so I used the blow dryer again, this time by hand, moving it up and down the walls.

Unfortunately, I started smelling the blow dryer overheating, and shortly after, it suddenly stopped. I had to go searching, but I found a desk fan in the pile of junk that took up one spot in our garage. I plugged it in and held it up, letting it blow against the wet paint.

Driven by the need to protect my sister, I didn't care about the tediousness of the work. I kept at it for hours. It was the only way I could cope with not punching John and not telling my sister. I felt dirty. I questioned my lack of action because it made me feel like an accomplice.

I'd started the last coat of paint when the floor creaked. I looked out of the bathroom, paint roller in hand. My sister appeared in the doorway.

"Jake?"

I opened my mouth to say something, then closed it. My mind wanted to say this: "I had to fix the holes in the drywall because your creepy stepfather gets his jollies by watching you shower." However, my mouth fumbled and didn't really say what my mind thought. Instead, only one word came out.

"Hey."

It's a good thing I didn't say more because Kendra stepped into the doorway just behind Sis. Four inches taller, she could easily see over Sis's shoulder. Her smile reached her blue eyes, and she tossed her long, golden brown hair behind her, as oblivious as Justine to John's act. She'd stayed the night here dozens of times over the past few years. How many times had she used the shower? Had John ever . . .

I'll kill him. I squeezed the handle of the paint roller until my knuckles went white.

"I didn't know you were planning on painting our bathroom today." Sis actually pouted her lips a little like she used to do when we were kids. "You didn't even let me pick the paint."

My mouth fell open. John had been watching her naked in the shower for who knows how long, and she was worried about the color of paint. The plastic handle to the paint roller cracked in my hand, and I felt it cut into me. It wasn't her fault; she didn't even know. I was the jerk who wasn't telling her.

"Sorry," I managed.

"No worries," she conceded. "It looks great anyway. Doesn't it, Kendra?"

"I like the shade of white you picked," Kendra spoke up, her voice shattering my numbness. "Get his picture with your phone," Kendra laughed. "You should see yourself, Jake."

I glanced in the mirror. My hair, my face, my shirt—
everywhere was covered in white dots of paint. *Click.* I heard Sis's
phone snap my picture.

"Mom's home," Sis added. "She's cooking dinner, and it's a
Monday. She never cooks on Mondays."

My reply was nothing more than a grunt. If Sis or Kendra
noticed something was wrong with my mood, they didn't say
anything, but walked on to Sis's room.

"You have to send me that picture," I heard Kendra say.

I skipped dinner and kept working. Mom saw what I was
doing and decided to avoid me and let me do it. Luiz called. He
was with the other jeeks, but I blew them off. I couldn't get the
thought of what John did out of my mind. Who would want
images of their sister showering running through their head all
day? Let alone deal with the added creepiness of a peeping
stepdad. My muscles writhed under my skin with a renewed
frenzy, and I wanted to scrape out the evil that caused it.

It was midnight before I finished the bathrooms. As I scored
the tape with a box cutter and pulled it off, I basked in what I'd
accomplished. I had patched the holes and put three coats of
paint on both bathroom walls. In the corners, a few paint drips
proved I'd used too much paint. Brush lines were visible where
I'd tried to paint behind the toilet. A professional painter would
say I'd done a terrible job. Still, it was a huge improvement on
how it looked before.

As I stepped in the hall, the silence of the house settled over
me. I walked downstairs. The lights were off. A blanket covered
a body on the couch. It was Mom. Had she slept there to avoid
interrupting my work? I decided against trying to wake her.

Light escaped the edges of the door to the den. John was still
hiding out in there. Sis, who had gone out with Kendra and some
other friends, was due back at any time.

The urge to protect my sister still possessed me, though, and as
much as I had done, it didn't feel like enough. I needed to do more.

I felt driven back upstairs, past my room, and into my sister's
bedroom. She was vulnerable there too. I looked at every wall, in
every corner. No holes in the drywall. Nothing that John could
use to spy on her. I turned the light on in her closet and checked
every inch of it. I breathed a sigh of relief. It was stupid of me to
look in her room. Two walls were exterior walls, one separated
her room and mine, and the other was partially the linen closet
and the hallway. I hadn't thought it through.

"What are you doing in my closet?"

I jumped. I hadn't heard Sis come in.

"I . . . uh . . . I'm thinking of cross-dressing," I tried to make a joke to deflect her curiosity, but my voice—which came out flat—wasn't really in it.

She eyed me as she walked toward me. She stopped inches from me, reached her hand past me into the closet, and lifted out a dress. She held it up to me. "Jake, you're over six feet and two hundred pounds. I'm five-two and a hundred and fifteen pounds. It would get shredded," she laughed.

I didn't laugh back. I couldn't. The compulsion to protect her overwhelmed me and took hold of my mouth.

"Be careful of John from now on," the words finally came out. "Never be alone with him again. Ever." The guilt flowed out of me with each word.

Sis froze. Her eyes fixed on my paint-spattered body, then they slowly dropped to the floor. It didn't take a jeek to figure out why I'd patched and painted the bathrooms. She crossed her arms over her body defensively. I watched her eyes dampen. I wanted to say more, but I didn't want to talk about it. I couldn't look at her without remembering John's act, which led to unwanted mental images. She needed a hug, and I left instead because thinking of what John had done made me feel like a creep too.

I walked to my room and closed the door.

CHAPTER 8
FRIENDS

Tuesday morning, I skipped football. I wasn't going to leave Justine home alone with John. Justine woke up at seven, which for her, was extra early. She showered, dressed, and got ready for the day. We had breakfast together in silence. She didn't ask why I had skipped football this morning and I didn't offer. I had three bowls of Frosted Flakes and Sis had one bowl of Lucky Charms. What went through her mind while she showered? I sensed a new awkwardness between us, which confirmed that she had figured out the gist of yesterday's atrocity. We couldn't figure out how to start a conversation without bringing *it* up, but neither of us wanted to talk about *it*, so we said nothing. I wanted the awkwardness to go away as soon as possible. I wasn't sure if it would take minutes, hours, or days.

What if it takes longer?

I couldn't take it if the awkwardness between my sister and me never went away. I hated my home so much. After grandma died, I had thought I couldn't hate it any more than I already did. I had been wrong.

The silence between us hurt my brain and dragged on past breakfast. She went upstairs to finish doing her hair. I sat on the couch, my mind unwillingly going over everything that happened yesterday. Even though I had fixed and painted the wall between the bathrooms and told her to avoid John, my actions felt inadequate. I had planned to watch TV, but half an hour later, I was still sitting there thinking when Sis came down. She walked over to the couch and sat next to me. She didn't move for a second.

"You make me feel safe," she whispered, and all at once she laid her head on my leg and started crying. *Man, I love my sister!* For the second time, the idea of killing John crossed my mind, but my sister needed me more than John needed to be murdered, so I pushed those thoughts away and stroked her hair.

"One year for me, and two years for you," I said. She knew I meant how long till we could move out. We'd been sharing that comment for a few years. This time, she cried harder. Why . . . Oh! I swore in my head. I had helped her realize that after next year, she'd have to live here without me for another long year. We needed a distraction, and we needed to get out of this house, at least for today.

"Want to see if Luiz and Kendra are up for going rock climbing?" I asked.

She sat up and wiped away the tears with her hands.

"Yeah," her voice cracked, and she laughed at herself in the strange half laugh, half cry that only a girl can pull off.

We made a few calls. Luiz couldn't come, but Kendra could. I called the other jeeks and both Ethan, the math genius, and Kevin, the coder and computer whiz, wanted to come. A half hour later, Kevin picked us up in his new Hyundai Tucson that his dad had recently bought for him. The license plate read BSD4ME. Both he and his dad were software developers—like father, like son.

Sis and I had backpacks filled with our climbing gear. We also had a rope bag. Kevin stayed in the driver's seat, but Ethan got out and grabbed Sis's gear. The speaker system rocked a Creed song from Kevin's smartphone. We threw our stuff in the back, and I conceded the front seat to Ethan and sat in back with Sis and Kendra. I sat on the right, Sis sat on the left, leaving Kendra in the middle. Ethan looked a little disappointed in the front seat. Maybe he was hoping to sit by Kendra. While I didn't prefer her hair in two braids, she was looking as hot as usual. She wore a sporty tank top and tight spandex dancer shorts that ended mid-thigh.

Oops. I was staring.

I looked up to see Kendra's blue eyes watching me stare.

Double oops. She caught me.

I turned away and pretended I hadn't been looking. As my sister's best friend, Kendra was off-limits for me, but not for Ethan. I'd ask him later if he was interested.

Rock climbing doesn't get much better than in the Rocky Mountains. It took half an hour to get to the trailhead in Big Cottonwood Canyon. Green leaves topped trees that lined the creek and stuck out from natural cliffs while the man-made cliffs had been cut bare to make way for the winding road. We went up and hit a climb called *The Slips*. Being July, the runoff had already come and gone, so the creek was not life-threatening like it was in the spring, allowing us to walk over the rocks without even getting wet. The trail to The Slips was short and wound around a crag for a few hundred yards. With so many small rocks in the path, we took care to avoid them and step on the carpet of dried pine needles that had fallen from tall spruces. A couple squirrels darted across our path. The hum of cars disappeared, replaced by the rustling of pine needles and water trickled under the rocks in the now-hidden creek.

Once at the cliff face, Ethan and I donned our harnesses first. He put on his climbing shoes while I hooked up my belay device to one end of the climbing rope. When we were both ready, he lead climbed the easier route on the right, clipping into bolts every eight feet or so while I belayed him. Lead climbing has some danger to it. You have to climb above the bolts you clip into. That means if you are eight feet above your clip, you can fall sixteen feet before the rope catches you—more if the rope has a few feet of slack.

When Ethan reached the top, he clipped in before threading the climbing rope through the steel anchors and chains that had become as permanent a part of the cliff as the rock itself. Then he tied the end of the rope to his harness.

"Take!" Ethan yelled.

"Gotcha!" I yelled back, and Ethan unhooked his clips and moved to a sitting position, his hands holding the rope. He pushed off the rock wall. I felt his weight as he dropped a few feet, the rope stretching.

"Lower!" he called down.

"Lowering!"

I lowered him the rest of the way down pretty quickly.

Now that the rope was up, the girls could climb top rope. Unlike lead climbing, there was less danger if done right—and we did it right. The only dangerous part of top-rope climbing is trust. A partner belays you. If you fall, and they don't belay you, you can fall all the way to the ground.

Ethan hooked up Sis and prepared to belay her. He made sure her harness was tight and the strap was double-backed so the harness wouldn't come loose. Her gear checked and ready, Justine moved to the rocks. She dipped her hands in the chalk bag that hung from her harness.

"On belay?" she asked.

"Belay on," Ethan replied.

"Rocking."

"Rock on!" Ethan laughed. We were supposed to say "climbing" and "climb on," but our way sounded cooler. While Sis climbed top rope, Kevin belayed me as I lead climbed a more difficult route to the left.

Sis scrambled to the top in a few minutes. Girls make great climbers because they are smart enough not to rely on upper body strength alone. They have smaller feet, and they don't weigh much. My lead climb was hard, so Sis was already down and Kendra was starting up when I reached the top. I clipped in and threaded the second rope through the anchors before tying it into my harness.

I was about to call down to Kevin when I felt a familiar tug on my chest. Kendra was at the top of her climb and looking over at me smiling, but the tug came from back toward the road. This was the first time I felt like it had a direction. It was time to ask Kevin to lower me down, but I hesitated. I took some time to examine the trail, trying to look through the tall spruces to see if someone was there.

"You all right up there?" Kevin yelled after a minute.

"Yeah," I called back. A couple of climbers were coming up the trail. I tried to convince myself it was them, but the tugging originated from a location higher up and farther away.

"Looks like we have company," I yelled down. I watched the other group of climbers approach for a second before I yelled, "Give me a second."

I closed my eyes and tried to relax. I took a deep breath. Then another.

"Jake," I heard Kendra call over.

Her voice triggered some kind of trance. My eyes remained closed, but I could see Kendra and myself as if I were floating in the air ten feet away from the cliff—an out of body experience.

"Lower!" Kendra yelled, and then she jumped from the wall. Her harness wasn't connected at her waist. Why was it left undone? Her hands, damp from sweat and no sign of chalk on them, slipped from the rope. She tumbled. Her head hit the rock face, knocking her unconscious and leaving her hanging upside down.

I watched her harness slide to her knees, catching there.

I yelled, "Get her down quick!"

The harness slid to her shoes and caught again as Ethan lowered her eight feet—nowhere near far enough or fast enough. Her feet slipped out, and I watched Kendra fall, headfirst to the rocky ground.

The trance ended, and I found myself back in my body, against the wall and holding the rope. I glanced over at Kendra, and she was still there looking at me. Her harness was not latched, and her hands didn't show any sign of chalk.

"Kendra," I whispered, then gulped, afraid my vision would come true. "Why is your harness undone?"

She glanced down and tightened her grip on the rope.

"Put some chalk on your hands," I suggested.

Hesitantly, she let go with her left hand and reached to the chalk at her back. Then she switched her grip and chalked her right hand.

"Lower," she yelled.

"Lower," I yelled down, too.

Kevin lowered me while Ethan lowered Kendra. We both made it down and off the rope in seconds, without anyone falling to their death. Shaking a little, I took off my painfully tight climbing shoes. I grabbed the cooler and guzzled some water, fighting to keep my shaking arms from splashing water all over my face.

"Give me some of that," Sis demanded, pulling the cooler away as I drank. Water splashed down my chin and down the front of my dust-covered white shirt. She laughed. It was a hot day, so a little wetness was just good fun. It took the nerves away that my strange premonition had left me with.

"Pay more attention," I told everyone. "Someone forgot to check Kendra's harness."

We climbed a couple of hours till everyone rubbed their forearms, too tired to climb anymore. We made our way back down the trail to Kevin's Hyundai Tucson sometime in the mid-afternoon.

"I'm going to be so sore tomorrow," Kendra rubbed her forearms as we drove back. She sat in the middle again between Sis and me. I should have thought to let Ethan take the back seat.

"Me too," replied everyone simultaneously—everyone except me. I didn't think anyone noticed that I kept quiet. I didn't want to bring any attention to the fact that I've never been sore. Good thing Luiz wasn't here. My smile fell away as Luiz's comment about being locked up for some pokin' and proddin' flashed through my mind.

The conversation continued, but I checked out—which means I stopped listening, forgot where I was, and let myself get lost in a memory.

It was the start of the second half of the first game of the playoffs last season. There was an early snow that melted during the day, leaving the field muddy. The second half kickoff came my way. I stepped into some mud as a tackler jumped on me and my right shoe sank. Another tackler arrived, pulling me to the ground. The problem was, my foot was stuck in a few inches of mud. I screamed as pain exploded from my ankle. The mud gave

35

way in time to prevent the bone from breaking, and mud catapulted twenty feet into the air.

I tried to get up, but I couldn't put weight on it. It was my first sprain ever, but I knew it was bad—season-ending bad. I needed help off the field and didn't play the rest of the game. I couldn't walk the rest of the night. Luiz had to drive me home and help me inside.

When Kevin sprained his ankle our sophomore year, he ended up not playing for six weeks and missed more than half the season. It should have been the same for me. But it wasn't.

The day after the game, a Saturday, it didn't feel much better. However, I could walk on it by Sunday. I sat out practice on Monday, Tuesday and Wednesday, but by Thursday, I couldn't even tell my ankle had been sprained. I told Coach it must not have been as bad as I thought. But . . . I was lying.

I played on Friday night like nothing had happened.

Part of me was happy to play again, but another part wished the injury had put me out for the season because I didn't want to be a freak. Maybe it was instincts, but I knew that my fast healing had something to do with my evil biological father. That was when my nightmares about meeting him started—the ones where he tells me I am a freak.

"Remember that, Jacob?" Ethan asked. He was laughing. So was everyone else. His phone now sent a Maroon 5 song over the speakers.

"Huh?" I said, feeling stupid because I had no idea what they were talking about.

"Man, you weren't even listening," Ethan complained.

"Yeah, someone was having an out-of-body experience," Kendra said looking at me. "Where did you go in there?" She pointed at my brain.

Sis's smile faltered, assuming I was thinking about what John had done.

"I just remembered my sprained ankle last season," I said quickly to save my sister from spiraling into her own John-centered emotional abyss.

"Uh . . . OK," Kevin replied. "So laughing our heads off reminds you of past injuries. Good to know."

Everyone laughed at me. I tried not to let it bother me. I forced out a fake smile. A few minutes passed, and everyone moved on to who was dating whom over the summer and if the relationships would last into the school year.

Kevin pulled into our neighborhood a few minutes after four. Too bad I didn't want to be home—not even a little bit.

"Hey, let's keep up the fun. What are we doing after dinner?" I threw out as we passed the houses that were newer and nicer than mine. The big tree in front of our house stood out because it was the biggest in the neighborhood. All the other houses had new yards and trees only a few years old.

"Are you skipping the weight room today?" Kevin asked.

My sister tensed up and cast her eyes my way. My mom wouldn't be home yet, and I couldn't leave her alone with John.

"Rock climbing was our workout today," I replied. Sis blinked and then smiled, and I could feel her relief.

"I'm up for something," Kendra replied, looking at me.

"Yeah, we are," Sis jumped in with some extra enthusiasm, glancing at Kendra then at me.

"I got some dinner thing with the family tonight," Ethan replied.

"I'm out too," Kevin added. "Call Luiz. He worked the day shift and is probably dying that he missed climbing."

"OK. We'll catch you later," I said as I got out of the small SUV.

"Thanks for the ride," Sis added.

I expected Kendra to follow, but she stayed in the back seat.

"See ya, Justine. See ya, Jake," Kendra said as they drove off.

"Wait, didn't Kendra say she was up for hanging out tonight?" I asked with too much interest.

"Yeah. She said to call her after dinner," Sis told me, a teasing smile on her face. I was about to question my sister about that smile when something pulled at my chest and distracted me.

Who's watching me now?

Kevin's Tucson turned the corner and the purr of its engine faded out. No cars were coming or going the other way. Two girls, not yet teenagers, were playing down the street. One of them laughed, but they weren't looking this way.

"Did you forget something?" Sis asked.

"No. Let's go inside."

As I closed the front door, the pulling sensation on my chest snapped like a broken string.

CHAPTER 9
OFF-LIMITS

I didn't want to shower because I didn't want to go into the place John had desecrated. The shower still represented John's act, which I preferred not to think about. I forced myself to shower anyway—chalky hands, dirty and sweaty body—a shower is required after rock climbing. I made it out in record time. If it was awkward for me to shower, it had to be more so for Justine, and she went in right after me. I wished there was something more I could do to help her, but short of punching John, I'd done all I could already.

Sis had left her phone on the arm of the couch, so I called Luiz with it.

"Hello."

"Hey, Luiz. How was work?"

"Greasy. I need a shower. Hey Jake, *te llamo* right back, OK?"

"OK," I responded, and he hung up.

I didn't recognize the number that he called back from.

"Hello," I answered.

"Now you have my new cell phone number," Luiz replied.

"You suck," I complained jealously.

"No, I work. Get a job, you lazy, white trash piece of . . ." He proceeded to call me some bad names. Don't ask me why guys sometimes do that. For some reason, because we're best friends, swearing at each other is allowed. It doesn't make sense, but we do it anyway.

"So, are you up for hanging out tonight?" I asked after I told him to shut up and called him some bad names right back.

"*¡Cómo que no!* What's the plan?"

"Don't have one. Call when you're ready—like in an hour or sooner."

"OK."

We hung up. I saved his number in Justine's phone.

I flipped on the TV and went into the kitchen to cook dinner. I went simple—spaghetti. On the five o'clock news, a blonde reporter stood in front of the Jordan Valley Medical Center, only a mile from my house, and reported that a break-in had occurred there and at three other nearby hospitals. The story caught my attention as I threw some water on to boil and put some hamburger meat in a frying pan. The only item found stolen: A rare type of blood called Bombay—it lacks all normal blood antigens *and* has a strange antigen discovered in the Fifties.

Mom came in the front door. She saw me in the kitchen, but she glanced away quickly to hide her eyes.

"Hey, Mom," I called, ignoring the way she hid her eyes. She didn't want to hear the question I was about to ask, but I asked it anyway. "Didn't you once tell me that my blood type was Bombay?"

Mom froze.

"Your pediatrician detected it. You were . . . you needed . . . extra tests," she chose her words carefully. She didn't like to talk about my birth. Actually, it was my conception that bothered her.

She glanced away from me to the TV and caught the end of the news story. Only four people per million had Bombay blood type, according to the newscaster. Another way I was a freak.

"I have spaghetti," I said, not wanting to disturb Mom further. She turned the TV off and set the table with awkward silence. I was mixing the sauce, hamburger, and noodles when Sis came downstairs, her hair still wet.

Mom asked John to sit up for dinner, and he had the nerve to accept, making dinner awkward. He talked with my mom over our spaghetti like he'd done nothing wrong. Thankfully, they left Sis and me out of their conversation. Mom treated him extra nicely tonight. She should be furious at him. She should be doing whatever she could to keep him away from Sis, but she flirted with him like a new boyfriend and . . .

Oh. My mom was trying to fix things her way. A wife way. *Oh, crap.* I wasn't letting my mind any closer to that thought. I started counting my bites as I ate. I finished my plate and scooped myself more—a lot more. I kept counting the bites. It was either eat more and count bites or throw up for the first time in my life. I finished my third plate before Sis finished with her first.

"Let's get out of here, Sis," I said as I dropped my plate in the sink.

I rushed her through her last bites, anxious to be as far away from John as possible. Sis didn't need to be asked twice to get out of there, even with wet hair. Mom didn't ask where we were going, and we didn't offer. We didn't have a car, and we didn't know where we were going yet, but Sis grabbed her bag, and we walked out the front door.

Our neighborhood was alive with summer fun. Kids played in our street, enjoying the overcast evening; their shouts and laughter merging with the hum of the distant busy streets.

"Luiz's or Kendra's?" Sis asked.

"Either," I replied.

"Let's go to Kendra's then. I can finish my hair there."

We walked the few blocks to Kendra's house, the clouds keeping the July heat to a minimum. Sis flipped her hair back and forth trying to dry it. She glanced at the clouds and frowned. Her hair didn't dry before we rang Kendra's doorbell. I liked the clouds. I wasn't even sweating.

Kendra answered the door. She had on a skin-tight shirt and a pair of plaid shorts. She'd traded in her braids for a long, straight hairdo that fell softly around her face and down past her shoulders. I'd seen her in that shirt during the school year, but she had filled out since I last noticed . . .

Oops. I was looking.

Kendra's blue eyes looked at mine, which were lower than they should be.

Double oops. She caught me. That was twice in one day.

"Come on in," Kendra said with a big smile aimed at me. "Do we have a plan, yet?" she asked as we slipped by into her air-conditioned house.

"Not really," Sis replied. "It's a no-plan night."

"Just us?"

"No, Jake called Luiz, and he'll call my cell when he is ready. He got a new cell phone."

"It's like a double-date." Kendra's smile grew bigger, if that was possible, and it was still directed at me. She was flirting with me. I liked it. *Uh oh!* My sister's best friend was forbidden fruit, and she'd kill me if I went there.

"Don't tell Luiz that," Sis replied. "Jake says the jeeks are off-limits for me."

"Hah!" Kendra replied. "None of the jeeks are off-limits to me." Her eyes didn't leave mine.

"Lucky you," Sis replied and winked at her. She and Kendra shared one of those inside-joke moments, and unfortunately, I was outside.

"You're starting something with Dylan anyway, aren't you?" Kendra reminded her.

Oh, yeah! I had forgotten to ask Justine how her date with Dylan went. I should have asked yesterday. *What distracted me . . . ? No! Don't think about that.*

Sis's cell rang, saving me from thinking about Monday and our stepdad. Sis looked at the caller ID.

"It's Luiz," she said and handed me her phone.

I answered, "Hey Luiz," putting the cell phone on speaker so that everyone could hear.

"Hey, Jake. I'm bringing Andrea," he warned. "I just have to swing by and pick her up."

"Oooooh, Andrea!" Sis and Kendra said in unison, then giggled.

"I see I'm on speaker," Luiz laughed. "I should have texted."

"Yeah, we are all at Kendra's, so come over here."

"OK, see you in a few."

Kendra's house had an immaculate room set up for visitors directly inside their front door on the right—the Nice Room. We chatted in there while waiting for Luiz and Andrea to arrive. Her parents were pretty strict about having visitors stay in the Nice Room, and they had a curtain barrier separating it from the rest of the house. Sis and I had seen the rest of the house. They had a harder time keeping it clean.

Kendra and my sister kept chatting, and I wanted to be part of it, but I couldn't find a way to join in. It drove me crazy. Fortunately, Luiz and Andrea finally knocked. I took the liberty to open the door. Luiz held Andrea's hand, which sent Sis and Kendra into a short giggling fit. Andrea glared at the girls, clearly not enjoying the attention. She was a senior and a cute brunette, geeky and curvy, exactly Luiz's type. My sister and Kendra danced on the drill team—the popular girls—the type Andrea usually stayed away from.

Luiz glanced at Andrea and back at the girls. "Do we know what we are doing yet?" Luiz asked, giving me a let's-move-it-along look.

"No," we all replied in unison.

"We could go to the Gateway and hang out there," Kendra suggested, meaning the local mall. "We can window shop, or hit a movie, or whatever."

"I know. Let's take swimsuits and hit the splash pad," Sis suggested.

"That's for kids," Andrea complained.

"That's what makes it fun," Sis responded, oblivious to Andrea's increasing level of annoyance.

"*¡Al verte mojada!*" Luiz winked at Andrea.

"Don't speak Spanish at me!" She glared, as unsure as I was as to what he had said. Luiz smiled back, and Andrea melted under his smile. "OK, fine, but I'll have to go back home and get a swimsuit."

"No, wait. I have a swimsuit for both of you," Kendra offered. Andrea, though older, was shorter than Kendra but heavier. How would one of Kendra's suits fit her? Sis was shorter, but the same slender build, and could fit in any number of swimsuits Kendra had outgrown.

"Come on upstairs," Kendra said with tiny excited claps.

As Sis and Kendra stepped through the curtain barrier, Andrea focused her wide eyes on Luiz, begging him to save her.

"Be nice," Luiz mouthed silently to her. Andrea let out a grunt and reluctantly followed the girls through the curtain. I heard their footsteps go upstairs toward Kendra's room followed by the mildly scolding voice of Kendra's mom. "Kendra, you didn't say you were going to have a new friend over. I would have cleaned up."

I laughed.

"They'll have to try them on," I indicated in the direction the girls had gone, "and that will take a while. Let's go get our stuff while they're up there."

"I'm up for joining them. Maybe they need our opinion as they try them on," Luiz smiled in jest.

I ignored him and walked out the front door.

"What?" Luiz laughed, following behind me.

I wanted to say, "My creepy stepdad ruined your joke for me, that's what," but I kept the comment to myself.

Luiz had borrowed his parents' Hyundai Sonata and we jumped in it and swung by each of our houses to get swim trunks and towels before returning to Kendra's.

Girls are never fast, especially when trying something on, so we waited another twenty minutes before they came down—still in regular clothes. Andrea came out of the curtain first and widened her eyes at Luiz as she approached him and then whispered in his ear through clenched teeth, "Never again!"

Sis and Kendra came out shortly after. Sis carried a large tote decorated with blue flowers. Towels stuck out of the top of it. She'd obviously found time to dry her hair.

"Let's go," Kendra suggested, and we all followed Luiz to his car. Luiz opened the door for Andrea. Kendra ended up in the back middle seat again with Sis and me on each side of her. The back seat of Luiz's car wasn't as roomy as Kevin's Tucson, so it would have made more sense for Sis to sit in the middle. Maná—Luiz's favorite rock band—blared from his speakers as he started the car. Someday I'd get him to translate their lyrics for me.

My shoulder and arm, bare in my sleeveless sports shirt, pressed against Kendra's equally bare arm. With her hair so close, I could detect the lavender scent of her shampoo. I tried to ignore both the touch and the fragrance. *I can handle it. It's only a mile to Trax,* I encouraged myself.

Trax is Salt Lake City's light rail system. Luiz needed to save on gas because he had to pay for it himself. Once at the Trax station, I opened the door, slid out, and walked halfway to the platform before I found myself alone. I stopped and looked back at everyone else still getting out of the car. Luiz grabbed my forgotten towel and swimsuit. As he walked, he tried to shove his stuff and mine into the girls' already overflowing bag, but something fell out.

"*¡Diantre!*" Luiz exclaimed, picking the article of clothing up. "This doesn't look like a swimsuit." He stretched out a pair of light pink panties that had a dark pink bow in the front. Andrea's hand struck like a snake, snatching them from his hands, her glare burning holes through him even as the heat reddened her cheeks.

"Give me the bag," she growled, snatching it from the ground next to Luiz and stashing her undies out of sight.

"We're wearing our swimsuits under our clothes, so we only have to change once," Kendra explained. "See?" She pulled the edge of her shorts down for a split second, enough for me to see the tied string of her swimsuit bottoms.

Wow. I refused to believe it. Kendra was wearing bikini bottoms? *No way!* I had never seen her in a bikini because, like my sister, Kendra normally held to high modesty ideals.

Off-limits, I said in my mind and turned toward the Trax station. *Off-limits.*

CHAPTER 10
GATEWAY

The red line train showed up a few minutes later. At this hour, we had plenty of room to sit together and talk. Once downtown, we switched to the blue line for the final leg of the trip.

The Gateway is like a mall, except the walkways are outside. The splash pad sits on the north end in between two rows of stores west of the Trax station. We didn't hit the splash pad right away. Instead, we window shopped for a while because the girls wanted to. Luiz and I actually didn't do much more than escort the girls and complain when Sis vetoed the sporting goods store.

Shoppers and other teens hanging out walked in both directions, and we weaved through them as we took the ground level south until the girls had seen all those stores. We rode the busy escalator up and started back.

"Orange Julius!" Kendra shouted. "I'm getting some."

Orange Julius—the name of both the franchise and their main smoothie—was sandwiched into a little nook past the AT&T store. I wished I could buy a cell phone, but a smoothie would do for now.

"Let's all get some," I glanced at Sis. She didn't know I had extra cash from John. I stepped up to order three smoothies. "I'll get yours, too, Kendra." Kendra and my sister exchanged looks, sharing a private inside moment again. I tried to ignore them. Andrea eyed their interaction and whispered something to Luiz. After my purchase, Luiz ordered and paid for his and Andrea's smoothies—they were on a date after all.

With our cold smoothies in hand, we sat down on a stone bench that overlooked the pathway below. The bench wasn't quite big enough for all five of us. Andrea smiled, not at all displeased to be forced to sit elsewhere. She grabbed Luiz's hand and dragged him away from us toward another bench that was quite a ways back.

"I love these so much," Kendra commented. "Thanks, Jacob." She flashed her blue eyes at me and sipped her smoothie.

"It was your idea," I reminded her, and she smiled back and flipped her golden brown hair from her face. I'd seen her flip her hair like that for years, and it had never really demanded my full attention before. I decided to keep my eyes on the cement at my feet and keep the straw in my mouth.

"When does football practice start?" Kendra asked me.

So much for keeping the straw in my mouth. "It never stopped." I locked my lips back on the straw immediately after answering.

"You know what I mean."

"First Monday in August." I glanced her way then hurriedly returned my eyes to the cement.

"Oh, drill team starts then, too. Justine is going to ride with me. Do you want to ride with me too?"

"Are your parents getting you a car?" I asked, a little jealous— straw out of my mouth and staring at her. I was *so* failing to ignore her.

"No, they are going to let me use one."

"I usually run to practice, and I go early," I answered.

I stood and walked to the trash can to toss in my empty cup. The distance let me escape her a little. Sis scowled at me. *What did I do?* They stood up, and we started walking past stores back toward the splash pad, forgetting about Luiz and Andrea.

"Hey, it's Aeropostale." Kendra jumped in front of me and looked at me with her big blue eyes and asked, "Can we go in?"

"Uh . . . go ahead." I tilted my head at her, a little dumbfounded to be the one giving her permission. Weird. Why ask me? Sis smiled at me encouragingly—scowl gone. Sis and Kendra tossed their empty smoothie cups into a trash bin and went inside. I stayed outside, but two seconds later, Kendra came back out.

"Come in with us, silly." She grabbed my arm. I let her pull me inside. She didn't let go of me until she'd led me all the way into the girls' section where she started looking at shirts. Sis looked at shorts a few racks away. Katy Perry's "Wide Awake" drifted down from the ceiling speakers. The guys' section was way over in the other corner, and it looked so . . . safe.

"Look at this one." Kendra lifted a shirt from a rack and held it up. "I like the gathers."

I had no idea what gathers were, but I went with it. "You could rock that shirt!" I said, playing along. "But you could rock any shirt." Her smile exploded. I shouldn't have added that last line. It was too much like flirting.

"I could, huh?" She looked around and grabbed the worst mustard-colored shirt I have ever seen. "What about this one?"

"You could rock that one, too," I lied.

"You're so full of it," she laughed and put the shirt back. "Nobody would look good in that." She looked at a few other shirts before picking up a reddish, purplish one and holding it up to her chest. "How about this?" she asked. "And your honest opinion, please." It had two flap things that crossed in the middle and some tie things in the back. I obviously didn't know anything about girl clothes. I stared at it, confused.

"You don't like it?" She frowned.

"Uh, not sure. I don't know what it looks like on you."

"Well, let's go see," she grinned mischievously and grabbed my arm again. She dodged racks of clothes as she towed me toward the dressing rooms. I fidgeted with my pockets as Kendra waited for a worker to unlock a room. Kendra stepped inside, then looked at me as if waiting. I didn't move.

"I'm wearing a swimsuit, silly." Another arm grab pulled me inside, and she closed and latched the door.

Is this really happening? I asked myself. I've never been claustrophobic, but the little boxy room tightened around both of us. Maybe Kendra was trusting her best friend's brother too much. She clearly wanted a guy's opinion, but did she realize what she was doing to my hormones?

Off-limits, my mind shouted. *Off . . .* My mind didn't finish as Kendra's shirt came off.

Bikini. Definitely. Two triangles. String. I'd thought earlier that she had filled out some. Confirmed. I studied her every movement as she slipped the new shirt on. It took her a minute as she fiddled with the flap-things and tie-things. She glanced at me through the mirror. I stared back with a red face that I hoped my tan hid for me.

"Well?"

I didn't say anything.

"Jake?" she asked again.

Yeah, I had zoned out looking at her.

"It . . . well . . . the . . . it's . . . I . . . um . . . like . . ." The shirt flattered her figure, and while I can't be sure what I said exactly, she figured out that I liked it. I wanted to stay and watch her change shirts again, but my heart beat rapidly, and heat spread through my body. I needed to get out of there *because* I wanted to stay.

"I just . . . I have to . . ." I stammered.

My body was about to embarrass me, so I slipped from the changing room before she could grab my arm again.

The song had switched to Ingrid Michaelson's "The Way I Am." I scanned the store for Sis. A Latina girl stood at the rack of shorts where I'd last seen her. A couple preteens stood by the wall of shirts, and a group of college girls laughed as the checkout worker folded their clothes into a bag. No Justine. I waded through the racks of clothes and went outside. Groups of all ages lined the walkways in both directions. Justine wasn't out there, either. I walked to the stone bench where Luiz and Andrea had sat down, but they weren't there anymore. Had they headed toward the splash pad without noticing we'd stopped?

I returned and looked through Aeropostale's manikin-filled windows. Sis and Kendra stood by the checkout. Kendra held a shopping bag, and Sis handed some article of clothing to the checkout girl. When they finished their purchases, they looked around, then saw me through the window and came out.

"Where did you go?" Sis asked.

Kendra looked at me without a smile, then her eyes lowered to her feet.

"I came out to," I tried to think of something, "to tell Luiz and Andrea we were here, but they must have already passed by."

"Oh, right," Justine smiled and nudged Kendra.

"Shall we head to the splash pad?" I asked, keeping my eyes on my sister. I determined to ignore Kendra the rest of the night. I definitely didn't want Sis to notice that I had been flirting with her best friend.

Off-limits! I shouted the words in my mind.

Kendra tried to thank me for helping her pick a shirt, but as a guy, I had mastered the one syllable, conversation-killing response long before puberty. I shrugged and grunted. I used that response for a few other questions as we walked.

The splash pad sat on ground level—a big circle in the cement with patterned holes that could spray water twenty feet high. Despite being late evening, the sun, hidden behind the stores, still illuminated the sky with an orange glow. Luiz and Andrea sat on a stone bench watching the few remaining kids run laughing through the spray. The flowered tote sat on the ground next to them.

"Shall we go change?" I said to Luiz.

"We don't need to go anywhere," Kendra's blue eyes grabbed mine. For the second time, Kendra stood in front of me taking off her shirt. I didn't have the willpower to look away, but I didn't need it because, at that moment, I felt a familiar string pulling at my chest sharply. I forgot Kendra completely and started looking around. The tug pulled stronger tonight as if an invisible thread hooked me and pulled me toward the watching eyes. I followed this imaginary thread to the stores down the path on the first level. While dozens of people walked in different directions, none looked my way. I let my eyes drift up to the second level as the thread angled upward. Far down the walkway, a man stood alone, staring back at me. He wore a long-sleeved black shirt, and in the middle of July, there wasn't another long-sleeved shirt around. He stood too far away for me to make out any other features.

"Jake!" I heard Sis yell.

"Huh?" I glanced at her and felt the thread snap, freeing me. I looked back, but only a group of kids walked where the man had stood a second before.

"I called you three times," Sis complained. "What are you looking at?"

Sis's eyes oozed displeasure. Kendra pursed her lips, and she moved her eyes disappointingly to the cement like I had spoiled something. She turned and meandered slowly toward the splash pad. I turned back and found Kendra in her bikini. *Off-limits*, I reminded myself again.

"Where did you go this time?" Sis scowled.

"This time?" I tilted my head at her.

"Yeah. Sometimes it's like you're here but you're not here, you know?" Sis scolded me.

It was true that I often got lost in my thoughts. OK, I could totally zone out sometimes. This wasn't a new thing. I've done it for years, but this wasn't one of those times. Should I tell her about the invisible string pulling at my chest and how it connected me to the man I'd seen? Luiz was already handing me my swim trunks and ushering me toward the public restrooms.

"Be right back," I told her instead.

We changed quickly in one of those square, one-room public bathrooms with only a toilet and a sink. We made it back to the splash pad in less than two minutes.

The girls ran through the spraying water, already drenched—at least Sis and Kendra were. Andrea eyed Kendra with displeasure. She hesitated joining in as she had all night. Once she did join in, she avoided getting her hair wet. She grimaced and tugged at the boy shorts and adjusted the tankini top. I didn't know her as well as Luiz did, but I pegged her for the uptight type. Kendra and Sis, on the other hand, were having loads of fun, laughing and trying to guess which holes would spray next.

When I joined the girls, their laughing stopped, and they had a moment of seriousness, but I ignored it. I put my hand over one of the holes, directing the spray at them, and they screamed as water splashed off their bodies. As Kendra spun to avoid my spraying water, I couldn't help but fixate on her painfully sexy, bikini-clad body. The spray stopped, and they replaced their screams with laughter as they sought to get me back. At first, I did my best to keep Sis in between Kendra and me whenever possible, but the effort didn't last.

We played for about forty-five minutes as the water sprayed us in patterned intervals before Andrea said she'd had enough. That meant Luiz was done, too. Suddenly Kendra stood next to me, her face inches from mine. She grabbed my bicep with both hands. Her touch, not the cold, caused my goosebumps.

"Stay and splash some more," she pleaded, her blue eyes begging.

I wanted to say yes. My body begged me to say yes. I glanced at my sister. *Off-limits.*

"Nah, I'm going to get changed," I said with great effort. Kendra dropped my bicep, and I saw that hurt, disappointed look again. I didn't know what the look meant, or maybe I didn't want to know, so I ran to catch up with Luiz and Andrea.

I overheard Andrea complaining to Luiz, ". . . tight little bodies make me feel inadequate. They're—" She cut her sentence short as I approached.

"I think you're sexy!" Luiz flashed a grin at her.

"Hush, Luiz." Andrea couldn't help but smile at Luiz's comment. She glanced my way, and her cheeks turned red, then she darted into the women's bathroom to change.

"I guess it's time to head back," I commented as Luiz and I slipped into the men's bathroom.

"I don't think the night is over yet," Luiz replied, grinning back.

CHAPTER 11
TEARS

Kevin called while we rode the Trax red line back toward where the car was parked. Kevin had arrived home earlier than expected and wanted to know what we thought of ending the night by watching a movie at his place. His house had an awesome theater room in the basement with a projector and a twelve-foot movie screen, making it a common place for us jeeks to spend the final hours of a group date night. We all agreed to go.

We had a hard time finding seats on the train. I could have sat by Kendra and Sis, but I chose to sit with Luiz and Andrea instead. I didn't look at Kendra the whole ride back. Without the other two girls right next to her, Andrea smiled and chatted comfortably with Luiz and me. When we got off Trax and piled into Luiz's car, Sis sat between Kendra and me.

"I think I'll go home," Kendra said, with a firm sadness to her voice. My insides divided into two parts—a huge part of me oozed disappointment, but the smaller part, which kept reminding me that Kendra was off-limits, celebrated. Andrea tried to hide her smile.

"OK, I can take you home," Luiz responded.

Sis leaned over and whispered in Kendra's ear as we drove. I looked out the window at passing houses.

"Fine, I'll come," Kendra agreed a minute later, despite how her eyebrows pulled together in a scowl.

"Yay!" Sis cheered and did a quiet little clap. Her whispered words had worked like magic. The two parts of me swapped emotions. Andrea briefly glanced back at Kendra, her smile gone.

Once at Kevin's, we piled into the theater room where four couches were arranged in two rows, the couches in back on a raised platform. Kevin started the movie and turned off the lights. Luiz and Andrea cuddled up nicely on the back couch farthest from the door, and I took the end of the one in front of them. Sis took the other end, and Kendra sat between us—right next to me. I tried to ignore her closeness until our arms touched. I fled to the bathroom—I really did have to go—but when I came back, I sat on the other front couch opposite Kevin. About halfway through the movie, Kendra stepped out of the theater room, and a moment later Sis came over and sat next to me.

"What the freak are you doing?" she whispered harshly in my ear, her scolding demanding my attention. The large movie screen reflected in her scowling green eyes. "Why are you treating Kendra like this?" she mouthed, exaggerating each word.

"Huh?" I mouthed back. *Oh, crap.* She'd figured out I'd been flirting with her all day.

"Out." She pointed toward the theater room door, and I followed her into the hall. She turned on me as soon as the door closed. "Why are you treating Kendra like that?" she demanded again, still keeping her voice down, but making it twice as harsh.

"Uh . . ." I stuttered, unable to say anything for a second. "I don't know what you mean," I lied.

"You know exactly what I mean." Her eyes drilled into me.

"Look, I know she is off-limits, and I didn't mean to flirt with her today. I'm sorry, but I'm doing my best to stay away from her for you."

A smirk formed on my sister's face. "Off-limits?" she giggled. "You are staying away from her *for me*?" she chuckled. "Jake, why would you . . . ?" she stopped, eyes softening in realization. "Because she's my best friend."

"Exactly!" I nodded.

"Jake, I know you told me your jeeks were off-limits to me, but did I ever tell you Kendra was off-limits to you? Think about it."

I thought about it and came up blank. It had never happened.

"You assumed that because you banned me from your friends that I had automatically banned you from mine?" She shook her head. "You're so clueless. Kendra's got it bad for you, Jake. She's been trying to get you to notice her all summer long, and all you've done is make her cry. That's twice now."

"Twice?" I tilted my head at her.

"She cried on the Fourth of July when I went on a date with loser boy, and you bailed on her. She really laid it on thick today, Jake. Even though I told her not to, she bought that bikini this summer for the sole purpose of getting your attention."

In my mind, I heard Kendra's words from earlier in the day. *None of the jeeks are off-limits for me.* Had she meant me? The answer to that question was so obvious I couldn't believe I hadn't seen it earlier. She'd sat in the middle between Sis and me on the way to and from rock-climbing. She'd asked permission from *me* to go into Aeropostale where she'd pulled *me* into her dressing room. I could still feel her hand on my bicep as she asked *me* to stay and splash some more. My mind provided me a nice montage of a half-dozen other ways she'd made it obvious for me, even before today.

My sister was still talking, but I hadn't been listening.

". . . your last summer at home, she asked me if I was OK with her going after you. I told her to go for it."

"So, she's not off-limits?" As I spoke the words, I tried to convince myself that they were true.

"She never has been." Sis smiled flatly at me, her head shaking again.

She's not off-limits.

"She's upstairs," Sis added. "Probably still in tears, thanks to you," she scolded.

Oops. I'm such a jerk. I hadn't meant to make her cry. *I can fix this,* I thought as I started upstairs.

The lights were off, except in the hall. Kevin's parents must have gone to bed. I located Kendra's silhouette sitting alone on a couch in the living room. She looked at me as I walked toward her. The hall light illuminated her face and damp blue eyes. She glanced at me, then looked down, perhaps hoping to hide the wet lines running down her cheeks.

I sat next to her on the edge of the couch. Three seconds passed as I listened to her shivering breath before I put my hands on her cheeks and wiped her tears with my thumbs. At my touch, her blue eyes opened wide and riveted on mine.

"Justine is . . . I . . . She . . ." I took a moment to breathe. "I'm sorry. I thought you were off-limits."

She blinked her confused eyes at me. I waited a moment for her to process my words. "You thought I was . . ." She didn't finish. She let it hang, and her eyes opened wide.

I nodded. Her lips parted slightly as if trying to find the right words to finish her sentence. I didn't wait.

I pressed my lips to hers.

I tasted the salt of her tears mixed with vanilla mint ChapStick. I lingered there, enjoying the feel of her lips on mine. I felt heat in my chest as a connection formed between us—as if a burning rope existed from her heart to mine. Her hands slid up my arms, and she kissed back, moving her lips with mine.

After long seconds, I slowly pulled back, keeping eye contact. I removed my hands from her face and took her hands.

"You're not off-limits," I whispered.

"I'm not," she cried more as she said it.

I pulled her toward me, and she pressed her wet cheek to my chest. Through my shirt, I could feel the dampness, either from her tears or hair, which was still wet from the splash pad—maybe both. I stroked my hand down her damp hair several times and breathed in a fading hint of lavender.

"Will this be real tomorrow?" she blubbered and raised her eyes to blink at me.

"I hope so," I answered. "You're not planning to break up with me now that you've kissed me, are you?" I teased.

She cracked out a laugh through her tears, and I couldn't help but laugh at the sound of it.

"Hey, don't laugh at me," she pretended to complain, but her smile reached her eyes. "I was about to walk home," she confessed, and her cheeks reddened.

"I'm glad you didn't."

"I'm glad I didn't, too."

"Let's go finish the movie." I stood, kept hold of her hand, and led her to the stairs. Her hand felt soft and warm, and her thin fingers fit perfectly into mine.

"Wait." She tugged my hand, stopping me. She put her arms around my neck and pulled me in for another kiss. Her lips tasted the same—minus the salty tears. I didn't have to lean down quite as far to kiss her as I expected—she hadn't just filled out, she'd grown, too. I wrapped my arms around her waist and pulled her body tight against mine. She shivered as we kissed, and then stepped back.

"I needed to try that one more time," she said, face flushed.

Should we stay up here to "try that" a few more times? I wanted to, but Kendra took my hand and led me downstairs. I wish I could have taken a picture of Sis and my friends' reactions when they saw us walk back into the theater room holding hands—especially Sis whose grin was as big and white as Kevin's movie screen.

Kendra and I took the empty couch in the back, and I pulled her into my chest. Kendra wasn't someone I'd just met. I'd known her as my sister's best friend for years. We knew a lot about each other. We were going into this with eyes wide open. She had pursued me knowing all about me. She knew I called other kids in the school barnacles. She knew why my mom flinched when I showed up unexpectedly. She knew I wanted to get away from my home life. She knew all that and still she had pursued me.

She didn't know I was a freak, but I ignored that for tonight.

CHAPTER 12
PAIN

I woke up Wednesday morning at six, smiling. I wasn't even bothered that I dreamed my biological father told me I'd turned out like him—a freak. I skipped football again for the same reason as yesterday, so I had a lot of morning time. I hadn't missed two days in a row all summer. I ate breakfast and watched an hour of the college chemistry course on the DVR. It covered complex molecules, which as a jeek, I found interesting.

Mom woke up first. I was normally at football at this time of the morning, so seeing me sitting on the couch must have caught Mom off guard because she flinched at the sight of me on the couch. She swallowed and tried to hide it. Oh, the joys of having a face your own mother loathes. The hurt was dulled this morning because of Kendra, even if our relationship could still be counted in hours. Mom went off to work without a word and with only a granola bar for breakfast.

Sis woke up early again—early for her meant after eight. I cringed as I heard her turn on the shower. It would be an hour before she finished getting ready and came downstairs. I had intended to wait till nine to call Kendra, but I'd been fidgeting with the phone since eight and got antsy, so I dialed her number. That's right! Even though a guy calling the next morning is akin to seeing Bigfoot, I did it. Of course, I'm a freak, so maybe I don't count.

"Hello," Kendra's voice answered. Of course, it was her. Was she home alone? Did her mom work?

Sis had coined the term "seventh and only child" for Kendra because while she was number seven, her next sibling was six years older and married.

"Hey, Kendra," I said. I could faintly hear music over the phone but not clear enough to recognize the song. I started pacing back and forth between the kitchen and the family room.

"Hey, Jake," she replied, the smile in her voice evident as she spoke my name.

"I wanted to call and make sure you knew that last night was *real*. You seemed unsure if it would be," I teased, recalling her words.

"Oh, I did, huh?" she mused. She had shown an amazing amount of confidence yesterday in pursuing me—at least until I made her cry and the vulnerable version of Kendra had come out. Her confidence was back, which made me smile, although I had this strange premonition that I would see her vulnerable side again someday.

"I just got out of the shower," she emphasized provocatively.

"And yet you rushed to answer the phone."

"I didn't rush. I have a phone in my room. It's the least my parents can do for withholding a cell phone from me."

"I don't have a cell either," I said from the living room, still jealous of Luiz's new phone.

"I know."

"So, what are you doing?" I asked, now in the kitchen.

"I am standing in front of my closet trying to decide what to wear."

"Are you trying to give me a visual?" I asked, because it was working.

"Maybe," she stretched out the word tantalizingly.

"You're evil," I laughed at her, now back in my living room.

"Uh oh! My towel dropped."

"Kendra!" I exclaimed, trying to hold the mental image at bay and failing miserably. *I'm not my stepdad,* I told myself. Back in the kitchen, I opened the fridge mindlessly and closed it.

"Just kidding," she said, her blush as evident in her voice as her smile had been earlier. "I'm going to Lagoon today," Kendra changed the subject. Her voice sounded labored, and I got this image of her holding the phone to her ear with her shoulder while using her hands to dress. "We're going as a family. All my brothers and sisters are coming. I won't be home until way late. I might not see you until tomorrow." We were already the sappy-want-to-see-each-other-every-second couple. "Wait, hold on a second . . ." A minute of silence passed before I heard her muffled voice talking to her mother. Maybe her mother didn't work? Or maybe she had taken the day off? You'd think that since I'd known Kendra for a decade, I'd know if her mom worked or not.

"Can Justine and her brother come to Lagoon with us?" I barely made out Kendra's muffled words. If she asked me to go, part of me wanted to say yes, but the reasons to say no piled up. First, she had referred to me as Justine's brother, which meant she hadn't shared last night's events with her mother—not that she'd had time. Second, Lagoon is major expensive, and I couldn't afford to pay for both Sis and me. Third, if Sis couldn't come, I had to stay home anyway. Fourth, she said all her extended family would be there, and I didn't care how much I liked a girl, I didn't want to hang out with her extended family in the first twenty-four hours, even if, in this case, I had met most of them already.

I made out bits and pieces of her mother's answer. ". . . pick up . . . sister . . . don't . . . enough room . . . car." I heard enough to know the answer was no and breathed a sigh of relief.

Hearing Kendra trying to get her mother's permission reminded me how much younger than me she was. She would turn sixteen in a couple weeks—July 31—a little more than a month before I turned eighteen—September 3. Since she was only a grade below me, it didn't seem like she could be two years younger, but she was.

Sis came down, dressed and ready for the day, and as I paced into the kitchen, she grabbed me and forced me to sit down at the table. She couldn't stop grinning at me.

"I'm back," Kendra's voice returned.

"I overheard." I saved her from having to tell me: "Mommy said no."

"Sorry," she replied, the embarrassment evident in her voice.

"It's completely fine." Besides, it saved me having to turn her down.

"So, are you excited for drill team to start?" I changed the subject. "I might take you up on that ride to school in the mornings, assuming the offer is still on the table."

We stayed on the phone for half an hour until her mom told her to quit flirting on the phone because it was time to go. She said goodbye with the embarrassment back in her voice.

Sis had been waiting patiently this whole time for me to hang up.

"So," she eyed me quizzically with a flat, knowing smile. I grinned back and waited for her to ask. I hadn't let her ask when we got home last night. But now it was sharing time. "Tell me what happened when you went upstairs," she nearly squealed.

I told her every detail, including how her kiss tasted like salt the first time but not the second.

"I don't think I'm her first kiss," I confessed to my sister. "She knew how to kiss."

Sis's cheeks turned red, and her embarrassment dimple appeared on her right cheek.

"What?" I asked. Whatever it was, she didn't want to tell, but we didn't really keep secrets, and after I eyed her for a few seconds, she spilled.

"You're the first *boy* that she's ever kissed."

"Excuse me?" My mouth hung open a little.

"Never tell Kendra I told you this. And don't get the wrong idea because we completely like boys." She pulled her eyes away from mine. "I . . . we . . . used to practice."

"Practice? On what?"

The red in her face deepened.

Oh!

"On each other?" I shouted, my mouth gaping.

She nodded, her eyes looking down and away.

"Let me get this straight. You and Kendra used to kiss? Well, maybe *straight* is the wrong word."

"It wasn't like that. It was only a few times. We were practicing for boys. We really were. And we haven't . . . practiced . . . since last year some time." If I didn't know how much Sis liked boys, I might not have believed her.

"Yeah, did one of you pretend to be the boy?" I teased. "Who'd Kendra pretend to be? Wait. Who did you pretend to be?"

"I am *so* not saying another word." She tried to hide her smile.

I smiled right back, unable to prevent the image of her pretending to be me while Kendra practiced kissing her. My sister had kissed my girlfriend before I had.

"You need a distraction, don't you?" I had no idea what she read on my face because I rarely felt grossed out, jealous, and turned on all at the same time.

"Xbox?" I offered.

"The dancing game?" she offered back.

"Only if you play Madden with me after," I agreed. She could score a mean virtual touchdown.

We played for hours until John walked through for lunch. We did our best to avoid him and then decided to get out of the house. We packed our swimsuits and rode bikes to the library over on Forty-Eighth and Ninetieth. We hung out there reading books and playing on the Internet. I don't sleep much, which gives me lots of time to read, and the geek part of me loves sci-fi and fantasy books, so I checked out three of them. After the library, we splashed around at the nearby private neighborhood pool until about half past three. Kendra must have borrowed a phone from one of her sisters because she texted Sis a couple times with messages for both of us.

Sis had her Wednesday piano lessons from four to five, which was perfect because it freed me up to hit the weight room with the jeeks. I rode with her to her piano teacher's house before continuing on to school. As I walked into the weight room, the jeeks were already there.

"Hey, it's Jake," Luiz called out as he and Ethan spotted Kevin at the bench press. Kevin was shirtless and his ribs stuck out through his white skin. Dylan was doing leg presses with a buddy of his. Despite his red-faced exertion, Dylan nodded at me. I nodded back.

"Man, you have some explaining to do," Ethan commented.

Oops. I hadn't asked Ethan if he was interested in Kendra, and I may have already stepped on his toes. He and Luiz grabbed the bar from Kevin and set it on the rack, allowing Kevin to sit up. Kevin left a lake of sweat on the bench.

"What happened to staying away from your sister's best friend?" Ethan's voice sounded strangely hopeful.

"My sister was part of the conspiracy to get us together," I confessed. I pointed out the lake of sweat to Kevin, and he used his tank-top to wipe it off.

"Does that mean Justine is fair game for the jeeks, now?" Luiz asked. I watched Luiz's eyes glance at Ethan and then back at me.

Oh. Dots connected in my head. *Could I be OK with a jeek dating my sister?* Before yesterday, I would have said no and prefixed it with a nice expletive to enforce its seriousness, but at that moment, I was inspired to look at things from a different point of view. If the jeeks were the best guys around, shouldn't I be making sure my sister was with the best? Maybe I could forgo being a total jerk when it came to my sister and my best friends.

I looked directly at Ethan. "Sure, Ethan, she's fair game."

"Hey!" Ethan scowled at Luiz. "You told him?"

Luiz held up his hands defensively. *"¡No dije nada!"* I knew that meant he hadn't said anything.

Ethan turned his eyes to Kevin, who held his shirt in a ball, wiping sweat from his chest.

"Come on, Ethan. I'm a jeek," I said, pointing to my brain. "I figured it out." I picked up a 45-pound weight and added it to one side of the bar.

"Then can I take your sister out on Friday?" Ethan asked.

"No," I laughed.

"Man, now you're messing with me," Ethan complained as I added another 45-pound weight to the other side.

"I'm not. She already has a date with Dylan. You'll have to try her another day." Everyone glanced over at Dylan.

"She's going out with Dylan?" Ethan lowered his voice as I grabbed some 5-pound weights and tossed one on each side, making the total 235 pounds.

"What? Are you worried you can't compete?" I challenged, as I lay down on the bench and grabbed the bar.

"Oh, I can compete," he replied, but the insecurity in his voice contradicted his words. He grabbed the bar and helped me stabilize it above my chest before I started pumping out reps.

"Enough about *su hermana*," Luiz cut in. "What's up with you and Kendra? Andrea was enjoying watching you blow her off all night, then next thing we know you were holding hands," Luiz continued.

"They cuddled up together pretty close, too," Kevin added. "I don't think there was an inch between them the rest of the night."

"Did you kiss her?" Ethan asked as I finished counting to ten. He helped move the bar to the rack, and I sat up.

"Yes," I answered, grinning. "A couple times before we went back into the theater room and again when I dropped her off. Don't worry; you'll be around us often enough you'll get sick of seeing us kiss."

"You two are going to be sappy, aren't you?" Kevin asked, with a hint of jealousy. Luiz started pulling off the 45-pound plates.

"Yes. Yes, we are," I smiled back at him. "We won't be as gross as Luiz and Andrea, though," I deflected, and Luiz grinned as the attention turned his way.

The conversation drifted as we leisurely lifted weights. I'd only worked out a couple muscles and it was already time to leave. Sis's piano lessons only lasted an hour, and I didn't want her to be home a single minute without me there.

The jeeks decided to leave with me, and we all walked down the hall together until Kevin realized he left his phone in the weight room so he and Ethan ran back to get it. Luiz walked out the school's glass front doors with me. The blue sky let the sun shine bright, and I heard the hum of cars driving down twenty-seventh. The parking lot was mostly empty. Could I throw my bike in the back of Kevin's Tucson and let him drive me home? Just then, the thread of being watched hooked to my chest, pulling so hard as if ripping out some ethereal part of me. I came to a complete stop. Luiz took another couple steps.

I felt a sharp pinch in my leg, and the glass in one door shattered behind me.

Time stopped. Shards of glass scattered through the air in slow motion. Luiz's eyes moved slowly from the glass to me. He didn't look at my face. He looked at my leg. His eyelids took a full second to blink. His head moved in slow motion to look to one side, his eyebrows pinched in the same confusion that I felt.

The pain receptors in my right thigh finally got through to my cerebral cortex and time restored to normal as I dropped to the ground, crying like a baby. My hands reached for my thigh where blood poured out of both an entry and an exit wound. Luiz's mouth moved, but my mind was too busy dealing with the pain to allow my ears to work.

In seconds, Kevin and Ethan stood over me. Luiz started looking around and yelling, but I couldn't tell what he was saying. Kevin pulled out his phone and stared at it, not knowing what to do. Luiz pulled out his own phone and dialed three digits.

My ears started working again because I became aware of sirens, which didn't make sense to me since Luiz had just finished dialing—he wasn't even talking yet.

It finally dawned on me that I might have been shot. I had never been shot before. The pain came in waves from my leg and prevented my mind from thinking clearly. Before this, my worst pain had been my sprained ankle. But my sprain hadn't hurt enough to make my body twitch uncontrollably.

"What do you mean someone called in five minutes ago?" Luiz shouted into the phone. "It just happened."

Sirens blared, and in less than a minute, an ambulance and a police car pulled in and screeched to a halt next to the school. The white ambulance doors swung open. One paramedic rushed over to me while two others pulled a gurney from the back of the ambulance. The paramedic asked me something, but the waves of pain continued to roll through me. What had he asked? I couldn't hear past the pain. He waved his partners over, and they moved me onto the gurney and then lifted me, gurney and all, into the ambulance. The police officer stood next to Luiz, asking him what happened. Then the ambulance doors closed.

I should have been wondering why someone shot me. I should have wondered who tipped off the paramedics and cops before I got shot. I should have wondered if I was going to die. Instead, I only felt the sharp screaming from my thigh that blocked everything else out.

The Jordan Valley Medical Center was only two miles away, so the paramedics barely had time to cut off my shorts before they were hauling me into the emergency room where white coats with large fuzzy faces hovered over me.

"He's losing too much blood," said one face above me.

"I'm his pediatrician," said a woman's face that I recognized.

"We don't need you," another face shouted.

"I was paged here, and it's a good thing, too. He's in the Bombay blood group!" My pediatrician shouted back.

"Oh, hell!" the first face replied.

I was going to die of blood loss. They didn't have blood for me. A single thought made its way past the pain and my hazy vision before I blacked out. *Who's going to protect my sister?*

CHAPTER 13
HOSPITAL

I heard the click of a door that woke me up. My leg felt like someone had stabbed it with a knife and twisted. I swore a few times in my head. Something odd inside me dulled the pain, though. *Are my insides glowing?* Wait, no, I wasn't glowing because no light was involved. *Maybe pulsing? A warm pulsing?* Yes, something warm pulsed inside my body that I'd never felt before. It wasn't exactly physical, but it wasn't exactly not physical either. As I opened my eyes, I caught sight of Sis sitting near the wall of the dimly lit room.

I slightly turned my head. Mom stood in the open doorway. Even with her back to me, I could see her wiping her eyes. A part of me had thought she'd be happy if I died, but seeing her wipe tears meant that despite who I looked like, she loved me.

Two officers in full uniforms stood on the other side of her. The left officer spoke, but I couldn't hear him. He was holding up a picture. Mom shook her head, then stepped out and closed the door. As the door closed, I could have sworn a vertical scar crossed the officer's eye, but in my delirium, I couldn't be sure.

I meant to say something to Sis, but I closed my eyes. I must have fallen asleep again because another click of the door woke me. Again, it took effort to turn my head. Mom walked into the room. She looked right at my now open eyes.

"Hey," I tried to say, but an annoying tube clogged my throat, so instead it came out as, "Hegh." Monitors surrounding my bed provided an ambient humming, and something like an IV stuck out of my chest. Mom and Sis responded to my attempt to speak. Justine wiped her cheeks as she stepped toward me. My mom no longer had any tears to wipe.

"Jake, you're awake," Sis's voice cracked. As she stood and hurried over to me, she asked, "What happened?"

I tried to say, "I don't know." But the tube wouldn't allow it. Three unintelligible syllables came out instead.

Mom scrutinized me with disapproving eyes, which was unexpected. Where had her tears gone? Trying to pull out the tube myself had triggered something on the monitors, and they had responded with a couple of beeps, and a very round and bubbly nurse came in. She reminded me of the character Bailey from Grey's Anatomy. She flipped the lights on, and the room became very bright.

"Oh, my goodness, you're awake," the nurse bubbled. "I'll page the doctor. You lost more than sixty percent of your blood. We had to put in a central line. Just the fact that you are alive is a miracle." She looked at me as if trying to believe it herself. "How you are awake and responding, God only knows. It's a miracle!"

No miracle. I'm just a freak.

"Honey, I'll pull this out," she indicated to the tube in my throat and started easing it out, "but don't you go touching the tube in your chest. It's a central line. You need that one. Promise me you won't go touching that one." I waited for the throat tube to slide out and a coughing spell to pass—both blood and yellow gunk came out—before I nodded my promise.

"Well, it's such a miracle you survived," the nurse continued. "You needed a transfusion, but you're in the Bombay blood group, and well, we shouldn't have had enough blood, but due to some recent donations, we did. A miracle." She fiddled with my IV. "You know you are the first person we've ever seen survive after losing that much blood. Another miracle."

"OK, it was a miracle, we've heard you," Mom cut in sharply.

The nurse's bottom lip pouted. What did the police say to Mom?

"Well, I'll be back with the doctor." The nurse eyed Mom sideways as she walked out and muttered, "Well, it was a miracle."

My mom's what-did-you-do-wrong eyes returned to me, and I wished the nurse was back. "Nobody is telling us anything. Who shot you, Jacob? Why did they shoot you, Jacob?" She had bags under her eyes and wore rumpled clothes.

"I . . . don't . . . know," I struggled to answer.

"If you are involved in something, honey, you can tell me," she tried to speak softly, despite clenched teeth. Justine stared open-mouthed at Mom and ran her fingers through her blonde hair.

I didn't answer.

"The police spoke with me, Jacob," Mom complained. "I need you to tell me what is going on."

I tilted my head at her and blinked. *Had the police told her that I'm involved in something?* Her behavior was off. I looked at Justine and then back at my mom. What did she expect me to tell her? I knew less than she did.

"Damn it, Jacob Matthew Stevens, what did you get yourself into?" she hissed.

The pulsing inside me kept my anger at bay, or I would have shouted back—or tried to. Sis scowled at Mom for me and then took my hand and squeezed it.

I would have figured my mom would be the last person to blindly accuse me. I almost died. I expected her to cry and hold me. Sure, she'd cried earlier. But failing to do so now that I was awake, regardless of what the cops may have suggested, was a new low for her. She wasn't the same anymore. John had happened to her. Did my mom wish I had died so she didn't have to look at the spitting image of the man who terrorized her so long ago?

"Does it hurt?" Sis asked softly.

"Yes," I replied, but the odd warmth slowly overcame the pain, making it bearable.

"Kendra is in the waiting room. They only let family in." My chest leaped when I heard Kendra's name.

"Tell them I want to see her."

"We don't need your friend in here," Mom scolded. Sis glanced at my mom, then let her eyes drop to the floor.

"She's . . . my . . . girl . . . friend," I forced each word out.

Mom's mouth dropped open, and she fumbled for something to say. "You're dating Kendra? She's Justine's best friend!" Mom shouted. She gave Sis a harsh look. "Justine, she can't stay over anymore."

"That ship sailed on Monday. John was the captain," Justine cut back sharply. Mom threw her head back like she'd been slapped in the face. Sis's eyes thinned, the muscles in her cheeks flexed, and for the first time in my life, I saw her dimple when she wasn't embarrassed. She looked both angry and . . . grown up.

"Go home, Mom," Sis ordered. "I'll stay with Jake."

Mom stomped her foot and clenched her teeth until her face shook. She appeared ready to unleash a fury worthy of John, but the anger turned to tears. For a second, I thought she'd apologize and give me a hug, but instead, she turned and left. I might have felt bad for her, but basking in the warm sensation emanating from inside me, I didn't really care. This really was a new low for her.

Sis and I sat in silence for a while—if you count the annoying humming and beeping of the medical equipment as silence.

Should I tell her about the warm pulsing that hung out all cozily inside me? I could tell her it was like laughing gas because I couldn't really feel other emotions—except it was nothing like that. What would Sis say? That meds caused it? If I believed for a second my warm insides came from the meds, I would have told her, but it had something to do with how I was a freak, and being a freak was the only secret I had never shared with her.

"Mom *was* sad and crying," Sis defended her. "Then after the cops talked to her, she came back in angry."

"What . . . did . . . ?" I started to ask.

"I don't know," Justine shook her head. "We can ask her later—maybe when she's calmed down. Do you want me to sneak Kendra in?"

"Uh, huh," I responded, nodding, and then painfully swallowed. That tube had scratched my throat.

"OK. Be right back," she said and slipped out.

As I watched Sis leave, strange words whispered through my mind like rustling wind.

Hælan mīn thēh.

Did my mind just talk to me in a language I've never heard before? Yes, it did. Should I know what those words meant? They had finesse to them, and before I knew it, I was whispering them over and over again. The warmth inside me pulsed in rhythm as I chanted.

"Hælan mīn thēh. Hælan mīn thēh."

Right in the middle of the chant, some guy in pink scrubs came in—a male nurse maybe—I clamped my mouth shut, cutting off the whispers.

"Time to redress your wound," he stated. The edges of his mouth curled up as if he were holding back a smile. *Uh! Did this guy just hear me?* Outside my control, my mind repeated the words. *Hælan mīn thēh.* I had to consciously prevent my lips from moving.

The guy had a face chiseled from stone and didn't look like a nurse. He removed the bandages on my leg carefully and inspected the wound. He pulled out a clear, unmarked container of blue liquid and dripped the cold ointment over the wound. He wrapped my leg back up, but the coldness remained.

"Drink this." He put a small plastic cup in my right hand, and I drank it. He took the empty cup from me and walked out without another word. He was definitely less chatty than the last nurse.

Uh oh! Did the cold . . . move?

Icy tendrils of pain spread over my leg, expanding from the center of the bullet hole. As bad as the pain of the gunshot had been, this hurt worse. I cried out. Alarms sounded all around me, the instruments crying out for aid on my behalf.

Sis and Kendra reached the door to my room. "Kendra," I tried to call her name, but I wasn't sure if my mouth actually said anything. Nurses ushered them away before they could take a step inside. I heard that sound—the one on television shows—the single uninterrupted high pitch that follows a flat red line across a monitor.

This is so not fair. I was supposed to be a miracle. I wasn't ready to go yet. My sister needed me. Who would keep John from being a creep around her?

God, I prayed, *I want out of my house but not like this. I'm supposed to get out with a scholarship.* Was this my punishment for being a jerk? What was God going to think of me? Of how I mocked kids in my school by calling them barnacles? Was I going to go to hell?

Come on, God! You could at least give me more time if I'm going to hell. I've only been Kendra's boyfriend since last night, and I haven't even seen her today. We're supposed to spend a lot more time together. We're supposed to kiss so much that the jeeks would complain that we were being gross.

None of it would happen.

I died.

CHAPTER 14
ALIVE

Fyr leoht!

I woke up to more strange words whispering through my head like rushing wind. I looked at my hands and touched my face. *Am I alive?* OK. I might have been a little mistaken about that whole dying thing. I mean, since I woke up and all. But the jury was still out because I woke up in a strange, all-white bedroom—not mine and not a hospital's.

Maybe I'm in heaven?

Scrap that idea—not heaven. That itches. I scratched at my right thigh as best as I could, but the itching didn't really go away. I couldn't be certain about this, but I doubt there is itching in heaven. Besides, I never did see a tunnel of light. Of course, how was I to know if the whole tunnel of light thing really happened anyway? I shivered as vague memories of darkness flashed through my mind. Maybe I had only dreamed about it being cold, but it didn't feel like a dream. An image of me on a sliding metal slab in a freezing, dark room flashed in my mind.

Where am I? I scanned the room's white walls that were incapable of answering my question. Sunlight flooding in through the window told me it was daytime. That warm pulsing still occupied my insides like an extra helping of Thanksgiving dinner. I scratched the bullet wound again, this time realizing I hadn't felt a bullet hole. I flipped the covers off my leg. The front of my thigh had a small circle of pink, still-healing tissue, with little stitches sticking out. I felt the back of my thigh and compared it to the front. It felt the same. I'd healed enough I didn't need the stitches anymore.

I nearly jumped when the door opened and a man stepped in. He wore an FBI hat and jacket and had a badge hanging from his hand. His other hand stayed on the doorknob. I made a wild guess that he was an FBI agent.

"Jacob, I am Special Agent O'Brien," the man said. He had a chiseled-from-stone face that looked familiar, but I couldn't place it. He could have been anywhere between thirty and forty. "You're in a safe house," Agent O'Brien continued as he flipped his badge closed and put it away inside his jacket.

The FBI? A safe house? I should have panicked at FBI involvement, but the warmth taking over my insides shut out my panic just as it had shut out my anger. Besides, I felt safe—extremely safe—safer than I had ever felt anywhere.

"Why don't you take time to get dressed? There is a bathroom and shower if you need them." He gestured to a second door inside my room. "We can eat and talk when you are ready. OK?"

"OK," I nodded, and the FBI guy stepped out of the room and swung the door closed.

It took a while to get all my muscles, especially those in my injured leg, to respond. I'm not Wolverine or anything; I heal faster, not instantly. I swung my legs off the bed, making its simple metal frame creak, and stood up. I found myself back on the bed a few seconds later, the blood rushing back into my head. I swung my legs off the bed and stood up again, but this time I leaned against the bed as I let the light-headedness pass. What did the FBI think of my superhuman healing? In a little more than a day, my bullet wound had pretty much healed.

Or was it more than just the next day?

A clock by the bed answered my question: Thursday, July 18, 3:12 P.M. Of course, it was only the next day. Four hours of sleep served as a full night, and except for the short time I'd been awake at the hospital, I'd slept since someone shot me. There was no way I could stay unconscious for longer than a day—that would be six nights of sleep for me. Unfortunately, that confirmed that I had mostly healed from a gunshot in a single day. I would have some explaining to do. Luiz's comment about being poked and prodded flashed through my head again. Only this time, with the FBI in the other room, the possibility felt far more real.

I made it to the shower, limping the entire way. It was small—a sink, toilet, and tub-shower combo—like home except for the superior paint job. Should I take a bath so I didn't have to stand? When had I last laid down in a tub? I might not fit, and my leg hurt worse when I bent it.

I turned on the shower and waited for it to warm up before stepping inside. The hot water eased the tension in my muscles that I didn't even know I had. While washing my hair, I wondered who shot me. Had I ticked off some clingy barnacle at school? Maybe. There were supposedly three gangs at my school, but I'd never really interacted with them. Perhaps a kid shot me by accident? I imagined a boy playing with his dad's hunting rifle and accidentally pulling the trigger with the barrel directed at me. I thought of dozens of other possibilities and entertained each one as I let the warm water wash over me, heating me on the outside while the pulsing sensation heated me inside. As much as I thought about it, my mind couldn't explain why I'd been shot, and each guess seemed unlikely.

What had Sis and Kendra thought when I nearly died in the hospital? I felt bad for not getting to talk to Kendra. Had the FBI talked to them? Maybe they're here? That idea perked me up and inspired me to wrap up my shower.

A single clean towel hung on a bar next to the shower. It only cost $5.99. I pulled the tag off before drying myself. The Target shopping bag on the sink had my exact underarm deodorant and hair gel. Either the FBI did their homework, or my sister had shopped for them. The bag also had a fingernail clipper, a razor, and shaving cream, so I shaved since I had some good scruff. I was almost eighteen. What if Kendra was waiting for me? I didn't want to have teenage stubble when I kissed her.

I removed the fingernail clipper from its package. My nails were fine, but my stitches itched, and apparently, I didn't need them anymore. I clipped them and pulled them out one at a time, wincing each time the string caught as I pulled its length through the loop in my skin. The stitches on the back of my leg were harder to get to, and my leg was ten times more sensitive in that area, so my wincing included clenched teeth. As I pulled the last stitch from my body, it caught. I tugged it harder and pain shot through me, but it didn't come out. I closed my eyes and took a breath and jerked it hard. I balled my fists tightly as the tender scar tissue screamed at me. A few trembling seconds later, the pain subsided, and I unclenched my fists only to find fingernail marks on my palms. Maybe my fingernails did need to be clipped.

There were clothes and a pair of shoes for me in my room in another Target bag and a shoe box. I pulled out three pairs of cargo pants and three V-neck shirts, each the same style but different colors. It definitely hadn't been my sister who bought those. I tried to keep my hopes up that I would see her and Kendra. I winced as I bent my injured leg to put my foot in the pant leg. Putting on my socks and shoes wasn't a joy either.

Why am I in a safe house? I wondered again, now fully dressed. Time to find out. I opened the door to a short hallway. It was a normal house, except the empty white walls and lack of furniture in the family room seemed out of place. When I didn't hear any voices, disappointment bubbled up inside me like a waking volcano. It erupted when I entered. It was actually a great room—kitchen, dining, family room combo. No Justine. No Kendra. My heart sank. What if Sis was home alone with John?

There was no "they" to the FBI, either. Four mounted stools hung from the kitchen counter that separated the kitchen and the family room, and Special Agent O'Brien sat in the last of them. He didn't speak. Instead, he tapped the stool next to him. I limped over and sat down. The counter held only two items: a thick old book and a gun. Agent O'Brien held a tablet and scrolled through a news article.

"Jacob, I'm glad you're sitting. This isn't going to be easy to hear."

More bad news. His upcoming words hung above me, waiting to drop down and bury me like a pile of dirt.

"First, the good news is you are alive and well. The bad news is that you and I are the only ones that know you're alive . . . and others in the FBI of course," he added that last part almost as an afterthought. He handed me the tablet, and I read the news story open in the browser. I breathed a sigh of relief that it didn't mention my not-so-immaculate conception.

Gunshot Kills Utah Football Prodigy

Last year's prep football player of the year, Jacob Stevens, was shot in what police are calling a drive-by shooting. He survived a few hours, allowing his mother and sister to say good-bye, but unfortunately, his father, John, never got that chance . . . [*read more*]

He's my stepfather. I clenched my jaw. I didn't click the link to read more. Instead, I blinked at Agent O'Brien. Everyone thought I was dead. Why? Sis must be devastated—along with Kendra, Luiz and the jeeks, and the whole football team. Oh, no. This was not happening.

"We have to tell them," I stammered. What about Justine? Who is keeping an eye on her? Was she home alone with John?

"I can't stay. I gotta get home. My sister . . . she needs me!" My voice came out a little higher pitched than it should have.

The agent shook his head. "Not happening. You're not out of the woods, yet. The best way to make sure you stay alive is to keep everyone thinking you're dead. I . . . we . . . the FBI faked your death, Jacob. It'll be a while before you go home." He forced eye contact.

"What do you mean a while?" I glanced away, unable to hold his gaze.

"I don't know," he shrugged. "First, we have to figure out who the hell's trying to kill us . . . I mean you." He took the tablet from me as he spoke.

"And then?"

His jaw clenched, and his eyes tightened. "Then we kill the bastards." He smacked his fist on the counter, and I recoiled, slipping off my chair. I grabbed at my leg as pain shot from it. His eyes followed my hands to my thigh. He took a deep breath and loosened his jaw.

"I have some questions for you," O'Brien continued. "Do you know this man?" He pulled up a picture on the tablet of some old guy whom I'd never seen before, but he held a staff that made me think of the cover of every *Harry Dresden* book I'd ever read—except the guy in the picture was ancient looking and wore a regular business suit; not a black duster. No cool hat either, just a full head of white hair.

"No," I replied. "Who is he?"

"His name is Caradoc Rhys," O'Brien responded. "We believe he is—or was—the leader of a secret society. He and all his followers were recently . . . uh, disappeared."

I gulped.

Did he just avoid saying killed?

He reached over and grabbed the thick book. Its cover had a little bit of green left, but most had rubbed off, leaving a dull gray. It had to be more than four inches thick, and the binding was cracked and torn, showing aged strings.

"Have you ever seen this book before?" he asked, dropping the thick tome into my hands. *I could work out with this thing,* I thought as I hefted it. *OK, maybe I couldn't get a workout from it, but Kevin or Ethan could.*

"I've never seen it," I replied, shaking my head. I opened the heavy book and thumbed through a few pages.

A montage of images flashed before my eyes, and my mind started racing through memories I didn't recognize—memories that indicated that I'd read this book a thousand times before. My vision blurred as my eyes raced side to side like I was dreaming. The same words I'd heard as I woke whispered into my mind like a gust of wind.

Fyr leoht!

I slammed the book shut and tossed it to the counter like it had burned me. The fed kept his gray eyes fixed on mine. He pressed his lips together, emphasizing his stony jaw. A single vein stood out on his left temple, and the beginnings of wrinkles lined the corner of his eyes. He held my gaze for a moment, then glanced at the book and then back at me, questioningly. He reached for the book and examined the binding.

"Sorry, I shouldn't have tossed it like that. Is it expensive or anything?" I grimaced. Damaging the FBI's evidence was the last thing I needed.

"It's not as old as it looks. This is a copy. The original was written only in Old English. This one was made in the Nineteen-fifties." He opened it and pointed to a publication date near the front. "This one is also a translation," he explained and flipped to the middle of the book. "It has an Old English page on the left and an English translation on the right." His eyes grabbed mine, suddenly intense. "How is it you speak Old English, Jacob?"

"I . . . uh . . . I don't speak Old English," I answered nervously.

"What does *hælan mīn thēh* mean?" he asked. "A nurse reported that you were chanting those words at the hospital."

Oh, crap. I gulped again. *Hælan mīn thēh. Fyr leoht.* Were both of those Old English phrases? Why were Old English phrases flashing through my brain? How could I explain something to him that I didn't understand myself? It's not like they teach Old English in school. Shakespeare is about as old as it gets.

"I'm . . . not sure," I managed.

"We looked it up," he added quietly. "It means: 'heal my thigh.'" He let that sink in as his eyes glanced at my thigh. "I find it interesting that you're caught chanting that phrase, and a day later, your right thigh doesn't have a bullet hole anymore. Can you explain that?"

"Good stitches," I evaded. I'd been expecting that question, and I still couldn't answer seriously. I didn't want to tell him that my biological father—though evil—had made me some kind of freak of nature. Sure, fast healing was great for Wolverine, but my healing wasn't anywhere near that fast, and this was no movie or comic book. This was real life. Freaks are treated . . . well . . . they're treated like the X-Men were treated—not good.

"Do you know what a druid is?" Agent O'Brien asked.

"Who doesn't? I've played World of Warcraft and read more than my share of fantasy novels, and I watch the History Channel. The druids built Stonehenge and—" I stopped as the craziness of his question finally hit me. Dots connected in my brain. Old book of spells. Old English chanting. The old guy in the picture with a Dresden-style staff.

"Caradoc Rhys was the leader of a secret society consisting of over a thousand people around the globe." He looked at me, as if waiting for something, then continued. "Those in this secret society claim to be druids."

My jaw dropped. What was I supposed to say to that?

He continued, "They claim that potential druids become aware of their powers during their teenage years. They experience something they call the *wyrman tiegan*. Have you heard that Old English phrase before?"

I shook my head. This conversation had turned weird.

"That translates to *warming connection*. They claim it is a warmth inside you, which doesn't actually raise your body temperature." His stone-gray eyes fixed even more firmly on mine, and the one vein on his left temple swelled to be even more pronounced. "They claim it is a connection to magic. It is often described as pulsing."

I shut my mouth quickly and swallowed as chills ran down my back. *Oh, crap!* I already knew I was a freak—I healed quickly, I didn't sleep much, I had the rarest blood in the world, and I could feel eyes watching me like a string. Now I was experiencing this warming connection—a supposed connection to magic. My muscles tightened, and I stopped breathing, my mind freaking out. I couldn't look at him, so I looked at the daylight streaming through the kitchen sink window and fixated on it.

"The doctors also mentioned that, while you were delirious, you claimed you had this warm feeling inside. Is that true?"

My breath came back, only it came back as quick short breaths—too quick.

"Are you planning on joining this secret society?" he pressed.

My breaths per second accelerated. Everything around my vision went blurry. I felt my head tingling as blood rushed to it. Then a hand touched my shoulder.

"It's all right," the agent spoke each word slowly. "Everything is going to be all right." His touch steadied my breathing. The fuzziness slowly cleared from my eyes, and the blood stopped pushing against my brain. The safety I'd felt earlier returned.

"I don't know anything about this, I swear. I'm not sure what you are talking about. I am not sure why I feel warm inside. It's just there, and I . . ." O'Brien grinned. *Crap!* I'd said too much.

"I knew it. I *knew* you felt it." He smacked the counter, overly excited. "Do you want to hear my current theory?"

I nodded, a little caught off guard.

"The druid secret society is actively recruiting you," he stated flatly.

I shook my head and started to say no, but he cut me off.

"Don't answer until you hear me out. This society is recruiting you—without actually telling you—and the attempt on your life has everything to do with them." He turned back to the tablet and brought up a list of thumbnail images and started scrolling through them. Hundreds of pictures, all different people, moved up the screen.

"These are all the known members of the druid society. Do you know what the one thing they all have in common is?" His face hardened.

"No," I replied.

"They are all dead or missing," he answered.

As the faces flipped past, I realized that I did know them. In fact, I recognized all of them.

"Wait, aren't they the . . . ?" I didn't finish as the History Channel's documentary came to the forefront of my mind, flashing the same faces as those on the tablet. "The Day of a Thousand Deaths," I breathed, "those are . . ."

"Yes. They are," O'Brien confirmed. "Some faction is trying to kill every member of this secret society. If they even suspected that the druids were recruiting you or that you are experiencing the *wyrman tíegan*, they would kill or capture you immediately."

I had thought of a lot of possibilities for why someone had shot me. I had come up with a lot of crazy far-fetched ideas. That was not one of them. "Someone shot me to keep me from becoming a druid." The words sounded absurd as they left my mouth. "That's crazy."

"Is it?" his voice deepened. His hand still rested on my shoulder, and he finally removed it. "You want to hear something crazy?"

I nodded.

He glanced to the ground for a few seconds, and I waited. He finally looked back up.

"I had an encounter with this secret society once about three years ago. They're good guys mostly—vigilante-like sometimes. I was on a case trying to bring in a pusher. You know, a drug dealer. These druids were after the same guy. The pusher and his buddies knew we were coming. They would have killed us, except this guy showed up—a druid." O'Brien looked me straight in the eye. "I thought the druid had a flamethrower, but you know, I'm not sure. If I didn't know better, I'd say he was throwing fire from his own hand." He pointed his palm at me.

"But it was dark." He broke eye contact and looked to his right. "It must have been some kind of flamethrower, right?" He didn't say anything for a long moment. I didn't believe for a second that he thought it had been a flamethrower.

"You really didn't know you were chanting Old English in the hospital?" His eyes returned to mine, drilling into them.

"I, uh . . . No, I didn't know. I swear."

"Humph." He looked up as if thinking. "Read this book." He handed me back the large tome. "Read both the English and Old English sides. Who knows, maybe a memory will jump out at you."

I handled the book again warily as he got up and walked over to the refrigerator, which wasn't full but had a stack of sandwiches wrapped in cellophane and a case of water bottles. My stomach growled, and my dry tongue licked my lips. He grabbed two sandwiches in one hand and two water bottles in the other.

"You must be starving," he said as he set down one of each in front of me. "Eat up. We're going to be here a while."

I set down the heavy book and removed the clear plastic wrapping around the sandwich. I devoured it in a few short, rapid bites. The water bottle lasted about three seconds. My stomach wasn't satisfied, and I looked at Agent O'Brien, wondering if I dared ask him for another sandwich. He glanced my way.

"I forgot, you're a teenager," he commented as he went back to the fridge and grabbed another sandwich and water and slid them my way.

As I ate, the enormity of the situation piled onto me. Someone had tried to kill me. The FBI made it look like they succeeded. My sister, Kendra, the jeeks—they all thought I was dead. I was in a safe house where the FBI could protect me—that is, where *one* FBI guy protected me. On TV there was always more than one agent. "Shouldn't there be other FBI guys around?" I let my thought spill out despite having a mouthful of sandwich.

"Actually, that depends on the situation," he told me, looking away. "When protecting a witness, we use a whole team, but you're presumed dead. Nobody is looking for you. We've also had budget cuts, so you're lucky the FBI is even involved."

I took what he said at face value, but I didn't feel lucky, and something about the situation didn't sit right in my mind. "Where's the furniture?" I asked.

"There isn't any—yet. We'll bring in a couple of things this afternoon or tomorrow. We only had time to acquire a few things before bringing you here." He glanced into the kitchen. "I need a coffee maker."

I regretfully took the last bite of my second sandwich. I thought about asking for a third, but I wasn't starving anymore, so I didn't.

"I have some paperwork and other things to go through online. Top secret. Stay in your room while I work on it."

He had clearly dismissed me. I got up and started to limp away.

"Don't forget the book," he said. "Read it."

I stopped and looked back, wincing. He grabbed the book, stretched his arm out, and dropped it heavily into my hands before I continued limping back to my room.

CHAPTER 15
MAGIC

My thigh itched as I sat on the bed with my back against the wall. The twin bed sat on an unstable metal frame that wobbled and squeaked as I scratched my almost fully healed bullet wound.

I had nothing else to do, so I opened the heavy book and started reading. I didn't need to be a jeek to realize that this book was a druid textbook. It read like last year's biology book, only instead of introduction chapters on life, it had introduction chapters on magic. The first pages explained that magic was another name for energy that could be found everywhere, and the *wyrman tíegan* temporarily connected potential magic users to it. A magic user was simply a person with the ability to feel, control, and manipulate energy. Even matter was nothing more than energy in a physical form.

I found the last third of the book held nothing but spells. *It's like reading a gaming manual,* I decided, grinning. My heartbeat quickened. *Are these spells real? Am I a druid?* I turned back to the first page and began skimming for clues to the ways in which I was different. I needed to make a list. For now, I flipped pages, skimming for anything describing my abnormalities.

My eyes caught a sentence with the words "an invisible fishing line with the hook in their chest." I had called it a thread the other day. The passage spoke of a druid called a Finder. I read the top of the page: "Finders are druids with the ability to detect youth with the potential to use magic."

I skimmed to the part about the fishing line: "When a Finder seeks a potential druid, some potentials claimed they felt a line between them and the Finder. In their stories, they say they were caught like a fish by an invisible fishing line with the hook in their chest. Likely an old druid's tale." Fading notes written in pen filled the margins of this page. There were too many to read right now, but the scribble to the left read:

Need to confirm.

Uh, it's freaking confirmed now!

I read on, but the text didn't mention it again.

This isn't happening. Stop thinking crazy. Druids aren't real. I am not a druid.

I tried to convince myself, but facing the possibility of being something more, I couldn't let it go. I believed this craziness, and I couldn't help it.

I searched the book for my other oddities but found nothing about fast healing except three spells. The first healing spell was a chanting spell, and it described the phrase I'd been repeating at the hospital: *Hælan mīn thēh.* However, according to the text, I hadn't finished the spell and cast it, because the *wyrman tiegan* was supposed to go away with the first spell cast. The second spell, which produced a blue liquid, nudged my memories, but I couldn't quite place it. The last healing spell involved enchanting a crystal called a healing stone.

I found nothing about sleeping for only four hours. In fact, I found the opposite. In the introduction to advanced spells, it mentioned druids needing more than eight hours of sleep as magic use could be draining. OK, maybe that was evidence I wasn't a druid.

Near the end of the book, I encountered a spell that I recognized from real life—well "real life" wasn't the right term either—I recognized this spell from virtual life. Every computer game involving a magic user that I'd played since I was a kid had this spell in one form or another.

The Magic Missile. Or in Old English: *Bealustræl.*

The spell required pressing the bases of my palms together with fingers spread, bringing the magical energy from all around, and compressing it into a single spherical area while simultaneously using a second source of energy to propel the missile at the target.

Awesome! I smiled excitedly.

I couldn't help myself. I followed the instructions to the word. I tried to call on the magic power through the *wyrman tiegan.* Nothing happened. I repeated the steps. Still nothing.

The spells in the book had difficulty ratings. Of course, this spell sat right in the middle of the most advanced spells. In all the computer games I'd played, the magic missile was usually available to a first level magic user. If this druid book was for real, that meant all the game makers had gotten it wrong.

The book also noted that very few druids could even cast these advanced spells. Perhaps one in a hundred.

Hurriedly, I flipped back through the spells until I found the beginner's section. I sucked in a breath as I read the first spell for a novice druid. The English side read, 'fire light' and the Old English side read . . .

Fyr leoht.

Again, the words flashed through my head like rustling wind.

No freaking way! My hand shook in anticipation as I read the spell's instructions. They were simple enough. Hold up one palm. Access the magic energy all around you and focus it into a compressed area rising from your palm. Release it as heat. It should create a very tiny one-inch candle flame.

I tried it. Nothing.

I tried it again. Nothing.

Reality started to set in, but I refused to give up. I was a jeek. I knew how to learn. I read the English side a second time. I tried to read the Old English side, but I didn't get much from that since I had no idea how to even pronounce the words correctly.

I tried again. Nothing.

And again. Still nothing.

I refused to give up despite how impossible it seemed. *I have to be a druid.* The evidence pointing in that direction had piled up. I ignored the one piece of evidence against it for now—my short sleeping habits—because I was desperate to find some explanation for every way that I was different. If I were a druid, I might still be a freak, but at least I'd know what kind of freak I was. I went to the front of the book, the first few chapters, and reread the passage about the *wyrman tíegan.*

The passage gave me new hope as I read: "A potential druid should close their eyes and listen and hear the magic as if listening and hearing the wind. Only then should they try to bring it under control. It may take hours to gain this control. Focus, feel, control."

I repeated the words. "Focus, feel, control." I closed my eyes and started using my mind. Focus, feel, control. I embraced the warmth and the magical energy. I focused on how the magic pulsated and flowed inside me, making my body hum. I lost myself in examining it. The *wyrman tíegan* took control of me. Hours passed and the sun set while I'd been completely enveloped. In those hours I'd come to understand the *wyrman tíegan.* It connected me to everything because magic was part of everything.

I opened my eyes to a dark room.

I no longer doubted.

I raised my palm.

"*Fyr leoht!*" I shouted the words so loud it hurt my own ears. I didn't pull the magic in so much as communicate with it and share my will for it to focus and compress. It obeyed. A faint light glowed above my palm. Then the air ignited.

I had *fire light.*

It was real . . . and it was too much. This was not a tiny and safe one-inch flame. Instead, fire erupted from my palm and rose high, spreading wide and engulfing the entire ceiling. The paint peeled, and the drywall blackened.

I was burning down the house!

"Ahh!" I screamed. I fake-died yesterday. I was in no hurry to die for real today. I panicked and cut off the flow of magic. The fire flickered, then disappeared. Thanks to the paint and drywall, the ceiling had only blackened and scorched but hadn't caught fire.

The door flew open, and Agent O'Brien shouted. "What the hell did you do? You weren't supposed to use that much magic. You shattered this house's threshold. You've just announced to every magic user and creature within a two-hundred-mile radius that a druid is right here." He pointed angrily to the floor. His eyes moved up and noticed the scorched ceiling, and he raised his blond eyebrows in disbelief.

I heard the words "every magic user," and since most of the druids were dead, my imagination went wild with who else he might have meant. And did he say *creature?*

I swore under my breath. I'd read enough fantasy to assume that other magic users can detect magic use. In fact, I felt pretty stupid for not considering this before trying to cast a spell.

"They're gonna come fast. We have to go now! Grab everything. We can't leave any trace of us here." He moved with urgency, grabbing the shoe box and both bags, the one from the floor with my clothes and the one from the bathroom with the toiletries. I got off the bed, but I stood there watching him as he hurried.

"Move it, damn it!" he screamed, startling me into motion. "Get the book."

I grabbed the book, and his fingers wrapped firmly around my forearm and dragged me out the bedroom door. My leg complained sharply at every step as he rushed me down the hall. He glanced at me, his pupils dilated, and the blood drained from his face. I'd never seen a man so obviously terrified in my life. How he could keep moving with such obvious fear was beyond me.

He didn't look like someone who scared easily. If a man like him felt that much fear . . . I increased my urgency to match his.

He stopped at the doorway and let go of me with his left hand. From inside his jacket, he pulled out a little vial of clear, glowing liquid and threw it straight down onto the tile floor. It shattered, but instead of splashing, the liquid expanded in a cloud of mist. A ripple of magic hit me like a heat wave. The *wyrman tíegan* had left me. The book had said it would leave after casting my first spell. Instead of being connected to the magic with a warm pulsing, the magic simply existed everywhere, and I no longer needed the temporary connection to draw it in.

"Keep moving. Let's get to the truck." O'Brien grabbed my arm again. He marched me outside. The moon and the city's ambient light barely illuminated the neighborhood of unfinished homes. A half-framed house stood like a skeleton as we passed it. Shadows made some homes appear complete, but as we passed them, they were nothing but wood, their yards nothing but rocky dirt. The builder must have run out of cash before completion. The entire area was deserted.

O'Brien led me to a home that was not quite finished. He lifted the garage door easily by hand and inside was an old truck. Rust hid all evidence that the truck had ever been painted.

"Get in," O'Brien ordered and handed me the two bags.

I got in and closed the passenger door.

O'Brien removed his FBI jacket and hat and stuffed them carelessly behind the front seat. Underneath, he wore a long-sleeved black shirt that pinged some memory, but before it came to me, he slipped on a black leather jacket that had silver buttons. I opened the passenger door. The mist from the vial had followed us this whole way. It came through as if the passenger door didn't exist. The mist erased any trace of us: our tracks, our scents, everything.

From under his shirt collar, O'Brien pulled out a crystal hanging from a leather cord and emitting light. "Damn it." His swearing told me that the crystal's glow was a bad sign. Under the crystal's light, tattoos peeked out from beneath his shirt collar. The inked symbols looked a lot like runes.

My mind finally caught up with the situation. O'Brien had used magic. The mist still trailed us. This magic crystal illuminated the cab of the truck. He started the truck and pulled out of the garage. He immediately stopped and got out to close the garage.

"We can't leave any evidence we were here," he repeated. He motioned to the garage and to the mist as he slipped into the driver's seat and started moving. His pale face and dilated eyes warned me of danger every bit as much as his glowing crystal. As we pulled out of the neighborhood, our headlights revealed someone ahead of us in the middle of the road, walking right down the yellow lines. Just a man. He stopped and watched us drive toward him.

"Shit! A transient." O'Brien slapped the steering wheel. "It thinks we're prey. It knows you used initiate magic, and it can sense that my magic can't hurt it."

He said *it* instead of *he*. "What is *it*?"

"An enemy."

It didn't look like an enemy to me. Just a normal man. O'Brien floored it, and the truck's engine roared. He planned to run the guy over, and that just didn't feel right to me. He rolled down the window with his left hand and drove with his right. I wondered about the wisdom of rolling down the window. If the man was an it, I wanted the windows up and the doors locked.

Just before the collision, I put my hands against the dash, ducking down. When the man jumped eight feet in the air and hung there long enough for us to drive by underneath, I finally agreed with O'Brien that he might be an it. As we passed, my muscles crawled under my skin like larvae. I'd felt it before—the day my stepdad had . . .

Evil. *I can sense evil.*

I turned to look. The man came after us faster than any man—or *it*—I had ever seen. It caught up to us and dove headfirst into the truck bed and rolled forward to a standing position, leaning against the cab. Its white-skinned hand swung into the driver's side window the same time that O'Brien reached out and tossed a vial into the truck bed. He shouted in pain as the creature's hand grabbed him, but an explosion shook the truck violently and cracked the rear window. O'Brien swerved, and I ducked my head protectively. When I looked up, the man—the it—was gone.

"What did you do? Where did he go?" I asked.

"It's gone," O'Brien answered without looking away from the road.

"I thought you just said your magic couldn't hurt it?"

"That wasn't *my* magic. It was . . . Shit!" He slammed on the brakes. I didn't have my seat belt on, so I hit the dash nose-first. I pinched my eyes closed and grabbed at it, trying to absorb the pain, and felt blood dripping into my hands. I forced my eyes open. Three more of them walked down the road toward us. Farther away, a fourth transient stepped into view. Then a fifth.

CHAPTER 16
BURN

I held my throbbing nose and looked past my hand at the five transients who stood on the dark road in front of us. O'Brien's eyes betrayed my hope. We didn't have a chance. They just walked toward us, calmly. Their tranquil yet persistent motion unnerved me. Whatever they were, they oozed evil, making my muscles thrash, but other than that, they appeared completely normal.

"We'll have to outrun them." O'Brien spun the steering wheel and hit the gas, swinging the truck around. The cab bounced as our tire hit the curb, then again as it dropped off. O'Brien ground the gears as he shifted. I dared to glance back. The transients gazed back without expressions. They maintained their calm walk until one of them launched forward with impossible speed. Another followed. We weren't accelerating fast enough. We hadn't really outrun the first one. Why did O'Brien think we could outrun more?

A high-pitched whine ahead of us grew louder. I thought it came from the engine, and for a second, I worried the truck might stall. But the sound didn't come from our engine; instead, it came from a fast-moving bullet bike speeding right at us. I couldn't make out the figure on the bike.

"Another one!" I shouted and pointed with the hand not holding my nose. "On a motorcycle." O'Brien shifted gears again, but the truck accelerated at a frustratingly slow pace. He'd already played round one of chicken with the first transient, and he drove right at the biker as if expecting round two. As the bullet bike neared, our headlights illuminated the figure sitting on top of it. It was a woman—more of a girl. She wore black leather and no helmet. Her eyes and light skin reflected our headlights back at us, and her black hair flapped behind her.

"What the hell?" O'Brien breathed. I got the impression the girl wasn't another transient. He didn't consider her friendly, though, because he kept the gas pedal floored. Just before colliding with us, she leaned left and zigzagged to my side of the truck, avoiding the head-on collision. I let go of my bloodied nose and swiveled my head, watching her pass within inches of my window. Time seemed to slow, and for a millisecond her eyes met mine. The light must have caught her eyes just right, making them reflect red. Then she passed behind us. She locked up the front brake, throwing the rear of the bike over the front wheel. She leaped off, using the bike's momentum to sling herself through the air. A glint of metal flashed in each of her hands, and two transients dropped as she flew between them. She flipped just in time to roll to her feet and start toward the next transient. O'Brien was still accelerating, though, and before I could see her next move, the scene disappeared into the blackness of night.

"Who was that?" I still held my nose, so my words came out nasally, but the bleeding had stopped. Whoever that girl was, she was helping us. Leaving her behind didn't feel right.

"I don't know, and I don't care." He glanced at me. "We're getting out of here while we can."

"She just saved us. We can't just leave her to die," I protested, looking out the cracked back window into the darkness.

"First of all, she is an *it*. Second, we don't know if it saved us. It's likely just defending its territory. Maybe it wants us for itself."

"But . . ." I started but gave up. I wasn't ready to know what type of an *it* she was right then. I was dealing with my own issues—like my bullet wound, my faked death, my sudden use of magic, and my smashed nose, which while no longer bleeding, throbbed with each heartbeat. I also didn't want to go back there and die.

I glanced at O'Brien. Something dripped down his jacket near his left shoulder. *Is that blood?* "Did it get you?" I pointed and halted my breath.

He swore and opened his jacket, removing some shattered glass and tossing it out the window.

"It must have broken a vial," he said. "No harm done except . . ." He didn't finish.

"Except what?" I asked, breathing again.

"It shattered a spell in my jacket. A truth spell," he said through a tightly clenched jaw. "I might be more . . . well . . . more open to honest communication tonight." He cursed under his breath. The spell was already working.

As we drove east, I realized we were only just a few miles southwest of my house. Once on the freeway, O'Brien turned south. He calmly drove a few miles under the speed limit, and it grated on my nerves. The color had returned to his face, and his pupils were no longer dilated. Instead, his face flexed and hardened. His yellow hair stuck up an inch off his head—a military cut that the fake FBI hat had covered up. He didn't look like a federal agent or a civilian.

He is a druid bodyguard. I heard the words pop into my mind like a memory, but I didn't recognize the voice as my usual thinking voice. It sounded like a voice from someone else's head. I eyed O'Brien, questioningly. *Did I just read his mind? No*, because the memory had been in third person. If I'd read his mind, it would have been in first person. Still, I stared at O'Brien. *Who is he really?*

I felt like I should trust him, but I didn't want to. He had played me this entire time. The whole FBI thing had been an act—a disguise. Acting as FBI, he had given me information that resonated with me so deeply that I had fully embraced it as truth. Yet he'd shared only partial truths meant to guide me so I'd figure everything out on my own. In fantasy books I've read, this exact thing had happened. The druid Allanon never told Shea the truth of the Sword of Shannara. Dumbledore never told Harry Potter he was a horcrux. Instead, both wisely let their pupils gain the needed knowledge on their own.

This guy Dumbledored me.

He hadn't even tried to explain about the discarded FBI disguise. He didn't have to. He was obviously not an FBI agent.

He was a druid.

I considered this repeatedly as we drove in silence. We traveled south to Orem and then into Provo Canyon toward Heber.

"It wasn't your fault," O'Brien finally spoke. His gray eyes had a faint glow to them, making them look blue. "It wasn't anyone's fault." He looked over. "No one could have known you would throw out that much power on your first cast. You nearly burned down that house." He had a slight grin as if my excessive use of magic excited him. "That is supposed to be a one-inch flame. Simple magic that shouldn't ripple past a home's mantel," he continued. "You overdid it."

I knew that the truth vial had broken and he'd answer anything I wanted to ask, but I just didn't know what to ask. Too much had happened, and I couldn't think clearly. Like an idiot, I just sat in the passenger seat and waited for him to say more. It was very un-jeek-like of me. He didn't speak again until we arrived in Heber and stopped for gas. I wouldn't call the truck fuel efficient.

"Stay in the car," O'Brien ordered. I obeyed. He finished gassing up the beater truck and went inside. Through the window, I watched him walk up to the cashier. He paid with cash. Hardly anybody uses cash anymore except . . .

Oh. Except for people on the run—like us. The weight of that realization weighed down on me.

O'Brien got back in the truck, and we drove away. We turned north, which I found a little strange because that would lead us back to Salt Lake City. I noted it but didn't bring it up. I spent the next twenty minutes as we neared I-80 worrying about being on the run and about Sis and Kendra and the jeeks and what they must be going through believing I died. I desperately wanted to call them and let them know I was alive. I worried about my sister being stuck home alone with John when Mom went to work. John's creepiness had escalated. Where would it escalate to next?

I wondered if, over time, Kendra would consider the few hours we had as a relationship or if our kiss would end up being just the Utah version of a one-night stand. I'd never taken her out on an official date. *What if it takes months before I can go back?*

She would move on, that's what.

I didn't like *that* idea at all. My mind conjured up the faces of some of the barnacles that Sis and Kendra had hung out with. Would Kendra end up dating one of them? Oh, no! What if Kendra started dating one of the jeeks? Yes, a jeek would be a great guy. Hadn't I just said yesterday that I shouldn't keep great guys away from my sister? Hadn't I told my friends that I now hoped my sister ended up with one of them? But with Kendra, if I came back and found her with some random loser barnacle, I would have no qualms winning her back; but if I found her with a jeek? What would I do? The reality was that I had lost her. I had lost everyone. Painful emotions shattered in my chest, leaving me aching inside.

It freaked me out that someone had shot me and that everyone, especially those I loved, thought I was dead.

It freaked me out that I had unleashed an inferno from my hand, confirming I was a druid.

It freaked me out that we had just survived a run-in with a half-dozen transients, leaving behind some bad-ass chick with blades to fight alone.

Any one of the above would be enough to make a teenager curl up and cry. I'd experienced all of them within twenty-four hours. So the whimpering sound that O'Brien surely heard— yeah, it was me.

O'Brien finally spoke again, pulling me out of my pounding self-misery.

"Don't get angry and overreact when I tell you this," he started, then under his breath muttered, "Damn truth spell."

Yeah, like I'm not already overreacting, I thought as I wiped my wet eyes. Still, he was going to share some information that he otherwise would not have shared, so I cleared my mind as best as I could and tried to brace myself for one more thing.

"Remember the picture I showed you of Caradoc Rhys, the leader of the druids?" O'Brien spoke loudly so I could hear over the truck's noise. "He was with me until just a few days ago. He . . . he disappeared." He stopped there and let me process that. While that information sucked, I didn't think it was what O'Brien thought would really cause me to "get angry and overreact." He was still getting to that. "Caradoc's blood type is Bombay—same as yours. You lost a lot more blood than I expected."

I heard those words individually. Especially the last two words: "I expected."

O'Brien's thumb rubbed nervously at the steering wheel, as he continued speaking. "Your blood transfusion—all the blood was Caradoc's. Recently—well, more like a few decades ago—druid scientists discovered that injecting druid blood into a potential would start the *wyrman tiegan* immediately and increase the new druid's power. Caradoc and the scientists kept the information hidden. They all forbade each other from sharing or using this knowledge. But after The Day of a Thousand Deaths, only the two of us survived—Caradoc and me. Caradoc is the leader, and I am . . . was just his bodyguard."

He is a druid bodyguard. The words rushed through my mind again. How had I known that?

O'Brien continued: "Caradoc made the decision to give potential druids his blood. We found a couple potentials in Boston, but by the time we got close enough to inject one of them, *they* found us. Caradoc and I barely escaped. *They* took the potentials."

"Took them? Or killed them?" The words shivered from my mouth.

"I don't know," he shook his head. He gripped the old truck's steering wheel so tightly his knuckles turned white. "Some . . . mercenaries tracked us to Chicago. Different mercenaries found us in Dallas. A third group nearly killed us in Kansas City. Caradoc got suspicious. There was no way they were that good at tracking us." O'Brien paused and glanced at me, then continued. "It was my fault." The words came from clenched teeth. "I can barely touch the magic. I didn't know that they put a tracking spell on me. Caradoc hadn't seen the tracking spell either because it only activated when close to a potential. The spell was intricately woven into my brain. Caradoc was working out how to best remove it without damaging my mind. He said he was close, but he didn't have the chance to try and remove it before he disappeared." He turned and made eye contact for long enough that I started worrying that he would swerve off the road. "I'd been leading them right to us." His eyes went back to the road, and he stopped speaking. The truck's loud engine and air whistling through the crack in the back window gnawed at my ears as I waited for him to say more.

"Who are these mercenaries?" I asked.

"A mix of secret societies—always different. But that isn't the right question. The right question is who sent the mercenaries."

He took a moment to breathe, then continued: "With the tracking spell on me, Caradoc wanted to find the potentials on his own, without me to protect him. I didn't want to leave him unprotected, though. But the tracking spell gave him another idea. He could put a tracking spell in his own blood and donate as much as possible to the blood banks. His blood type was Bombay—a universal donor. His blood would go everywhere, and his tracking spell would alert us when it was injected into a potential. With his healing magic, he could give blood three times a day.

"We started here in Salt Lake because a huge portion of the population in Salt Lake are descended from England—places like Herefordshire and Worcestershire. It's also the genealogical capital of the world. Ancestry.com started just south of here and the LDS Family History Center is here. Together, they're a Finder's greatest resource. Salt Lake has the highest genealogically documented population of druid descendants."

He glanced my way again as we neared Park City. Lighted lines ran down the mountain from the ski resorts. The ski resorts had zip lines and speed slides that were open during the summers. I'd never gone at night. I'd take Sis and Kendra and the jeeks, the next chance I got . . . which would likely be never.

"Why me?" I asked, trying to refocus my thoughts.

"You topped the list of Salt Lake potentials. Caradoc and I kept a tight watch on you, except when he was giving blood. Monday, he'd detected evil near your home. He convinced me to stay nearby and keep watch on your house while he went to give blood. I shouldn't have let him go. I haven't seen him since." O'Brien's hard face trembled. My muscles had crawled that day—it was the first time I detected evil. A monster had been at my house—just not the kind Caradoc and O'Brien had thought. In a way, my stepdad was responsible for Caradoc's disappearance.

"Without Caradoc, I didn't know what to do," O'Brien explained. "I couldn't get close to you without alerting our enemies. Until I had the idea to use my other skill." He hesitated. The vial of truth spell forced him to keep speaking, but he didn't want to. "My way worked without getting close."

Some subconscious part of me guessed what he would say next, but I couldn't bring it to the forefront of my mind. I was already torn up emotionally and mentally, not to mention my nose still throbbed and the noise of the truck had built up pressure in my ears. I was buried deep in crap I didn't understand already, and he was about to drop another dump-truck load on top of me.

"I broke into the different hospitals and blood banks and removed any Bombay blood that wasn't Caradoc's. I expected you would only need a pint or two, but you lost more than half your blood. They gave you two quarts, Jacob. Two full quarts of Caradoc's blood. Giving a potential that much of another druid's blood has never been done before. That must be why your first spell had so much power." He stopped. The dump-truck load of bad news hung above me waiting to crash down.

He needed to inject me with Caradoc's blood, but he couldn't get close to me. Dots connected in my mind. *Oh. That means he . . .* My mouth opened despite a tense jaw. My voice quivered as I asked. "What did you do?"

"I didn't even know it, but I'd been using magic for years as a Marine," he replied. "I had so little magic. I just thought I was the best. I never missed."

"Oh, hell no. Did you shoot me?" That was exactly what he was saying. The entire dump-truck load fell on me all at once. The muscles throughout my body tensed.

"In the Marines, I was a sniper . . . I . . ."

"You freaking shot me!" I screamed, magic pouring into me at the same rate as my anger. I wasn't thinking clearly. I couldn't see him as someone ordered by Caradoc to protect me. I couldn't see him as a druid bodyguard trying to keep both of us alive. I could only see the bastard who shot me, and I felt the hate spread stickily from my gut.

"Yes. I . . ." He kept speaking, but I didn't hear him. I lost it. My ability to cope broke. I lunged at him, my fist missing his face by inches only because my seat belt stopped me short. I swung again and again, but he used his right hand to fend off my punches while still steering with his left. I swung at him without reservation, using all my strength, yet he blocked my punches like I was a child. So I reached for a bigger fist—a magical one. Actually, my palm, since I only knew one spell.

His eyes widened, and he flashed an oh-crap face at me. Before I could cast the spell, he slammed on the brakes, pinning me to my seat with the tightened seat belt and breaking my focus. The truck swerved off the freeway and lurched to a stop. More magic filled me, and I added it to the only spell I knew.

"*Fyr leoht!*" I growled. Fire exploded from my palm, and the entire cab went up in flames, engulfing both of us. Just like at the safe house, the fire light didn't burn me. The magic protected me because I was wielding it.

Except I couldn't breathe.

I had just burned away all the oxygen in the cab. Magic or no, I needed to breathe. I couldn't see anything because the flames surrounded me, and I sat motionless inside them trying to figure out what to do next when a wave of air rushed in. Had O'Brien opened the door? I couldn't see through the flames. A few seconds later, my door opened, and more air rushed in as flames rushed out. A hand grabbed me and yanked me out, dropping me to the ground. My back and head hit the hard dirt first. The impact knocked both the wind and the magic out of me, but the flames didn't stop. The fire no longer needed magic. It fed off the plastic in the cab—a real fire now—spewing up a cloud of black smoke even darker than the night.

As I tried to catch my breath, the gravity of what I had just done filled my mind like the flames had filled the cab. I had just destroyed our truck—our only means of transportation, and we were currently on the run. What if the transients were still after us? Worse, I had tried to kill a man—attempted murder. I was worse than my stepdad because, while he was a creep, he had never once been violent. I couldn't even compare the bad things he had done to attempted murder. My muscles writhed under my skin, recoiling from the hate that I had allowed inside me, and I wanted to wash it away.

I looked up in time to see O'Brien's fist coming hard at my face. Pain spread from the impact above my left eye. As I twisted, he hit me again in the left cheek. I flailed my arms trying to create some distance between him and me, but the next fist came down unobstructed, right on my already throbbing nose.

CHAPTER 17
TRUTH

I regained consciousness the next morning in a hotel bed. My left eye didn't open all the way. Was it swollen? O'Brien sat in front of me, eyes on me. The silencer-extended barrel of his handgun pointed between my eyes. His other hand held a coffee mug with steam rising from it. He thumbed the rim of the cup nervously.

"You're a damn fool, you know that!" he growled at me. "I never tried to kill you. I made the bullet special. I call it a slicer. It's the opposite of a hollow point. It goes in and out like a knife with minimal damage."

He sipped his coffee as I eased into a sitting position. I was still dressed, but my clothes had some nice scorch marks and a few burn holes. I reached down and scratched the scar on the front of my leg, then scratched its twin on the back of my leg.

"Good thing I paged your pediatrician to the ER. I thought I'd made a perfect shot, but I must have nicked your femoral artery. You needed a lot of blood. I thought you were going to die, and it would have been my fault. I overestimated my accuracy."

He was finishing the story he'd started telling me the previous night as if nothing had happened—as if I hadn't unleashed a fiery inferno to kill him. As if he weren't holding a gun on me. This guy was on a mission to tell me what happened and nothing could distract him from it. Maybe that was exactly it. Caradoc had ordered him to watch me—his final mission. Was he still on a truth high from the broken vial?

"I figured if I could get to you, I could heal you, but I had that tracking spell on me. As I drove south away from the scene, I found a possible solution staring me in the face." He sipped his coffee.

"Certain cathedrals in Europe are old and quite powerful. Religion is faith. Faith is power. Power is magic. The threshold of an ancient cathedral will strip away even the strongest spells.

Only it usually takes hundreds of years for such power to build up. The building usually has to be big and hold a lot of people worshipping at one time. We have a documented list of cathedrals that are strong enough to strip spells. Worldwide, it's a large list. Unfortunately, this is the western United States. Few buildings are old enough to have accumulated enough power to fortify a threshold with spell-stripping power."

He squinted at me and lowered his gun as he took another sip of his coffee. I recognized the handgun from the Xbox—a Glock.

"Caradoc had suggested we fly back to Boston and use King's Chapel. It's been on the list since the late eighteen hundreds. But Caradoc disappeared, and then I got my other idea."

I clenched my teeth. His "other idea" had nearly killed me.

"While I drove away, I saw one of the Mormon temples." O'Brien shook his head. "None of the temples are on our list. We usually test religious buildings, but not until they are at least two hundred years old. Of course, the temple I drove by wasn't likely to be strong enough, but I thought just maybe the one downtown just might be. That building is a fortress, and it looks like one, too. If any religious building west of the Mississippi could strip the spell from me, it was that Temple. I drove there as quickly as possible, but rush hour slowed me down. I had to walk around to find the entrance as it wasn't where I expected. I made quite a scene when I hurried past a couple of old guys that I wouldn't really call security guards."

"You went into the Salt Lake Temple!" I exclaimed, my mouth hanging open as he took another sip of his coffee.

"That temple didn't disappoint. Its threshold easily stripped away the spell. I left before the geriatric guards could call for real security." He spoke with excitement, his thumb nervously rubbing back and forth on the rim of his coffee mug.

"So why didn't you just do that in the first place?" I tilted my head at him. "Hello. You shot me!"

His eyes dropped to the floor. "As I said, we were rushed and desperate. We never thought about it. Perhaps Caradoc considered it, but he never mentioned it."

"You screwed up!"

"You don't know a damn thing!" he said, defensive. "You don't know what it's been like the past year." His eyes turned wild as if filled with fire. If his hands weren't full, he might have hit me again. He took a deep breath and calmed himself. He holstered the handgun, which allowed my shoulders to relax. I hadn't even noticed them tense up.

"So you are an ex-Marine?" I asked.

"I was," he nodded.

"And while in the Marines, you were a sniper."

"That's right." His nod continued from my last question.

"And you snipered me, then tried to save me?"

"Well, snipered isn't really a word, it's sniped, but yes, I shot you and then saved you. It took me far too long to get back to you at the hospital. I assumed you would be dead when I arrived, but you survived. Caradoc's blood must have helped. No other explanation makes sense, except if you were a prot—" he cut the last word short. "No, his blood did it. I arrived just in time. You were chanting in Old English and about to cast a healing spell on yourself, which would have attracted the wrong crowd at the wrong time."

"How come I have Old English words floating in my head?" I interrupted and waited for him to finish another sip of coffee to answer.

"Along with the tracking spell, Caradoc embedded some of his own memories into his blood; knowledge that can only be activated by a druid."

"I have Caradoc's memories?" That explained the Old English and how I knew he was a bodyguard before he told me.

"Not all of them. Probably just a few memories of some of the more basic spells." The ex-Marine thumbed the rim of his mug.

"So what, can Caradoc talk to my mind?" I asked. The voice in my head had not been my own.

"No. They are just memories. They will pop into your head randomly just like your own memories do. However, different than your own memories, you can't just remember them. You're basically stuck waiting for them to pop up."

I stopped and considered that for a moment. I had a handful of memories that weren't my own. Could I live with that?

"How did you fake my death?" I was on a roll now. I should have been asking him questions last night instead of trying to burn him up with the truck. I must have been in shock last night and not realized it.

"I don't have much magic myself, but druids can bottle it. I used a healing vial on your leg and then . . ."

The blue vial, his stone-cut face; I recognized him now. "The guy in the pink scrubs—that was you," I interjected.

"Yes," he nodded. "I also used another vial—one that stills the heart and cools the body. It should have lasted three or four days. Did I dare wait until they sent you to a mortuary? What if

I didn't get there before the scheduled autopsy? I figured you'd be more useful *with* your organs." He grinned and just stopped short of laughing.

Apparently, he thought that my near-autopsy was funny.

The image of my body being cut open alive on a cold, stainless-steel slab forced its way into my mind. I shivered and didn't find it funny at all. OK, maybe the fact that I had been only "mostly dead" was a little funny.

"I rescued you easily from the morgue—no security. It's a good thing I did because the vial didn't last three days. Maybe the healing spell weakened it." He looked off to the right, considering while his thumb went nuts rubbing the rim of his coffee mug.

I wondered which was more unbelievable: the story of a near druid genocide, tracking spells, and memory-embedded blood transfusions, or that I believed every word. I was still overwhelmed, but a good night's sleep always had a positive effect on me, and I had slept for at least six hours—two hours more than I normally needed. My body felt strong and my mind felt . . . well, it still felt freaked out but at least it was dealing. I wasn't swearing and throwing fire at O'Brien. That was a good sign.

The ex-sniper rubbed his fist. "I dripped some of the healing fluid on your eye just now. It woke you up." His coffee must have cooled because he drank down what remained and set his mug on the hotel desk behind him. "Sorry, I hit you. Your black eye should be gone soon."

I touched my slightly swollen eye, and it felt cold and damp. I didn't really care about his apology, or that he'd knocked me out last night. My mind connected bigger dots. As a jeek, thinking wasn't new to me. Why had O'Brien been so desperate he'd resorted to sniping me? Because a bunch of bad guys hiding behind mercenaries had almost entirely wiped out the druids—a very powerful secret society. A coordinated genocide like that would have taken another powerful secret society with a hell of a leader and a major grudge.

"Who's behind this?"

"I don't know," the ex-Marine replied.

My mind kept thinking. There couldn't be that many secret societies, could there? My mind threw out a random mathematical guess—one secret society per hundred million people in the world. *Crap.* I didn't like that math. With seven billion people on the earth, that made at least seventy secret societies. Of course, I might be shooting low. What if one secret society existed per ten million people . . . that would be seven hundred.

My estimations were getting me nowhere. Sometimes the geek side of being a jeek was distracting.

"Who could have pulled it off?" I wasn't asking an easy question. The United Nations had been asking the same question about The Day of a Thousand Deaths for over a year and had no clue, and I was expecting this druid bodyguard to know.

He shook his head. "Caradoc and I had this conversation daily," he replied. "We just don't know for sure. We could only speculate."

Crap. This wasn't a simple case of catch the bad guy and go back to my life. O'Brien and I were going to be on the run forever. I wasn't going to have to worry about Kendra having a boyfriend when I returned, because it didn't look like I'd ever return. The dump-truck loads of tough information just kept burying me deeper.

"Speculate with me like you did with Caradoc," I suggested.

The druid bodyguard took a breath. "There are many secret societies," he stated. "However, most are not organized well enough to pull something off. Some secret societies are not actually societies at all. They lack leadership, or the leaders lack obedient followers." He paused as if to think, and I got the impression he was deciding what to share and what to hide. "Caradoc says that there is only one secret society that had enough information about us to catch us off guard."

"Who's that?" I asked eagerly.

"Us. The druids." He sighed and looked down. Admitting he and his fellow druids had been betrayed from within stressed him out enough to make the vein on his left temple stick out. His answer didn't make sense to me. Not that any of this made any sense. "We haven't confirmed that all the druids who are missing were assassinated," O'Brien added. "Caradoc believed some of the druids faked their assassination. He thinks these druids have taken over one or more smaller secret societies. We are up against an enemy as intelligent and powerful as ourselves that has one or more secret societies under their control. But again, that is just speculation."

I shook my head. So basically, it was him and me against some evil druids and their armies of minions. It sounded so surreal. Two days ago, I was weight lifting with the jeeks and now I was a druid and a target of mass genocide—one perhaps led by other druids. *I miss football.*

"I need to teach you a containment so you can practice magic," O'Brien told me.

"OK. What's a containment?"

I'd read a few references to containments when skimming the druid text. Had I burned up the book with the truck?

"A containment is exactly what it sounds like. It's simply magic used to contain magic and other things. Magic performed inside containments doesn't ripple out and broadcast your whereabouts to the rest of the magic world. Also, magical fire doesn't leave the containment, so it is harder to burn something down."

"Sorry about the truck."

He raised his eyebrow at my apology. "That beater? We had to ditch that truck anyway. They'd seen us in it. You mostly did us a favor, except I had to pack you fireman style to the nearest parking lot and steal a car."

"You stole a car?"

He ignored me. "Your fire broadcast our location again, but I guess your magical tirade just made it look like we were heading east. Whoever is tracking us is hopefully searching for us in Colorado or Wyoming right now."

"Where are we?" I asked, suddenly realizing I had no idea where he brought me after he punched me out.

"Sandy," he supplied. Sandy City was about ten minutes west of my house in West Jordan.

"Wait, didn't we just run from here?" I questioned.

"What better place to hide than the place where everyone thinks we left."

While that sounded pretty smart on the surface, he was hiding something. We were staying in this area for another reason—a reason he wasn't sharing. The truth spell had most likely worn off.

"Why are we *really* back here?" I asked.

"How about I tell you that later," he said firmly enough that it wasn't a question. "For now, you need to learn to cast a containment and practice magic."

I took a breath. Words like "cast" and "containment" and "magic" were going to be commonplace, so I'd better just get used to them.

"So, let's get started." I slid my legs, scorched pants and all, off the bed.

"We have a problem," the druid bodyguard admitted.

"What's the problem?"

His eyes lowered again. "I don't have the power to cast a containment. I don't even know how. Remember, I have little magic, and I can only use it in two ways. Finding and . . ." He put his arms up like he was holding a rifle and pulled an imaginary trigger. "I'm the best sniper because I don't miss."

"Don't remind me," I frowned.

He had mentioned his lack of magical ability before, but I hadn't understood what he meant until now. This guy was a magical dud—a bullet with no black powder. He was nothing more than an ex-Marine with a gun, and we were likely up against some traitor druids and their armies of minions. I reevaluated my chances for surviving. They had gone from so impossible I was pretty sure I was going to die to . . . well, so impossible I was pretty sure I was going to die. I guess his being a dud didn't hurt my chances of surviving any, but they didn't help them either. I needed to find some way to improve the odds.

"You'll just have to use the book," he continued. "Don't forget, you should have some knowledge embedded in Caradoc's blood you can tap into," he pointed out.

I blinked at him, and he turned away quickly, trying to hide his gulp. I interpreted the gulp as if he said the following: *Oh, and by the way, Caradoc disappeared, which probably means they killed him. He was a full-fledged druid, the leader of them all, and they got to him. So, guess what you have coming soon?* He, of course, didn't say that, but I'd bet money his thoughts were along those lines.

My jaw tensed up, and I said, "This all freaking sucks!"

He nodded and reached back to the desk behind him and grabbed the druid textbook.

"Hey, I didn't burn it up." Relief swept over me as he handed the book to me.

"That book doesn't burn so easily," O'Brien laughed.

"Enchanted?" I asked.

"As a matter of fact," he grinned. "How about you study containments in the book. I have to hit a store. Unlike that book, our spare clothes didn't make it, and I'd just bought yours."

"Can I come?" I asked and jumped off the hotel bed and winced. I reached down and grabbed my thigh. The bullet wound wasn't fully healed yet. I *so* needed a change of clothes. Pants with holes were in style, but not fire-scorched holes.

"No. Stay here and read the book. Start with reading about containments. Then just start at the front and read the whole thing."

"Seriously?"

He ignored me. "Don't try to cast any spells. Just read. Don't leave this room. Don't call anyone." He walked over to the phone and pulled the cord from the wall and took it with him. "That should alleviate one temptation." He walked over to the TV and reached behind it, pulling out a tightly strapped bundle of cables.

He reached into his jacket and pulled out a knife and cut them all. "No internet on the TV either." I hadn't even known I could get internet on the hotel TV. I hadn't really stayed in a hotel since I was a kid, back when Grandma had forced Mom and John to take us to Disneyland.

"I get it," I said, raising my hands and eyeing the knife defensively. "I've seen enough movies where the idiot calls home, and the bad guys find him. I won't be that idiot. But what do I do if someone comes for me here?"

He was already halfway out the door. He stuck his head back in and answered, "If something comes for you, burn the place down and pray that fire can hurt it."

Oh crap. I had said *someone,* hadn't I? He'd changed some*one* to some*thing.* Just like *he* and *she* had become *it.*

"It's daytime. You should be safe enough," he finished, pulling the door shut behind him.

Double crap. I was safer in the daytime.

CHAPTER 18
HUNGRY

O'Brien's comment about being safe because it was daytime echoed in my mind. Dots connected in my head. I'm a druid, which I didn't think existed two days ago. The transient had jumped eight feet as our truck drove underneath it. What even was a transient? Its speed was unforgettable. It had easily caught up to us even though O'Brien had floored it. What other creatures existed besides transients? *Are we talking team Edward or team Jacob?* Except, were the monsters coming for me friendly? Maybe I had it all wrong. The monsters might not be from this world. Maybe I should be thinking about something wearing an Edgar suit. Or perhaps these creatures were daemons escaped from hell. Too bad I didn't have a beastie-like red devil with a giant hand to help me out of this situation, but at least I could throw some fire. Unfortunately, identifying with the character of Liz was not that comforting.

I'd just have to *bump back* myself.

I could bump back by being a hunter like Sam and Dean Winchester. That made me feel better for about two seconds until I remembered all the different monsters that they dealt with. I could quote books and TV and movies with the best of them, but I needed to get out of fiction-land. This was real life. I needed to learn what was real and what wasn't. I needed to learn more magic than just throwing fire.

I grabbed the druid text, sat down at the desk, and started reading. The druid tome contained twelve hundred pages. Well, actually it was twice that size, but that was just because every other page was a modern English duplicate of the Old English page. I had read some of this book already. I should have started with the section on containments. O'Brien had been right to tell me to read the whole thing, as daunting as it sounded. To give myself even a chance at surviving, I needed to understand every line, so I turned to page one.

I was a jeek. *I can do this*, I encouraged myself. Then I dove right in.

When I started, it was morning. O'Brien hadn't left any food. I couldn't order room service because he killed the phone. I thought about going to the front desk, but I had promised not to leave the room. Since I had nothing to eat, I drank a ton of water. That started an annoying, forty-minute cycle of read, drink, pee, read, drink, pee. Add two naps in there, and that made up my entire day. Of course, the naps weren't long—twenty minutes energized me and left me wide awake. Even the extreme dullness of the druid text couldn't bring me to sleep longer or more often.

I reached the beginner's section on the containments. It was pretty short, so I read it twice. It mentioned a more advanced section later on in the book but didn't give a page number. I'd get to it eventually.

I got sick of reading the textbook straight through, so I turned to the Magic Missile spell again. I read and reread it. That single spell stood out as the coolest part of the old tome. I had killed so many virtual monsters with magic missiles in various computer games, doing the same in real life would be freaking awesome. Unfortunately, the spell fit on one page, and it didn't take me long to study it thoroughly. I still needed to read the book straight through, so I went back to working on that.

The red numbers on the clock told me it was after five. I didn't want to drink another cup of water, read another page, or make another trip to the bathroom. I stood, and my muscles begged me to go for a run, jump up and down, work out, or something. My stomach argued against exercising in its deprived state.

Why wasn't O'Brien back yet? I was seriously worried. This worry didn't sneak up on me. It had grown with every passing hour. I had batted it away constantly, but my mental swinging arm was tired and started striking out.

Where the freak is he?

Hadn't O'Brien said that Caradoc had just disappeared? What if O'Brien just disappeared, too? What if he left me alone? Where would I go? I was so not prepared to be a druid on my own. I'd been planning to leave my house for years, but I had always planned to leave with somewhere to go, like college with a full-ride scholarship.

Doubt crept in with the worry. I didn't know anything about this O'Brien guy. Was O'Brien really his name? The only thing I knew for certain was that despite sniping me, O'Brien wanted to keep me alive and protected, but after that, what did I know? That O'Brien was a druid? He'd used no magic whatsoever except a few vials of something, which might not have been magic at all. I even started doubting my own use of magic. With a little natural gas, O'Brien could have easily tricked me into believing I'd cast fire light. I could feel the magic around me, but the ability to feel magic was only since the hospital.

What if he had drugged me, and now, I was hallucinating?

I paced back and forth with tense muscles, no longer able to read. What would happen if I just walked home right now? It had to be less than five miles to my house. I could easily jog that in an hour. I rubbed my still tender thigh. OK, I could walk my way to a bus stop and ride home in an hour. I imagined the look on Sis's face when I walked in. Kendra would be crying again, and I could kiss away her tears. I needed them. I preferred not to see my mom flinch, and I really didn't want to see John again, but I longed to be back with Sis, Kendra, and the jeeks.

Besides, did these secret societies even know I existed? Hadn't O'Brien said they had captured and taken every potential druid from them until now? Maybe they had no idea who I was yet. Maybe I could just walk away.

Of course, there was the whole *I died* thing, but my mind had already started forming a story for that. Maybe I woke up shivering and delirious with amnesia in the morgue and wandered away. Maybe my memory returned and I went home. People are mistaken for dead all the time. The hospital will look stupid, not me.

I'm going home! I decided. I just needed to gather my stuff. Except I didn't have any stuff—just the charred clothes on my back, so I decided to just go. Well, I needed the book to learn how to be a druid. I picked it up. So much for doubting the reality of magic. I took one last look around the hotel room before opening the door and stepping out.

"Get back in that room," O'Brien hissed at me as he walked toward me down the hall. He had a couple of bags, again from Target. I guess he expects more but pays less. My stomach growled in anticipation at the sight of the other bag of food.

I didn't acknowledge the relief that swept over me at seeing O'Brien. I helped him carry the bags back inside and then move the food from the bags to my mouth. I courteously let some food go to the refrigerator. He scowled at how much I ate anyway. I had been so famished, I had delayed asking him where he had been. With food in me, however, the time for questions had arrived.

"Where were you?" I demanded, my voice abrasive with frustration.

"I had business to attend to," he responded.

"I waited here, hungry, while you were gone all day!"

"Why didn't you order . . ." he trailed off, and his eyes quickly switched from the phone to the severed media cables. "Sorry about that. Well, you've eaten now."

"Yeah, but where were you?" I demanded.

"It is none of your concern."

I find that whenever someone says the words "It is none of your concern," it is most definitely your concern. It is likely more your concern than theirs, and they are trying to protect you when it would just be best to communicate. I pressured O'Brien for ten minutes straight, arguing and digging in every way I could. Unfortunately, the truth spell had definitely expired, and he was overcompensating by being extra closed off.

"How far did you get in your book?" he asked, changing the subject.

"Page two-hundred and forty," I replied. "Reading that book is like watching paint dry," I said, remembering holding up a desk fan while literally watching paint dry.

"I guess that is a start," he commented.

That is a start? What did this guy expect? I read a fifth of a freaking huge, twelve-hundred-page textbook.

"Can I try a containment?" I didn't want to stay cooped up in the hotel room anymore.

"Let's wait till morning. It is too close to nightfall. If we make a mistake . . ." He looked out the window at the sun, which was still a good three hours or more from setting. "Well, let's just try when we have a full day of light ahead of us."

A part of me wanted to ask for the list of creatures that could come for us at night, but another part of me didn't want to know and wasn't ready to know.

"Can I get out of here for a while?" I begged.

"Sorry. Too dangerous." He didn't even look up as he answered.

My hope deflated. The clock read 6:07 P.M. I wasn't planning on sleeping till two in the morning. What was I going to do for the next eight hours? I looked at the magic tome and cringed.

CHAPTER 19
DUALITY

I reached the section in the druid text about Finders just after ten. I glanced up at O'Brien who, like me, sat on his bed with pillows behind him. My eyes drifted to the darkness visible through the crack in the blinds. The darkness worried me. Actually, not knowing what could come for us in the darkness worried me. Still, I kept the worry in the back of my mind.

I had read part of the page on Finders already, including the part about the fishing line, but I hadn't read everything. I read it again with new interest because O'Brien had mentioned he was a Finder. Finders could detect potential druids, but not actual druids. As soon as a potential used magic for the first time, Finders could no longer detect them. According to the book, a potential rarely used magic without guidance. Not that I was an expert yet, but the word "rarely" sounded like a load of crap. Maybe living in the Wikipedia age made me less trusting of such statements. How would they ever know if a potential druid used magic on their own? I found the answer a few paragraphs later. They didn't unless they caught them using magic later in life.

A handwritten note in the margin jumped out at me. I hadn't noticed it the last time I'd read this page.

> *Duality of Druids - Potential druids never found alone. Found in twos. Find a druid, second druid near. Phenomenon not understood. Holds true in last hundred years. Has it always been this way?*

Why hadn't O'Brien told me about this?

"O'Brien," I called over, "question for you." He looked at me and adjusted one of the pillows behind him. He'd kept his nose in his tablet since he got back and hadn't said a word in hours. He deliberately held his tablet turned away from me so I couldn't see what he was doing. Maybe he didn't want me to know how much he liked Angry Birds. Except I pegged him as more of the zombie-killing type.

"Ask away."

"Who is the other one?" I asked.

"Who's the other what?"

"You know who," I countered, and I read him the note.

He finally looked away from his tablet and swore. "I thought that was unpublished information," he complained.

"Someone published it the old-fashioned way." I showed him the note written in the margin.

"Oh." He didn't answer my question. He just turned back to his tablet.

"So, who is it?" I asked.

"I've been working on that since last Friday when we confirmed you as a potential," he replied. "I guess there's no use not telling you now. A potential druid is always someone fourteen to seventeen. I've ruled out the obvious choices, like your three friends and the football team. I have a long list of your classmates, and I've ruled out most of them."

"What about my sister?" I asked.

"We did rule her out, but just to be thorough. Your sister isn't likely. In only extremely rare cases is the other druid a different gender. That has only happened a few times in history—only once since Merlin found Arthur and Morgan la Fay in the fifth century. Still, we weren't taking any chances, especially since Justine is your half-sister, just like Morgan la Fay was to Arthur."

"Wait, Arthur didn't have magic."

"Without magic, how could he have pulled the sword? Of course, he had magic, just very little, like me," he clarified. "Only hints of it made it to your history books."

Of the Arthur movies, it was the Disney cartoon that came to mind. The part where Wart reaches for the sword and a light shines down from above, allowing him to pull the sword from the stone. Disney got it right. I'd have to ask O'Brien sometime about the possibility of turning into a fish, squirrel, or bird.

"So we are looking for a guy my age or younger," I stated.

"Uh-huh," he replied, thumbing through his tablet.

"Why didn't you tell me?"

He looked at me consolingly. "Wouldn't you worry about him if we had to leave? If we can't find him soon, we will."

Oh. I swore to myself. If they wanted to kill me, they wanted to kill this other potential druid, too, and we could only guess who *they* were. Someone I knew was about to become the unsuspecting prey to a secret society he hadn't even known existed. Whoever he was, we shared the same fate and the same threats.

O'Brien's eyes gazed at me with intensity. "I don't want them to take you or him like they took the others. We have to find who is responsible. The future of the druids depends on our survival."

"At least you are here looking for him still. We need to find him fast."

"Patience," he said, but he didn't seem patient himself.

"But what if we don't find him?"

"We'll leave!" O'Brien's jaw stiffened with resolve.

"I can't leave one of my friends to die!" I argued. "I'd risk my life before bailing on him!"

"We will do what is necessary to survive. Right now, our survival would be greatly improved by finding another druid. He will be someone you know and interact with a lot, usually for years."

Using his tablet, O'Brien showed me a spreadsheet of every teenage boy whom I had possibly been in contact with regularly.

"I got this list from your high school's database," he told me. "I've crossed off most already."

He handed me the tablet and let me look over the list. He had the majority of them checked off. He'd compiled a thorough list. I scanned through the names looking for a few guys my age I knew the best.

"You left off a couple guys from church," I told him. "They go to a different high school even though they live by me."

"Really?"

"Yeah, but I don't go to church that often, maybe once a month."

"That's enough to make them possibilities. Give me their names," he instructed, taking back the tablet. I gave him the names, and he added them. "We'll check them tomorrow," he assured me excitedly.

"I can come?" I smiled.

"I meant I'll check on them tomorrow. You have to stay out of sight."

"There has to be a way I can come."

I tried to convince him for several minutes, yet he made it obvious I couldn't go driving around my neighborhood when I was supposed to be dead, so I gave up.

I wondered who the other druid could be. I went through the list of guys in my grade. I thought of the jeeks, even though O'Brien had already crossed off their names. I let my mind entertain the possibility of joining with another jeek and opening a can of kick-ass druid magic on some secret society. O'Brien had crossed off Sis, who was the only girl on the list, but I still thought about how cool it would be for Sis and me to cast spells together as brother and sister druids. Of course, I didn't want her to be in any kind of danger, so I pushed that idea away. O'Brien had checked Dylan off the list, too. So, my sister's current boyfriend wasn't in any danger. I went through every member of the football team, but I only found a couple names not checked off.

"I have no idea who it could be. How did you find me?" I asked, curious.

"Oh, your mom's side of the family is on a genealogical list. And you stood out for . . . well . . . for other reasons."

"What other reasons?"

"Well, the records listed your father as unknown, so we looked into you further, and when we came across your blood type, Caradoc suspected that . . . well . . . that was enough for us to focus on you."

What had Caradoc suspected? O'Brien had answered my first question, so I let my new question go. Besides, the topic was too close to my biological father, which wasn't something I chatted about casually.

"I shouldn't tell you this, but your funeral is tomorrow."

Ouch. The shards of my already-shattered emotions cut at my heart again. *You shouldn't have told me,* I thought. "Thanks," I said, instead, not really meaning it.

Once the wave of emotional pain passed, I had a morbid desire to hear what everyone would say at my funeral. Very Tom Sawyer of me. Would my stepdad, John, even attend? Mom would cry. Justine would stand by my grave with people all around and despite her tears, she would refuse to let my mom comfort her. Kendra would stand by her. They would turn to each other to get through this. The jeeks would be there too. I don't think I have ever seen any of them cry except Luiz. I had a hard time imagining Ethan or Kevin crying. Instead, I could picture them cracking jokes over my grave as if making one last attempt to cheer me up before my spirit took a trip to . . .

To where? Where was I going when I died? Surely not hell as I'd thought before. I was technically on the Utah Jesus train, but I didn't attend church that often, and when I did, I mostly sat in the foyer, so I didn't know much. We believed in heaven—three of them—but I couldn't remember which of the three I wanted to go to. Since dying was likely, I resolved to find out more about my possible final destination if I ever got the chance.

At least I'd see my intended final resting place. Wait a minute . . . How would they handle my missing body? Usually, a Utah funeral started with a viewing, which consists of an open casket allowing people to say goodbye to the deceased. Except my body definitely was not going to be in there.

This whole sequence of thoughts sucked. I didn't want to be dead. I should tell my sister that I'm alive. Except, if anyone questioned her, would she let something slip? Even if it was by lying poorly?

But would it matter? If some evil secret society found out I was a druid, would it matter if my sister knew I was alive? And if they didn't know about me, why would they ever question my sister? I searched for a hole in my logic, but couldn't find one. I resolved to find some way to tell Sis. I couldn't do it now, but I would find a way to do it later. I couldn't stand that her grief was a lie. I thought for a while about clever ways to give her clues, except I couldn't think of anything easy and obvious. I would have to tell her without seeing her in person, but also without using technology that could be tracked, such as phones or the internet. My plan needed time and thought. I'd also have to look into the future consequences of telling her. It was like playing chess with Luiz. I needed a strategy and the ability to foresee the future, and I wasn't very good at either since Luiz still checkmated me every time.

She would tell Kendra. Would that be foolish? I wanted Kendra to know I was alive, too, but I also wanted to make sure she stayed far away from my being-hunted-down, druid life. I thought about how our relationship began. I'd enjoyed that Tuesday so much. I couldn't believe that only three days had passed. The connection I made with Kendra hadn't faded. It felt as strong as ever. Even if our relationship had only lasted hours before my untimely, yet very fake, demise, I would think of her as my first love for the rest of my life.

O'Brien had the tablet now, and I struggled to remember all the names on the list. Should I ask him for the tablet again? I'd gone over the list thoroughly. My mind meandered as I pondered the names I could remember.

The other potential isn't on the list. Why I had that thought was beyond me, though. It was more than a thought—perhaps intuition; either way, it concerned me. Should I share my concern with O'Brien? He might decide to pack up and leave, so I kept it to myself. Something obvious evaded me—like when I

can't remember a name, but it is on the tip of my tongue. It would come to me soon enough.

"Time to get some sleep," O'Brien called at half-past eleven.

I pretended to sleep until O'Brien breathed rhythmically. I actually wished I could sleep longer. I didn't have an Xbox or a computer. The TV, of course, wasn't working. Should I try to slip the tablet from O'Brien? Where was it? Was he sleeping with it under his pillow?

O'Brien had brought food to stock the little hotel fridge, so I had a second dinner. I wiped out the contents of the fridge. He should have brought more. After that, my only option was reading the druid text.

Why didn't I tell him that I only needed four hours of sleep? Maybe because it wasn't normal for a druid any more than it was normal for a regular person.

As I slept, I dreamed of my biological father. He stood in front of me. I could have been looking into a mirror, except for the slight wrinkles around his eyes and the few strands of gray in his hair. "I knew you would turn out just like me—a freak," he laughed. "You are a druid now, but even for a druid, you're a freak."

That last bit was new.

CHAPTER 20
CONTAINMENT

I woke up at six in the morning with Kendra at the forefront of my mind. I couldn't complain about waking up to thoughts of my girlfriend, except I'd likely never see her again. My thigh itched, and I let that distract me. I scratched it lightly, but that didn't alleviate the itching, so I applied some pressure and really dug at it with my fingernails. I prepared to wince but didn't have to because the deep pain was gone. I got up to hit the bathroom and found I could walk with far less of a limp than the day before. The mirror showed me that my black eye had healed, too.

O'Brien sat on the edge of the bed when I came out of the bathroom. I'd woken him by flushing the toilet. I should have forgone flushing and let him sleep. *If it's yellow, let it mellow.* I'd try that tomorrow. I didn't want him finding out that I only needed four hours of sleep. The longer he slept, the easier it would be to keep that secret.

He made coffee, and the aroma filled the hotel room. O'Brien didn't offer me a mug. I didn't drink coffee anyway, but the smell made my stomach growl.

"I need some food and some exercise," I told O'Brien. I refused to let him leave me to starve again, and I wouldn't stay locked in this hotel room like a bottled genie. He thumbed the rim of the coffee cup as he considered my request.

"I'll bring some food up soon. Do as many push-ups and sit-ups as you want."

"O'Brien," I said, frustrated, "you're trying to confine a seventeen-year-old with phenomenal cosmic powers to an itty-bitty living space!" I included the hand gestures and all. "It didn't work for the genie, and it's not going to work for me." He raised an eyebrow at me in confusion. I didn't try to explain. He obviously didn't watch many movies, let alone Disney ones. Besides, if he had, he would've made some crack about the genie lasting thousands of years in his itty-bitty living space.

"I need access to the gym and pool, and I'm coming to breakfast with you."

He sipped his coffee then answered, "The gym and pool I'll allow if I check them out first and they are empty. But there's no way you are coming down for breakfast."

"Why not?" I complained. *Did I really just sound that much like a whiny teenager?*

"Well, let's start with the fact that you're supposed to be dead and that your face is on the front page of the local papers scattered all over the lobby."

"Oh." Until that very moment, I hadn't fully grasped the concept that everyone, even people I didn't know, thought I was dead. I couldn't go around showing my face just anywhere.

"There's free breakfast downstairs. I'll bring you some." He downed the rest of his coffee and left.

Alone again.

I should have taken a shower while I waited for him, but instead, I lay in bed, my mind racing. He'd left the coffee on, so the aroma dominated the room, tormenting my taste buds. *What is taking him so long?* It was forty-five more minutes before I heard the hotel door click, and O'Brien walked in with another bag.

"I'm up here starving, and you went to Target," I said through clenched teeth, my muscles tightening as I glared at him. He threw the Target bag at my chest. I caught it and looked inside to find workout clothes and a swimsuit.

"Oh, I guess I'll need these," I conceded but looked around to see where he had hidden the breakfast.

"One thing at a time," he growled. He left before I could grumble about the missing breakfast. He returned ten minutes later with three plates. He held one plate in each hand and balanced the other on his forearm. How he opened the door was beyond me. He slid the plates down on the table, like he'd done this before.

"You expecting a tip?"

He didn't respond, but I saw him crack a grin as he turned away.

"Which plates are for me?"

"Are you kidding? You eat more than a horse. All three are yours. I ate before I went to Target."

I would have given him another dirty look, but the three plates had my full attention. The tall plate of pancakes with butter and syrup smelled like heaven. OK, the syrup and butter came in those annoying little square plastic containers, so it wasn't quite heaven, but close enough. Scrambled eggs nearly fell from the second plate, but bacon rimmed it in like a fence. The third plate held cantaloupe, watermelon, and other ripe fruits.

"Hotel breakfasts rock!" I exclaimed as I dug in.

For just a moment, I forgot that I had been shot. I forgot I could use druid magic and that some secret society was trying to kill or capture me. I forgot that I missed my sister and Kendra and the jeeks. I ate in a moment of peace. Unfortunately, I finished the three plates too quickly, and it all came crashing back as I threw them away.

"The pool is empty," O'Brien said, drinking another cup of coffee.

I changed into the swimsuit in about ten seconds.

O'Brien threw a hotel towel over my head. "Just in case someone sees you."

I grabbed the towel and hung it over my head. "You *will* take me to the pool." I waved my fingers like Obi-Wan Kenobi.

O'Brien raised his eyebrows in confusion. My mouth dropped open. There was no way he didn't get that reference, was there? As if the wave of my fingers had worked, O'Brien led me out of the hotel room. We used the stairs, avoiding the busy elevator, and walked down a hall to a door he opened with his key card. The indoor pool looked clean and the water motionless. Each long chair held a rolled towel.

O'Brien lay down on a white chair and pulled out his tablet. I glanced at the numbers painted on the pool wall, disappointed they only indicated a depth of five feet. I dove in horizontally to avoid hitting my head, and broke the perfectly still water.

Oh! I wasn't ready to feel the water.

Not physically. Magically. The water felt new and powerful.

I got out and dove in again. My splash created waves and the waves created energy. The book had a note about using bodies of water for major spells. If my splash at the pool released ripples of magical energy, imagine how much magic ocean waves released.

I swam laps for quite a while, basking in the energy. If hotels had deeper pools and diving boards, they would be much more fun. I played around doing flips off the edge into the water, enjoying the immersion in both water and magic. I had the pool to myself for more than an hour before hearing girls' voices just outside the door.

"Hey," O'Brien yelled. He threw a towel at me, then he mouthed, "Cover your face."

I caught the towel, keeping it out of the water. I waded to the edge of the pool and jumped out. I dripped over to O'Brien, drying my hair with the towel just as the group of girls walked in. The girls weren't from around here. Over their swimsuits, they wore pink volleyball T-shirts with little images of the state of Idaho. I hung the towel over my head like a hood, covering half my face. I shouldn't have bothered though. Their eyes fixated below my neck. They didn't care about my face. They liked my chest and abs.

"I should have brought you a shirt," O'Brien groaned as we stepped out into the hall. "They paid more attention to you than I would have liked."

I laughed. "At least they weren't looking at my face."

O'Brien grunted back in response.

The girls' attention was a double-edged sword. It felt good. But it also reminded me that my muscles came from my evil biological father. He was why I healed fast and never got sore. He was why I was a freak. Except, even though working out never left me sore, it still mattered that I had put in the time. That effort was all me. I needed every asset to survive whoever hunted us. Before this was all over, my muscles would be the difference between life and death.

When we got back to the hotel room, I sighed. Could I survive being stuck here another day? Probably, but I wouldn't enjoy it.

"Can I try a containment now?"

O'Brien checked his watch, considering my request. "OK. But not here," my bodyguard added. "If you make a mistake here, you will give away our location."

I smiled, energized by the hope of escaping the hotel.

"There's a safer place," O'Brien added. "Let me shower first."

"I better shower after you. I need to wash off all this chlorine."

An hour later, we headed downstairs. Well, I jumped down the stairs with another excited wave of energy. I went out the back door and waited for O'Brien in the parking lot. Wait, hadn't I torched the beater truck? I winced.

The hum of traffic mixed with the fluttering leaves in the slight breeze. He led me to his stolen replacement. A beat-up Jeep Grand Cherokee.

Why is it always a beater? I kept my mouth shut and got inside. I set the heavy druid text on the seat behind me. The ignition casing had been stripped, and instead of a key, O'Brien inserted a flat screwdriver and turned.

He saw me looking.

"No, the screwdriver in the ignition thing doesn't just work. It takes a few modifications first."

O'Brien took us north on I-15 before telling me our destination.

"The druids have caches hidden around the world. Every capital city has one, including Salt Lake City. They are hidden in plain sight, and even most druids don't know about them. The cache here is newer. It's a mostly empty storage unit," he explained. "Salt Lake City keeps its nose clean, so the druids haven't had a reason to stock up on spells here. There won't be much. The storage unit has a containment spell around it, so you should be able to make as many mistakes as you need without alerting the magical world of our location."

We drove to an old storage unit in Murray just off the freeway on third west. O'Brien parked and pulled out his tablet. I caught a glimpse of numbers on the screen: 3-27-18. O'Brien got out of the jeep and used the numbers to unlock the padlock, and with wheels grinding, he raised the garage door. Inside, he flipped one switch, and I heard a hum. He flipped another, and the lights came on. He closed the garage door behind us.

Inside, I could sense the containment surrounding me like I could feel the heat in the air, though I hadn't noticed either while outside. The storage unit didn't store much. A single wooden shelving unit stood at the back, holding vials and boxes. A huge battery sat in one corner with thick cables rising to the ceiling. A card table and four folding chairs leaned against one wall.

"This place is solar powered." O'Brien gestured toward the battery. "A lot of the new caches are equipped with solar power instead of lamps and oil."

Lamps and oil. Was everything the druids did old school, like the druid textbook?

O'Brien set up the table while I set up the chairs. We sat down, and I opened the druid text to the section on containments. According to the book, there were dozens of types of containments and many ways to implement one. The hardest way was to imagine the containment area. But if your imagination runs wild, so does the containment. Size also matters. If a magic user contained an area too large, they could burn out their energy and pass out from overexertion.

The book explained that each containment had the dual purpose of keeping magic in *and* out. To keep another magic user from blasting you with a spell, a containment makes a great shield. However, while inside the containment, you can't blast them either.

The easiest containment spell covered small areas, like a circle around one person, which is likely why chalk circles were popular. Druids used to believe that the quality of the circle affected the containment's strength. That was just a mind trick, though, because only failure to believe made a chalk circle weaker. If only the book listed the page number for the section about complex containments. Oh, well. I'd come across that part eventually.

A thin copper ring about twice the diameter of a Hula-Hoop stuck out from behind the shelf. I hadn't noticed it until O'Brien slid it out. "Here is your circle." He tossed the ring onto the cement floor. "Get inside it and start practicing."

"No advice?" I asked. I moved my chair into the circle and sat down.

"I've never formed a containment." He shook his head, reminding me he was a magical dud. "Use the book." I'd left it on the card table, so he tossed it to me. Good thing I played football and had good hands.

I set the book on my lap and thumbed through it. I found the spell for a basic containment one page after the spell for fire light. I quickly read the instructions to cast a containment. Step one, feel the magic from everything around you. Step two, gather the magic in. Step three, focus on the outer rim of the containment. Step four, release the magic. An easy spell with easy steps.

Except I couldn't do it.

It took time to concentrate enough to even get to step two. I could feel the energy around me, but I struggled to gather it in.

Twenty minutes passed as I worked on gathering the magic from the elements around me. I'd only cast fire light twice. I fumbled with the magic like a useless newbie.

The *wyrman tiegan* had handed me the magic on my first cast of fire light. On my second cast, magic had poured into me with my anger. So this was my first time trying to cast a spell where I had to consciously gather the magic.

"You are trying too hard," O'Brien commented. "For beginners, they often recommend you close your eyes, breathe, and examine the magic without trying to use it."

His suggestion mirrored what the book had recommended when I had first cast fire light. It worked for me once, so I closed my eyes and tried it again. I examined the magical energy around me. Magic existed everywhere; in the air, in the ground, on the walls, in the ceiling. I couldn't help but think about how electricity required wires to direct it where it needed to go, but magic existed and moved everywhere, completely wireless. What had the book said? Matter is energy and energy is matter, they are just two forms of the same substance, like water and ice. Or perhaps more like water and steam. Time passed. The magic became more tangible, there for me to take, so I did. I looked at the copper circle and released the energy.

A cylinder of grayish light appeared, encircling the copper ring, glowing from floor to ceiling. The magic organized itself in a perfect pattern. I thought of the college chemistry class when they showed how molecules of certain crystals formed intricate patterns.

"Wow!" I exclaimed.

"Wow's right!" O'Brien agreed and stood staring at the circle. He raised both eyebrows in amazement. "That's never happened before. I've seen plenty of containments cast before, but I've never *visibly* seen one."

As I held the containment together, my body tired. Or maybe my mind tired. Either way, the magic sapped my energy. I released the containment.

"That wore me out," I breathed. My shirt clung to the sweat on my body.

"It wore you out?" O'Brien pinched his brow in thought. "You put way too much energy into it. Tone it down. Containments should be one of the easiest and least draining spells. Keep it calm and controlled."

This time, when I reached for the magic, it came immediately. The visible cylinder of light returned.

"You're still using too much."

I tried to tone it down, to keep it calm and controlled. I failed. The magic stopped completely, and the containment disappeared.

"Again." O'Brien sounded like my football coach, barking at me to run sprints faster *or else.*

I repeated the attempt, trying to use less energy. It worked! The cylinder of light appeared with about half the opacity. For a second, I thought I'd had it; unfortunately, O'Brien shook his head.

"Close your eyes," O'Brien directed. I closed my eyes. "Try to decrease the energy but don't release it."

With my eyes closed, I could focus more on the magic. I could feel the energy pulsing from everything around me. Without sight, I cut the energy flowing into the containment by half. I opened one eye and peeked at the magic barrier.

"Keep your eyes closed," O'Brien coached. "You're doing it. Decrease it some more."

I dialed down the energy flow, and compared to the first try, I felt like I would never tire.

"Still too much," O'Brien growled.

I decreased it as much as I could without releasing the magic. "Good. Now open your eyes."

I could barely see the energy field that remained.

"See how it is invisible now?" my mentor asked. Should I tell him I could still see it?

He opened a vial and held it next to the containment. A misty substance began seeping out of the vial like smoke from a blown-out match. He only let a little out before he capped the vial back up. Then he blew the mist at my containment, and it wrapped around the faintly visible cylinder of gray light.

"See how the containment acts as a barrier," he noted.

I nodded.

"What's that?" I eyed the mist curiously.

"This." He held up the vial. "Same stuff I used the other day. This spell erases any trace of humans. I used it to show you magic can't cross a containment. That's enough for today. Let's have lunch," O'Brien suggested.

"Lunch already?"

"It's been three hours." O'Brien showed me the time on his tablet.

We had arrived just after nine in the morning. It felt like I had only been trying for thirty minutes, but three hours had passed.

"Let's put everything away in case we don't make it back."

He knew how to ruin a good moment. I wanted to celebrate my success, even if it *had* taken three hours, and he had to go and say we might not make it back. Yes, we could be dead before we got the chance to come back, but did he really have to remind me?

"It wasn't completely invisible," I said. "It still had a hint of color."

"Really?" he asked, raising both eyebrows again. "Interesting. Usually, druids can only see large amounts of intense magic. I've never heard of a druid seeing small amounts of magic."

I filed that knowledge away. I put the chairs and the ring away while O'Brien put away the table. He then walked over and inspected the contents of the solitary wooden shelving unit. It held a half-dozen metal boxes on the bottom shelf. O'Brien took one and opened it.

"That's a lot of money," I said, looking over his shoulder. I left my mouth hanging open. Four stacks of bills fit perfectly inside—three stacks of twenties and one of fifties. The box stood six inches tall.

"The druids have never been poor," O'Brien informed me, moving on to look at the thin vials of spells on the shelf. Each had a colored fluid inside and a slight glow of magic.

"The vials contain liquid magic," I exclaimed. I had seen the effects of four vials already, but I hadn't seen them up close or read about them. The glass cylinders were a little thicker than a fountain pen, except they flared out, cone-like, at the base. Some had lids and some didn't. I assumed the ones without lids were meant to be shattered, and the ones with lids could be poured or drank.

"Yes. Some of these spells can help us," he told me.

"How?" I asked.

"Depends on the magic in the vial." He pointed at a clear vial with a phantasmagoric display of swirling colors but didn't pick it up. "A teleportation vial."

"Here, there," I said, but I doubted O'Brien would get the reference to the autistic superhero Shep. I could have gone with something more traditional like "Beam me up, Scottie."

He grabbed two deep-yellow vials and slid them into a protective cloth sleeve custom-made to hold them. "A couple sunlight spells."

"A light to use in dark places." I grinned, but O'Brien ignored me again. I'd figured out by now my comments were lost on O'Brien. I guess the comments were more for me than for him, anyway. If we survived to be on the run together for our whole lives, I'd make O'Brien read some books and watch some movies.

"Four healing spells." I recognized blue vials from when O'Brien had used one on me in the hospital. He took them all and moved to a silvery one. "Bones of steel," he named it as he collected it.

I couldn't think of a book or movie reference for either healing or bones of steel, so I just said, "Cool."

"Not as cool as flesh of steel, but serviceable."

"What's the difference?" I asked.

"Well, with bones of steel, you can still be cut, shot, or bitten—your flesh is still vulnerable. Only the bones are strengthened," he answered.

The word "bitten" sort of stuck out. Why did so many monsters have to bite?

"The best is when you combine them both," he added as he scanned through the selection of vials. "Hmm. I had planned to take you back to the hotel, but . . ." O'Brien held out a vial in each hand. One vial was clear as water; the other had a hint of red. Both had lids. "Disguise and Finding."

"Can the book show me how to create vials of disguise?" I asked.

O'Brien ignored me. "Each lasts a day or two. I could use your help crossing your peers off the list. How would you like to attend your own funeral?"

CHAPTER 21
FUNERAL

As we got into the jeep to drive to the funeral, O'Brien handed me his tablet and said, "Read this."

Jacob Stevens' Body Sent to U of U

The Jordan Valley Medical Center released the results of its investigation into the missing body of Jacob Stevens, claiming that it had been sent by mistake to the University of Utah Medical School to be used as a cadaver. Attempts at locating the body have been unsuccessful. Jacob's parents are pursuing legal . . . [*read more*]

"Liars," I commented, and O'Brien grinned.

I usually never clicked to read more, but this time I did and found myself reading boring statements from the U of U denying having received my body. I shouldn't have bothered clicking. Too bad the article hinted that Jordan Valley Medical Center told the truth and the U of U lied. The media rarely got the details right.

I drank from both the disguise and the finding vials. O'Brien drank part of the disguise vial, too. He didn't think *they* were aware of me, but just in case, he didn't want to confirm their suspicions by showing his face at my funeral. His face slowly altered in little ways until I didn't recognize him anymore. What did I look like now?

We took our disguised faces over to Target where I helped O'Brien buy us funeral clothes: white dress shirts, dark slacks, ties with muted colors, and basic dress socks and shoes. O'Brien paid with cash. We changed in the Target restrooms.

O'Brien and I arrived at the church building just as they rolled my casket from the viewing room to the chapel. I guess even without my body, the viewing had still happened but with a closed, empty casket, which didn't make sense to me.

A big yellow-and-green flower arrangement, centered around a football, adorned the top of my casket. A chill ran up my spine as *my casket* rolled past. I stared at the football. Signatures covered the ball. Had every guy on the football team signed it? Luiz Espinoza's was the largest.

Then I saw the girls. Sis and Kendra followed my casket, walking behind my mother. Despite wet eyes, Sis glanced at everyone she passed. Kendra held her hand and whispered something to her. Aunt Rita walked behind them, her two daughters and young son in tow. They were cousins from California whom I hadn't seen in ten years. The jeeks followed them.

Sis's green eyes finally fell on me. They glanced off me as if I didn't exist, moving on to the next person. I wanted to shout to her, to let her know it was me, but I just stood there. The reality of being hunted and being supposedly dead bowled over my brief gratefulness and unleashed a hurricane of emotions in my chest. My face contorted in a manner that I desperately wanted to hide.

I detoured past the drinking fountains to the bathroom, gesturing to O'Brien so he knew. In the bathroom, I leaned against a sink and looked into the mirror and trembled. The many small changes to my face had added up until I looked like a stranger, so of course Sis had looked right past me. She had no clue who I was. I'd expected it. I swallowed the lump in my throat anyway.

I ran cold water over my hands and splashed my face to cool off. The magical feel of the running water calmed me.

The toilet flushed and Mike, our team's quarterback who I'd punched just the other day, came out of the stall. At the same time, Jason and Gunther walked in. They looked funny in shirts and ties. Two more boys came in a few seconds after them, crowding the restroom. There was no hiding out in the bathroom.

I took a breath. *I can do this!* I told myself. I shook the water from my hands and then consciously took one step at a time out of the bathroom.

Thankfully, O'Brien waited just outside the door for me. As we walked into the chapel, I recognized everyone, but nobody recognized me. Even though O'Brien walked with me, and even though we had to wade through a crowd, I'd never felt this alone in my life. I knew so many of them, but I couldn't talk to any of them.

O'Brien and I sat in the back—way back. I wasn't prepared for the number of people who attended my funeral. It wasn't just my family, friends, and neighbors; it was everybody. Latter-day Saint church buildings have a slide-away wall that separates the chapel from the gymnasium. When needed, the wall can be opened, and the gym can be used for overflow seating, making the chapel and gym one large room. The chapel and the gym had filled up, and more people were coming, so the ushers added chairs to the stage. I didn't know half the people there. I gazed without understanding at row after row of barnacles from my high school and their families. I didn't understand why so many people came. They had nothing to gain by pretending to like me now. I was dead . . . well, supposedly dead. Kids from other high schools had come, too. The chapel and gym hummed with a hundred different conversations and men setting up folding metal chairs.

The surprising attendance would allow O'Brien and me to cross a lot of teenage boys off the potential druid list. The ex-marine opened the spreadsheet on his tablet, and I looked around the gym and chapel to find guys who were not yet checked off the list. We split them up and got started.

Finding wasn't fast. At first, I had assumed that just glancing at someone would be enough. It wasn't. It required staring at someone for about ninety seconds, like casting your fishing line, waiting for a fish to bite. It wasn't a physical tug. If not for the book, I wouldn't have compared it to fishing. I'd compare it to a football player fielding a punt. The ball hangs in the air and everyone wonders whether the player will catch the ball or drop it. You know by the player's reaction if he drops it or catches it.

The noise of additional chairs being set up in the back and people entering delayed the funeral's start time for about five minutes. We would have had time to scan about six guys, but O'Brien didn't trust me. He took extra time to scan each boy even if I already scanned them. His lack of trust in me really slowed us down.

Finally, the bishop stood, and the crowd quieted. He welcomed everyone to the funeral and explained the program and sat down. The funeral began with a hymn and a prayer, after which my mom stood.

"Wow. I've never seen this many people at a funeral," my mom started. "I loved having Jacob as my son. I will miss him. Someone who has so many people who know and care for him is certainly in a better place."

Hah, you got that wrong! I thought. *I am in the same place as you. Oh, and by the way . . . some evil druids and their minions might be trying to kill me, and the only help I have is from a druid who can't really use magic.* I definitely was not in a better place.

I couldn't focus on finding while my mother spoke with real tears about me. I'd expected those tears in the hospital, but instead, I'd received accusations. At the hospital, she'd just spoken to the cops. Had they suggested to her that I'd become involved with something I shouldn't? I wondered if we would ever talk face to face again as mother and son or if our angry encounter at the hospital would be our last. For her, the way she treated me in the hospital would haunt her for her entire life. She'd ruined the last time she'd ever see me. The night of my conception already haunted her forever, and she didn't need something else to haunt her that long.

My mom finished and stepped away from the pulpit. I realized that it didn't matter that she flinched at the sight of me or that John had screwed her up plenty because neither were her fault. She was my mom. She'd raised me despite everything. Whether she really loved me back or not, I loved her. I couldn't allow her to hate herself for how she treated me the last time she saw me. I'd find a way to talk to her—to fix things. I had to.

My sister stood and gave Mom a hug, then wiped her wet eyes as she stepped up to the microphone. She hesitated and scanned the crowd before speaking. We should have sat closer so I could see her better. People were talking to my left and the speakers weren't the greatest on the stage, so it was already hard to hear.

"Jacob, I want you to know you were the best brother a sister could ever have," Justine began. She spoke as if she were talking directly to me, which ironically, she was. "Jacob, you always made me feel safe and protected. You've made me feel safe at home. You've made me feel safe at school. You've made me feel safe everywhere. I want to thank you for painting my bathroom. Each time I go in there, I remember your hard work and feel safe."

My emotions shattered at her words and the shards cut at my heart. Until that moment, I had assumed that she cringed at the thought of going into the bathroom because of our creeper stepdad. I had no idea that she felt completely safe showering or that I'd given her that safety. I turned my head, wiping at my wet cheeks with the backs of my hands, hoping O'Brien wouldn't notice and think I was weak. I'd already cried in front of him in the truck. Did he already think I was soft?

"Jacob, you and I shared everything," Sis continued. "Life will never be the same without you. I will miss you forever." She barely got out the last words before she broke down and grabbed a tissue from the tissue box next to the microphone. She stood at the pulpit for a minute, unable to say anything, just wiping her eyes, before she composed herself and continued. "I know that I will see you again in heaven."

She finished speaking but stayed up at the pulpit. She looked over at Kendra, who stood and walked over and joined her. The pianist started playing a song called "Where is Heaven?" It was an old song I had liked when I was a kid. I had forgotten all about it, but Sis must have remembered. Nobody in my life was more important than my sister. She hadn't ruined our last moment together as Mom had.

Sis and Kendra had sung together before, and while neither would be going to Hollywood, they had decent voices under normal circumstances. Unfortunately, nobody sings well at a funeral. My sister's voice cracked, and she stopped singing. Kendra covered for her by singing louder. Kendra's voice didn't crack. She sang strong. Zero tears. No red eyes. Kendra? She finished the song, hugged Sis, and walked back to her seat.

The jeeks walked to the pulpit together and shared a few short words. Kevin told the story of how I'd gone cliff diving in the middle of the night at Lake Powell and lost my swim trunks. Ethan told everyone how, at fourteen, Tina had a teen crush on me. At our eighth-grade Halloween dance, she wore a Batgirl costume. I thought I'd danced with her three times until I found out *two* girls had worn a Batgirl costume. I had, of course, danced with the wrong girl each time. The whole audience laughed.

Luiz spoke last. He stood, looked around at the crowd and paused for a second, a little overwhelmed. Then he cracked a grin.

"Uh . . . I'm Catholic. Only an annoying *gringo* like Jake would go off and die just to get his best friend to finally come to his church. *Ay sí*, he was a *gringo*. When Jake tried to speak Spanish, he sounded like a translation of Forrest Gump confessing, 'I am not a smart man.'"

He proceeded to do an imitation of me speaking Spanish that was surprisingly accurate. The crowd's reaction blared into my ears. So many people packed the chapel and gym that it sounded like a stadium of cheers at a football game.

Then Luiz did something I'd rarely seen him do. His mouth closed tightly and he gulped. He took a breath and blinked a few times.

"Jake inspired me to play American football instead of *fútbol* or soccer as you *gringos* call it. I love football. I loved playing it with Jake. I don't know if I'll ever love it the same."

Wow. I had spent so much time resenting football for putting me in the spotlight. I'd only kept playing because it was the only way to get away from my crappy home life. I hadn't taken time to realize how much fun I'd had playing it with my friends.

I shivered, though it wasn't cold. My mind felt like collapsing. My legs just wanted to get up and run out of there. My throat didn't want to move yet still screamed for me to swallow. Despite that, I kept breathing. I had thought that, since I was alive, I could laugh this stuff off. Truthfully, even though I wasn't dead, I was cut off from Sis and my friends, and there was a real chance their good-byes were valid. We might never see each other again.

O'Brien turned the tablet my way and tapped on the screen, reminding me that we had work to do. I would have glared at him but I had to wipe my eyes—again. Had he really brought me here to help with finding, or did he just see me as an all-he's-got Caradoc replacement? I doubted he cared at all about my feelings. He just didn't want to lose another druid.

Whatever his motives, it didn't matter. He was right. We needed to keep trying. I looked at the list and started locating the remaining possibilities. We had about a dozen boys left to scan when the funeral ended. The jeeks, Coach Ferguson, Dylan, and a couple guys from the team lifted my casket and started carrying it outside. I realized how few relatives I had. Not a single pallbearer was related to me.

O'Brien had hoped to avoid going to the cemetery, but he wanted to cross off the last few boys from the list. I was already less than hopeful. I still didn't think the list had all the right names. O'Brien had grouped the kids by how much contact they had with me, and we were pretty much scraping the bottom of the barrel. I'd have thought he would have lost hope after scanning the boys from my church and coming up empty, yet he seemed undeterred.

A police car escorted the black hearse and the procession of cars to the cemetery. We slowly followed the long line of cars until we reached the cemetery on thirteenth west. The whole thing felt so surreal—as if I were sitting in a theater watching a tragic movie and as soon as the movie ended, everything would go back to normal.

Sis, my mom, Kendra, the jeeks, the football team—I couldn't focus on the reality that, despite not actually being dead, my life was over. Would I start using past tense when talking about them? Would I say Sis *was* my sister? Or Mom *was* my mother? Was Kendra my *ex*-girlfriend?

The cemetery was little more than a long rectangle, a fourth the size of a city block. It extended east from the corner of Thirteenth and Seventy-Eight Hundred South. Grass covered the cemetery grounds, providing a canvas for the tombstones of various sizes and shapes and the temporary flowers that adorned them. The pallbearers carried my casket from the hearse to a lump of dirt covered by green miniature golf carpet. They set it down on the special frame with green cords and pulleys that would lower the coffin into the ground. Everyone gathered around the casket as it hovered over the rectangular hole.

I didn't recognize the names on any of the nearby tombstones. It was strange to think that my supposed final resting spot wouldn't be next to a family member. I had to remind myself that I wasn't *in* the casket, so it really didn't matter.

An old girlfriend of mine, Teresa, crossed in front of me. She eyed me as she walked by. She had added purple streaks to the front of her hair. Even though my face no longer looked like mine, I expected her to recognize me. But just as Sis had done, she just walked on by. She walked over to some guy and then headed over to Justine to offer her condolences.

As I wandered around my empty grave, traffic hummed on Seventy-Eight Hundred South, and another group of people mostly dressed in black stood on the east side of the graveyard, mourning their own loss. As I watched, a bullet bike pulled up and parked. A girl dressed from head to toe in leather got off the bike. She had her back to me when she removed her helmet. Before she turned around, she pulled out a black cape and wrapped it around herself like a hooded dress. Then she covered her head with a veil. When she turned around, she still wore her large black sunglasses. It wasn't part of Utah's culture to dress in all black at funerals, so she stood out.

"O'Brien," I whispered, nodding toward the girl, but he was already looking her way, as were most of the guys. "She looks like the girl who saved us."

He shook his head. "Couldn't be." He glanced at the sun. "It's daytime." O'Brien kept an eye on her, though.

I nodded back, as if I understood, even though I could really only guess. I wanted to ask more, but this wasn't the place.

O'Brien let me pick where to stand. I chose a location twenty yards away from the grave where I had a clear view of Sis and Kendra. I wanted to talk to them but I couldn't. I had always longed for anonymity, to be *out* of the spotlight. I used to worry about what would happen when my friends found out about how

I was conceived. Well, not a single person had any idea I was even alive. I stood alone, next to O'Brien, anonymous. I finally had my wish, but I wanted to take my wish back.

After ten minutes at the cemetery, we checked off the last few names on the list. We'd failed to find the other potential druid in the pool of boys from my school and church.

"Let's go," O'Brien ordered in a whisper. He pulled his eyebrows tightly together, emphasizing the bulging vein on his left temple. With every name checked off the list, he could no longer hide his frustration.

"The dedication of the grave will be over in a few minutes," I whispered back. "Everyone will notice us if we leave now."

O'Brien nodded. He didn't want any unwanted attention if it could be helped.

Besides, I wanted to stay. I glanced at Sis and Kendra. I wanted to talk to them. They didn't have to know it was me, but I could talk to them, couldn't I?

I stood there fidgeting with my pockets until the bishop began the prayer to dedicate the grave. Everyone closed their eyes and bowed their heads, except a few little kids who were oblivious to anything but the joys of being outdoors. The moment the dedicatory prayer started, a warmth brushed at my skin.

I took the opportunity to watch Kendra. With her head bowed and eyes closed, she wouldn't catch me staring. She still wasn't crying. She didn't have a single tear mark on her cheeks either. Her lack of tears made my jaw clench. She was beautiful, though. Her birthday was coming up on July 31, and I wished I could be there. Sweet sixteen and never been . . . Oh wait, I'd already kissed her. Remembering our kiss gave me energy. Yet knowing I wouldn't be there to share her sixteenth birthday cut deep inside my chest, canceling out the energy. I should have looked away, but I couldn't take my eyes off her. I longed to touch her cheeks with my hands again and press my lips to hers.

Subconsciously, I used my Finder power on her until it clicked, confirming she was not a potential druid. At that exact moment, Kendra opened her eyes, lifted her head, and looked directly at me as I stared back.

Oops. She caught me staring.

The burning rope that connected her heart to mine flared up as it had when we had kissed, as if it had never left. Her gaze held mine for the last seconds of the dedicatory prayer. After everyone said amen, Kendra broke eye contact and turned and said something to Justine. Sis looked my way, then turned to Kendra and shook her head.

O'Brien grabbed my arm firmly. His eyes widened at me, and he indicated toward the jeep with his head. "Let's go," he said through gritted teeth. I wanted to ask him what was wrong, but I'd have to wait.

People had already started to leave, so we faded into the crowd as he rushed me to the jeep and we jumped in. O'Brien immediately checked his crystal. It was not glowing. He took a deep breath and let it out, then drove calmly, but without hesitation, away from the cemetery. As we drove away, I looked back to see Kendra standing exactly where I had been standing. She spun around, looking in every direction—looking for me. *Had she been able to see through my disguise?* The girl in black with the cape and veil started talking to her. I lost sight of them as we turned out of the cemetery.

"Someone besides the religious leader used magic," O'Brien interrupted my thoughts.

"Bishop used magic?" I asked, totally missing his point.

"Of course, he did. A couple hundred people all focused on a single grave as a religious leader blesses it; there's a lot of power in that." He glanced at me with eyebrows tight. "But that is not what is important. Someone else just used magic." He emphasized the last sentence as I remembered the warmth that brushed my skin as the prayer had started.

"I used my finding power on Kendra," I suggested. "Kendra isn't a potential druid." My words came out a lot more disappointed than I thought they would. We'd crossed every guy off the list, so I subconsciously started to let myself hope it could be her. I wondered if O'Brien could detect my disappointment.

"No, it wasn't you." He brushed my words off as insignificant. "It was someone else."

"Who?"

"I don't know." He shook his head. "I'm only certain that someone used magic, and it wasn't part of the prayer."

"What does that mean?" I asked, putting my seat belt on. If something jumped out at us, I didn't want another bloody nose.

He took a deep breath. "It means that there is a hostile magic user attending your funeral. If so, someone found out about you. They'll be looking for the other potential druid too. They may even be looking for us, assuming they know we are here, and that you aren't dead." He thought that over for a minute. The thumb on his right hand rubbed the steering wheel nervously. "I guess another possibility is that the other potential druid has already used magic;

which would explain why we haven't found him yet. But that's not likely. That is extremely rare . . ." He trailed off.

Why did I get the feeling it was the second extremely rare possibility? Why did everything about me stretch the bounds of extremely rare?

"So, what do we do now?"

"Stay on our toes in case a hostile magic user is nearby." He took his right hand off the steering wheel and used it to check his crystal again, even though it still wasn't glowing.

"What if the other potential has already used magic?"

He sighed. "Did I mention that's how it was for me? I used magic on my own. Remember that story I told you about the druid casting fire without a flame thrower. That was only three years ago. Caradoc arranged for my release from the Marines. After six months, it was clear I couldn't cast spells, so Caradoc made me a bodyguard."

I just sat there blinking at him. Had he just shared information about himself, willingly, without a truth spell? I'd known he couldn't cast spells, but I hadn't known he had only been a druid three years.

"I guess we have to teach you some new magic." He grabbed the steering wheel and took a deep breath. "There is a spell for detecting a druid, but I can't cast it. Once you learn it, we have to re-check every last name on our list."

CHAPTER 22
NIGHTWALKER

Back at the hotel, I had the joy of reading the druid tome for the rest of the night. Again. I would rather drink sand after football sprints, but hey, I felt the same way about studying football film, and I still worked hard at that.

I stopped reading the text straight through and focused on the section about detecting other druids. Finding a potential was far different than finding a full-fledged magic user. Detecting a magic user required a careful feel while pushing magic at them. With a regular person, the magic wraps around their body, but with a magic user, the energy flows in and out of them like a conduit.

It sounded easy at first, but it wasn't. I read that if I used too much power, I'd immediately alert the magic user to my presence. If I sent too little, it would be impossible for me to feel the reaction of the magic. People who could barely use magic, like O'Brien, were only able to conduct the smallest amount of it, so they didn't appear to be magic users at all. To make matters even more difficult, a magic user could easily deceive the spell by forming a containment around their skin, making them appear as a normal person.

A normal person. My desire to be a normal person had only grown over the past few days. If I were normal, I'd still be with Kendra. If I were normal, my mom and sister wouldn't have had a funeral for me while I was still alive. I could have dwelt on that further, but I didn't want to, so I pushed the thought away before I let it drag me down.

Pushing magic around was as easy for me as breathing. However, pushing a small enough amount to remain undetected was like trying to palm a playing card without noticeably bending it. Was I doing it wrong? I had no one to tell me.

Sensing magic takes time and experience. I had neither. What if I cheated and sent a stronger thread of energy so that I could faintly see the magic with my eyes? If I used enough magic, I would see its glow either spread around them or enter them. Unfortunately, that amount of magic was akin to standing up and screaming bloody murder in the middle of a crowded room. Every magic user around would turn and look at me.

I set my book down on the bed to think. The bed was the perfect size for the border of my containment. O'Brien hadn't given me permission to practice magic in the hotel room, but I made the containment easy enough. With its barely visible glow around my bed, I felt safe enough to practice magic without sending magical beacons rippling out to broadcast my whereabouts.

I grimaced and felt the strain as I created a small hole in the barrier to send magic at O'Brien. I tried to look up an easier way, but the druid book clearly stated that opening a hole in a containment wasn't even possible. Well, I could put a hole in it whether the book said it was possible or not.

O'Brien could detect magic use, but he wasn't strong, so I didn't think magic would wake him. He lay under his covers and had his back toward me. I sent a dim thread of magic toward him and watched how it wrapped around him except the smallest amount, which seeped into him. He stirred, so I cut off the flow, but he didn't wake.

While thinking of better ways to detect a magic user, my eyes glanced around the room and rested on the useless TV. I couldn't believe O'Brien had cut the cables. Watching TV sounded great right now. I could go for some sitting back and relaxing with some mindless entertainment. Should I just go to sleep? I'd been reading by the light of the bedside lamp. Why would anyone ever make a lamp such an ugly mustard color? The translucent plastic cord suffered from the same ugly color. I reached over to turn it off, then hesitated.

The cord. Electricity. Cables. Dots connected in my mind. The cable was nothing more than a *containment* for electricity.

Could I cast a cable-shaped containment and send my magic through it? I could definitely try. I found nothing in the druid book to help me with this, so I had to figure it all out on my own. I failed a dozen times. I fist-pumped the air when I finally succeeded. I glanced at the clock: 1:14 A.M. Just enough time left to test it.

I created my new cable-like containment between O'Brien and me. The magic cable was too thick, so I made it smaller and smaller until it could barely contain a hair-thin line of magic. I limited the magic I used for the cable so that I couldn't see it glow at all, but inside the cable, I created a slightly stronger thread that I could faintly see and sent it through. If it were true that I could see magic better than other magic users, then perhaps the thread I sent would be invisible to everyone but me. Being fiber-thin and wrapped in a containment, it probably wouldn't cause any ripples.

My magic cable sort of worked. I had to leave the magic cable open on the ends. Like any cord, it had a beginning and an end—the beginning connected to me. If I used this on an experienced magic user, they'd follow the magic cord right back to me. I needed to fix that.

The lamp's power cord turned and twisted to the plug.

Can I make my containment conduit twist and turn?

I tried it. I had it working about ten minutes later. It took a combination of imagination and concentration. Sadly, despite the twists and turns, my conduit spell still led directly to me. The twists and turns hadn't really solved anything. While contemplating, I glanced at the cables O'Brien had cut between the TV and the wall. Could it be that easy?

I created a containment and sent a six-inch fiber of bright-orange magic through it. When the magic traveled more than halfway through the conduit, I cut the conduit in half, and the connection to me disappeared. When the energy hit O'Brien, I watched how part of the magic spread around him, and a smaller part passed into him.

O'Brien snapped awake. He sat up and turned toward me. Seeing me awake, he swore. "What just happened?"

Oops. I'd pushed too much. "I just figured out how to safely detect a druid," I defended myself.

"You used magic here?" He swore again and grabbed the crystal from under his shirt and breathed a sigh of relief. It was not glowing.

"I only used magic inside a containment," I assured him, not sharing that I had just invented a magical cable. If only it were patentable.

He grunted and glanced at the clock: 2:11 A.M. "Sounds like enough progress for tonight. Get some sleep," he ordered.

His face still hadn't fully returned to normal yet. My face had changed back hours ago. His disguise was lasting longer.

I closed the book and set it on the nightstand. I undressed and wrapped the blanket around me, letting my head settle onto the soft pillow. Sleep came quickly. So did the dream.

A needle stuck in my arm, and I watched the blood pump out of me. This dream didn't make sense because I had never given blood, yet it felt like I had recently done this dozens of times.

130

While the blood left me, my body already began generating new blood at a rapid pace. In a few hours, it would be like I hadn't given blood at all.

The nurse gave me a cookie as I left. Oatmeal, my favorite. Except it had raisins. If I could go back in time and find the person who thought it was a good idea to put raisins in oatmeal cookies and change their mind with a good smack across the face, I would. I picked out the raisins as I ate, walking down the sidewalk, rune-covered staff in hand. I used the staff to walk even though I didn't need it. I finished the cookie and tossed a handful of raisins into the bushes that lined the sidewalk. I stopped and leaned the staff against me. I removed the taped cotton ball from my aged skin. I already couldn't find the spot where the needle had pierced it.

I felt a sharp pinch in my chest on the left side. I looked down at a growing red stain. It wasn't until I touched it and saw the blood transfer to my hands that I realized I had been shot—in the heart no less. That shouldn't have been possible. My enchanted shirt should have stopped the bullet, but instead, it had penetrated my defenses. I finally understood how so many of the other druids had fallen so easily. They had felt protected, as had I, until the very moment they realized they weren't.

Desperately, I reached for my magic, pulling a healing spell that was already prepared as a rune in my wooden staff. The rune flared to life as energy transferred into me, augmenting the healing spell that was already regenerating my blood. Ripped flesh began to heal but not fast enough. I was going to die.

I could still sense my blood in the building behind me. I could still send it more memories. I started a conduit from my mind to the blood I had just given, even though it was in the building behind me. I embedded more memories into it. In my desperation, I sent them all.

I touched a crystal hanging from my neck and felt its power. Since obtaining the crystal, I'd never ceased to be amazed by it, not even while dying.

I called for the crystal's power.

I snapped awake as O'Brien yanked me out of bed. The light of the crystal dangling from his neck forced me to squint. His neck and face were lit up like my Scoutmaster holding a flashlight under his chin while telling ghost stories. He held his finger to his lips. The clock read 3:27 A.M.

O'Brien and I had already prepared a plan to follow in case we needed to flee in a hurry. The glowing crystal told me it was time to follow the plan: keep everything in a duffel bag ready to grab it and go. O'Brien grabbed his bag as I went for my clothes.

O'Brien had told me to sleep with my clothes on, but wearing just my boxers, I'd obviously not listened. My clothes lay on the floor, and the book sat on the nightstand.

He swore at me.

"Dress in the car. We have to go," he whispered urgently. "Now!"

With one hand holding my duffel bag and the other holding my clothes, I stumbled out into the hall after O'Brien. I turned toward the stairs.

"Not the stairs," he mouthed silently, grabbing me and pulling me toward the elevator.

We hadn't taken the elevator yet. He had always wanted to steer clear of it, but we took it this time. We were only on the second floor, so we made it in and out of the elevator in seconds. A single concierge sat behind the front desk talking on the phone. When he saw us, he froze and dropped the phone. It had to be a funny sight from his point of view—a teenage boy in boxers holding his clothes and running behind a guy who looked military, carrying a similar duffel bag and a . . .

I swore. *When did O'Brien pull out the handgun?*

The poor concierge put his hands up as if O'Brien aimed the gun at him, but O'Brien didn't slow down. He continued outside and rushed to the jeep. I sprinted behind, feeling the cool pavement under my bare feet, and jumped in the passenger side. O'Brien started driving before I had even thrown the duffel bag into the back seat. He pulled out quickly but made sure the wheels didn't squeal. He turned us south onto State Street and floored it.

Even before four in the morning, State Street had a couple of cars here and there. We swerved around them like they were standing still. O'Brien braked hard at One Hundred and Sixth South and turned right, taking us west toward the nearby freeway. He ran the red light at the mall. At the light at the freeway entrance, he swerved into the left lanes, blowing by a half-dozen cars stopped at the light, annoying the drivers, before turning onto the southbound onramp. If any of them flipped us off, it was too dark to know.

O'Brien pulled his crystal from under his shirt. Its glow hadn't dimmed at all. He let out a couple of expletives through gritted teeth. He dropped the crystal back down his shirt where its light seeped through.

At the very last second, O'Brien swerved to take the Bangerter Highway exit, almost taking a sign with us. I hadn't tried to put on my pants or shirt. It had taken some work just to get my seat belt on. Since then, I had just been holding on.

"What's after us?" I asked.

"I don't know." He glanced at the rearview mirror and swore. "But we're about to find out."

I looked behind us. What was coming toward us? I could only see a car-sized blackness that absorbed the light from the fifty-foot-high street lamps. Whatever the blackness was, it was gaining on us. I watched it come closer until it started to take a cloaked, humanoid shape. The area between my skin and my muscles started to crawl as if larvae wiggled around inside me.

O'Brien swore again.

"A nightwalker." He cursed under his breath, his pupils already dilated—the same eyes I had seen during our last flight from the empty house.

"What's a nightwalker?" I asked.

He looked at me. He started to speak but stopped, trying to find the right words to explain the creature coming after us.

"Is it worse than a transient?" I asked, but I already knew the answer. The sensation of writhing larvae between my skin and muscles intensified, telling me that it was far more evil than anything I had yet encountered.

He nodded. "Much worse. Think of the Grim Reaper, a banshee, a vampire, and a flesh-eating zombie—then add extra intelligence."

"Oh, that's all," I said sarcastically. I swore, too.

More cars blocked the intersection where Redwood Road met Bangerter Highway. O'Brien had to swerve into the turning lane again to run the red light. That slowed us down, allowing the nightwalker to gain on us. I couldn't tell if the creature ran or floated toward us.

O'Brien reached into his jacket and pulled out one of the magic vials. "Sunlight." He flashed a smile at me. Of course, his still-dilated pupils and his pale face warned me that he wasn't expecting it to work. "It makes them burn like charcoal," he told me while spinning the vial between his finger and thumb nervously and steering with the other hand. "It takes more than this to kill them, but it might give us time to escape. I'm going to let it get close, then hit it." He glanced in the rearview mirror. "Take the wheel."

He rolled down his window, and the roar of the air filled my ears. Again, I wasn't so sure I wanted the window rolled down when a black, humanoid shadow of darkness approached at bullet bike speeds. He didn't wait for me before letting go of the steering wheel. I reached over and grabbed it to keep us on the road. O'Brien grabbed the roof and twisted his body, hoisting himself to sit in the open window. From where I sat, the only visible part of his face was his chin, which pointed behind me to the creature chasing us.

I glanced into the rearview mirror in time to see the nightwalker jump at us. With a scrape of metal, it grabbed the top of the jeep on the left rear. The SUV lurched, nearly pulling the steering wheel out of my hands, but I firmed up my grip and stabilized the jeep. I heard another loud scrape of metal as the creature moved forward on the roof.

I almost didn't hear the vial shatter. Sunlight lit up the sky for as far as I could see.

A chilling wail screamed out into the night so loudly that it drowned out the rushing air from the open window. The cry carried with it tainted magic that shrouded my mind with frigid darkness. I wanted to curl up and hide. I let go of the steering wheel and shrank back into my seat, curling up protectively. I lost awareness of where I was. The imaginary larvae under my skin must have procreated because the writhing doubled. I wanted to pull out of my panic, but I couldn't. A part of me wanted to give in—to embrace the darkness—but another part of me fought back, threatened by it. I fought back both emotionally and mentally, but I was losing the battle.

The sunlight lasted about four seconds before nighttime returned.

O'Brien, not quite as affected by the scream as I was, grabbed the steering wheel just in time to keep us from heading off the highway into the cement sound barriers. Consumed by the battle that raged inside of me, I barely acknowledged what he did. If I embraced the cold, dark void, my mind would break—go insane. I would lose the ability to think rationally and the ability to fight back. The void threatened my memories as well. If I gave in, the cold darkness would take my past from me. Part of me wanted to embrace the darkness and disappear into its abyss. If my memories were erased, I would be at peace.

Except I wanted my memories.

Mentally, I fought back. I reached into the very memories that the void threatened and grasped at them. Images of my sister's face from her birth to my funeral flashed through my mind. These images strengthened me and encouraged my mental and emotional struggle. I grabbed for memories of my friends, focusing on images of Luiz and the other jeeks.

The part of me that wanted to give in grabbed some memories too. I flashed through a dozen images from different times when my mom flinched at the sight of me. In my mind, I heard my mom yelling at John who had just been caught watching my sister through the wall and relived my failure to act as they walked past me. Oh, how I wanted that vile memory to go away. That memory infected and corrupted me. It would go away with all my other memories if only I embraced the void.

My mind weakened.

I pulled up images of Kendra's face—smiling, confident, vulnerable. I focused on the memory of her crying—her cheeks lined with tears. She had needed me at that moment, and I had taken her cheeks in my hand and leaned forward and kissed her. The memory affected me almost as much as the original kiss had. The same fiery rope that had connected us flared to life again, fueled by the memory.

Awareness of my surroundings returned.

"Fight it, Jake!" I heard O'Brien screaming. He had been shouting at me nonstop, but my mind had been unable to process his words.

The cold darkness hovered just outside of my awareness as if looking for a way to surround me again, but the memories of my sister, my friends, and my girlfriend lingered like a shield. Despite it being a warm night, my teeth chattered as I tried to speak. "Wha-what th-the f-f-freak w-was th-that?"

"The nightwalker's scream," O'Brien responded. "Most people who hear it up close lose their minds. You're lucky you're in the minority." He breathed a sigh of relief. I was glad to be in the minority, too.

As I sat up, we were already approaching I-80. That meant I had fought the effects of the nightwalker's scream for more than ten minutes. It had seemed like just seconds.

Brake lights came into view ahead—a lot of them. The high, sound-suppressing walls that lined Bangerter Highway prevented us from seeing the immobile traffic soon enough to escape it. In Utah, there were only two seasons, winter and construction. There was no way to exit the highway.

O'Brien gulped then swore. "It's still coming for us."

CHAPTER 23
BEALUSTRÆL

W came to a stop behind a long line of cars. O'Brien's pupils returned to normal, and the color returned to his face. He looked peaceful. His hand grabbed his crystal, and the light spilled through his fingers. My imaginary larvae friends once again twisted and writhed between my skin and muscles, confirming the crystal's warning. The sunlight potion had barely slowed the nightwalker down.

"Put it in reverse," I suggested.

O'Brien just sat there. Cars pulled up, stopping behind us, pinning us in. He looked around and pressed his eyes closed to clear his mind. I hoped he'd think of something fast.

"Get out," O'Brien ordered.

I didn't hesitate to obey and couldn't help but feel exposed, wearing nothing but boxers.

"Are we going to run?" I asked. I hoped not. I wasn't exactly up to full speed yet. Sure, my wounded thigh had healed amazingly fast the past few days, but I wasn't anywhere near ready to make a run for it on foot. I wasn't even wearing shoes. Not that there was any chance of running from this thing anyway.

"No," he said, hopping out of the jeep too.

We hustled to the right shoulder of the road, between the white line and the sound-suppressing wall. The wall towered over us, too high to scale. The cars stacked up bumper to bumper in both directions. There was nothing to do but stand and fight.

"What's going on?" we heard someone yell.

O'Brien whipped around and pointed his gun at a man who'd seen us step out of his car.

"Get back in your car. Keep the windows rolled up." He moved his gun to another driver in a baseball cap. "You, too." Both men jumped back into their cars.

"Drink." O'Brien handed me a half-full vial of silver liquid with one hand as he wiped his mouth with the other.

I couldn't remember which spell was silver, but I grabbed it and drank it down. I felt its magic spread out inside me. I had no idea what drinking the magic did to me, but I was pretty sure I'd figure it out at some point.

A high street lamp a distance away dimmed and flickered as it went out, drawing my attention. Then another street lamp extinguished. The nightwalker approached. Car headlights dimmed too, furthering the darkness.

"It's coming." O'Brien cursed and pulled out another vial that I recognized as sunlight. We had taken only two of them from the cache, and he'd already used one.

"Stay back," he cautioned. His warning was useless. It didn't matter if I stayed back or not. This creature was more than I could understand. I was new to this darker side of the real world and unfamiliar with its dangers—unfamiliar with its predators.

A containment wasn't an option. On TV, any supernatural creature would stop at a chalk circle, but in the real world, against this creature, I'd need four steel walls and a roof. I only had the tall highway sound barrier behind me.

"Run. I'll try to stop it. If I don't . . ." O'Brien swallowed.

Run? I had nowhere to run. And even if I did, I would never be able to run far enough fast enough. My survival depended on O'Brien. If he died . . . Wait. Maybe his survival depended on me. Could I bring enough flame to incinerate this thing?

A mist billowed toward us like unwanted smoke from a campfire that I couldn't brush away. I felt the corrupt magic inside the mist, and its icy darkness thickened.

The nightwalker stalked toward us out of the mist, only visible because its silhouette was blacker than the surrounding night. The mist brushed at my skin. This time I recognized the deceptive nature of the cold, dark void. I gathered the memories and thoughts that had saved my mind from collapsing in despair. Then I wielded them as a mental shield.

O'Brien stood in front of me. Resolute.

The nightwalker spoke. "Charles O'Brien."

Goosebumps prickled on my body. If the darkness hadn't been so thick and suffocating, I would have been able to *see*, not just *feel*, the hair standing up on my arms and legs. My hold on the memories of my sister, my friends, and my girlfriend cracked. The creature's voice held a similar power as its scream, and I fought to restore my mental shield.

O'Brien's first name is Charles? Why hadn't I ever asked him his full name? I had no idea how this creature knew that detail, but it disturbed me that my enemy was better acquainted with my companion than I was. Since I had met O'Brien, my only concern had been myself.

So selfish.

If there was ever a time to be unselfish it was now. I needed to help O'Brien if there was any chance of both of us surviving. I needed to risk my life.

I grabbed the magic around me. A lot of it.

"*Fyr leoht!*" I screamed, unleashing a wave of heat far greater than any flame I had yet created. The nightwalker didn't move. The flames engulfed the creature completely. The dark shrouds around the creature burned and peeled, curling off the nightwalker layer after layer like pages of a burning book. Its black, rock-like face appeared to grimace in agony and . . .

Uh oh.

It wasn't a grimace. The nightwalker smiled. Then laughed. It twitched its hands, fingers tipped with arrowhead-like claws.

I'd burned the reaper-like cloak that had shrouded it, but that was all that burned. Its obsidian skin remained unharmed and stretched tightly over the visible shape of muscles and tendons, like a disproportionately tall statue of Bruce Lee. Except Bruce Lee had a full head of hair and a movie-star face. This thing's bald head absorbed light with skin that hugged tightly to its skull. The rib cage seemed excessively pronounced, but it didn't look starved. I understood O'Brien's description now. The cloak and its skeletal structure made it look like the Grim Reaper. The skin stretched around its muscles and bones made its body look like a zombie. It screamed like a banshee. But since this thing didn't have fangs, I wondered what made it comparable to a vampire.

I stood there unprotected and a little exposed—yes, I still wore nothing but my boxers. I almost laughed because I was suddenly better dressed than the nightwalker—who, by the way, was unmistakably male. *Yuck!*

Unfortunately, disrobing the creature with a magical torch had only made it cackle like it was about to introduce the next episode of Tales from the Crypt, making it all the more ominous. All humor drained from my mind.

It took its dark eyes from O'Brien and looked at me, hammering against my shield of happy memories, leaving it broken and weak.

"Is that the only spell you know?" it cackled at me. "It is," it answered itself. "I can read your feeble young mind."

O'Brien used that moment of distraction to slip his hand behind his back and let the vial of sunlight drop. The nightwalker didn't see it. For the second time, daylight interrupted the darkness of night. The light traveled faster than the sound of shattering glass, and its rays lit up the nightwalker just as my fire had done. The creature emitted another banshee-like scream. Whereas my fire had failed to even leave a mark, the light charred the obsidian skin like a piece of charcoal. With amazing speed, the creature fled under a high suspension truck only a couple cars away, crouching in the patch of shade. But the scream continued.

The creature would remain vulnerable for a few brief seconds. I *should* have taken advantage. But that horrid scream pounded at my mental shield until it shattered, and the black icy void invaded my mind, putting me on the defensive. I had a battle in my mind to fight before I could attack. I grabbed so many happy thoughts that if I had any fairy dust at all I could have flown to Neverland.

O'Brien pinched his eyes closed and covered his ears. He couldn't act while it screamed either. I walled off the dark mental abyss as quickly as I could, but just as I did, the sunlight disappeared. The screaming stopped.

A long moment of silent blackness passed. We couldn't see. Our pupils had reacted to the light and needed time to adjust anew.

A lot of drivers rolled down their windows or opened their doors. I could hear them cast their voices loudly, asking complete strangers if they had witnessed the same miraculous moment of daylight. Why weren't they going insane? Perhaps the scream had been unable to penetrate their cars, whereas the sunlight had. Or maybe a few drivers had gone insane. If so, they'd be the ones still in their cars.

The dome light flashed on in the truck under which the nightwalker lurked. It briefly illuminated the silhouette of a driver who stepped out. Before I could see more, the driver was yanked down and out of sight. Another scream, this time human, echoed between the sound barriers. But it was only a half scream, cut short in death.

Had the driver been a woman? It had sounded like a woman's scream. *A woman is dead because of me.*

My chest felt like an oversized linebacker just ran his facemask through it at full speed. The muscles under my skin moved beyond writhing and crawling and literally spasmed. How could *anything* be this evil? I was unprepared for the realities of a fight to the death with a creature that didn't value life. I knew O'Brien might die. I might die. But I had not once considered an innocent woman might die. Had she been a wife? Had she been a mother? Nausea swirled inside, but I didn't throw up. My nerves refused to accept what happened, forcing my muscles to flex in anger. I clenched my fists until my fingernails dug into my skin and my body shook.

I heard O'Brien shout out a very bad word. He hadn't liked the death of the woman either. He threw a vial underneath the truck, releasing more magic from broken glass.

Time slowed—at least it slowed for everyone in front of O'Brien and me. Whichever vial the druid bodyguard had tossed, it hadn't been one we'd picked up at the druid cache.

As if watching a slow-motion instant replay, the nightwalker slid out from underneath the truck—its movements deliberate. As it stood, it raised the woman's upper arm—unattached and dripping. Blood covered the thing's obsidian skin in a spray pattern except where a second layer of blood dripped down from its mouth like spilled paint, adding to the gruesome scene.

I glanced at O'Brien who was searching inside his jacket for a vial to use next. Other than sunlight, which we'd already used, I couldn't think of any other bottled spell that could help us now.

Still in slow motion, the nightwalker opened its mouth, revealing blackened teeth, and it bit into the dismembered arm's triceps. I cringed but could not look away as the nightwalker chewed open-mouthed. Its eyes, its blood-stained grin—the thing reveled in ecstasy as it fed. Beneath the blood and gore, its charred obsidian skin began slowly healing.

Without warning, I heard rapid gunshots. Holes appeared in the nightwalker's chest. In seconds, O'Brien, also not slowed by the vial, had emptied at least twenty rounds into the nightwalker, which sluggishly but deliberately stepped toward the sniper.

The nightwalker continued forward, ignoring the wounds. As it took a second excruciatingly slow bite of flesh, the bullet holes began healing and closing at a visible speed.

A few shouts distracted me. The people in the parked cars reacted to the gunshots by closing their car doors and windows and trying uselessly to drive forward. Frantic honking and shouting filled the air. One SUV started driving forward, hitting the car in front of it and pushing it forward into the car in front of it. I heard shattering glass followed by a half-second of grinding metal.

The druid bodyguard ejected his clip and I heard it hit the ground. He started sliding in another clip, but about halfway through, time returned to full speed for the nightwalker who shot forward with an unnatural quickness and viciously swung its claws at O'Brien's head. The ex-Marine tried to dodge but barely had time to move an inch. The impact lifted him off the ground. He flew back against the sound wall, landing with a sickening smack of flesh and the clatter of bones of steel. O'Brien dropped to the ground, his body completely motionless.

The nightwalker turned its bloody, obsidian body and flashed me a crimson smile. As it stepped toward me, it thought me insignificant. It had beaten O'Brien, and it planned to consume me as its victory celebration. My trembling, my chattering teeth, my screams of pain—this creature would suck that in like bite-sized hors d'oeuvres. It planned to kill me slowly and feed on my screams.

Since the moment the nightwalker pulled the woman under the truck, I had been gathering in magic. I let it flow into me but not out, amassing a reservoir of power. I couldn't contain the flow much longer. I needed to use my magic soon or it would cripple me just to hold it. I wanted to attack the creature, but how? Fire had been completely ineffective, and the only other two spells I had ever cast, a containment and druid detection, were useless. I searched my mind for some way to defend myself or attack it. Yet all I got was a very unhelpful thought: *I am going to meet my maker wearing boxers. I should have put on pants.*

The nightwalker continued toward me, much closer now. It planned to feast on my emotions as it feasted on my flesh. In fact, it had already started to enjoy my fear. A nightwalker reveling in a victim's fear; something about that ignited the memories embedded by the druid whose blood flowed in my veins. Suddenly I knew everything about nightwalkers as if I had studied them for years. Their joys, their fears, their needs. Everything. This creature was planning to eat me alive. It would drain me, body and soul. I wasn't going to live on as a spirit either. It would simultaneously feed on both my flesh and my soul. According to Caradoc, it could do that. I would be entirely consumed.

I wasn't just facing death. I was facing the erasure of existence.

A new desperation set in, and my mind and my spirit worked together, searching for any possible solution to survive, for anything that could prevent the end of my entire existence.

And then I knew what to do.

I had studied one other spell but had never cast it. I had forced myself to read that druid book for hours. Whenever I got bored, I had turned to this spell—and I'd felt bored a *lot*. My attempts to cast it had been halfhearted at best. Caradoc, however, had cast it before, many times.

I placed the base of my palms together, my hands forming a V, and pointed the V toward the nightwalker.

"*Bealustræl.*" I barely whispered the word, pronouncing it perfectly from Caradoc's memory. I didn't shout because the volume of my voice had no effect on the spell's power. The dam that held the magic I'd absorbed collapsed, and magic rushed into the spell, compressing into a sphere of white and blue light between my palms.

Just minutes before I'd had nowhere to run. Now neither did it.

The nightwalker's bloody grin vanished. It snarled and opened its mouth extra wide revealing a gray tongue before clenching its black teeth and hissing. It gave up the idea of making me suffer. It darted at me with the intent to kill me instantly.

But I acted at the speed of thought. I cast the magic missile.

The glowing orb traveled the half-dozen feet to the swift nightwalker, striking the obsidian creature like a ball of lightning. Unfortunately, it only staggered. Its obsidian skin illuminated briefly as it absorbed the immense power of the magic missile. Although its stride was broken, its momentum kept it coming directly at me. Stumbling but still moving extremely fast, it collided with my chest, throwing me backward. I crashed back against the wall, my insides rattling with clattering steel, as O'Brien's had. As I slumped to the ground, pure light broke through the nightwalker's skin in various places. The light spread and brightened until the creature exploded into nothingness.

I'd had the choice of sending a missile that attacked only its body or a missile that attacked both its body and soul. I'd chosen the latter. I'd done to it what it had intended to do to me.

A tremor of pleasure replaced the way my skin writhed with evil. I'd hit the barrier wall so hard, I should have passed out right away, but the pleasure sustained me.

I tried to stand, but blood rushed to my head and dripped from my nose. I had overextended in a big way. Despite the pleasure, I couldn't stay on my feet. As I collapsed, I saw a semi-truck coming fast. It was not carrying a trailer, but it was driving at full speed toward the unmoving cars.

Just then, a small, lithe form swung from the driver's side window to the top of the diesel's cab. The figure leaped toward me as the semi crashed into the tightly packed cars. I listened to the screeching of metal for what seemed like a full minute, but it surely didn't last that long—did it?

As my eyes drifted closed, the dark silhouette of the second creature came for me.

I swore in my head.

I had survived the nightwalker only to incapacitate myself in the process. I couldn't stand up. I couldn't defend myself.

Unconsciousness took me.

CHAPTER 24
BEAUTY

For the fourth time in a week, I woke up in a bed after passing out, and once again found myself surprisingly not dead. So far, I'd been shot, pronounced dead, punched out by a druid bodyguard, and this time . . .

Wait. What happened this time?

I had to stop doing this. Except if the alternative meant *not* waking up, maybe I didn't mind so much.

Where was I? Trying to remember my most recent near-death experience caused my breath to quicken. I tried to sit up. I couldn't. I hurt in a way that I couldn't understand. Every muscle shouted at my brain when I tried to turn in bed. I couldn't move without being aware of parts of my body I had never really thought about. The same thing happened with my mind. Even thinking hurt.

Then it dawned on me: for the first time in my life, I felt sore.

Not just physically but mentally, emotionally, spiritually, and magically sore. I wished Luiz were here. He'd always complained about his soreness after weightlifting. He felt that it wasn't fair that I had never shared his pain. Well, I could finally identify with his suffering. Even a freak like me, when in pain and vulnerable, could feel a little more like a normal person. Except I couldn't tell Luiz because he thought I was dead. Sore or not, I was still a druid, which isn't normal at all.

I sat up even though my every molecule protested. I tried to lift my arms but couldn't. Chains held my wrists to the bed. Definitely not something I had expected. A chill started at the base of my spine, running up and ending at the hair follicles on my head. After the chill passed, I gulped.

I tested and rattled the chains because that is just what a person does when they are chained up; they test and rattle the chains.

Yep. Strong chains.

I looked around. Daylight poured in from three large windows on the wall to my right—which had to be about a dozen feet away. My bed lay in the exact center of the room, which was bigger than my kitchen/dining/family room combo back home. Just as far to the left, a mahogany desk with hand-carved patterns on the drawers stood against the interior wall. The wall in front of me was closer. Aged paintings in thick gilded frames as big as the windows hung on each side of the door. The wood molding atop the walls also looked hand carved. A chandelier dangled ominously from the high ceiling directly above me, its crystals shaped like spikes. I had never been in a house owned by "old money," but that was exactly where I found myself. I'd never used the term "old money" before, either. Where had that phrase come from?

Standing to the right of the door, an older woman with gray hair and age-lined skin glanced up at me, but quickly lowered her eyes. She wore a gray dress with a white bodice and a white apron. I don't think I've ever used the term "bodice" either. Before I could say anything to her, she moved to the door and slipped out. I'd seen people similarly dressed in movies. They were called servants.

The room. The servant. Was I in a home fit for royalty? Was it possible I had time traveled? Nope, the triple-paned windows were framed with vinyl, a digital alarm clock sat on the expensive desk, and electrical outlets lined the room every three feet.

So after moving around, I realized that I had a blanket over me but not a stitch of clothing. This was a first. I'd never in my life slept naked. Even at the hospital, I'd woken wearing a hospital gown. Couldn't they at least have left me in boxers? I usually slept in my boxers. I couldn't for the life of me remember how I ended up in this bed without them. Of course, I couldn't remember how I got to this bed in the first place.

Not only was the bed centered in the room, but metallic lines in the floor intricately surrounded the bed. Were the lines made of silver?

I traced the lines until I saw the pattern: a Star of David wrapped in a perfect circle. The inner points of the star formed one hexagram and lines connecting the outer points of the star formed a second larger hexagram. Additional patterns filled the space between the star's six points. How very . . . eccentric. It didn't take a genius to realize that the silver pattern marked a containment.

I gulped again then reached for magic. Ouch! It just plain hurt to try to use magic. It felt like a headache except the pain was somewhere inside my soul, not my head. Ignoring the pain, I grabbed the magic around me, which wasn't much.

With magic, I tested and rattled the containment because that is just what a druid does when they are contained; they test and rattle the containment.

Yep. Strong containment.

OK. I didn't actually rattle it. I had recently figured out how to make pinholes in a containment, at least to let magic out if not in. I pushed at it with magic and tried to form a pinhole, but I couldn't penetrate it. According to the beginner's section of the druid's book, the design and pattern of a containment didn't matter. This had either clearly been wrong or I had made assumptions about the statement that I shouldn't have made. I wished I'd read further. I could faintly see the energy forming this containment. The intricate pattern fortified it in a way that I had little ability to comprehend.

Where was my book?

The last thing I remembered, I'd been up late reading and flipping pages in the hotel until I fell asleep. Something else had happened; something after I'd woken up; something that was worse than just bad. Something that was so horrible my mind had tossed the memory out like the smelly gym socks I once left in my locker over the weekend.

As I reached for the memory, my heartbeat and breathing sped up, which I hadn't expected. I'd never experienced a panic attack before. I didn't like it at all, so I stopped reaching for the memory, much to the relief of my heart and lungs.

I didn't need any help from a memory to panic anyway. I sat in the middle of a scene from *The Exorcist*, chained to a bed and surrounded by an eccentrically decorated Star of David. For all I knew, some freaked-out members of a cult would show up and cut my heart out and offer it to their make-believe god. Before I had time to evaluate my situation further, a servant woman opened the door. She held the door open and lowered her head as if bowing to someone who was about to enter.

"Leave us!" I heard a soft but commanding female voice. The servant left immediately, keeping her eyes down.

A woman walked in dressed like Trinity from The Matrix, wearing a black leather outfit that fit like another layer of skin. Her pants hugged her hips and her tall boots extended just above the knee. Her shiny black leather shirt had a zipper down the front and a high collar. She had it zipped to the chin as if trying to cover as much skin as possible.

An enticing aroma of pumpkin spice emanated directly from her. I can't remember being able to smell a girl without being inches from her hair, like when dancing or kissing. And yet from across the room, this woman's scent had definitely reached me. I reacted to the aroma as if pumpkin pie were my favorite food in the world and I hadn't eaten in a week.

Everything about her pulled my senses to her. Her hair, as black as her outfit, draped in straight lines, covering the light skin of her face. She wore large, black sunglasses. For some reason, I really wanted—no, not just wanted—hungered to see her eyes.

Compared to my attraction to Kendra, this felt unnatural. I tried to use my feelings for Kendra as a shield. I imagined Kendra beside me. Also chained. No. Dragging her into my new, deadly, monster-filled world wouldn't be love. That shield cracked.

The temperature in the room had to be approaching eighty, so I would have expected her to sweat profusely in that tight, leather outfit, but she rocked it just fine. Nobody dressed like that in July. Was it even still July? Maybe I'd been in a coma for a few months.

"Yes, it is July," she said. Her velvety voice caressed my ears.

Had I verbalized that thought? I didn't think I had. Actually, I knew for certain I hadn't. The idea of someone picking a thought from my head disturbed me to a new level. Who was this woman?

She tilted her head curiously at me as if just realizing something. "You don't know me," she stated.

I shook my head no.

She removed her large sunglasses and eyed me quizzically, allowing me to see her face and eyes. Her irises . . . they were blood red. I'd seen them before. The motorcycle girl who had saved O'Brien and me from the transients stood before me. O'Brien had called her an it. She didn't look like an it. She looked like a . . . a young woman, actually.

Or are you a vampire? I questioned, wondering if maybe she only looked young.

"Not exactly," she replied, again answering my thought.

Uh, OK. *What does not-exactly-a-vampire mean?* I thought at her. Either she was a vampire or she wasn't, right? And what kind of vampire smells of the most alluring pumpkin spice ever?

If she'd heard my thoughts this time, she ignored them. "Your name is Jacob."

I nodded, unable to look away from her eyes, which attracted me with a power equal to her aroma. Besides being mesmerizing, her eyes were the safest place to look. I had already just looked her up and down, and I had to consciously fight off the temptation to do it again.

She smiled at me knowingly. Uh oh. I needed to shut her out of my mind.

Why wasn't the containment keeping her out of my head? I found an answer in Caradoc's memories. *Thoughts are different than magic,* Caradoc's memory told me. I needed a "thought containment" to wall off thoughts, and those required more refined magic. Caradoc had cast thought containments many times. Still sore, I winced as I reached for the magic. Then, following Caradoc's memories, I created the thought containment. I tried to access more of Caradoc's memories, but they retracted to the back of my mind at my effort.

"Such power!" the girl remarked, eyes widened by the fact that I had just closed off her telepathic highway into my head. "I must tell grandfather about you," she noted.

"Shouldn't we at least have a first date before I meet your family?" The words came from my mouth before I could stop them, and I don't know where they came from. What idiot while chained to a bed and trapped in a Star-of-David containment and facing a not-exactly-a-vampire feels the urge to mouth off? It was quite unlike me.

Or was I flirting? Flirting was definitely more like me. At least, it was more like the football star part of me who I let out now and then to get me through parties where clingy barnacle girls flung themselves at me while I did my best to pretend to be like them until I could escape.

"The new druid can speak," she grinned. "Good. I need your *friþáp* before your containment and chains are removed."

"You need my what?" I asked.

I couldn't be sure, but I could swear she just made up some weird word to throw me off.

"*Friþáp.* Oath of peace." She raised her eyebrow at me quizzically.

This time, I heard the word better. It sounded like Old English. I reached for Caradoc's memory and once again, they pulled away from me. I guess I'd have to wing it.

"Uh . . . OK," I replied, wondering what the freak she was talking about. "You have my oath of peace."

"I don't find that humorous!" Her eyes went dark—the red in them disappeared, leaving them as black as night. I felt pressure against my thought containment, and my sore mind screamed at me. I pressed my eyes closed and tried to will the headache away. Her aroma changed to copper—the smell of blood—except strangely still enticing. The pressure stopped, and I opened my eyes to find her standing at the edge of the containment. She'd pulled in magic, so to me, her body faintly glowed.

"You can use magic?" I asked.

She raised her eyebrows, pulling her eyes further open, emphasizing her now-black irises. Then her brow lowered into a scowl. Her stance changed and she pulled in more magic so quickly that the colors of it swirled into her. She was preparing herself to defend against me, which made no sense. I was no danger to her while stuck in this containment.

"How did you know I could . . ." She didn't finish.

I saw traces of her magic as she pushed it toward the Star of David containment, strengthening it. I could now see the magic forming the containment.

"Your oath, druid, or you die." I followed her eyes up to the chandelier above me—the one with spiky crystals that would put a hundred holes in me if it fell. It dropped six inches and jerked to a stop, causing the spikes to rattle and bounce. I yelped like a frightened puppy.

She considered me a threat. Maybe she thought I could break out of her containment because I had detected she could use magic. What she didn't know is that I had *seen* the magic. I had no chance to break out. The containment had me trapped and helpless. She could kill me with a thought.

I was pretty sick of the whole almost-dying thing. What even was an oath of peace? I tried to find a Caradoc memory to explain it to me, but his memories moved further to the back of my mind as I tried to access them.

"I promise. I promise," I spit out rapidly, my voice shooting up an octave or two. "You can have my oath. Whatever you need. Just tell me what to say."

"Oh." She looked at me quizzically. Her eyes faded back to red and her aroma switched back to pumpkin spice.

I breathed a sigh of relief that she had believed me—until I realized that I had dropped my thought containment. She believed me because she had read my freaked-out mind.

"How is it that you are powerful enough to blast a nightwalker into oblivion; powerful enough to create a thought containment; powerful enough to detect my magic through this containment; but you have no idea how to give an oath of peace?"

Because I've only been a freaking druid for a few days, I thought at her.

"Really?" She smiled at me like I was a child. "You are just learning? Oh, no. O'Brien is teaching you? Where is Caradoc? Caradoc disappeared? How? Of course, you wouldn't know. How has O'Brien been teaching you? Only from the book? Yes, I have your book. No need to worry, you shall have it back. No, I don't mind if you look at my body while we speak, I am quite aware of how attractive I am. Your body is quite attractive as well." Her grin returned.

"Stop that!" I yelled and brought the thought containment back up around my skull.

She'd just had a conversation with me without ever letting me speak, picking the answers from my mind. It was quite awkward and intimidating. Not to mention I had a lot of other thoughts that I preferred to keep to myself, and she had already gotten to a few of them. My cheeks flushed, but fortunately, my tan skin hid it well.

"Now why did you do that?" She pouted. "We were making such progress."

"Because it freaks me out!" I shouted. "You can't just go around invading my mind."

"Obviously, I cannot as you can block me out whenever you want." She glanced at the window, then slipped her glasses back on and let her hair fall forward to once again cover her face. Was I imagining it or did she noticeably relax?

"I suppose I need to teach you how to make an oath of peace," she admitted.

As soon as she said those words, Caradoc's memories finally flashed into my mind. Probably because I was no longer trying to access them. Better late than never.

I started speaking: "I speak to the magic inside this house. I give my oath of peace that while in this dwelling I shall not harm this girl—er, this woman—unless my life is threatened. By magic make it so."

"Did you read my mind?" She eyed me with renewed suspicion.

"I don't think so," I answered, unsure. Hadn't it been a Caradoc memory? Or had I read her mind? How was I to know? Maybe it was better she thought that, though. No way was I going to tell her that I had masses of undiscovered memories embedded in the liters of Caradoc's blood flowing through my veins.

She motioned with her hand. The shackles released from my arms, and the faint glow of the containment disappeared. I rubbed my wrists where the cold iron had wrapped around them. I made a move to get up, but I quickly stopped. Despite being free of the shackles and the containment, I was still trapped in my bed because a terrifying, beautiful, not-exactly-a-vampire girl stood in front of me and I was totally naked under the blanket.

"I gave no oath!" she breathed harshly. "You would be wise to remember that."

Yeah, she had definitely just threatened me. Another day, another death threat. I thought about telling her to get in line, but then I wondered if she already was in line. She could easily be a part of whatever group assassinated the druids.

She turned and opened the door. Outside, a servant woman stood waiting, her hair silver and skin creased with age.

"Dress him and bring him to the dining hall," she ordered as she walked out.

A part of me felt disappointed to see her leave. I hadn't even asked her for her name. I wanted to call out for her to come back, but I didn't. The smell of pumpkin spice hung in my room, dissipating slowly.

Maybe I couldn't ever be with Kendra again, but no way was I going to let this *not-exactly-a-vampire* mess with me—or my subconscious avoidance of dealing with losing Kendra.

The older servant brought me a folded pile of clothes. She didn't look me in the eyes, nor did she hesitate to pull the blanket away from me before I thought to stop her. I jumped off the bed and ducked down a little, trying to gain some coverage from the bed. She set the clothes down on the bed and lifted a pair of black jockey shorts, preparing to dress me herself.

"I'm good." I snatched my undies from her, again grateful my tan hid my flushed cheeks. No way was I letting some old woman help me put on my underwear. "Just let me dress myself, please."

She looked me in the eyes when I said please. She blinked multiple times. Apparently, she was not used to hearing that word. She looked back down to the floor and left. That look in her eyes had meant something, but I didn't have time to figure it out right then. I was just glad to be rid of her and free to dress myself.

It wasn't lost on me that my skin felt clean. Someone had bathed me while I had slept and that weirded me out. I put on the black pants. What material were these made of? They looked runway expensive and felt amazingly comfortable. The black shirt felt silky. I wasn't the type to dress in all black or in nice designer clothes, but if I was in the house of some type of royalty, as was my guess, such clothes were likely all they had to offer. I scratched my head at the thick black socks and combat boots. Really?

Again, it was July and while the not-exactly-a-vampire girl could pull off something like this without sweating, I certainly couldn't. Still, even though they were a little too hot, the socks and boots felt comfortable.

"The lady would have you come with me." The older servant woman stood in the doorway, having returned to my room the moment I finished dressing. Had she been watching? I followed her out of the room and down a long hallway lined with closed doors.

She led me into what looked to be a huge, formal dining room. It had to be the size of a small basketball gym. The friendlier chandelier didn't look like it was designed to impale but rather to decorate with its ornate crystal. That would have comforted me except that the chandelier and all other lights were off. The room had many windows, but unlike those in my bedroom, every single one of them was well covered with tightly closed, mahogany blinds.

My nose detected the Matrix girl before my eyes did—the same arousing pumpkin spice beckoned me toward her, urging me to bend to her will. The sight of her contributed to my attraction.

She sat at a large oak table. Two places were set with expensive dishware. She sat at one of them. I guessed the other was for me and started toward it. The servant confirmed this by gesturing to the seat with her arm. As I sat down, the servant lit a single candle on the table between the girl's seat and mine, and I was grateful for it because it was the only light in the room.

I was about to ask her name but she spoke first.

"You are perspiring," she remarked, her nose wrinkling slightly.

"I was given warm clothing," I answered without apology.

"Cool yourself," she commanded.

Everything about her made me want to obey, and the only reason I didn't was because I didn't know how.

"What do you mean?" I asked, eager to comply.

She looked at me questioningly with red eyes shaded by her straight, black hair, and if possible, the alluring aroma of pumpkin spice increased. She was hoping my skull wasn't wrapped in an anti-read-my-thoughts blanket, but it most certainly was. No way I was letting her burglar my brain again.

"May I?" she asked, putting her hand out for me to take.

I nodded and placed my hand in hers.

Her skin felt cool but not cold. Touching her ignited a desire greater than either her aroma or her looks, and I never wanted to let go. My mind sent out a warning, telling me to jerk my hand away. I dropped all magic.

Think of Kendra.

The girl's red eyes locked to mine.

Think of . . . who?

I smiled, already lost in her touch.

CHAPTER 25
BEAST

While holding my hand, she used magic on me. Flows of energy—visible to me—cooled the air around me, shaping a barrier—or maybe a filter—so that heat flowed around and through me in a controlled manner. Goosebumps formed on my arms.

"Heat is energy, and all energy is part of magic, so you can control it. Did you feel how I did that?" she asked.

Her voice hummed beautifully to me, and despite being lost in the velvety sound of it, I nodded. She let go of my hand. A part of me wanted her to never let go.

"That is much better." She smiled at me. "Please, eat."

A servant brought us plates with a fancy meal. A seasoned chicken breast sat over rice with a side of cooked vegetables. It looked as good as it tasted. She ate the same meal as me. Whatever she was, she could eat food.

"What's your name?" I finally asked.

I didn't immediately pick up my fork, which was unlike me.

"Alexis Kaloyan," she answered, smiling.

"OK. Who are you?" I asked.

"I am the granddaughter of John Kaloyan," she replied, expecting me to know who that was.

"I am the grandson of the late Michael Stevens," I replied, grinning as I watched her take a bite of chicken.

"I have not heard of Michael Stevens," she stated. "Was he a powerful druid?"

"Well, I haven't heard of John Kaloyan, either." I smiled wider, ignoring her useless query about my mom's dad.

"Oh." Her eyes thinned. "Were you mocking me, Jacob Stevens?" she said, her monotone voice firm. The tips of her fangs touched her lower lip. My goosebumps returned.

"Sorry. Just trying to play along," I replied. "By the way, you've saved me twice. Why?"

"So many questions."

She set down her fork and gave me her undivided attention. I'd moved my hand to my fork, about to pick it up, but she placed her hand on mine. For the second time, warning lights started flashing in my head, but her hand felt so good I couldn't pull mine from under hers.

"Let me get you up to speed on how much I know about being a druid," I offered, perhaps too eagerly. "I was shot in the leg last Wednesday . . ." I began. And I went on to tell her things I should never have told her. I told her I healed quickly and that O'Brien had increased my already-fast healing with a vial of blue liquid. I told her O'Brien had faked my death and my family believed I was dead. I told her about the *wyrman tiegan* and the first spell I had cast, *fyr leoht*.

"Can you cast it for me?" she asked.

I nodded, anxious to do anything she asked. I controlled the magic better this time. Only a small flame, a little larger than the candle's, rose from my hand.

"The first time I cast the spell, I lost control and nearly burned down the house, causing transients to come for us. Wasn't that you who helped us?"

She nodded and said, "Go on."

I explained the druid cache, casting a containment, and the magic vials.

"We've been looking for another potential druid," I said, then I explained the duality of potentials and drinking the vials. "O'Brien and I searched for him at my funeral."

"You attended your own funeral?" She laughed. Her cheeks and eyes joined her smile. I didn't want her to stop. I wanted to share everything.

I skipped something about the funeral, something I should remember but couldn't. I moved on to discussing how I invented a new way to detect a magic user without them knowing it was me. I started telling her I was given Caradoc's blood, and that randomly his memories, which were embedded in his blood—my blood—had helped me . . .

Then I stopped. Something was wrong. Why had I just told her so much? I was talking to her like she was the only person in the world I could trust. Like we could share anything. And it felt good.

Except now *it feels wrong!*

"Did you find the other potential?" she coaxed, still holding my hand. Her voice pushed me to share more, but I just stared at her. I fought the urge to keep talking, and I won. I thought back to our meeting and tried to determine when she could have instilled this false trust in my mind. I mentally checked the thought containment and found it was still in place.

What else had she done besides showing me how to cool down?

I looked at her hand on mine. I jerked my hand from underneath hers.

"What did you do to me?" I demanded.

For a brief second, her eyes went completely black and her smile disappeared. But then her eyes dropped guiltily.

"Who are you, really?" I demanded. I grabbed a fork in one hand and a knife in the other and started eating so she couldn't touch me again.

"I was honest with you, Jacob. I am Alexis Kaloyan," she answered.

"OK, then *what* are you?" I pressed.

"My mother is . . . she *was* a dhampir," she told me. "Like you, Jacob, I have no idea who my father is, except I do know that he was a druid."

"What's a dhampir?" I asked, though I already had an idea. According to books and movies—and I've read and watched plenty since I hardly sleep—a dhampir was some type of vampire offspring. However, I was certain that books and movies were inaccurate.

"A dhampir is half vampire, half human. My mother, Carina, is the daughter of John Kaloyan, the Vampire King. My grandfather takes human wives because he likes children. Unfortunately, he does not like *old* wives. I never knew my grandmother. I do not even know her name. I already told you I do not know who my father is. My mother has refused to tell me his name."

Her words made me want to hold her, to comfort her, to do anything to make her feel better. Her pumpkin spice aroma, her red eyes, her soft face framed in straight black hair: they had a power over me. I wanted to succumb. Yet I knew I was dealing with a predator who might be luring me in for the kill. Except for the same reason I trusted O'Brien, I trusted her—at least I trusted she had no plans to kill me. I had remained unconscious and incapacitated for hours. If Alexis had wanted me dead, she could have killed me at any time. Of course, if she just wanted information *before* she killed me . . .

"So not-exactly-a-vampire means you *are* one-fourth *vampire*." I emphasized "are" and "vampire" to block my desire to hug Miss Dangerous and tell her everything would be OK.

"I suppose." She pouted her lips again. "I do prefer to think of myself as half dhampir."

"Half dhampir, huh?" I preferred to think of her as one-fourth vampire—it helped remind me of how dangerous she could be.

"So you don't burn in the sun?" I asked. She had stood unharmed in the room I had woken in despite the bright sun that had shone through the large windows.

"I can handle the sun for a short time," she replied. "It is hard on me."

"And you're not the type to go water skiing without SPF ten thousand," I added.

"Actually, water skiing at night is quite fun." She smiled widely. "Would you like to go sometime?"

I almost spit out a quick yes, but I caught myself. Alexis was still trying to restore the control she had held over me. I wasn't done getting information out of her yet, though, and I wanted to see how much *she* was willing to share. So far, she hadn't shared much more than what she expected a druid to already know.

"Do you kill to eat?" I asked.

The same black fury took over her eyes, but it was gone even quicker this time. Her smile went from wide to mocking. She glanced at the remaining chicken on her plate. "This chicken is quite dead, I assure you."

"You know what I mean," I retorted.

"What of the rest of your story?" Alexis deflected. "You did not finish."

"What of yours?" I countered. "You still haven't told me why you've saved me twice."

Her eyes thinned again. "I only saved you once. You saved yourself the second time."

"I saved myself?"

She grinned mischievously. "I suspected it was something your mind has forgotten."

Her words twisted inside me. I had forgotten. *What had happened before coming here?* When I had pried into the memory earlier, a panic had swept over me. That same panic crawled back into me now. I didn't like it any more than I had liked it the last time.

"Have you forgotten what made you pass out? Why O'Brien is in a coma?"

"O'Brien's in a coma?" I asked, grasping at anything that would quench the anxiety burning through my chest.

"Yes."

"Where is he?" I pressed.

"He is here."

"Can I see him?"

"Of course. You had but to ask." She smiled.

I stood, ready to go that very second. With the panic had come the need to move, to do something.

"Please, have the courtesy to finish eating," she ordered, taking another bite of her chicken. Her words still mesmerized me, and I saw no reason to let food go to waste. I sat back down and shoveled my food in, elbows on the table and everything. Alexis glanced multiple times at my elbows but said nothing. I didn't say anything either. I kept my mouth too full to either ask her questions or foolishly give her more information.

"Can we see him now?" I asked, scraping my plate clean.

"You are very impatient," she observed. "It would be proper manners to let the lady of the table finish her plate as well." Once again, her words compelled me to obey. I sat there watching her eat and regretted my empty plate, wishing I had taken my time.

My eyes had adjusted to the darker room and the candlelight. Alexis was beyond beautiful. I struggled to fight off the desire that she stirred in me. I watched her lift the fork. Her mouth opened, and she surrounded her fork with her lips. I couldn't help wanting to feel those lips pressed against mine.

I closed my eyes and tried to take back control of my mind.

I reminded myself that the touch of her hand had completely overcome me. I couldn't imagine how completely in her power I would be if I let her lips touch mine. I made a note to avoid skin-to-skin contact with Alexis. My body groaned in protest, urging me for more skin-to-skin contact as soon as possible.

Thankfully, she finished eating and stood up.

She looked at her chair, then at me. I didn't move. Was there something I was supposed to do? What did she expect? She gave me a frustrated look and moved her own chair aside.

Oops. She had been waiting for some old-fashioned courtesy, and I had totally missed the cue. She stepped toward me, and my heart beat faster. She smiled as she approached, aware of her effect on me. She moved to within inches of me and then stopped, staring at me expectantly once again. I'd already proven I couldn't take the cue, so she spoke up.

"Offer me your arm," she ordered flatly.

I offered it against my better judgment. She slipped her hand into the crook of my elbow. I waited for her touch to overpower me, but it didn't happen. I wore long sleeves. Her hand only touched my silk shirt. I breathed deeply in relief, but that didn't help because I sucked in her aroma and that nearly overpowered me itself.

I focused on putting one foot in front of the other and counted my steps. Counting helped, but her allure was too much for me. At least my containment kept me from being an open book to her—mentally, anyway. She didn't need to read my mind to know that she was affecting me physically. She could reach out and touch my hand or face at any moment. I was hers for the taking, yet she just walked with me. Why didn't she touch my skin and take control of me? Is she working just as hard as I am to avoid a touch? She was.

In sixty-seven steps, we were standing by O'Brien's bed. I couldn't say which direction we had gone from the dining hall. I couldn't remember anything but counting steps and trying not to be overcome by the desire for the girl walking next to me.

"Here he is," Alexis announced. "We did not bandage him in case he healed rapidly. Unfortunately, it seems he is healing poorly."

The room would have looked like a normal bedroom, at least normal for a mansion, but the equipment surrounding O'Brien made it look like a hospital room. A tube stuck out of his mouth and connected to a ventilator, which breathed for him. An IV pumped fluids into him. Other equipment monitored his heart and brain functions. I stared at the black and swollen skin around his ear, held together with a lot of stitches. A piece of his ear had been ripped off.

"He took a hard blow to the head. We were unable to relieve the pressure in time. His skull was . . . unbreakable."

"Bones of steel?" I whispered, remembering the silver vial. *Why would he have used that?* I felt the panic stir back to life as I searched for the answer to that question.

"When the spell wore off, we were able to drain the excess fluid."

I spotted two small holes above O'Brien's ear, spaced about two inches apart. *Had she . . . ?* I searched for the fangs hiding behind Alexis's lips as chills ran down my spine.

"We used a drill," she said.

Was my thought containment still in place? It was. She hadn't needed to read my mind. She had just read my eyes.

"What happened?"

Alexis looked at me and didn't answer. I tried to remember. *Oh, crap.* I felt the panic rising up from the pit of my stomach. The memory pressed upward from a deep abyss in my mind, threatening to come back, and I couldn't stop it.

"O'Brien needs healing," she stated. "Magical healing. Unfortunately, I do not have that skill."

I barely heard her as my breathing increased. Panic set in.

"I've never healed anyone," I whispered between breaths. "But we had some vials of healing with us . . ." I couldn't finish. I was remembering and . . .

Am I hyperventilating?

"Are you OK?"

My body quivered, and my legs gave out. I dropped to the floor. The previous night came crashing back, and it hurt. The nightwalker's screams returned to my mind. The woman being pulled from the truck. The nightwalker feeding off her upper arm. My stomach turned, but the food stayed in.

Guilt ignited inside me, accelerating the panic. I had power the whole time to destroy the creature, but I hadn't seen it. I was responsible for the innocent woman's death. I had stood there and done nothing while the nightwalker tore her limb from limb and while it attacked O'Brien. O'Brien's coma, his damaged ear; they were both my fault too. I shivered at the memory of the nightwalker's cold mist of darkness and overpowering scream. I recoiled at the idea of not just dying but of its threat to feed on both my body and soul. I had failed to fight back until *I* was the one in danger.

I grabbed my knees, my breathing rapid and sporadic. I couldn't get enough air.

When the nightwalker approached, I had consumed so much magic that I almost failed to hold it inside me. I had let in more power than I should have—until I was about to explode. The pleasure of releasing the power and how it had destroyed the nightwalker came back to me. I had done to the nightwalker what it had planned to do to me. I wasn't sure what type of soul a nightwalker had, but however evil a soul it was, I had destroyed it. Had I broken some kind of spiritual law, perhaps God's law? The nightwalker had threatened me with the same. Hadn't I acted in self-defense? Which rated higher on the evil scale, the nightwalker or what I had done to it?

As the hyperventilating began to threaten my consciousness, two hands touched my cheeks. I opened my eyes and looked into the most beautiful, red eyes.

"Relax," Alexis whispered calmly, kneeling in front of me. "Breathe slowly."

With her hands on my face, each word she spoke took charge of my body, which obeyed. I relaxed and my breathing slowed to a controlled rhythm.

I lost myself in Alexis's touch. I gave in, turning over my will to her. I would do whatever she asked. Nothing mattered but her. I wanted her to have me. I felt the urge to share my life—my blood—with her. I lifted my hand to my collar and moved it aside. Maintaining eye contact, I turned my head, exposing my neck.

"Please," I whispered, begging her to take me.

Her lips parted, exposing her teeth, and I watched her canines extend slightly. I ached for the touch of her lips on my neck. I wanted to feel my blood flow into her. If only she were to bite and drink from me, she and I would become one, and that was all I wanted. Desire also reflected in her eyes. She thirsted for my life-blood as much as I wanted her to have it. She wanted, *needed*, to pierce the neck that I bared as an offering.

Her irises turned black, then red lines forced their way through the blackness and extended into the sclera. *Hunger.* The word traveled from her mind to mine. At the same time, the scent of honey replaced that of pumpkin spice. She leaned toward me, eyes on my exposed neck.

But she stopped.

Her lips and lower chin quivered. She jerked away, trying to stand. Her left boot caught on a power cable that ran under O'Brien's bed, and she fell to the floor. She scrambled backward on her feet and hands until her back hit the door. The black drained from her eyes, which turned white. She flailed one arm up, grabbed the knob, and pulled herself to her feet.

She fled the room.

My heart broke. I felt like the person I loved had just died in my arms. I cried. The emotion became physical pain in my chest, and I doubled over. Why had she rejected me? Why had she not taken me? My heart felt like it would never stop aching. I watched the door, wishing she would return so that I could feel the touch of her hands again. I imagined her pressing her lips to my neck and taking my blood. If only my life could flow into her, she and I could become one.

I curled up, leaning against O'Brien's bed. My anguish lasted for long minutes. Eventually, it faded. The hospital equipment beeped, restoring my focus. I finally moved. I leaned back and placed my hands on the floor behind me. I felt the texture of the

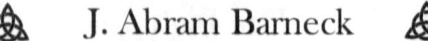

hardwood floor. I remembered where I was and what I was doing here. I sat in O'Brien's room. He lay in a coma. I had come to check on him.

Instinctively, I reached for the magic around me and created a seal around myself that blocked everything out—magic, thoughts, emotions, scents—everything. I liberated myself from Alexis's unnatural power.

I breathed a sigh of relief to be thinking clearly again. Then I swore.

What had I been thinking?

Why had I offered to give my blood to Alexis? Stupid! I had just offered myself to a monster. Was she the most beautiful girl ever? Maybe. But she was a monster all the same. Except even as I thought it, I didn't believe it. She couldn't be a monster. Alexis had backed off. Her eyes had turned black with red lines and her scent turned to honey. She had wanted my blood more than I had wanted her to take it. How had she found the willpower to pull away?

Monsters don't do that.

She looked scared of herself—of her powerful hunger. I could identify with that. In fact, she was better than me. I had failed the woman in the truck, letting her get ripped to shreds while I did nothing. I had failed O'Brien. Then I had killed the nightwalker. I could have limited my attack to the nightwalker's body, but I'd mercilessly erased both its body and soul. I'd fed my hunger. Alexis had shown restraint where I hadn't. If she was a monster, she was less of a monster than I was.

CHAPTER 26
CRYSTAL

As I sat in O'Brien's room, another servant woman came in. Unlike the other servant who had been completely gray with aged and wrinkled skin, this woman's hair only had a few gray strands and her mostly smooth skin only wrinkled at the corners of her eyes. I placed her in her mid-thirties. She carried my druid textbook open in her hands. For a second, I thought she was using a red Ring Pop as a bookmark.

"The mistress wishes you to read this particular passage." She held out the book for me to take. "She also says it is best if you stay in here or in your room until you have protected yourself. She wanted you to know that when you are done," she indicated the open page, "you will be able to help your friend as well."

I stared at the red ruby, wedged in the crease where the pages met inside the book. It wasn't a Ring Pop, those were round but this one was a rectangle and its cut . . . *Radiant*. That was the third time today I'd used a word I'd never used before. "Radiant" described the jewel's rectangular shape and the cut.

This has *to be a fake*, I told myself.

I took the book and stared into the ruby, half expecting it to glow or put me in a trance or something, but nothing happened.

I turned my attention to the words on the page. If one of O'Brien's monitors hadn't beeped, I wouldn't have glanced up to notice the servant leaving.

I returned my eyes to the book and read the title of the spell: "Protection Stone." Below that, I read an alternate name: "Vampire Protection Crystal."

Oh. The spell included instructions for enchanting the ruby to ward off the effects of vampires or other creatures that had influential powers. This ruby was no fake. I felt a wave of trust toward Alexis. Perhaps her allure still influenced me slightly, causing me to read far more meaning into her gesture than it really held. Even so, handing me a gem worth a fortune and showing me how to protect myself against her power created a foundation of trust that I couldn't ignore.

I glanced at O'Brien's comatose form then continued reading the spell. Actually, the book called it an enchantment rather than a spell. Of course, it had to be in the back of the book, smack-dab in the middle of the uber-complex section of spells that only one in a hundred druids could cast. This one was supposedly even harder as it required the rare ability to manipulate energy and matter. Perhaps that answered the question as to why Alexis didn't enchant the crystal herself.

The enchantment's intricacy overwhelmed me. The idea was to make the enchantment slowly feed off the crystal while still supplying plenty of strength to the protection spell. One particle of the crystal would feed the magic and its energy should last up to one second per particle. It was important to determine the pattern the magic should use to consume the particles. Consume them in a straight line, and too soon the crystal breaks in half. The book talked in concepts of thousands of years. I didn't care whether it lasted that long.

The druid text recommended I practice with cheap, abundant crystals, such as bits of salt. I'd been told to stay between my room and O'Brien's, but I risked going to the end of the hall to flag down the thirty-something servant. She brought me a small bag of rock salt a few minutes later.

I read the enchantment twice and then closed my eyes, reaching for the magic around me. Magic came to me instantly. Even with the magic and the book's instructions, I again found myself clueless. I searched for a hint from Caradoc's memories, but as before, when I reached for the memories, they scurried away into the back of my mind. If I had just been patient, would the right memory have just come to me?

I might as well just give it a try, I thought.

I grabbed a granule of salt and got started. I mistakenly enchanted it with barely any magical strength. When I altered it to have more strength, the salt crystal glowed brightly, then shrank and faded into nothing, as completely erased from existence as the nightwalker. I felt remnants of the pleasure of erasing the nightwalker. I pushed the feeling away because, despite the nightwalker's evil, it felt wrong to have gone beyond just killing it; to have gone so far as to destroy its soul. I tried not to admit how much I had enjoyed the power. I imagined erasing John, my creepy, peeping stepfather. I dwelt on the thought too long. Despite the nasty things John had done, he didn't even deserve the death penalty, let alone having his soul obliterated from existence.

I put another granule of salt in my palm. The book was right. Salt was convenient and abundant, making it easy to experiment and play. I sat at the desk against the wall of O'Brien's room and worked on trying to understand the intricacy of the spell. Sam and Dean Winchester used salt all the time. Fiction often has a basis in reality. Perhaps salt was an easy crystal to throw power into. I skimmed for more info about salt in the druid text. Turns out that salt should only ever be used to test enchantments. It is a weak element that crumbles easily.

Reading about the salt inspired me to look up more information about each step of the enchantment. I engrossed myself in studying. The thirty-something servant came in and out, checking on O'Brien as if she were a nurse. I didn't realize how many hours passed until she walked in with a covered, silver tray and offered me dinner. I had been studying for hours, and my stomach lurched at the smell. I lifted the domed cover and saw salmon over a foundation of long asparagus and discs of zucchini. A side of browned-ribbon mashed potatoes sat on top of yellow cheese as if intended to look like a flower. I asked for a second helping as I started on the first. I could eat a lot, and I wasn't ashamed of it. I finished my first plate long before the second serving arrived, which had two salmon steaks over a mountain of vegetables. The servant gave me a knowing smile, as if she knew something about me that I didn't know. I should have asked her about it, but I just let her leave. I finished the second plate and felt truly full, a rare feeling for me.

I kept glancing at Charles O'Brien. Each time I saw his mangled ear, the image of the nightwalker swiping its clawed hand at him jumped into my mind, causing my whole body to tremble. To avoid this repeating pattern, I headed to my own room. When I reached my door, I grabbed the knob, then stopped. Two servants were talking on the other side. I leaned closer and put my ear against the door.

I heard a few broken words: "help the mistress" and "offered her blood" and "she collapsed." I swallowed nervously. I pieced together what those words meant. I strained to hear more but they lowered their voices. I waited, still barely hearing their muffled voices. I gave up trying to hear more and opened the door.

Both servants glanced my way, suddenly silent. They hid their gossiping well. If I hadn't heard them talking before I had walked in, I wouldn't have known they had cut off their conversation mid-sentence. They worked together putting clean sheets on my bed. This was like a hotel. Clean sheets every day.

One of the servants was the thirty-something woman who had recently brought me the ruby and the salt. I had expected the other to be the older servant from earlier. Instead, this servant was much younger. She had healthy auburn hair and soft eyes. Her well-fitted dress hugged a little to her slight figure. She couldn't be much older than twenty.

"What happened to the older servant?" I questioned.

The servants' eyes looked everywhere but at me. They didn't answer my question. They just finished their tasks and walked toward the door. The servant who had brought my food couldn't help but glance my way as she walked out. A single tear rested on her cheek. She turned away, but not before the tear fell.

Oh, no. I didn't like what the tear implied, especially coupled with the broken conversation I'd just heard. I sucked in a quick breath and held it. *Had Alexis drained the older servant dry?*

I assumed she had. Alexis had spared me, but perhaps to her, the older servant was disposable. Or food. I tensed my muscles, unable to calm myself. My resolve to create the protection stone renewed. What would it take to kill Alexis? Could I pull it off? I didn't know for sure, but nothing could survive decapitation, could it? For the moment, I pushed the thought out of my mind.

My room had a bathroom, which was good, because I needed to use it. I got to choose which of the two sinks to wash my hands in. The shower was as big as my entire bathroom at home and its marble tile covered the entire wall and ceiling.

I examined the walls to see if there was any way I could be spied on. Did I do it because of my creeper stepdad or because I felt uneasy in the luxurious mansion? Perhaps the false trust Alexis had infected me with had me overcompensating with extreme distrust.

I went back to the room, grabbed my book and some rock salt, and settled at the mahogany desk to continue practicing the enchantment. With Caradoc's help, I had pulled off the magic missile, which was a highly advanced spell, so I assumed I'd be able to pull off this enchantment quickly. But the magic missile was advanced because of the massive amount of power required to cast it while the protection stone enchantment was advanced because of its complexity. I kept failing in different ways. I kept getting the rate of conversion wrong, either too quick or too slow. I couldn't connect the magic so the molecules converted to magic that dispersed into the air instead of feeding the enchantment.

Getting the spell right would take time. I worked on it most of the night and well into the early morning hours.

At 4:00 A.M., I found myself glancing at the bed. I hesitated to get into the same bed where I had woken with shackled wrists. The chains were gone, but the metal pins still stuck out from the headboard. Despite no longer sustaining a containment, the silver Star of David pattern on the floor discouraged me further. I decided not to chance it. I tried to move the bed, but the frame was bolted down so I grabbed the top mattress and dragged it to the floor and away from the circle, making a mess of the perfectly made blankets and sheets. As I lay down, I hoped the servants would forgive the mess. I fell asleep before I could think more about it.

I woke up a little after 8:00 A.M., content to have no recollection of dreaming. A silver tray of food already sat on the desk. A note lay next to it. I felt my heart jump, knowing Alexis had written it. I reined myself in, reminding myself that the infatuation I felt for her was not real but just the result of her vampiness. Still, I went straight to the note and read it.

> *Interesting sleeping arrangements. The women of the house were quite confused, though I believe I understand. You shall not find me in the house during the day. Finish the protection stone.*
>
> *Alexis K.*

The shortness of the note disappointed me, as did Alexis saying I wouldn't see her. I shouldn't have wanted to see her, but I did. I turned to my breakfast, looking for a distraction. The servants had prepared me a huge skillet of eggs and hash browns and a dozen different vegetables. It must have taken a dozen eggs to make the scrambled mound. The skillet still sizzled. Each bite was heaven.

After breakfast, I showered. Yes, it felt like I should be playing basketball in there, not showering. I couldn't touch the sliding glass doors and the opposite wall at the same time. A second showerhead stuck out from the marble wall behind me. At first, I assumed the second showerhead would allow hot water to spray me from both sides, but this shower was built for two.

I spent much of the day in my room trying to work out the enchantment. I slipped out a few times to check on O'Brien. By early afternoon, I was tired of being inside, so I went outside for a walk or perhaps a good run. The servants protested, urging me to stay inside, but I ignored them.

The mansion topped a hill halfway up the mountain on the southeast side of Bountiful City, a suburb north of Salt Lake. I hadn't known this area existed. I had never seen houses so large. Each must have cost as much as my entire neighborhood. As big as the surrounding houses were, the vampire mansion dwarfed them all. It had pillars and not just one set, but three sets of three pillars, spaced evenly. Did the mansion have as much square footage as my high school? Probably.

The sun warmed my face. Both the grass and the fluttering leaves on the trees seemed extra bright and green. The sounds of nature mixed with the sounds of the city. It felt good to be outside. I ran a dozen laps around the house to get some much-needed exercise. I breathed in the clear air, grateful the mansion had been built high above the smog that distorted my view of the Salt Lake valley.

I thought about just taking off—disappearing and never coming back—except I had nowhere to go. Could I just go home? No. I didn't dare put my sister in danger. I'd already thought out the repercussions of that, so I dropped the idea and went back inside.

True to her word, Alexis was nowhere to be found, which allowed me to focus on the enchantment. I spent a lot of time at the desk in my room. Shortly after dinner, I started to get close to casting the enchantment correctly.

It is difficult to explain what it is like to work with magic. Magic is energy that is somewhat sentient. I communicated with it, but I had to communicate a dozen different things at once. It took practice. I kept ironing out small kinks and little mistakes, trying to make it resemble the enchantment described in the book. Twice Caradoc's memories helped me through some misunderstandings, basically guiding me through the two parts of the enchantment that made it so complex. I wished his memories would just show me how to do the entire thing, but no such luck. This went on until almost midnight when I finally felt ready to try it out on the ruby.

The ruby cost more than my life was worth. Of course, a vampire's ruby could only be perfectly blood red, but it wasn't just the color, it was the size. At just shy of an inch in diameter, I made a wild guess that it cost at least a half million dollars, which was more than twice as expensive as my house.

I couldn't even comprehend how I'd feel if I caused the ruby to disappear in seconds like I had done to the first piece of salt rock. Messing up would be the greatest financial catastrophe of my life. So, I practiced a few more times just to make sure. I got it right every time.

I inhaled deeply as if sucking in confidence.

I took the ruby in my hands and gathered the energy in small tendrils. I hooked a line of energy to one molecule. For an intricate spell like this, both my ability to handle massive amounts of magic and my ability to see magic were useless. My understanding of the periodic table and elements and molecules was critical to making this spell work. A ruby is made up of aluminum and oxygen but has traces of chromium, in the formula of $Al_2O_3{:}Cr$. No, I didn't know that off the top of my head. Sure, I'm a jeek, and I have a memory that borders on photographic, but I still had to look that up. The mansion didn't have a computer or internet, which I found strange; however, it had a library. That library had a very complete, though dated, encyclopedia set that had all the information I needed.

The book recommended using the particles that gave the crystal its color to avoid compromising the crystal's integrity. If it were to crack or break, the enchantment would die. That meant I should set up the enchantment to convert only the chromium molecules. I wanted to set it up so it would only flare up in the presence of a vampire, but that was way too complex and would take weeks, so I decided to just make the protection stone work non-stop. A single molecule of chromium would provide one second of power.

Would that make it last? Yes. I did the math. There are sixty seconds in a minute and sixty minutes in an hour and twenty-four hours in a day. That is eighty-six thousand, four hundred seconds in a day. In a year we are talking just over thirty-one and a half million seconds. The number of molecules in this large crystal could only be counted in scientific notation. With only the chromium molecules, the protection stone would last thousands of lifetimes.

With the enchantment complete, I proudly held the ruby in front of my eyes and examined it, excited that I had accomplished such a difficult enchantment and happy to have protection from Alexis's vampiness.

"You will want to wear it always," Alexis spoke into my ear.

I jumped and dropped the ruby. Without the ruby, her power came crashing down on me. Her voice, her looks, her enticing scent: it all combined to make up her allure and I could lose myself in it again. I quickly got off my chair, reached down, and picked up the ruby, clenching it tightly. Her allure dimmed.

Alexis laughed. I didn't share her laughter. I tensed my muscles and glared at her for startling me.

How did she hide her smell until she snuck up on me? I didn't ask her that though. I had something else to ask her.

"How is the older servant woman?" I accused with my question.

I expected her eyes to turn black with anger, but instead, her irises turned white. She gulped and glanced away.

"She is alive." She sighed. I could have sworn I detected a hint of relief in her voice.

"Nice of you not to drain her dry."

Alexis lowered her eyes. Had my sarcasm caught Alexis off guard? She hadn't expected me to drill her about her bloodsucking habits. Her white eyes reminded me of the expression on her face when she fled after I offered her my blood. The question of how many people she had drained crossed my mind, but I couldn't bring myself to ask it.

She closed her eyes and took a long breath. When she opened them, her irises were red again.

"Take this," she ordered, holding out a silver chain that coiled in her hand like a snake ready to bite. A setting with fang-like prongs dangled from the end. "Put the stone inside it."

Did I want to wear a red ruby on a silver chain? It was a bit girly. But hey, I preferred keeping my blood *inside* my body, even if most of it was once Caradoc's. As I took the necklace from her, my hand touched hers. I could feel the power of her touch but the ruby warmed, dimming its effect. With the protection stone, she was just a regular pretty girl . . . mostly.

At six-foot-one, I stood barefoot in front of her and she was as tall as me in her boots with three-inch heels. She had to be five-foot-ten.

She wore a different version of the same black leather outfit. Her fitted leather shirt was much more revealing. What type of shirt was it? A *bustier?* Another word I had never used before. Her bustier had tank-top straps, then curved inward, barely covering her breasts. It laced down the middle with a string instead of a zipper, leaving gaps down her entire front that exposed her skin. The shirt ended an inch above her tight black pants, leaving her navel exposed.

Her hair, still straight, now hung to the sides, and she had no sunglasses. Why would she need them at one in the morning?

I had an unobstructed view of her face. The light skin of her soft cheeks contrasted well with her red lips and eyes. Had her lashes always been that long? Maybe I had looked right past them to her red irises.

She was stunning.

I'll admit that once under the safety of the protection stone, I had foolishly expected her to look hideous. A part of me felt disappointed that she didn't turn into a hag, but the rest of me enjoyed the view a little too much. OK, a lot too much.

I pulled my eyes away from Alexis and looked at the necklace and the setting she had given me. The prongs needed to be bent around the ruby to hold it into place, but I couldn't bend them. It would take some special jewelry tools.

"Let me help you," Alexis offered.

I let her take the ruby. As soon as it left my hand, I regretted it. I wanted it back because her pumpkin spice aroma, her red eyes, and the way her body fit in that tight black leather made me hers again. I hadn't noticed when I'd briefly dropped the protection stone but her allure was much stronger today—a lot stronger. It held me hostage like when she had taken my cheeks in her hands. She gracefully slipped the ruby into the setting and then, with a small knife that appeared from a hidden pocket, she bent the silver prongs to lock the ruby into place.

"Here." She slipped the necklace over my head. To my relief, her power once again dimmed. I had full control of myself. Mostly.

Then she kissed me.

CHAPTER 27
FIREWORKS

I kissed back, and not because of her vampire powers. I kissed back because when a freaking hot girl kisses me, pulling away is not my first reaction. As she pressed her lips to mine, her right hand moved to my side and lifted my shirt just enough that a single finger touched my skin. She did it on purpose. A couple seconds that felt like a minute went by with our lips together and her finger on my skin before she pulled back.

Wow. I hadn't expected that. Why did I feel guilty for liking it? Why did I just picture a girl with golden brown hair?

"Did it work?" she asked with her red eyes fixed on mine.

It took me a second to respond.

OK. So even though her allure was no longer involved, she still had the power of a regular freaking-hot girl. It doesn't take vamp power for a girl's beauty to overwhelm a boy with a kiss. Plenty of movies depicted some hottie owning a boy to the extent that the boy had killed for her. *She is still dangerous,* I told myself, which allowed me to finally answer her question.

"Yes," I nodded. "It works."

She smiled slyly at me.

"Why'd you kiss me?" I asked.

She hesitated. Her eyes, which were normally strong and demanding, softened.

Does she look scared and vulnerable?

I felt like comforting her, which freaked me out. So instead, I took the opposite approach and snapped at her defensively.

"Well, don't do it again, OK?" I retorted coldly.

"Of course not!" she hissed, her eyes turning black. "I was simply testing the ruby and now that it is tested there would be no need."

I didn't like how my heart cringed at her reaction. I didn't like how I wanted to fix her anger and make her eyes calm back to red. I wished I didn't care if she hissed at me or not, but obviously, I did, and that made me uncomfortable. Enchanted ruby or not, this girl had me.

I needed a distraction.

"Are you ready to tell me why you saved me?" I asked. "O'Brien suggested you were just defending your territory."

She smiled. "Most of Utah is off-limits. It is not anybody's territory," she answered.

I was actually interested in hearing more about that, but I tried to stay focused. "Are you avoiding my question? Why are you helping me?"

She blinked at me while the black in her eyes faded back to red but didn't say anything right away. I thought she was just going to ignore me until she spoke.

"My grandfather owed Caradoc a very large favor. Caradoc contacted him and requested that he honor that favor. Hence, Grandfather sent me."

"Why you?" I wondered out loud.

"Why not me?" she challenged, her eyes thinning slightly.

I didn't have an answer for that except . . . she might not be my age. Was it true that vampires didn't age? I assumed so, although she was *not exactly* a vampire. She preferred half dhampir. I was about to ask her age but she spoke first.

"It is time for us to help O'Brien." She picked up my book and thumbed forward a half-dozen or so pages. "Since you successfully created a protection stone, we should now be able to do *this*." She held the book toward me, pointing at the title on the modern English side of the page.

I read the title: "The Healing Stone."

I took the book and skimmed through the section. The healing stone worked the same way as the protection stone, by feeding off its own elements. However, the similarities ended there. The healing aspect looked to be orders of magnitude more complex.

"O'Brien needs to heal and this is a better way," Alexis told me.

"A better way than what?"

"Than giving him my blood," she answered. "In his state, he may turn."

"Turn into a vampire?" I questioned.

"Yes. A little of my blood goes a long way for healing. Most people are immune to becoming a vampire, but we are unsure of the state of O'Brien's immune system. It may not fight off the impurity in my blood."

"Most people are immune?" I questioned. "I've never heard that."

"Not everything is accurate in stories. If most were not immune then the whole world would be vampires by now. That should be obvious."

I breathed a sigh of relief that the old servant wasn't going to turn into a vampire.

"So it is a disease?" I asked.

"It is like a virus; however, it is a much more complex organism, many times larger than a virus. It is quite easy for most immune systems to fight off."

"Were you born with this . . . disease?"

"In a way."

"Could you be cured someday?"

"No. I am only a carrier. If a cure were found, I possibly would not be a carrier anymore. But that would not change me. I was born as I am."

"So, your DNA is different?" I asked.

"Only slightly," she replied.

"So, you could bite me and I wouldn't become a vampire?"

"Actually, the disease does not live in our saliva. It is in our blood. It is only transferred through blood."

Then why did she freak out when I offered her my blood? I'd donated blood before. Why didn't she drink a pint? I wouldn't have missed it. I decided against pursuing that question.

"So to turn someone, you drink their blood until their immune system is nonexistent, until they are only slightly alive, and then feed them your own blood?"

"Yes. This is common knowledge. Bram Stoker announced it to the whole world in 1897."

"Uh, *vampires being real* isn't common knowledge. Most people think Bram Stoker's book was fiction," I countered.

"It was fiction, mostly. Some parts were accurate. I meant that most druids already know this."

"Actually, you just informed fifty-percent of the remaining druid population. There are only two of us left," I reminded her.

"Not true, there are—" she cut her words short. "We need to focus. We need to start working on the healing stone. It will take both of us to make it."

"Both of us?"

She pointed at a line in the instructions, and sure enough, it said the spell required two druids to combine their magic.

"It says quartz makes the best healing stones."

"Yes, but I don't have quartz. Use this instead." She handed me a pear-shaped black diamond that looked slightly larger than the red ruby. "It will work just as well," she assured me. She probably had quartz, but wanted something black.

"OK," I agreed, taking the black gem, then continuing to read. "We can practice with salt again," I commented.

"Of course. All crystal enchantments recommend practicing with salt." She looked at me like I was an idiot, which when it came to being a druid, I was. I had been a druid less than a week.

We each took a salt crystal and got started. We worked on the healing enchantment for a few hours but got nowhere. Except for setting up the molecules to fuel the magic, it was nothing like creating the protection stone. A few hours later, I thought about sleeping since it was once again approaching 4:00 A.M.

"Why don't we work on it until sunrise, and then we can both sleep," Alexis suggested.

"You want me to sleep when you sleep?"

"Yes."

"Sure," I conceded. I only needed four hours of sleep, but that was still my secret, and I had no plans to share it. It was one of the few secrets that I hadn't spilled to her that first day when she had vamped me into telling her way too much.

We worked on learning the enchantment for a few hours, after which we took a break for another meal in the oversized dining hall. The servants were obviously accustomed to cooking for Alexis at all hours of the night. I suffered through the formal meal, trying to eat slowly this time so as not to be rude. The chandelier was turned on this time, radiating light throughout the room.

"Your powers are stronger than before," I commented as we dined.

"My powers?" she questioned.

"Your, uh, vamp powers."

"Of course," she replied.

"Um . . . why of course?" I asked, frustrated she expected me to just know everything.

"Blood," she explained, her face suddenly rigid and still. "I fed."

"Oh. You fed off the older woman," I reminded with an accusing tone.

"Yes," she answered, her voice now flat.

"But you let her live." Again I couldn't help but wonder how many people she had *not* let live.

"Yes."

I was searching for a reason not to be angry at her for feeding off her servant. The woman's survival was a good reason, yet it wasn't good enough. I couldn't quite fight off the desire to know how many people she had killed. I held my curiosity at bay for now.

It got quiet, except for the scraping of our forks and knives on our plates. We finished eating and Alexis stood. She waited for me to pull her chair out, and this time, I remembered my manners.

We went back to the desk in my room and continued to work. It was a tedious process. We needed to merge our separate parts of the enchantment together perfectly. It required focus and concentration, which I didn't have. How many people had she killed? The question rattled around in the forefront of my mind, preventing me from focusing as another hour passed. Her outfit didn't help either. Needless to say, we didn't make any progress.

Finally, I had to ask the question, if only to get it out of the way so I could concentrate.

"How many people . . . have you killed?" I struggled with the words.

Her red eyes met mine and turned black.

I offended her! I cursed at myself. *I shouldn't have asked.*

Her straight, dark hair swung as she turned her head to the east wall where the dawning light burst into the window. I could hear birds chirping outside.

"It is dawn," she announced, avoiding my question. "Let us sleep. I will return at dusk."

She turned away from me, and I watched her leave. A tattoo marked the center of her lower back—a red ribbon bow like you'd see on a Valentine's Day present. I would've expected her tattoo to be something darker, like a skull or a black widow. Alexis opened the door and walked out of my room without looking back.

I hit the bathroom and brushed my teeth. When I came out, I glanced at the healing stone sitting in the valley of the tome's pages, but I hesitated. The mattress, still on the floor, was perfectly made and needed someone to mess it up. I walked over to it and slipped under the covers.

I fell asleep a little after 8:00 A.M. and woke up about four hours later. I didn't really remember dreaming, which I didn't mind.

I expected my breakfast to be cold or perhaps skipped as it was noon, but it wasn't. Did the servants know that I only needed to sleep four hours? Had they timed my breakfast accordingly? I didn't know what to think about that, but I ate anyway.

Delicious, as always. I loved their cooking.

Unfortunately, as I ate, a disturbing thought crept into my mind. Are the servants slaves? How had I not considered this before? That added another uncomfortable question to ask Alexis.

I didn't really have anything to do until Alexis returned at dusk, so I practiced my part of the healing spell for a few hours, after which I thought I would go for another run. As I was about to step out the front door, the young redhead appeared. She followed me around. The thirty-something servant had been assigned to O'Brien as a round-the-clock nurse. Had this servant been assigned to me as a round-the-clock spy?

"The mistress would have you come with me."

I cracked a grin. "Is this a ploy to keep me inside today?" I asked.

She brushed a single loose strand of her red hair away but otherwise just stared at me. She had no intention of answering my question.

"OK. I'll come."

"This way," she turned.

I hurried and caught up to her.

"What's your name?" I asked.

She glanced at me then kept walking, refusing to answer. I got the impression the servant women obviously didn't like talking to me—or maybe they were ordered not to.

"In here." The servant opened the door and I stepped into a workout room any football player would dream of owning. It had a huge, windowed wall that provided a view of miles and miles of the Salt Lake Valley—the lake to the east of Bountiful and most of Salt Lake City to the south. The treadmills, the elliptical runners, and the stair steppers all faced directly out the window. A large universal gym—essentially a versatile weight-lifting machine—took up a ten-foot-square section of the room.

I turned back to tell the redhead thanks, but she was already gone.

I usually preferred to bench press with free weights rather than a universal gym. But as I had no spotter, machine weights sufficed. My body had healed completely during the past few days, so I was back to working out without getting sore.

My mind had at least partially healed as well. The panic attacks came and went when my memories touched on the nightwalker, but I was sort of handling them. At least, I hadn't collapsed or hyperventilated again since that first time. The cable on the machine weights let out a high-pitched screech as I bench pressed. That, of course, reminded me of the nightwalker's scream. My heartbeat still increased when the frigid, dark abyss threatened to grab me, but I was able to pry its fingers off me and calm myself down.

After three sets of a dozen reps, I took a deep breath; not because I was tired, but because bench pressing led to thoughts of the jeeks. I missed them. It would have been nice to have Luiz there to spot me and to make me laugh. Of course, thinking of my friends made me miss my sister. And thoughts of her led to thoughts of a girl with golden brown hair and blue eyes. I couldn't picture my sister without picturing her too. Who . . . ?

Kendra! How had I not thought of Kendra in days?

I felt a stab of guilt.

I kissed Alexis.

I felt a second stab of guilt.

OK, *Alexis* had kissed me—supposedly just to test the protection stone—but *I* had kissed back. Had I betrayed Kendra? Had I cheated on her? To some extent, I felt I had. I could be a real jerk sometimes. Yes, Kendra thought I was dead and entering her life again would put her in danger. I could never see her again, right? I had to stay away. I had to because that meant keeping her safe. I had to stay away from my sister and the jeeks for the same reason.

As far as I knew, only a few people knew I was alive: Alexis and her servants. O'Brien would, too, when . . . well, *if* he woke up. But what if Alexis told her grandfather about me? Was I a fool to trust her? I didn't even know her. Of course, even if I couldn't trust her, there was little I could do about it. The moment I had become a druid, I'd lost everything. I stayed here because I had nowhere else to go. I had trusted O'Brien because I had no one else to trust. Now O'Brien lay in a coma, and I was giving Alexis my trust for the same pathetic reason. I had no one else. I didn't have a choice unless I wanted to go out on my own.

Even knowing I shouldn't go home, I couldn't stop wondering about the possibility. Maybe no one was hunting me. Maybe they were only hunting O'Brien and Caradoc. Maybe I could simply return to my house and everything would be fine. Except how would I explain that I was not dead? The news would run with the story, forcing me to come up with some kind of lie.

I again contemplated The Day of a Thousand Deaths. O'Brien said that whoever set it up was targeting druids, making me a target too. No, I couldn't just go home, even if that was what I wanted to do, which was strange because of how much I had hated home and had wanted to get out of there.

After working out for hours, I returned to my room. I read the druid manual for another few hours, picking up where I had left off in my effort to read it front to back. I waited for night to come. The servants said little to nothing whenever we crossed paths. The house, which had tens of thousands of square feet, felt empty.

I lay on the mattress on the floor just reading and waiting. But I got bored and let my eyes wander up to the chandelier. Had it ever really been *dropped* on someone, impaling them a hundred times with its pointy crystals? The spikes would have creeped me out, except I imagined my room as a battleground in Mortal Kombat. The chandelier could easily be a special stage fatality that involved an uppercut that knocked the opponent up into the spikes.

"I hope you were not bored."

I jumped. *Again.* Alexis laughed at me. *Again.*

I hadn't seen or heard the door open. In fact, I felt certain it hadn't. Of course, if the door never opened, how could she possibly have entered my room?

"Stop doing that," I snapped. It came out a bit harsh. I was still mad at myself for forgetting Kendra.

"Why? It is so much fun to see you jump."

I lowered my eyebrows, scowling at her. Unfortunately, the sight of her melted my scowl away. She wore a shirt even skimpier than the one she'd worn the previous night—another leather bustier, just less leather. It didn't even try to cover her stomach, resembling a sports bra more than a shirt. It was also low cut and zipped down the front. I couldn't tell if her pants were different or the same. It was hard to tell one pair of snug, black leather pants from another. I assumed they were different. The boots were definitely the same.

She caught me looking and smiled. I needed a distraction.

"Do you want to get started?" I glanced over at the mahogany desk.

"Not yet. Come with me," she said it as a suggestion, but it bordered on a command. "The fireworks will begin shortly."

"Fireworks . . ."

I had forgotten today was the twenty-fourth of July. In Utah, that date is a state holiday called Pioneer Day. The pioneers first settled the Salt Lake Valley on July 24, 1847. Salt Lake City puts on a Days of '47 parade, a rodeo, and fireworks. It's like a miniature repeat of the fourth of July.

But since just last year, Pioneer Day had another meaning for the rest of the world—The Day of a Thousand Deaths. The state of Utah had been trying to decide whether to celebrate our state holiday while the rest of the world mourned the first anniversary of one of the greatest world tragedies ever. In the end, the state voted to keep the holiday because it had been a tradition for more than a century and a half. However, they set aside an hour from nine to ten in the morning to commemorate the tragedy. It had completely slipped my mind. *I can't imagine why,* I mocked.

Alexis interrupted my thoughts. "We will continue our efforts on the healing stone after."

"OK."

Alexis turned and led me out of my room. I followed her to the top floor of the house, through a large gathering room, and out to a balcony that faced west and overlooked the city of Bountiful. The night scene impressed me plenty and the fireworks hadn't even started. City lights dotted the night for miles to the north and south. Of course, the lights didn't go very far to the west because the Great Salt Lake left that area devoid of light. To the north, Bountiful's white temple seemed to float as it glowed on the dark hillside.

"The fireworks will appear there," Alexis pointed slightly northwest.

No sooner had she spoken than the first blast of colored light spread into the sky followed by a loud crack five seconds later. My jeek mind reminded me that sound travels a mile in five seconds.

Alexis said nothing during the fireworks. She just watched them. I found it strange that she would be fascinated by something so simple. How could a vampire—er, half dhampir— find enjoyment from fireworks? She could use magic. Couldn't she create similar explosions of light on her own? I kept glancing at her throughout the fireworks show. The grand finale arrived and lasted a few minutes, but I found myself watching Alexis the whole time. Except for her perma-grin, her face looked more relaxed than ever, her hands resting lightly on the balcony railing. She didn't blink much or look away. The fireworks reflected in her red irises. I didn't know what to think about her. Until this moment, I had assumed she only looked my age but was much older, but I had seen girls from my high school acting like her just twenty days before on the fourth of July. She was acting . . . giddy.

Monsters don't act that way, do they? They don't enjoy fireworks with the wonder of a child seeing them for the first time.

When the last explosion of light faded into the night, Alexis turned to me. She gave me that same cunning smile. Yeah, she caught me staring. Again. At least this time my eyes were on her face, and from what I knew about girls, guys never got in trouble for looking above the neck.

We stared at each other long enough it became awkward.

"How old are you?" I blurted out to avoid the awkwardness.

She looked at me and smiled and didn't answer. She looked my age. She had just acted like girls my age during the fireworks. She could be any age, though.

"Come on. How old are you?" I pushed.

"I am only half dhampir. I am as old as I look," she responded. "I grow old and die."

"How old are you, *exactly*?"

"I turned eighteen on April seventh."

"You're really only eighteen?"

"Yes."

"I thought you'd be older."

"I am sorry to disappoint you," she said with a shrug.

"You didn't, I was just curious. I thought maybe you didn't age or something."

"I am not a vampire, Jacob. Being half dhampir will only increase my life span a few decades, but I will live much longer than that because I can also use magic. I will have a lifespan similar to any druid."

"Two hundred years, huh?" That's what I had read in the druid manual.

"Yes."

I refused to forget Kendra, but knowing I couldn't bring her into my new life left me empty. Maybe this was stupid for a seventeen-year-old boy to think, but was Alexis the only girl who would live long enough for me to spend the rest of my life with? I didn't like that thought, so I changed the subject.

"How come you have servants?"

"They are my grandfather's servants. He has always had servants."

"Nobody has servants anymore," I protested.

"My grandfather has had servants for almost a thousand years. Why would he stop now?"

"He's a *thousand* years old?" My eyes widened, which was silly because most stories about vampires that I'd read or watched had vampires who were centuries or millennia old.

"Excuse my exaggeration. He is just over eight hundred."

"*Only* just over eight hundred, huh? So . . ." I said, moving my hands around to indicate the entire building, "is *this* his mansion?"

"Yes."

"Why would he own a mansion in Utah?"

"He owns a mansion in or near every capital city."

"In all fifty states?"

"Yes, and elsewhere," she affirmed.

"What do you mean *and elsewhere*?" I pressed.

"*Every* capital city," she emphasized.

"In the world?"

"Yes."

"Like every country and state and everything?"

"Yes."

"Oh," I gulped. I hadn't expected that. Until that moment, I hadn't understood how rich and powerful her grandfather, the Vampire King, really was.

"Should we go work on the healing stone enchantment?" I asked.

"Yes."

"You say 'yes' a lot," I noted.

"You ask many yes-no questions." She widened her smile back at me.

CHAPTER 28
SILENCE

"**W**e are so bad at this!" I laughed despite my tense muscles as we failed once again to join our magic. Alexis laughed too. We'd been practicing the enchantment for hours. It wasn't going well. I didn't mention to her that her distracting outfit was part of the problem.

"We should take a break," Alexis decided. "It is time to eat."

Chills rose up my spine and spread into my scalp. When a one-fourth vampire says it is time to eat—even one who looks like Alexis—it can be unnerving.

Alexis must have noticed because her smile faltered.

"The servants prepared us a meal," she explained, defensive. "Will you accompany me to the dining hall?"

She held out her hand. I glanced at it, and yes, this time I got the cue. I offered my arm, which she took. The protection stone warmed. Her allure did little more than brush against me. Even still, despite both the crystal's power and a long-sleeved black shirt, her fingers felt too present in the crook of my elbow.

The chandelier lit the spacious room. Its muted light reflected off the table's dark wooden surface. Like before, only two places were set, the head of the table and the adjacent corner. A doily-like place mat sat under stacked plates with two forks on the left and two spoons and a knife on the right. A stemmed glass sat at the top right of each plate—just like the first time I'd eaten here. The perfect place settings didn't mean I'd used them correctly.

I pulled my elbow from Alexis's hand and pulled out my chair. Alexis sighed and pulled her own chair out. *Oops.* I changed direction like I was juking a linebacker and hurried over to slide her chair in before sitting down myself.

I looked at Alexis. What should I say? Only offensive questions came to mind: How many people have you killed? Or the more vulgar: Do vampires use the bathroom?

I wisely kept my mouth shut.

The servants brought me two salmon steaks and about three times as much rice as Alexis had. They poured wine in Alexis's glass but didn't offer me any, as if they already knew I'd turn it down. Instead, they filled my glass with water.

While working on the protection stone, we had spoken easily. Of course, that was about the enchantment. Why was it so hard now? I thought about bringing up the servants again but the silence already had my muscles tense. Did I want a controversial conversation? I kept glancing at Alexis as I ate.

"You're older than me," I spit out. It was the first non-offensive sentence that came to mind.

"Yes," she answered.

That wasn't fair. Guys were supposed to rule the one syllable responses, not girls. I forged ahead anyway. "But only by five months. I'll be eighteen soon. My birthday is September third."

She nodded. I guess I hadn't asked her anything. I said three sentences about me. I knew better than to talk about myself with girls. I glanced at her and almost started telling her something else about me but my brain stopped my mouth just in time.

"So how did you celebrate your birthday?"

Her eyes thinned.

Seriously? How did that question annoy her?

"I did not exactly celebrate my last birthday. I spent the day entertaining Keagan. He is one of Grandfather's generals," she answered icily.

"Your grandfather has generals?" I asked.

Her eyes remained thinned and she continued eating.

"They forgot your birthday? That sucks. They didn't forget it last year, too, did they?"

"They certainly never forget. They just . . ." she pursed her lips. She took a few more bites and the silence returned.

"Well, when did you last celebrate your birthday?" Curiosity and the renewed silence kept me prying, even though I'd stepped into a touchy subject.

She blinked at me. Her pursed lips slowly softened. And then she smiled.

"I was twelve. We had returned to Newport Beach from visiting Grandfather. He lives in a . . . in Romania." Her hesitation meant she'd hidden something but I didn't want to interrupt. "Mom was in an extra good mood after the trip. I realize now . . ." She glanced at me and decided not to share that thought with me either. "Mom and I slept days. She homeschooled me until she started working nights. Then she left me homework to complete. My birthday night, she said she had to work and left extra homework, pretending to forget. She surprised me by returning home an hour later. She swept me up and wished me a happy birthday.

"She drove us to the beach. She had a birthday cake hidden in the trunk. It had a big candlestick shaped like the number twelve. At the beach, we lit a bonfire. We listened to music and danced and talked. Then she lit my candle and sang happy birthday to me. She even let me watch the sunrise before dragging me home." She smiled flatly as she finished. Her eyes stared off to the left.

That was the first time Alexis had spoken about herself. "That sounds like a good birthday." I smiled back at her.

"So, what happened on your thirteenth birthday? Why didn't you celebrate it?"

Her flat smile faded to pursed lips. Instead of answering she continued to eat. The silence grew with every second that my question went unanswered. I realized I'd finished my plate of food and she was only halfway through her salmon. I wasn't sure I could stand the silence while I waited for her to finish.

"So, tell me more about your mother," I urged.

She gave me a long look but kept eating. Now two questions hung in the air unanswered, emphasizing the silence. I didn't dare ask a third question for fear she'd ignore that too.

Finally, I watched her take her last bite. Relief!

She stood up. I jumped up and offered her my arm. She didn't take it. She looked at me without expression and spoke.

"My mom died," Alexis told me.

I should have said something, but I didn't. When my grandma died, nobody said anything worth hearing. Maybe that's why I said nothing. I just stood there, my arm still offered.

"We should continue working on the healing stone. I will meet you in your room shortly," she excused herself. Then she turned and walked away, leaving my offered arm hanging.

We were making a healing stone. Did Alexis need one too?

I headed back to my room, contemplating how my questions hurt Alexis. I needed to be more careful. If every question about her past hurt, what did that say about her past?

I hit the bathroom. In fact, maybe Alexis did the same. She seemed as normal as any girl—except for red irises that changed colors with extreme moods, extendable fangs, her allure, and the ability to use magic.

I waited for her back at the mahogany desk in my room. Was any part of her life not painful? She didn't share much. She was different from Kendra, who'd been my sister's best friend since we were little. I didn't have to ask about Kendra's past. We grew up neighbors. Perhaps that was why it bothered me that I knew so little about Alexis. She was only helping O'Brien and me because her grandfather owed Caradoc a favor, assuming she told the truth about that. What would happen if her grandfather found out Caradoc had disappeared? Would he tell Alexis to stop helping us? Maybe. I didn't know where her loyalties lay. She was more human than vampire, and though her father was a druid, she seemed more a part of the vampire's secret society than the druid's. Not that the druids had many members left.

Alexis returned. She spoke less and smiled less than before our meal. But she grabbed a piece of salt and we started trying to merge our magic to create the healing stone. To my relief, the awkward silence faded after an hour.

Multiple times, her outfit distracted me. In many of those moments, my protection stone warmed, reminding me that it dims her allure, not eliminates it.

"We still suck at this," I commented.

"Yes, we do," she laughed and glanced out the window at the coming dawn. We still hadn't made any progress with the enchantment. And Alexis was about to disappear for the day.

"Where do you go during the day?"

"To sleep," she answered. "I need sleep the same as you."

Well, she slept from dawn to dusk, about fourteen hours, so she definitely didn't sleep the same as me. I didn't tell her that.

"In a bed?"

"Yes. Would you like to come and see my bedchamber?" she offered, grinning and biting her lower lip. My protection stone warmed to almost hot.

My mouth hung open. I had struggled to focus the whole night. Her allure constantly warmed my protection stone, and whatever small amount broke through grabbed onto my reaction to her revealing outfit. If I went to her room, I might do something I wasn't ready for.

I lowered my eyes, but that led to her chest, so I lowered them further and that led to her navel, then her hips and legs. I finally turned and looked past her to the door. "N-no thanks," I stuttered. "I'm going to get some sleep."

"Good night, Jacob," Alexis said with that obnoxious smile.

I tried not to look at her as she left. But my protection stone was extra warm, and her skintight leather jeans and her red-ribbon bow tattoo called to me, and my eyes obeyed.

Once in bed, I tossed and turned for a couple minutes until I fell asleep and dreamed.

The boy hesitantly took Caradoc's outstretched hand. Caradoc thought of him as a boy, but he had to be in his twenties. He eyed Caradoc awkwardly, uncomfortable with the physical contact. His dark brown eyes looked so familiar—like mine. Did his face look like mine because it was my dream? They stood in a room, perhaps an office or library. A quill and ink sat on the desk. The boy could convert mass to energy. A rare gift. Caradoc was the only living druid who shared that gift and agreed to tutor him.

"After I convert salt to magic, try to reach for it," he instructed. Caradoc and the boy connected magically just long enough for Caradoc to demonstrate the conversion process. He converted a few tiny particles of a grain of salt, then he dropped the boy's hand. New magic expanded from Caradoc, and the boy grabbed at it greedily, but the magic wouldn't respond to him.

"Why can't I?" the boy complained, his eyes furious. Caradoc ignored the anger in his student's eyes, convincing himself that he'd imagined it.

"When you create magic from solids, it binds to you because magic is sentient. It chooses only you. No one else can use it, except those you have become one with," Caradoc responded.

"But we connected. Shouldn't that connection have allowed me to use your magic?" the youth demanded in frustration.

"Ours was but a temporary connection. It must be a permanent *myndtiegan*," Caradoc answered. He blinked nervously at the boy. Had he revealed too much?

I snapped awake to the thud of my door closing. A servant had dropped off breakfast. Great. Another boring day of reading and working out with nobody to talk to.

I tried to remember the dream as it seemed important, but my warm breakfast distracted me. If I didn't concentrate on a dream immediately after waking up, it faded away.

After breakfast, I checked on O'Brien. I slipped in and noticed the thirty-something servant—who was as attentive to my comatose friend as a nurse—was not alone. She stood next to a short, dark-haired man with a nose too large for his face. He wore a white doctor's coat. Hearing me enter, he turned. His eyes bored into me as if he could feel how much I wanted O'Brien to recover.

I stepped through the door and continued toward the bed.

"Hello. I'm Dr. Stewart." He offered a thin hand, which I shook. "And you are?"

"I'm Jake Ste—" I cut my name short. I couldn't tell him I was Jacob Stevens. So what should I tell him?

"Jake Stee," the doctor repeated my name as if I hadn't cut it short. "I'm sorry about your friend. I don't normally do house calls." He blinked as if just realizing he was here. "In fact, I am not even sure why I agreed to come here every day."

I stared at him, pretty sure I knew how he'd been convinced to make this house call.

"Are you related to him?" the doctor asked.

I shook my head.

"Do you know who his next of kin is?"

That question caught me off guard. Did he have a family? Perhaps he hid them after The Day of a Thousand Deaths and made plans to return to them when everything was safe.

"I'm not sure. Why?" What about all the druids who were assassinated? How many of them had relatives that knew they were druids? O'Brien had told me so little. I needed him to live.

He sighed. "I haven't seen Alexis since the first day. And a nurse who doesn't answer questions is not helpful at all." He glanced at the servant, pulling his eyebrows together.

I wondered what he would think if he knew she wasn't even a nurse. Of course, what did I know? Maybe she had been a nurse before coming here.

"What exactly is wrong with him?" I asked.

He hesitated to speak. Perhaps he wasn't supposed to tell me since I wasn't the next of kin. Or perhaps it was so bad that he needed time to prepare himself to deliver the news.

"I'm sorry to tell you this, Jake, but your friend is . . . not likely to improve. Look here?" He flashed a chart at me with a pattern of lines. I might be a jeek, but that didn't mean I could read brain scans without having ever seen them before. "There is no brain activity," the doctor spoke on, his monotone voice trying to show empathy. "He won't wake up." He licked his lips and waited for me to speak. I didn't. I couldn't.

I swallowed dryly. *I have to finish the healing stone. It will fix him. It has to,* I thought. But all I said to the doctor was, "Yeah."

Clearing his throat, the doctor lowered the chart and said, "I'm sorry for your loss. Do you know what his end-of-life wishes were?"

I shook my head but said nothing.

"I'll speak with Alexis about it next time I see her."

I nodded and left.

CHAPTER 29
MODESTY

Visiting O'Brien had been less than fun, but it fired me up. After a two-hour workout, I spent the rest of the day practicing my part of the enchantment.

The second night passed identically to the previous, minus the fireworks. Alexis was dressed in her usual fashion: distractingly sexy. We had fun working together—at first.

"This sucks!" I complained when we failed to connect her part of the spell and mine. Our magic wasn't joining.

"We are improving, but it is slower than I had hoped," she agreed.

"You think we have improved?" I asked.

"Yes. Yesterday, we were unsure if our magic was even working. Today we know it is working but not melding correctly. That is an improvement."

"I guess," I conceded.

"Does Caradoc have anything to offer?" Alexis asked.

"No," I responded. Caradoc's memories had helped me through a few tough spots with the protection stone, but none had popped up while working on the healing stone. Had Caradoc ever created a healing stone? I didn't like Alexis knowing I had Caradoc's memories. I glanced at her hands. Contact with her skin had convinced me to spill way too much information.

My eyes moved from her hands to her bustier, which exposed even more cleavage than yesterday's because it connected with stretchy loops, leaving an inch-wide line of skin showing all down her front. It did, however, continue down past the top of her leather pants in a V, covering most of her midriff and hugging her hips.

As usual, she noticed me looking, and her allure warmed my protection stone. Was that her outfit's fault? Or mine for stealing glances?

"Do you ever wear anything modest?" I asked before I could stop myself.

She raised an eyebrow at me behind her long black hair. "Of course! Modesty is required whenever I venture out in the sunlight!"

An image of her completely covered and wearing a veil at my funeral flashed through my mind followed by another of when I first woke in this mansion and she had worn enough leather to cover all but her hands and face.

"No, I mean—uh, never mind. Let's get some sleep." I turned away. "See you tomorrow . . . or tonight . . . or whatever." I let the annoyance color my voice. The spell wasn't going well, again. The rest of the day would be boring, again. Worst of all, the more time I spent with Alexis, the more I liked her. And I did *not* want to like her.

And yet we had worked so well together the past nights. Guilt bubbled up as if I were still committed to Kendra, even though, as far as Kendra knew, I was dead. Alexis wasn't at fault. She was just trying to help out O'Brien and me. But she dressed in a way that attracted me to her. Why was I still attracted to her? Was it just remnants of her allure? With the protection stone, I no longer believed that. That left only one conclusion. One I couldn't accept because I refused to believe that I had a crush on a half dhampir.

"Are you vexed with me?" she asked.

"No," I lied, my back still turned to her. "Just tired and hoping to get this done soon." Who used the word vexed anyway? And she'd called her bedroom a "bedchamber." Who talks like her?

"Sleep well then."

I didn't turn around, but I could hear that her smile was gone from her voice. I could be a total jerk sometimes. I delayed taking off my shirt and getting in bed, waiting for her to leave. When I didn't hear my door open, I turned to see if she was still there. She was gone.

I hate it when she does that.

I lay in bed for an hour, too perturbed to sleep. I finally drifted away around seven. I had the extreme displeasure of dreaming about the nightwalker. In my dream, the nightwalker kept pulling women from cars. The women became my mother, Justine, and Kendra, then past girlfriends, and even Alexis. When the nightwalker had killed that woman, the high suspension truck had blocked my view. In my dream, that was not the case. I watched the obsidian-skinned creature rip limbs from her, and then from every girl in my life, one at a time. The worst part was that the girls never died. They just screamed in agony, their shrieks sounding like the nightwalker's shriek. So I put each girl out of their misery, erasing their existence with a magic missile one at a time.

Pleasant dreams, I mocked when I woke up.

The clock on the desk said it was 12:08 P.M. My dream had disturbed my sleep, so I had slept an extra hour.

I slipped into the bathroom, stripped down, and jumped in the shower. When I came out, the youthful, auburn-haired servant was setting breakfast on the desk. She glanced at me, towel around my waist—good thing I wasn't drying my hair. She looked away, but not before I caught the corners of her mouth rise in a half smile. She didn't say anything as she left.

I settled down at the desk and took the lid off the breakfast platter. They'd made me a huge stack of French toast with bacon, sausage, and a plate of fruit.

Servants rock! I thought, then guilt hit me. I had asked Alexis about them but I hadn't asked the right questions. Were they paid? Or were they slaves? The answer mattered to me.

Every morning, the servants left clothes laid out for me. Were they new? The tags were removed and the fold lines ironed out, but they had the new smell. If they could afford this mansion and those jewels, I didn't have to feel guilty about them buying me new clothes, right?

Once dressed, I went exploring and found a new room: the garage. Or should I say *garages?* There were two of them, lined with expensive cars. A Lamborghini. A Porsche. A couple of practical cars, too, if you consider a dark blue BMW and a maroon Audi sedan practical. I'd never seen anything like some of the cars. Perhaps they were concept cars. A wicked-looking bullet bike caught my attention. It had to be the same one Alexis rode the first time I'd seen her.

I decided to go for a little drive. Not far and nothing crazy, as I didn't have a license, which was my stepdad's fault. Like refusing to give me a phone, never letting me get a license was one more thing he'd denied me.

Near the garage door opener, I found a key box. It had a slot for a padlock but didn't have one. The lack of security surprised me, but then again, who had the courage to steal from the Vampire King? That gave me pause, but I wasn't stealing—just borrowing one for a test drive.

I circled each car. I wanted to take a sports car, but I didn't dare. I couldn't help but wonder if the Vampire King had similar cars at all his mansions.

"The BMW 335i it is," I said to myself.

I opened the door and sat in the driver's seat. The key wasn't exactly a key. The thing was a little square piece of technology. It took some figuring out but I got the car started. I looked around for a garage door opener and found it in the console between the seats. I clicked it and the door opened, letting in a lot of sunlight.

The passenger door opened, and I jumped.

"Where are you going?" Alexis asked, leaning toward me.

Uh oh. Am I in trouble? I wondered.

"Uh . . . I just thought I would take a drive," I told her. Red silk draped loosely around her like a cape. She held it closed, her left hand gripping the silk at her right shoulder and her right hand pinching it at her hip. I'd never seen her in anything but black before.

"This is my grandfather's car," she half scolded. "Using his vehicles is not part of repaying his favor to Caradoc."

"Sorry." I turned the car off.

"You did not sleep long," she commented. "Was your room too bright?"

"No," I answered, not explaining my sleeping habits. She waited for me to get out of the car.

"Do you feel imprisoned here?" she asked.

"Kind of, yeah," I said, admitting to myself as much as to her.

"O'Brien needs you. We need to work on the healing stone. Also, people think you are dead, Jacob. You cannot be seen in public. This is not a prison," she assured me. "We can work on the healing stone elsewhere tonight. I know a place. Perhaps that will make you feel less like a prisoner."

"OK," I replied.

"I must go." She looked at the bright daylight flooding in from the open garage door. Her shoulders tensed and her face tightened, like she was about to break into a sweat. I pressed the remote and the door hummed closed. Square windows still let in the sunlight. I cracked a grin at the irony.

I followed Alexis into the house, watching the outline of her legs shift beneath the red silk with each step. She reached the shade of the darkened hallway, and as she closed the door to the garage, she breathed a deep, exaggerated sigh of relief. I'd seen her breathe before, but I just realized that unlike vampires in books, she breathed.

"How long did you say you can be in the sun?" I asked.

"It depends on how long it has been since I have fed," she explained. "The more recently I have fed, the more affected I am by the sun."

That was interesting. I would have expected the opposite.

"When did you last . . . feed?" I asked tentatively.

"The servant woman is fine," Alexis replied defensively. "She returned to work today."

So, she hadn't fed since then. What day had that been? Sunday? Was it already Thursday? Was this really my fifth day here? Yes. So why hadn't she fed?

"When do you need to feed next?"

"That is none of your concern."

I wanted to ask more but I was annoying her, so I changed the subject. "Since you're up, should we work on the healing stone?"

"There is too much sunlight, even inside."

"We could cover the windows," I suggested.

"You should get more sleep as well."

"I'm wide awake," I scoffed. "I couldn't sleep more if I wanted to."

"I need more sleep," she countered.

"You look wide awake to me," I challenged. Being awake and alone in this house was driving me crazy. I needed to convince her to stay awake.

She thinned her eyes and pursed her lips. Then she shifted her red silk ever so slightly, revealing her leg and a wide line of skin that ran from ankle to shoulder.

"I am not dressed, Jacob," she scolded. "Did you not say just last night that modesty is important to you?" With that, she turned, the silk billowing up to show her bare legs, and stormed down the hallway and around the corner.

I just stood there for a few seconds, stunned, before I could recover from her scolding and well . . . from other feelings her state of dress stirred in me.

"Well, just get dressed," I finally shouted, but she was already gone. If she heard me, she ignored me.

CHAPTER 30
GROVE

I suffered through the rest of the boring day, waiting for dusk, which in July isn't until nine at night. I didn't try to drive away again, though I thought about it multiple times. If I tried again, would I want to get away with it or have Alexis stop me again?

I tried to shove away the feelings I had for Alexis. I argued with myself that I was drawn to her because she was the only person to talk to, the only girl here, which was the only reason I found her pretty. Yeah, I lost both arguments with myself.

I found I could replace my infatuation with anger, so I did. It wasn't the best solution, but it worked.

Someone knocked on my door just before nine. I assumed it was a servant.

"Come in!" I yelled.

Alexis walked in and brought her pumpkin spice aroma with her.

Wow, she knocked, I thought.

She looked different. Covered. She wore a black leather shirt that, while tight, zipped to the chin and showed no skin. Over it, she wore an open black leather jacket that kept the tightness of her shirt in check. Her pants fit as tightly as ever, but the jacket hung low enough to hide the way they clung to her hips.

Whoa. She was being modest for me.

She grinned. I almost lost hold of the anger I was using to ward off my infatuation.

My protection stone warmed.

"We should go," she stated. "We need the book and the rock salt."

She hadn't asked for the stone, which meant she didn't believe we would succeed tonight.

"I'll bring the stone, too. In case we actually make this spell work," I said coldly, trying to hold onto my anger while she smiled at me.

"Of course," she agreed.

She held out her arm for me to escort her. I pretended not to notice and walked by without taking it. I didn't say anything on the way to the garage.

"Which car are we taking?" I asked.

"Which would you like to take?"

"Whichever," I replied.

"That is not very fun." She pouted her lips. My anger slipped a little. I was trying not to have fun with her, but it was hard not to have fun picking a car in this garage.

"Would you like a ride on my bike?" Alexis suggested.

I glanced at the bike, black and sleek except . . . I hadn't noticed the scratches on the left side earlier. Alexis leaping off it to attack the transients flashed in my mind. I did want to ride that bike, but staying angry after wrapping my arms around her waist was not gonna happen.

"Nah, we wouldn't want to draw too much attention. The 335i is fine," I said. I walked over and sat in the passenger's seat, but not because I didn't have a license. If she drove, maybe she'd be too occupied to notice my efforts to kill my attraction for her.

She grabbed the key from the box and slid into the driver's seat with far more grace than humanly possible. Feeding must affect her in every way. I reminded myself that she drank the servant woman's blood and had almost killed her. I told myself that she was not a regular girl, and she was not for me. I didn't really believe me. Not that I believed she had real feelings for me either. She was a predator who knew how to catch her prey, and any pretense of feelings was likely how she hunted. Sure, she had saved me after I collapsed from fighting the nightwalker . . .

Wait . . . had she saved me or captured me?

Wasn't she the other . . . person . . . who had driven the diesel into the parked traffic? I had collapsed from being knocked against a wall by a massive obsidian creature just after overexerting myself with a magic missile. But I still knew it was her.

"What happened that night after I passed out?" I asked her accusingly as we drove.

"I brought you and O'Brien to the mansion," she answered.

"No, I mean to the other people who were still in their cars."

She glanced at me then focused back on the road. She didn't want to answer. I let the question hang in the air.

"You and O'Brien and the nightwalker made quite a scene. I helped clean up the mess," she admitted.

"You call crashing a semi-truck into stopped traffic 'cleaning up the mess?'" I accused angrily.

"I crashed into the *empty car*," she emphasized. "It took the force of the crash. A lot of other cars were hit, but nothing serious," she insisted, glaring at me. "I meant that I cleaned up because the news reported nothing more than an accident. If anyone reported sunlight in the middle of the night or a dark-skinned monster or magic use, the news didn't report it."

"Where did you get a semi from anyway?"

"I borrowed it. The driver was asleep in the back."

"Did he die?" I shouted at her.

"I . . . am not sure," she responded, her voice not as strong as it had been. "No, wait. He lived. Yes, the news reported only a single casualty, and the nightwalker, not the crash, killed her."

She didn't even think to check on the sleeping driver. Is she even capable of knowing right from wrong? Can she even feel remorse? I used those questions to fuel my anger.

"Are you vexed with me?"

She had asked me that last night too. Who used the word vexed anymore? I didn't respond because I was trying to be angry with her, even if it was forced.

"I came to join a fight against a nightwalker, Jacob. You do not understand what that means, do you?"

"Why don't you tell me what it means then?" I demanded.

"Not everything is as it seems. You have no idea what the real world is like." Her eyes went black. She could sense my anger from the way the tension in my muscles had me sitting straighter and talking louder. I had infected her with it. Her knuckles whitened on the steering wheel, and I wondered if she wanted to take a swing at me.

"You mean that I don't understand the danger of a nightwalker? That I don't understand what it is like to be the only druid alive or not a vegetable?"

"I am a druid . . ."

"No, you're not!" I cut her off. "Access to magic doesn't make you a druid. Otherwise, O'Brien would've told me about you. But he thought of you as an *it*. Did you know that?"

She snarled, flashing her canines at me. It happened quickly, but I saw it as if time stopped. Her black eyes turned toward me. Her mouth opened, her canines extended slightly as she growled, and then her mouth closed.

That shut me up. It also made me cringe away from her and press against the passenger door. She turned back to the road and drove in silence until the blackness faded from her eyes.

"What is wrong, Jacob?" she asked without looking at me.

"Everything," I answered.

My answer was pretty accurate. Everything was wrong. I didn't want to think or feel anything, so I pushed everything away—even magic. Unfortunately, the thoughts came crashing down anyway. I was alone. Everyone I had ever cared for thought I was dead. I was a druid, but pretty much the last one alive. They were likely hunting me, whoever *they* were. I was a freak, and worse, I was stuck with an even bigger freak. A deadly one-fourth vampire monster who was as likely to kill me as help me. I just wanted to get out of here and away from Alexis as soon as possible.

"I understand," she said, an unexpected quiver in her voice.

Oh, crap.

Why had I let her hear any of that? My thought containment had faltered when I pushed magic away with everything else. I had broadcast all those thoughts from my mind to hers. I brought the thought containment back up. Should I tell her I didn't mean it?

"Perhaps my grandfather will consider the favor complete after we heal O'Brien." All emotion left her voice. "You and O'Brien can be on your way."

Silence overtook the car. I felt terrible. I had just wanted to curb my infatuation for her, but my anger tactic sucked.

The pavement ended, and she drove on dirt for about a mile before pulling off the road. She had driven us up the canyon while I foolishly hadn't paid attention. Where were we? There were no other cars around. We were completely alone.

Alexis got out and shut the door. I remained seated. I didn't want her as an enemy, but the truth was, she might *be* my enemy. What if she were only helping O'Brien and me to get information from us? She had said I had no idea what was going on. That I didn't understand. Wasn't she only here to fulfill her grandfather's favor? She followed his orders. She didn't make her own choices. She obeyed an all-powerful eight hundred-year-old Vampire King. Those words hinted that I couldn't trust her.

I finally got out of the car. I followed Alexis toward a circle of trees when it dawned on me what I was doing. I was walking into a remote forest at night with a part vampire who could drain me and leave my corpse to rot. Oh, and I had just verbally shouted at her and mentally called her a freak and a monster. Chills ran up my back and ended at my hair follicles, but I kept walking anyway, hoping she wasn't planning to use the canines she had flashed at me.

"It is a grove of evergreens," Alexis spoke, her voice even once more. "A natural containment."

I stopped and looked around. I could barely make out the perfect circle of trees. I had read about these in the druid textbook. A druid's grove, they were called. Natural containments. Magic was stronger inside, yet not as wild. These were rare and most of the known druid's groves were in Europe. The Americas—or the new world as the book still called it—was not as explored. Of course, the book was half a century old or more. For all I knew, there was a secret druid website that overlaid clickable icons onto a map marking all druid groves.

When I stepped inside the grove's boundaries, a magical calm settled on me. It calmed my tense muscles and urged me to release my anger. So, I did.

I looked at Alexis, who stopped walking in the very center of the grove.

"I'm sorry," I offered, and I meant it.

"There is no need to apologize. However, I accept your apology all the same." Alexis smiled at me and a moment passed as we looked at each other. "Jacob," she spoke my name softly.

"Yeah."

"I am sorry for my anger as well."

"Yeah." Guys like me are masters of one-syllable responses. We could even use them to accept apologies.

Our apologies broke the tension enough for us to start working on the healing enchantment. She grabbed a few salt rocks and set the bag on the ground.

Four hours later, I was shivering and jealous of Alexis's leather jacket. We were high in the mountains and it was cold at this elevation even in July. I had a long-sleeved V-neck and dark pants that weren't quite as warm as I would have liked.

"Warm yourself," Alexis recommended.

Oh, right. I had learned to cool myself but I hadn't thought about warming myself.

"Would you like some assistance?" she inquired.

For a second, I thought she was offering to cuddle with me, and I paused. But she was just offering to demonstrate how I could use magic to warm myself.

"I can manage," I told her, disappointed that she didn't want to cuddle. My infatuation was still running strong despite my best efforts to tackle it. I gave in. I wasn't going to fight my feelings for her anymore. Unfortunately, I didn't have to. After what I had said—er, thought—Alexis was all business. She seemed focused on finishing this enchantment, after which we would never see each other again.

I decided I was fine with going our separate ways. I could live with having feelings for her for a few more days. We just needed to figure out how to connect our magic together and make the healing stone. I had never worked with another magic user before and Alexis had only done so in practice. If only I had experience in this.

I pulled the magic in and felt its energy. I didn't need a spell to warm myself. I wrapped energy tightly around my body, creating a barrier between the cold air and my skin. I'd never need a coat again. Heck, for that matter, I'd never need clothes. I looked at Alexis. OK, clothes were still important.

As my shivering subsided, I felt a memory trying to surface. The memory wasn't mine, so I tried to help it along.

Caradoc, if you have something you want me to know, I'm willing to hear it.

I tried not to focus on the rising memory, because I didn't want it to pull away. Instead, I patiently let it come closer and closer until, finally, I had it.

Connect first, and then work the spells.

It was Caradoc's memory, but it wasn't his voice. Someone, perhaps a teacher, had spoken those words to Caradoc.

"Alexis." I felt awkward saying her name. Since meeting her, I had never actually spoken her name. Not even once. This was the first time.

"Yes?" She looked at me. She wore a soft smile, and I could swear her eyes filled with water as if about to shed tears, but no tears fell. Was I just imagining it?

"What if we connect to each other first and then work the spells?" I said, quoting the memory.

She raised an eyebrow at me. "Connect how?"

"Magically, I guess."

"I was unaware that was possible."

"It is," I said, a little less sure, but I pointed to my brain. "Caradoc finally shared something."

"I have not been trained to do that," she added. "Does his memory include instructions?"

Shouldn't I know how? In fact, I almost remembered this morning's dream but I couldn't quite bring it to mind.

I shook my head no. I grabbed the druid book and started flipping pages. I'd read something about "connecting" while

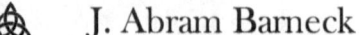

skimming through it, but it was too dark to see. I cast fire light, but instead of putting the fire in my hand, I hung it in the air above the book. I hadn't done that before, but hey, it worked. The small floating fire illuminated the pages while I flipped through the druid text until I found the section on connecting. It described connecting spells, calling them "mind-shares," but it didn't explain how two druids could connect before casting a spell.

"Let's just try it?" I offered. Maybe I could do it even though Caradoc's memories were vague.

I pulled the magical energy around me and reached out toward Alexis with it. I could feel the power she held as well. We tried several different ways to connect, but my magical energy pushed hers away. We pushed and pulled and tried to connect the magic we each held but to no avail.

"It is not working," Alexis commented a few minutes later. "Maybe . . ." She didn't finish. I felt her drop her magic. She stepped closer to me and grabbed my hands. When she touched me, the protection stone began to hum. Instead of reaching for the magic around us, she reached for the magic already inside me. My inner magic resisted at first, refusing to accept her. But I urged it to trust me, to trust Alexis, to let her in. It did, and just like that, *I* let her in too. I wasn't ready for what happened.

We connected.

CHAPTER 31
CONNECTED

Our minds joined. She was me and I was her. Her hunger hit me first. Her loneliness hit me next because it merged with mine.

Hello, Jacob. Alexis thought.

Hello, Alexis. I responded.

I could feel everything she felt. Her mind nearly overpowered mine. Whatever I had gone through was nothing compared to what she had gone through.

She longed to be free, but free of what? I moved toward her memories and neared the answer. Instead, I found her sympathy, strongest of all. She had never in her life killed to feed.

It was her most guarded secret.

Her grandfather suspected it and thought her soft. She was not soft. While she had never killed for blood, she had killed in self-defense. I had called her a monster. No, she was a weapon. Her grandfather constantly sent her on deadly missions, hoping to get her killed. She was constantly disappointing him by surviving—by ruthlessly killing those who threatened her.

I collided with a third mind already connected to Alexis, cutting off my probing. The connection was distant, but I couldn't break it. Despite its distance, it controlled her with overwhelming strength. Did it belong to her grandfather, the Vampire King? Alexis's fear increased as I approached that mind. She shivered.

Jacob, focus on the enchantment.

Alexis pushed my thoughts elsewhere. We each prepared our part of the spell. We were both intimately aware of how the other used magic. We used magic differently. I could use energy of any type—any power that existed—but Alexis could access only certain types. She couldn't enchant the crystals herself because she couldn't convert elements to magic. Her thought confirmed what I'd read in the book. Very few magic users could do these spells.

She couldn't see magic like I could. She could only feel the energy that flowed freely and only select types.

With new understanding, we knitted our spells together for the first time. After a few tries, we did it perfectly, balancing our magic at the right moments. Even connected, it was not simple. Still, we joined our parts of the enchantment. We never would have succeeded without connecting first. The complexity of this spell could have taken us decades to master. Once finished, the salt crystals slowly crumbled under the perfectly proportioned power, exactly as the book said would happen if cast correctly.

Again, Alexis thought to me.

She dropped my hand and grabbed more rock salt from a bag on the bed of pine needles at our feet. She took my hand again, pressing the salt between her palm and mine. We performed the spell a second time. It was easier, like we had performed it a hundred times together.

I let go of her hand and pulled the black diamond from my pocket. I pressed my hand to hers, pinning the crystal between our palms. We worked the enchantment without saying or thinking a word, reacting to each other's magic.

I pulled the healing spell into the gem and created the necessary magical connections to the atoms in the black diamond. It took a lot more energy than the vampire protection enchantment. I quickly estimated how many atoms this gem had. It would last a couple thousand years. More than O'Brien needed.

Then came the part where our magic had to weave together.

Alexis and I merged our magic flawlessly.

We'd done it. The healing stone came to life. It started working on us. I hadn't known I needed healing, but my mind healed. Would I ever experience another panic attack when thinking about the nightwalker? I wasn't panicking now. Alexis had been traumatized in so many ways that I couldn't absorb a fraction of them. It would take a long time for the stone to heal her mind.

We didn't need to stay connected, but we did. I held her hands tight, not wanting to let go. We couldn't hide our mutual attraction, and we didn't want to. We just wanted to be together.

She encountered the remnants of the wall of anger I'd used earlier to push my feelings for her away.

You were *vexed,* Alexis confirmed.

I shuddered in shame at her realization and thought both, *Yes,* and, *I'm sorry.*

Well, if she was trying to get answers to her questions, so would I.

Why are you here? I voiced the question in my head.

The memory of her entering a large room rushed into my mind.

Alexis's grandfather sat on a dais. A throne room? Vague paintings—no, tapestries—decorated the walls. He had shoulder-length white hair and a young face with pale skin and ancient creases. Even sitting, he looked tall. Servants sat below him on the lower level of the dais. Others near Alexis waited for an audience. A black-cloaked nightwalker stood in the center of the hall, looking up at him. Alexis heard her grandfather's order.

"Find him. Kill him. Kill the bodyguard."

"Why would I do this? I don't take orders from you." The nightwalker's grinding voice echoed through the hall.

The Vampire King's eyes shifted to Alexis and he held her gaze. "Because if you do this, I'll give you the gift you've asked for. Feel free to kill all who stand in your way. Eat the flesh from their bones." The power in his voice was only outdone by its creepiness. Something was off about the way he spoke—like he should have an accent but didn't. Perhaps it was his overemphasis of consonants.

The nightwalker turned, glanced hungrily at Alexis, licked its black teeth, then left.

Alexis approached her grandfather. He'd summoned her two days earlier. She'd caught a flight to Romania. All for a two-sentence command he could have given over the phone. But he still insisted on giving orders in person.

She stopped exactly where the nightwalker had stood and looked up at her grandfather.

"I owe Caradoc a favor," he said. "He has requested that favor now. You will be his favor."

Alexis started to speak, "He will not—"

Alexis shoved at my mind. The memory went fuzzy, but then it continued.

"Not as a gift." The king laughed with a soft chuckle that made Alexis cringe. "You are to defend him against those who seek to kill him."

"But Grandfather," Alexis challenged. "You sent the nightwalker to kill him. Should I back off when the nightwalker attacks?"

"Back off?" The Vampire King's eyes went black. "Back off? And how would that reflect upon my honor? I owe Caradoc a favor. I will honor that favor completely. Do you understand?"

"Yes, Grandfather. However, if he attacks while I am defending Caradoc, one of us will die."

"How unfortunate for one of you." His smooth pale face contorted into a pleased grin.

Alexis had grown up in a life of fear and learned to deal with it. She fought to keep that fear off her face in front of her grandfather. Against a nightwalker, she had no chance. She'd always suspected her grandfather wanted her dead. As she walked out of his presence, she knew her suspicion was confirmed.

The memory ended. My eyes locked onto Alexis's.

You were coming to fight the nightwalker?

Yes. I had been practicing the sunlight spell to defeat him.

But you couldn't cast it yet.

I am still working on it.

So, you came to die? Had she been willing to give her life for us?

But you saved me. You are my hope, she thought to me.

I gave her hope of safety and freedom. For the first time in her life, she felt the possibility of a relationship with someone she could trust—me.

You started crushing on me because I killed the nightwalker?

Yes, she answered.

I expected her mind to fill with embarrassment. But I could feel her every emotion, and that one seemed the most subdued.

My crush augmented my vampire allure. That is why the touch of my hands affected you so greatly on Sunday. It is not normally this strong.

It took me a second to understand. Her allure hadn't just doubled. It had grown more out of control than my first spells. Killing the nightwalker for her had kicked off a teenage crush.

Your allure isn't usually this powerful?

Only while my crush is new and exciting.

I contemplated that as we stood in the druid grove, looking into each other's eyes and sharing our thoughts.

Can you make the black diamond a protection stone as well? Alexis asked.

Yes. I hadn't thought of that but it was a good idea. With Alexis's allure on overdrive, O'Brien would need a protection stone. It would shorten the gem's life span, but it would still last over a thousand years. I worked the second spell, enchanting the black diamond to protect against vampires exactly as I had done with the ruby. Being in the grove and magically connected to Alexis, I performed the intricate parts of the enchantment with ease.

That left Alexis and me looking at each other. Joined together. Alone at night in a grove of trees far away from anywhere.

CHAPTER 32
BETRAYAL

Holding hands and looking into each other's eyes was not enough, so we embraced. We held each other for what seemed like hours, rapidly sharing thoughts, memories, and emotions. I couldn't hide from her that I thought I was a freak, that I healed faster than I should, or that I only needed four hours of sleep. She could access everything about me. All my sins, my shame, were laid bare before her. She found the parts of me I hated. She didn't recoil. She hugged me tighter.

She was part dhampir and a druid—far from normal herself. We shared the same desire to be normal, hers maybe stronger than mine. She ached for it. She hated her dhampir part most. She feared her own desire for blood—the addictive ecstasy of biting and drinking from her prey. I compared the thrill of erasing the nightwalker to how she felt when drinking blood. Each time she fed, she gathered the empathy and guilt, using them to bury her addiction.

I found happy memories from her youth, though not many. Her mother Carina stood out in most of them, but there were few others. Each person in these rare happy memories called her Lexy.

May I call you Lexy?

Yes. I felt her smile expand from inside as she answered.

I reached the end of her happy memories. Why were there so few? Then I saw the memory that ended the happy ones. We entered the memory as if it were a dream.

Lexy sat reading in a cheap apartment. Dingy but not dirty.

"Dinner is ready, Lexy," her mother, Carina, called from the kitchen area.

There was an edge to her mother—a nervousness that Alexis sensed, but at thirteen, was too young to understand. Alexis marked her book, set it aside, and walked to the kitchen. Lexy had a childlike face on the physique of a grown woman.

"Mother." Lexy's voice pitched in complaint. She looked around with distaste. "How long will we remain here?"

"I am not sure, Lexy." Her mother's eyes flashed black, then returned to red immediately, trying to be patient.

"Why did grandfather send us here?" Her question came out like a whine.

"I told you. That is my business," her mother snapped sternly. "Please get some bowls."

Lexy grabbed two bowls, the only two bowls, from an ugly green cupboard.

"We've been here for a week and . . ." She looked at the boiling pot on the old green stove. "Ramen noodles? Mom? That might leave us . . . undernourished."

"I know, Lexy." Worry lined Carina's face. She scooped noodles into the bowls. They sat at a card table that wobbled and had swollen bubbles of water damage. The black rubber lining had long since fallen off.

Lexy and her mother ate in silence until a knock came at the door. Carina stiffened, then held her breath. She slowly walked to the door. The knock came again, and she twitched as if startled. She looked through the peephole and let out her breath.

"The landlord is here to fix the shower," Carina said with relief. She unlocked the deadbolt, unhooked the chain, and opened the door.

"You called about the shower not working."

Lexy glanced at the landlord from the table. He looked like any regular guy with a tool belt. She could smell the small scrapes and cuts on his hands—the kind all handymen had— reminding her that she was hungry.

"Yes. Please, come in."

Carina walked the landlord to the bedroom and Lexy returned to her noodles. She smelled two familiar scents a second later, but before she could turn, a hand cupped over her mouth. Dane's hand. One of her grandfather's generals. He gripped her like a vice and pulled her from her chair. Lexy didn't understand why he held her the way he did. He jerked her around and she saw Keagan, her grandfather's other general. Lexy had always felt uneasy around him.

"Take her to the car," Keagan ordered. As Dane pulled Lexy to the door, Keagan looked toward the bedroom, pulled out a long knife and smiled.

Lexy realized why her mother had brought her to this cheap apartment. She'd taken her on the run. The last thing she heard was her mother screaming her name, followed by breaking glass.

If Dane's hand hadn't held her mouth so tight, she'd have screamed too.

With effort, Lexy pulled us out of her memory. Her sadness led me to a dark area of her mind filled with memories that I couldn't access. The foreign mind, her grandfather's mind, blocked me from those memories. Lexy shivered as I tried to open the darkness. A memory of hers slipped out, but it disappeared into the recesses of my own mind because Lexy pushed me elsewhere, distracting me with the openness of other experiences. I followed them instead, learning more about her.

We held each other, her face just inches from mine. We pulled closer, and our lips met. For the second time, we kissed. Her lips tasted of a mix of pumpkin spice and honey. Very different from . . .

Kendra!

My kiss with Kendra had tasted of vanilla mint ChapStick and salty tears.

With Lexy's mind wrapped around me as tightly as her arms, she had a front-row view of my memory. She watched me put my hands on Kendra's cheek, wipe away her tears, and kiss her lips.

Lexy broke off the connection and shoved me away. I dropped to one knee, disoriented by the sudden disconnection, and grabbed my head to stop it from spinning. The last emotion I felt coming from her was not jealousy. It was a mix of realization and fear.

"I . . ." Lexy tried to speak but she couldn't. She pushed her eyes closed and breathed. Perhaps the sudden disconnect had disoriented her too. She came out of it before I did.

"Bring the stone." She pointed to it in the pine needles. It must have fallen when we separated. She turned and started toward the car. "We need to hurry," she called back over her shoulder.

"What happened?" I asked.

I stood in the grove, stunned. We had just experienced the most wonderful moment of our lives only to have it cut off. I wanted more. How could she walk away from me after that?

"What happened?" I yelled at her back.

"Bring the stone!" she repeated, not looking back.

I couldn't see the stone. It was night and the stone was black, and the pine needles were deep. I cast fire light again, and the black crystal reflected the flame. I grabbed it and grudgingly followed Lexy to the car. By the time I reached it, she had it

started. I jumped in and she floored it before I even had time to close the passenger door.

She drove emotionlessly, as if she hadn't just shared everything with me. One second we were in each other's mind, sharing everything, and the next, she'd walled me off.

"What happened?" I asked the third time.

"It worked," she replied. "We created a healing stone. We have to take it to O'Brien."

"I mean why did you break the connection? Was it the memory of Kendra? Are you jealous?" I asked, even though I already knew it wasn't jealousy. I wished we were connected again so I could know what she was thinking and feeling.

"No," she denied. "Jealousy has no relevance to the situation."

"Huh? What situation? What scared you?"

"To save a soul, sometimes one must risk their own," she whispered cryptically.

"What does that mean?" I asked.

"Do you remember our fight earlier? There is much you do not understand and much I cannot tell you."

"What can't you tell me?" I demanded.

"I cannot say more."

I pressured her for more information the entire way back to the mansion, but she became as impenetrable as a rock wall. She refused to say anything to me, like I wasn't even there. We arrived at the mansion as the sun crested over the eastern mountains. She hurried inside. I followed her to O'Brien's room, not stopping till we stood at his bed.

She handed me another silver chain.

"Put the stone in the necklace," she ordered.

"Can't you do it?"

"I dare not touch it," she said, glancing at the door.

I wanted to ask why, but she was in such a hurry and was so adamant that I acted with the same urgency.

"Here." She handed me a knife from one of her hidden pockets. I used the tip to bend the little silver prongs around the stone. The knife slipped and cut my thumb. Lexy stiffened and her irises turned black. No, not all black. Red streaks remained, like when I'd offered her my blood. It creeped me out. Her aroma changed to honey. She licked her lips, and her eyes fixed on the crimson drop of blood on my thumb. I wasn't about to offer it to her, so I wiped it on my black shirt. Lexy swallowed nervously and looked away.

With the black diamond secured, I gently lifted O'Brien's head with one hand, but I couldn't manage to clasp the necklace.

"Set the healing stone on his bare chest," she instructed. "It's more effective if it touches skin."

"OK."

O'Brien wore a hospital gown and I moved the neckline aside. He already wore a stone on a leather band. It had glowed whenever something was after us. Thankfully, it was not glowing. I had read about his stone in the druid manual. A rare warning stone. I set the healing stone next to it, so it rested on his skin, not bothering to clasp the chain around his neck.

Nothing happened. I looked at Lexy.

"It will take time," she said, already turning away from me. "I must feed and sleep."

Before I could argue, she darted out of the room at an unnatural speed. I tried to follow, but when I reached the door, I couldn't tell if she'd gone left or right.

Had she said *feed* as well as sleep? No way was I going to let her feed on another servant! I tracked down each servant, but they were all fine and hadn't seen Lexy. I asked them where I could find Lexy's room, but they said they didn't know. I didn't believe them. I went hallway by hallway and checked every room in the house. She was nowhere to be found. I cursed myself for not taking her up on that offer to visit her bedroom. Had I done so, I would have known where it was. There had to be a secret door somewhere. I searched every wall, then the grounds, but found nothing.

At noon, I finally gave up. I had looked everywhere. I returned to my room and sat at the desk. I closed my eyes to think and found them too tired to reopen. I had been awake for twenty-four hours straight. Sure, I only slept for four hours, but I *needed* my four hours. Especially after the magical exertion of putting two powerful enchantments on the black stone while connected magically to Lexy.

I forced myself to stay awake long enough to check on O'Brien, but there was no change yet. I went back to my room and lay down on the mattress on the floor. Despite my heavy eyelids, I thought there was no way I could fall asleep while thinking of Lexy, but sleep came a minute after I closed my eyes.

I woke to the young auburn-haired servant bringing me dinner. The clock on the desk told me it was after 5 P.M. She apologized for waking me, but I told her it was fine.

Sleep had not wiped away my annoyance at Lexy's behavior. But I didn't try to find her room again. Instead, I checked on O'Brien. After finding him still comatose, I went and worked out for a few hours. It was the only thing I could think to do to pass the time.

After working out, I went back to my room and showered. I dressed in a hurry because I was expecting to see Lexy as dusk approached. The door opened, but instead of Lexy, the twenty-something servant stepped in. I should have known that it was too soon for Lexy. She hadn't been showing up until an hour or more after sunset.

"O'Brien has awakened," the servant told me in her usually soft voice.

I skipped to O'Brien's room. Excitement rose inside me, pushing away all other emotions.

The older servant whom Alexis had nearly drained stood over O'Brien. She must have removed the tube from his throat because she held a plastic mug and urged O'Brien to drink from the straw.

The healing stone was working. Besides bringing him out of his coma, his small scrapes and the two drill holes had disappeared. And while the missing piece of his ear wasn't growing back, it already formed a pink scar.

"O'Brien," I breathed his name in relief as I stepped to his bed. I didn't have many people in my life, and I hadn't realized how important my druid mentor had become despite only knowing him a few days.

He stopped drinking the water and tilted his head in confusion. Then he gave me a weak smile.

"How are you?" I asked.

He coughed and didn't answer.

"How did . . . we . . . survive?" he asked through more coughing.

"A magic missile," I replied.

"You?" He raised his eyebrows in disbelief.

"Yes."

He nodded, and his eyes closed.

"He needs his sleep," the elderly servant said with a gravelly voice. "I just gave him a sedative."

"No!" I elevated my voice more than I intended. "I wasn't done talking to him."

The servant glared at me with one eye thinner than the other. I decided to sit and wait for him to wake up again. So I grabbed the druid's book from my room then came back and read. At first, I read with total concentration, but once it was well past dusk, my focus failed me. I had Lexy to blame for that. I kept bouncing my knee and looking away from my book, forgetting what I had read. I sat through two hours of torment, waiting for her.

O'Brien finally woke up again, a happy distraction from wondering where Lexy had gone.

"You're awake," I breathed softly.

"What happened?" O'Brien asked. His voice sounded stronger than it had earlier.

"We survived." It felt so good to tell him that. He had not given up so much as he had accepted his fate. He had chosen to die fighting to protect me and had never expected to wake up.

"You . . . cast a . . . magic missile?" he croaked.

"Yes," I said with pride.

"Where are we?" O'Brien asked.

"My grandfather's mansion," Lexy answered.

I jumped, startled to find her standing right behind me.

"Who are . . . you?" O'Brien tilted his head.

"Alexis Kaloyan, granddaughter of John Kaloyan, the Vampire King," she replied formally. She even curtsied.

O'Brien's pupils dilated and his face trembled in fear as she leaned over him and put her lips close to his good ear.

"It's OK. Lexy won't hurt you." I tried, but O'Brien's face continued to tremble.

"Grandfather sent me to save you," she spoke softly. "I watched Jacob destroy the nightwalker, but he overdid the spell and passed out. I cleaned up the mess and brought you both here," she finished, giving him the very short version. Then she pulled away.

I didn't understand why she had leaned over him until she stood up. The healing-slash-protection stone—O'Brien no longer wore it. Lexy had taken it.

"Why'd you take the stone?" I asked her.

She looked at me then dropped her gaze to the floor as if my eyes were so bright that she couldn't look at them. When she looked back up, they were wet. One tear dripped down her cheek. Why was she crying?

"You made a healing stone!" O'Brien swore and fought off a wince as he sat up.

"It is more than that." Lexy blinked away her tears and smiled at O'Brien. "It is also a protection stone."

O'Brien trembled at her words. He looked at me, eyes wide. "What have you done?"

My shoulders sank. So did my heart. I looked at Alexis. Her eyes met mine. Her betrayal reflected in her wet eyes. She had used me to get the stone for herself, and I had been foolish enough to let her. Alexis broke eye contact with me and looked at O'Brien.

"I must go now. Grandfather is on his way, and he is not happy," she said, lifting the black stone. "I advise you not to be here when he arrives."

In a flash, she was at the door. She moved even faster than before, which reminded me that she had fed. At the door, she looked back at me.

"You saved me." Lexy smiled, her eyes filling with tears again. "Your secret is out, Jacob. Grandfather knows who you are, and he is coming for you and O'Brien." She took a step to leave then hesitated. "He knows who the other potential druid is, too. She's already used magic. She used it when you kissed her." With that, Alexis slipped out the door.

I looked back at O'Brien. His warning stone illuminated his neck and chin.

CHAPTER 33
KENDRA

"Why did you . . ." O'Brien coughed, ". . . make *it* a healing stone?" he demanded. His voice was more animated than he was ready for.

She is not an it! I wanted to shout back but I held it in. Instead, I defended myself. "I didn't. I made *you* a healing stone."

What had just happened with Alexis? I replayed the past few days. How had Alexis deceived me? Was Kendra really the other druid? Could it be true?

I thought back to my time with Kendra. I had known her for years. She had given me thousands of stolen glances as my sister's best friend and I had returned them. Then last week, we had kissed. As that memory took center stage, I recognized how a connection had formed between us—like a rope from my heart to hers. I had felt it again at the funeral. It wasn't just your average twitterpation-inspired butterflies. I'd felt magic. I recognized it now. That is why O'Brien had sensed magic at the funeral. When Kendra looked at me, her magic flared.

"Why didn't you . . . just use one of the vials? Were . . . they destroyed? You could have cast . . . healing on me directly . . . that is a far easier spell." His reprimand brought my mind away from Kendra. "That spell is . . . difficult. I can't believe you were . . . even able to do it." He struggled to string words together. One of the servants helped him sit up.

Why hadn't I looked for easier healing spells? I hadn't even thought to do so. Hadn't O'Brien used a healing vial on me? I never considered that another healing spell would be easier. I had trusted Alexis far more than I realized. She had said that there was so much I didn't understand. I had been a fool. She had been right. I had let my few successes go to my head. Sure, I had beaten the nightwalker. Sure, I was able to create a protection stone myself.

However, I had only survived Alexis's allure because she had let me live. I had even begged her to take my life before I had the protection stone.

"Its blood and," he coughed again, "its saliva . . . can heal too," he added.

Had Alexis lied about O'Brien's immune system? She'd at least skipped telling me that vampire saliva heals—a lie of omission.

"It'll be unaffected by sunlight with that healing stone," O'Brien told me, his voice stronger now that he was sitting up, "It'll be able to feed both day and night." He shook his head at me. "Why did you think it needed its own protection stone too?"

"The. Stone. Was. For. YOU!" I wanted to punch him like he'd punched me for repeatedly calling Alexis an it.

He pointed to the book in my hand and gestured for me to give it to him. I handed it over. I had a bookmark near the back marking the page for the healing stone and he turned there then flipped about a dozen pages back before stopping.

"Read this," his finger traced a line on the English page.

"Spells beyond this point are restricted. Permission from the druid council required." I swallowed. I hadn't read that page yet.

"The Vampire King keeps its vampires in line. The king controls them. It keeps them from going on killing sprees." He breathed hard. "By giving it the protection stone, you set that vampire free. It is no longer under the Vampire King's control, so it can kill at will."

"She wouldn't . . ." I stammered.

"Of course, it would. That is its nature!" O'Brien snapped back.

"She's not an it!" I finally shouted.

"How do you know?" he growled. "She's confused you." He coughed. "You don't know anything about her."

Except I did know everything about her, didn't I? We had connected—bound our minds together with magic. We had shared who we were with each other. She had hidden nothing except . . .

Oh.

While connected, a part of her had been sealed off from me. I hadn't been able to see her memories and experiences in that part of her mind. Could it be possible that she hid from me the very part of herself that made her a monster, the part that could kill without remorse?

Did I just set a monster free?

O'Brien's clothes sat folded in a drawer. The servant helped O'Brien dress. The clothes were similar to my own, black and expensive. His tablet, his phone, and his Glock, still loaded with that last clip; they were under the clothes. I wished I had known that earlier, I could have used the phone or tablet. I grabbed them.

"We need to get out of here." O'Brien touched his glowing stone.

"We need to get to Kendra," I corrected. A familiar alien need to protect her grew inside my chest. Protecting her was all that mattered. "She's the other druid."

He nodded.

I grabbed the druid textbook and ran to my room. I packed some clothes before returning to O'Brien. We shuffled slowly to the garage. I clutched him around the middle and held his arm over my shoulder, shoring up his trembling legs as we made our way to the garage.

The 345i was still there but the bullet bike was gone. Alexis must have taken it. I grabbed the BMW's key from the box. O'Brien was in no shape to drive. I would have to take the wheel—who needed a license anyway?

O'Brien's crystal shone even brighter now. We had to get out of the Vampire King's house and fast. It was ten thirty at night, so we didn't have the safety of sunlight. I helped O'Brien into the passenger's seat, then got in. Alexis should have left the healing stone on him longer. Her betrayal burned inside me as I opened the garage. I glanced at O'Brien's glowing crystal and heard his raspy breath, and then I screeched the tires and drove out of there, heading toward the freeway.

"Give me your phone," I held my hand out expectantly.

O'Brien hesitated, eyeing me, then handed it over. I steered with my left hand and held the phone in my right. Kendra didn't have a cell phone. She was supposed to get one for her sixteenth birthday. That was about a week away. I dialed her mom's cell. No answer. I dialed her dad's cell.

"Hello," Kendra's father answered.

"Mr. Duncan?"

"Yes," he responded.

"Is Kendra there?" I asked.

"She's in bed." His voice lowered, carrying a hint of daughter-protecting attitude. "Who is this?"

I couldn't tell him who I was. "I know it's late, but can I speak to her? It's important."

"Nothing is so important it can't wait till morning. You'll have to call back then." He hung up.

For normal boy-girl stuff, Mr. Duncan had acted like a dad should. If I were just a boy calling to talk to a cute girl, or trying to resolve some silly high school drama, he was right to hang up on me. Unfortunately, the Vampire King just found out his daughter was a druid, putting her on a short list of people targeted for assassination to complete the druid genocide.

I dialed the number again. No answer. I swore a little bit. OK. I actually swore a lot.

"Watch the road," O'Brien tried to shout but only the first word came out loud, the rest sounded weak and raspy.

I swerved back into our lane, barely missing an oncoming car.

The healing stone had helped O'Brien, but even so, he had just woken up from days in a coma after nearly having his head crushed by a creature moving at eighty miles per hour. So yeah, he was still weak. This wasn't a movie where he would suddenly be fine and lead us against the bad guys to save the day. This was the real world, where people who wake from a coma can barely move and even riding in a car wears them out.

Bountiful Boulevard turned into Eaglewood Drive, which has some serious curves, so I focused on driving. Constantly hitting my brakes to slow down gnawed on my nerves. I hoped we could get to Kendra before anyone—or anything—did.

How'd I miss Kendra's magic when we kissed? She'd connected us with a magic rope of emotions. It wasn't the same as what I'd shared with Alexis, but it had still been magic. I smacked the steering wheel, hurting my hand.

At the time, I hadn't known magic existed. But how'd I miss it at the gravesite? The magic had flared up when our eyes met. O'Brien felt it but didn't know the source.

If the Vampire King was a part of The Day of a Thousand Deaths, and I assumed he was, then the bad guys knew I was a potential. That meant Kendra wasn't the only one in trouble. My family would be in trouble, too. The need to protect my sister flared to life. I glanced away from the road to dial her number. I got her voicemail. I didn't leave a message, because, well, she thought I was dead. Hearing my voice would freak her out. Should I send her a text? No, she'd never believe a message from a random number. She'd assume someone was playing a cruel joke. I needed someone who could deal with being freaked out. My mom was out of the question. John wouldn't be freaked out, but he wouldn't care either.

I needed Luiz.

I dialed my best friend, tapping in his new cell number, glad I memorized it. I got his voicemail. In Spanish, he asked the caller to leave a message. Then he repeated the request in English.

"Luiz, this is Jake. Look, don't freak out. I'm not dead. Uh . . . some people are trying to kill me. My death was . . . faked so they'd stop looking for me. They found me. They know that Kendra is . . ." I stopped. I couldn't tell him she was a druid. "They know she was my girlfriend, so she is in trouble, too. They're going to try to use her to get to me. I know it's late, but get her somewhere safe as soon as you get this message. It really is me." I ended the call.

"Please get the message soon and take it seriously," I whispered. Luiz would surely recognize my voice—the voice of his supposedly dead best friend. Hopefully, the message wouldn't freak him out—too much.

I dialed Kevin's cell—another voicemail. I decided not to leave a message. I didn't try Ethan.

I breathed a sigh of relief when I pulled onto I-15 and accelerated. As I drove, O'Brien's warning stone dimmed.

We were twenty minutes away when I drove past the orange barrels. It was still construction season in Utah. I hadn't paid attention to the signs, so I missed the chance to exit and take surface streets, the same mistake O'Brien had made when fleeing the nightwalker. Our twenty minutes was going to be longer—a lot longer. I swore. I slapped the steering wheel a second time with the same result—a stinging palm.

We crawled forward. Minutes ticked by. Traffic still held us trapped as we approached the I-215 exit when the phone rang. I didn't recognize the number.

"Hello," I answered and put the phone on speaker.

"Jacob?" Luiz asked, voice suspicious.

"Yeah, man, it's me."

"You estúpido, basura blanca, pedazo de—" Luiz continued calling me a string of swear words in Spanish.

"Call me names later," I cut him off. "Did you get to Kendra's house?"

"My dad and I are on the way."

"You told your dad?" I shouted.

Luiz's dad was cool, but I hadn't even considered involving other people. Mr. Espinoza was only going to get himself killed. How did I feel about putting my friend's dad in danger? I'd put Luiz in danger by asking him to find Kendra, so why not his dad too? I didn't feel good about either.

"Yeah, my dad overheard the message when I played it. He agrees that you are a stupid piece of . . . Wait. Papá wants to talk to you."

The phone rustled as Luiz handed it to his dad.

"Jacob, this is Mr. Espinoza." Luiz's dad had a far thicker Mexican accent than his son did. The last time I had seen him, he'd been sick. His weak voice and raspy breath proved he hadn't gotten any better. "Jacob, we are on a disposable cell phone. It can't be tracked, so if your phone is secure too, we can speak freely."

"The phone is secure," I answered.

OK. Why would Luiz's dad, a world-renowned chess master, have a disposable cell phone? Was Luiz's dad involved in illegal activity? I'd have to worry about that later.

"I've been in situations like yours before, back when I was young in Mexico. I can help protect you from dangerous people . . . like drug dealers," Mr. Espinoza continued in his heavy accent.

Drug dealers? What was he talking about? Maybe Luiz had made something up. I went along.

"Thanks," I offered.

"Jacob, I have friends with a cabin a few hours from here. Nobody is using it. We can hide out there. OK?"

"Where at?" I asked.

"How about I don't tell you right now."

I looked at O'Brien. Was he awake? He must be because he nodded.

"OK."

Again, the phone rustled as it passed hands.

"We're at Kendra's," Luiz announced.

"We're still fifteen minutes away," I told him as we exited onto I-215, finally out of the construction and heading west to Redwood Road. "What about her parents?" I asked.

"We'll take care of it," Luiz said. "Gotta go." He hung up.

A few minutes later, we took the Redwood Road exit and headed south. I kept hitting red lights, and on this road, they could take over a minute to turn green. It was eleven at night. Should I run the red lights? Still too many cars. I was approaching the police station. Getting pulled over wouldn't help Kendra. I impatiently waited for the lights to turn green.

As we approached Ninetieth South, the phone rang again.

"Luiz?" I asked.

"We have Kendra and we're headed to I-15," Luiz told me.

"That was fast." I had expected them to argue with Kendra's parents until I arrived.

"I *knew* you were alive, Jake!" Kendra shouted in the background. When not in use, the magic rope had shrunk to a tiny thread. Now it thickened as her excitement poured through it. I could sense her approaching.

Kendra really *had* known I was alive? That explained why she hadn't cried at the funeral. She hadn't believed for a second that I was really dead. Then I had gone and let her eyes meet mine during the dedication of the grave and the connection had kicked in, confirming that she was right.

"I want to see you!" she shouted again, her voice two octaves higher than usual.

Unfortunately, she didn't understand the world she was about to enter. What if she heard a nightwalker scream? It had almost obliterated my mind. I needed to make her a protection stone as soon as possible. It would weaken the effects of a nightwalker's scream as well as protect her from a vampire's control.

"Her parents are going to stay at a hotel tonight," Luiz informed me.

"How did you convince them to do *that*?"

"It wasn't easy," Luiz answered back. "I had help."

They had only been there a few minutes. To me, that meant it *was* easy.

"Wow, your dad convinced them?" I guessed. "Tell him good job."

I had expected to meet them there and find them still arguing, and I'd hoped that seeing me would be enough to convince them. How had they been convinced so easily? Something felt off, but I was too preoccupied to dwell on it.

"Where are you now?" Luiz asked me.

"We're on Redwood Road approaching Ninetieth South," I answered.

"Hey, we're on Ninetieth South about to hit Redwood Road. Should we pull over and meet you?" Luiz responded.

"No, keep going. I still have to get to Justine." As we reached the intersection, their Hyundai Sonata pulled up to the light, "I see you now," I told them.

"Which car are you?"

"The BMW, turning right," I explained.

"There you are."

"Get to safety, OK?" I hung up and waved at them.

Luiz's dad drove and Luiz sat in the front seat. I could barely make out Kendra in the back seat with . . . Was someone with her? At first, I thought there was, but no, it was just her. I waved at them and they waved back.

My muscles, which I hadn't even realized were painfully tense, relaxed. Luiz and Kendra had seen me. Alive. The charade was over. Unfortunately, things weren't any better. I was still being hunted by some unknown secret society, and according to Alexis, her grandfather, the king of vampires, was coming for Kendra and me. Alexis and her grandfather were either fully or partially responsible for The Day of a Thousand Deaths. I worried about Luiz and his dad getting involved. Whatever secret society was after me wouldn't hesitate to harm those close to me. If I didn't protect them, they would succeed.

We turned west and Kendra, Luiz, and his dad continued east toward the freeway.

Then I felt magic like a sound. It reminded me of the loud boom of an aerial firework, like the ones I had watched with Alexis the other day. Only it was magic, not sound. It came from my neighborhood, a little west of my house. Kendra's house?

Luiz had saved Kendra with barely minutes to spare. I had almost not called Luiz, but I had been right to do so. A moment earlier, the threat had only been a possibility. Now a magic user was nearby. O'Brien's warning stone illuminated the car.

Then a thought hit me. My house was next.

Justine. Mom.

CHAPTER 34
CHOICE

I hit the gas as I headed toward my house.

With Kendra safe, the alien need to protect her hadn't exploded from my chest and disappeared. It simply switched its target from Kendra to Justine. If she were in danger, I would do anything to save her.

What if Mom wouldn't let me take Justine to safety? Once Sis saw me alive, she would come with me in a second. I just had to ask. But would Mom get in the way? Even worse, John might get in the way, too. If only Justine would come with me, would I be willing to let my mom die? No way!

The phone rang. It was the number Luiz had called from earlier.

"Hey," I answered.

"Jake." It was Kendra. "You're not going to your house, are you?"

"Yeah, I gotta get to Justine."

"Your mom and Justine don't live there anymore. They moved out the day after your funeral. Your mom is talking about divorcing your stepdad."

I pulled over to the curb after the turnoff to my house.

I had only been supposedly dead for just over a week, and everything about my life had changed. My mom and stepdad were divorcing. Kendra and I were druids, and the Vampire King—and possibly others—was targeting us. My best friend's dad just happened to have a secure cell phone. Did that mean illegal activity? Not to mention every way I had changed.

"Where do they live now?" I asked.

"She doesn't want John to know where she moved, so they haven't told anybody," Kendra answered.

"Do you know where it is?"

"No. Justine won't tell me. She's been avoiding me because I kept telling everyone you're still alive. I just never could believe you really died," she continued. "But Justine is on a date tonight with Dylan, anyway."

I breathed out some tension. Mom was safe in a new apartment. I hoped the bad guys didn't know where she had moved. Justine was safe with Dylan. Except if they knew anything about me, they would know they could get to me using Sis. My need to protect her didn't dampen at all.

"Where were they going on their date?" I asked.

"I don't know. Did you try her cell?"

"She didn't answer."

"I have Dylan's number." She rattled it off. I'd have to ask her sometime why she had his number memorized.

"Thanks," I exhaled. "I'll try calling it."

Neither of us spoke for a second. It was time to hang up but neither of us wanted to. I took a deep breath.

"Jake," her voice trembled as she said my name.

"I know," I told her. "I gotta find Sis." I hung up.

O'Brien had fallen asleep in the passenger seat. What did I expect? He was worn out and healing.

I dialed Dylan's number, trying to decide what to say. I got his voicemail. I tried again. Still voicemail. I swore.

I called my sister's cell. No answer. I sent them both a text that read: "Answer your phone." Then I waited a minute and called Sis's phone.

As her phone rang, my house came into view down the road. It was dark except for one window in John's den. He was home and likely in danger. Something writhed beneath my skin as a black silhouette even darker than the night appeared in the road ahead of me. It crossed into my front yard and disappeared behind my house. Chills ran up my spine and into my scalp. My heart beat faster.

What if Kendra hadn't called? What if I'd gone to my house? What if I'd been standing at the door when that silhouette moved into my yard?

"Hello," Sis answered. I had to decide. Should I hang up and die trying to save my stepdad, or stay on the phone with Sis? I stayed on the phone.

"Sis, don't hang up! It's Jake. I'm not dead," I spit out, unable to take my eyes off my house.

"That's not funny! Who is this?" she shouted into the phone.

"Sis, it's me, Jake, I swear. I'm not dead. Listen to my voice."

"Jake?" she cracked out my name, already crying.

"Where are you?" I asked, but with a loud bang, the phone went dead. I sucked in a quick breath and held it. Had something just happened to her? The sane part of me told me that I'd just freaked her out and she'd dropped the phone. I let out my breath. I dialed again, nervous. "Please be OK. Please be OK," I whispered to myself as the phone rang.

As I waited for her to answer, two more darker-than-night silhouettes glided from the road to the back of my house. The unnatural writhing below my skin increased. I touched my protection stone. I had no chance against three nightwalkers.

"Who is this?" Dylan shouted.

"Who do you think it is, Dylan?" I threw back. I had to say something to keep him on the phone, to make him believe it was me. "A week ago, you were disappointed that I didn't ride with you to go water skiing."

He took a deep breath through the phone. Did it work?

"Kendra's been telling everybody you weren't dead since your body . . . she said the whole story about accidentally sending your body to the U of U as a cadaver was a cover-up," Dylan replied. "Her parents were thinking of sending her to therapy."

Thank you, Kendra. It was easier to believe an unbelievable truth if someone else had already been saying it. I recalled a phrase from church about the truth needing two or more witnesses. Maybe it applied in this situation.

"Where are you? Let's meet up and you can see me for yourself," I suggested.

"We're at Jordan Commons," he answered. "I took Justine to a movie to get her mind off *you*. We just got out and are headed to the car."

Jordan Commons was a theater complex just on the east side of the freeway. I wanted to turn the car around, but I hesitated. Should I rush to my sister or try to save John? I didn't even know if I *could* save John. I had barely survived one of these things.

"Meet me at Maverick off Ninetieth by the freeway!" As I spoke, two more figures slipped behind my house, but they didn't look like nightwalkers. It was an older couple. Still, that made two against five. O'Brien's warning stone brightened. He was out cold. OK, one against five.

"No," Dylan said. "We'll wait for you here. Look for us by . . ." Was he deciding on a safe place to meet? "By the ice cream place." Dylan didn't trust me. I didn't mind because he was protecting my sister. I needed him to keep filling that role.

"OK. I'm coming soon."

"You're tripping your sister out, you know." He called me a name that I shouldn't repeat before he hung up. I didn't blame him. I was just trying to keep myself, Kendra, and anyone else in danger alive. If he kept helping my sister, he could call me names all he wanted.

I sensed a tremor in the . . . magic. Even as scared as I was, the familiarity of that phrase wasn't lost on me. A small magic spell had been cast behind my house. Perhaps they had opened my back door with the unlock spell I had read about in the druid text.

OK, so three obsidian Darth Mauls just entered my house along with a Darth Sidious and . . . his Darth Wife?

Time to choose. Hurry to my sister or stay and help John? Did they know where Sis was? I felt an overwhelming urge to protect her and no such urge to protect him. But he was still a person.

Wait! Luiz's dad had asked if O'Brien's cell phone was secure and I had said yes, but Alexis had O'Brien's cell phone for days. I'd called Sis with it. What if Alexis had tampered with the phone? The Vampire King might know where Sis was now. What if I died helping John and left Sis alone? Unprotected? Chills ran up my spine and danced around my hair follicles. What if they weren't going to kill John? They might see Sis and Mom weren't there and just leave. But what if they didn't?

I couldn't wait any longer. I made my choice.

CHAPTER 35
SISTER

I chose Justine. It wasn't just brotherly protectiveness; it was more than that. Was it magic-enhanced? Except, wouldn't I know if magic were involved? Once I turned the car around, I didn't even think about my creeper stepdad. The impulse to protect my sister erased him from my mind.

What would I tell Sis when I got to her? Should I convince her to come with me? Or should I tell her to get in her car and drive? If I sent her away, should I tell her to stay away for one day? Two days? A week? Would she ever be safe as long as I was alive? What about Kendra's family? It was just her and her parents left at home. Her extended family had too many branches, and we couldn't protect them all from being pruned. There was no way that she could go on the run and leave her family, but she couldn't stay here and stay alive with some unknown secret society planning to assassinate her.

How could Kendra and I keep those close to us safe?

Then it hit me. We were planning to hide out at some cabin because of fear. Fear for myself. Fear for my life. But I didn't dare leave because I feared for the lives of my family and friends. The only way to protect them was to make those after me more afraid of me than I was of them. I decided right then and there what I was going to do. I'd imagined casting the magic missile again many times while bored at Alexis's mansion.

I'd tried to push away the craving to use it again, to feel the pleasure of erasing a soul. I wasn't going to push it away anymore. Just the opposite.

I wouldn't hesitate or ask questions. If someone or something tried to kill Sis, they were going to die—and not just their body. I was going to erase them from existence. The more people—or things—I erased, the more others would avoid messing with my family and friends. I scared myself a little, but the need to protect them overrode that fear.

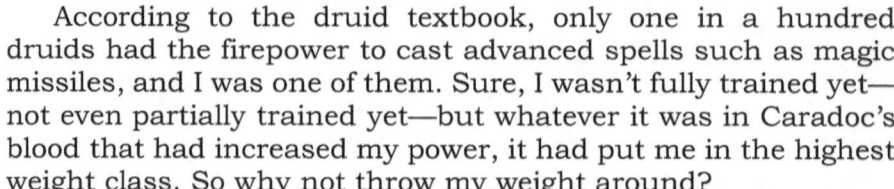

According to the druid textbook, only one in a hundred druids had the firepower to cast advanced spells such as magic missiles, and I was one of them. Sure, I wasn't fully trained yet—not even partially trained yet—but whatever it was in Caradoc's blood that had increased my power, it had put me in the highest weight class. So why not throw my weight around?

I turned into Jordan Commons in just under ten minutes. I pulled through the parking lot. Since it was approaching midnight, it wasn't very full but was plenty dark. Most of the movies were already out. I slowed to let a group of kids pass. Behind them, a couple on a date held hands as they walked. As I approached, the guy looked right at me. He reached into his pocket. I held my breath. He pulled out keys. *Why was I so nervous?*

I parked. O'Brien sat in the passenger seat. Did I dare leave him in the car? I decided he was fine as long as his head wasn't visible. I reached around him and leaned the seat back. He stirred a little but didn't wake up.

The warning stone still lit up O'Brien's neck and chin—not as bright as when I was parked near my house watching three nightwalkers enter it, but bright enough. Something was close. I had made the right decision to protect Justine. I only hoped I had time to get her to safety. If we didn't hurry, we would have to fight our way out. I moved the crystal under his shirt to hide its light.

I took a breath. Then without even glancing around for danger, I got out and sprinted to the entrance as if it were the end zone and I had to outrun the safety.

As I entered, I passed under the glowing sign that read "Megaplex Theatres."

This Megaplex had about twenty movie theaters extending off a long walkway. Restaurants lined both sides like an extended food court. I couldn't remember where the ice cream shop was, so I walked to the right first. I passed the sandwich shop and continued on past a number of screens. I reached the end where the largest 3D movie screen took up the rest of the building, but I hadn't passed the ice cream shop. I turned around, irritated.

I retraced my steps and found the ice cream shop. Dylan and Justine waited for me there. They sat at one of the empty tables. Dylan had his arm around my sister, comforting her. She wasn't crying, but streaks of mascara proved she had been.

I walked toward her. She turned and looked at me. Her spoonful of ice cream dropped to the floor.

"Jake!" She stumbled off the chair, ran around the other tables, and fell against me, wrapping her arms around me. She broke into tears, then let out one loud sob. I put my arms around her and held her.

"I'm sorry, Sis." I stroked her blonde hair. "I'm alive. I had to fake my death because . . ." I didn't finish because that wasn't exactly the truth, and I didn't lie to my sister. I hadn't faked my death, O'Brien had.

Dylan's eyebrows pulled together, and his teeth clenched—not quite as happy to see me as my sister was.

"What's going on, Jake?" he demanded. "You have some freaking explaining to do."

I ignored him and pushed my sister to arm's length and lifted her chin. I looked into her confused, tear-filled green eyes. What could be going through her mind? To see me after attending my funeral had to be more than she could understand. I regretted not having time to talk to her and understand what she was feeling.

"We need to go," I told her firmly. "I'm in trouble. You're not safe. They'll use you to get to me." She just looked at me, unable to process my words. She could only understand that her brother, whom she thought was dead, stood in front of her. Anything else was too much for her.

"Let's get outta here!" I looked at Dylan. "Quickly!"

I started pulling my sister toward the exit. Dylan hesitated and his eyebrows scrunched together. He wasn't going to make things easy on me.

"What did you get yourself into, Jake?" he demanded. "Why isn't Justine safe?"

"Some . . . some people are trying to kill me," I whispered.

"Jake," Dylan whispered back, and he hurried to catch up. "First you tell us that you faked your death, and now you tell us someone is after you. You realize what this means?" His low volume didn't hide the rough anger in his voice.

"Yes, it means we have to get Justine somewhere safe."

"No, it means you're schizophrenic, Jake. You know what that is, right?"

"I'm not schizophrenic!"

Dylan didn't know all the facts. O'Brien had faked my death, not me. He'd sniped me in the leg. I had no part in that. I'd also watched a scary obsidian-skinned thing rip a woman apart and nearly kill O'Brien. I guess it made sense that Dylan thought I was crazy, that I had faked my own death. I had just told him someone was trying to *kill* me, but I didn't even know who. The Vampire King was involved, and possibly Alexis who'd just betrayed me, so whoever the bad guys were, they included vampires and at least three more

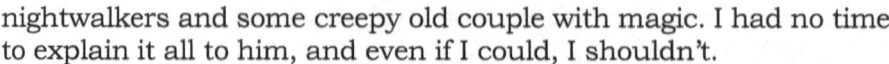

nightwalkers and some creepy old couple with magic. I had no time to explain it all to him, and even if I could, I shouldn't.

"It isn't your fault," Dylan continued. "You got shot by a stray bullet during that drive-by shooting. Have you heard of post-traumatic stress disorder?"

"Yes, I've heard of it!" I snapped back. He was interfering. The need to protect my sister caused every muscle to tense, and I barely held off from punching him. "And I don't have it!"

That was not exactly true. I might have PTSD. But if I did, it was from the nightwalker's scream or perhaps from watching it walk toward me while eating a woman's arm. I didn't have PTSD from getting shot in the leg. That was one of the highlights of last week.

Wait . . . hadn't I felt the healing stone repair my mind? Was it PTSD that the healing stone had worked on? I couldn't share any of this with Dylan, so I kept walking, trying and failing to unclench my muscles.

A teenage couple approached the ice cream shop. The boy had his hand in the girl's back pocket, and she leaned against him in a way that said she wanted the date to get a bit more serious. They shared a set of earbuds. The girl had familiar purple streaks lining the front of her hair. Her eyes lifted and looked at mine.

Teresa. An old girlfriend of mine.

"Jake, is that you?" She stopped and held on to her boyfriend's arm, pulling him to a stop as well. The earbuds pulled from their ears and fell, dangling just above the floor. They didn't notice. Their eyes locked on my face. I'd seen the guy around. He played football for another school, but I couldn't remember his name.

I had dated Teresa for a few months my junior year. She didn't want me. She wanted a star football player. We made out, a lot, but I kept things on first base. One night, she wanted me to go all the way and pulled me as far as second base, but I wasn't ready. I left. The next day, she apologized and asked me to take her out again. I said I would. I had lied. I hadn't talked to her since.

"I went to your funeral." Teresa's face drained of color and her mouth hung open as she looked at me.

"Me, too," her guy added.

It was true. I'd seen them there. I turned away without responding to them, pulling Sis with me.

"Just keep walking," I said, ignoring Teresa and her boyfriend. They didn't follow us, but I could feel their eyes on my back as we walked away. After a few steps, Teresa yelled to a group of kids from my high school to come and see.

"Hurry," I said, picking up the pace. I *so* did not want to have an audience. It had felt good to tell Luiz and Kendra and Sis that I was alive, but I suddenly didn't want anyone else to know. I hadn't understood until that moment that I still planned to remain dead to the world.

"Let's run," I urged. Dylan grunted but complied. We were out the doors before any more of Teresa's friends saw me. I hustled Justine and Dylan toward the parking lot, moving them at more of a hurried walk than a run. "Where's your car?" I asked.

Dylan pointed and took the lead. "This is nuts," he growled. "I'm taking your sister home."

"You can't take her home, Dylan. Trust me, just this once," I begged.

"Sure," he said. "What do you want me to do?"

"Just drive. Pick a direction. Don't tell anyone where you are going and just drive. Don't stop and don't come back until you hear from me."

"Sure. Will do," Dylan agreed.

I didn't like his voice. It was off. It was laced with . . . pacification. He only agreed with me so I would leave.

I swore silently.

We reached Dylan's tan Ford Explorer. It was only a few years old but still looked new. It was a bad time to be petty and jealous, but I couldn't help wondering why all my friends had cars and cell phones and I had neither. I didn't even have a driver's license.

I needed to convince Dylan I wasn't crazy. That the danger facing us was real. Seeing me alive wasn't enough and nothing I could say could convince him. He needed proof and that was something I could give him. I reached for the magic. As I pulled magic in, I felt it ripple ever so faintly, like a whisper. It was so subtle that if I hadn't reached for the magic right then, I wouldn't have felt the disturbance. There was another magic user nearby and it wasn't O'Brien. He was asleep in the car.

"Get down." I grabbed Justine and pulled her into a crouch behind the Ford Explorer.

As I dropped, a bullet whizzed over my head. I'd reacted just in time. There was no sound of a gunshot. The bullet missed and shattered the rear window of the car behind us, making plenty of noise. Dylan, who had remained standing, dropped immediately, just before a second bullet passed where his head had been. Another loud crack echoed in the parking lot when the bullet embedded itself in a stone pillar.

We were pinned down.

CHAPTER 36
PARKING LOT

"They have bullets," I breathed. I swore. How stupid could I be? I hadn't even considered bullets. I had considered another nightwalker. Vampires. Rogue druid assassins. Bullets had never crossed my mind. I was traveling with O'Brien, a sniper who never went anywhere without a gun. He'd even shot me, which started all this. I should have thought about bullets. I was such a rookie. Worse, I wasn't even a rookie yet. I hadn't even been through training camp.

Dylan cringed on the asphalt, hands over his head like a scared puppy. Good. Nothing like being shot at to convince someone that our danger was not just a figment of a psychotic mind.

I peeked over the car. I couldn't see anyone in the dim lighting of the covered parking. While the parking lot wasn't walled in, the exits weren't everywhere. I dropped back down as another bullet whizzed by, its wind brushing my hair, before ricocheting loudly off a concrete pillar. I'd survived by an inch.

I gave up trying to look with my eyes. Instinctually, I sent out magic, using it as if I were just looking and listening hard. I couldn't see or hear the people my magic touched. I could, however, *feel* their shapes as the magic spread around them. Soon, I located the shape of one person holding a rifle and wearing headgear.

I had already decided how to attack. Human or monster, whoever shot at Sis and me would get worse than death. I was going to wipe them from existence. I put the base of my palms together, hands forming a V, and gathered enough magic for a small ball of compressed energy.

"*Bealustræl!*" I whispered the spell. I formed a smaller magic missile than the one I'd used against the nightwalker. I still pulled a lot of magic in, but nowhere near enough to pass out.

While crouched and holding the glowing orb, I moved left to the front wheel well. I stood, illuminated palms already aimed toward the gunman hidden in the dark, and fired the glowing missile. I ducked down to the right, but a bullet skimmed my left shoulder, cutting my shirt and burning my skin.

Dylan and Sis both gaped at me in awe. I had just lobbed a glowing, white orb of magic.

Yes, the magic missile was *awesome*. But the bullet that grazed me, not so much.

"Ow!" I clenched my teeth and sucked in a quick breath.

The gunman had no idea what I'd thrown at him. The magic missile traveled too fast for him to dodge but slow enough for him to experience a second of terror. I sensed through magic when the missile hit. It ended his everything.

A man cried out near the vanquished gunman. I pushed away the pain in my shoulder and focused on the magic near the yell. Another humanoid shape with a rifle and odd headgear. The fool had given himself away. I released another magic missile, erasing the body and soul of that shooter as well.

Evil pleasure danced around my insides, making my skin prickle, but with my sister to protect, I tried to ignore the negative side. Except, I'd just killed two normal men. Not transients. Not vampires. Not nightwalkers. Two regular men.

I heard Clint Eastwood's voice in my head. *It's a hell of a thing, killing a man. Take away all he's got and all he's ever gonna have.*

"Yeah, well, I guess they had it coming," I said out loud. What would Will Munny have said if he could have obliterated a soul's existence with his guns?

"Jake!" Dylan shouted. He sat, back leaning against his vehicle. He cringed like a puppy. It was odd seeing him like that. He was a big guy, taller and heavier than me, built like the middle linebacker he was. Too bad when threatened with his life, he'd reacted no better than Justine, who also sat leaning against the vehicle, shivering, her green eyes wide.

I followed Dylan's eyes to two people—or creatures—running toward us. They wore black, military-like outfits and moved at speeds beyond what is humanly possible. For a second, I thought they were Transients, except they reminded me of Alexis.

I didn't have time to take them both out. I picked the closest one and pulled the magic into an orb and released it. Like a ball of lightning, it flashed into the vamp's chest just ten feet away from me, wiping out his body and soul.

Pleasure shivered through me. Did the thrill increase each time? Or was destroying a vampire more pleasurable?

I didn't have time for a second missile, but I tried anyway. Time seemed to slow as I compressed magic into a missile. The light from the forming orb illuminated the face of the creature coming toward us. With his pale skin and white hair, he resembled Alexis's memories of her grandfather, but he was shorter and had a thinner face. He bared fangs much longer than Alexis's, extending more than an inch beyond his other teeth.

He's coming too fast! If only I knew just one *defensive spell!*

Three feet from me, the vampire jerked awkwardly. Matter exploded from the side of his head. His change in trajectory gave me almost enough time to step aside. The vampire hit my right shoulder like a linebacker as he went by, knocking me against Dylan's Explorer before slamming against its tan exterior himself, leaving a massive dent. I pinched my eyes closed as pain started at the back of my head and spread out. I should have worn a football helmet.

A few seconds passed before I opened my eyes. The vampire writhed a dozen feet to my right. I began grabbing magic. A small hole marked one side of its head and a larger hole opened on the other side where its ear should have been. A bullet's entry and exit wound? I glanced around. O'Brien stood behind a car, gun resting on the hood, too weak to keep his aim steady without it. Had my magic woken him?

A bullet in the ear, however, only slowed the vampire. The skin and tissue around the hole began healing as he tried to stand. Unfortunately for the bloodsucker, another magic missile already hovered between my palms.

I wished that Sis and Dylan didn't have to watch me erase this thing at point-blank range. Their eyes riveted on our fanged attacker as I unleashed the magic missile, which shot from my palms to its chest. The impact knocked him to his knees. The light and energy of the magic missile disappeared into the vampire. He looked up at me, irises not red but white with fear. Light shot out of its skin, with a big beam coming from the hole in its head. As the light spread, his physical body erased. Every atom separated from the one next to it, diffusing into the black night. Then, the thing's soul floated upward—yes, it had one. The soul separated into tiny particles that faded away like a dust cloud.

My fourth kill sent a new level of ecstasy surging through my entire body. I trembled in pleasure from my head to my toes. I grinned wickedly. I'd killed four fiends. I looked around wanting something more to come for us so I could erase it with magic and raise my pleasure up one more level. Five fiends alliterated just as well as four fiends. Unfortunately, the fiends were finished. *I'd always wanted to use the word fiend in real life.*

No other creature came for us. My eyes found O'Brien, the man who *shot* me. The man who had failed to protect me. The very man who pulled me into all this nightmare.

He's earned some erasing, too, I thought.

I reached for magic.

Wait, no!

I cringed, recognizing the corruptive, addictive nature of my erasure-induced pleasure. My sister's tears fell from wide eyes. She trembled and sucked in short breaths. Was she trying to catch her breath between sobs or was she hyperventilating?

I reached for her, and she flinched. She slid away from me, shivering her way next to Dylan and grabbing at his arm until he wrapped it around her. My muscles tensed in anger. My addiction wanted to erase her for flinching and sliding away. But the need to protect her rose up and cast out the thought, washing the ecstasy from me. My stomach twisted, revolting against me in a way that would have caused anyone else but me to expel its contents.

How could I ever think of killing Sis? What was wrong with me?

I pinched my eyes closed and took a deep breath. O'Brien dropped to a sitting position, gun in hand, too tired to remain on his feet. *I've gotta get a gun.* Magic was awesome, but guns worked, too, and there was no reason not to have options— especially options that didn't include evil addictive side-effects.

I looked at Dylan. His chest heaved and shook.

"Dylan, do exactly as I say!" I ordered. "Get in your car. Pick a direction and drive. Don't stop for anything but gas. Keep driving until you hear from me!" By the end, I was talking way too loudly. I needed to calm down.

Dylan stood and then helped my sister up.

"Please give me your phones," I requested, with false calmness. "They can track you with them."

They slowly handed them over. It would sound so cool to say I burned the phones in my hand with fire light or something awesome like that. But they had nice phones, and being a jeek, I knew how silly destroying a cell phone is in real life. Instead, I took out the SIM cards, put their phones in airplane mode, and handed their phones back. I still needed to get rid of the SIM cards so . . .

"*Fyr leoht,*" I whispered, and a small, controlled flame melted the SIM cards in my hand.

Sis cringed away from me again. OK. Maybe casting fire light with Sis standing right next to me, already freaked out, hadn't been the best idea for disposing of the SIM cards.

"I love you, Sis," I told her, but she wouldn't look at me. I looked Dylan in the eyes. "Keep her safe." I turned away.

"Jacob, what the hell just happened?" Dylan asked.

"Nothing, I'm crazy. Remember?" I said, facing O'Brien.

Dylan grabbed my shoulder. Unfortunately, he grabbed the one that had been skinned by a passing bullet.

"Ouch!" I snapped and shrugged out of his grip. "It's better if you don't know. Pretend that you never saw any of this; you never even saw *me*. Don't ever speak of this to anyone," I warned.

Dylan gulped.

I turned and hurried over to O'Brien.

I helped O'Brien up. His lips moved like he wanted to say something but nothing came out. He'd exhausted a huge amount of energy that he didn't have just to walk this far and get one shot off. I was grateful. He had been too weak to lead the fight, but that one shot had made a difference. If that vampire had killed me, Sis and Dylan wouldn't have stood a chance. We owed him our lives.

I watched Dylan and my sister drive away in his now-dented Ford Explorer. Would I see them again? If so, would my sister ever look at me the same? Would I even live through this to find out? Could I live through this? As long as O'Brien, Kendra, and I were alive and vulnerable, someone or something would come for us. We either had to die or become invulnerable.

John Kaloyan, the Vampire King, was coming for us. The vampires I had just shattered into nothingness had been his minions. I had no idea who—or what—he was bringing with him. I swallowed away a shiver.

I put O'Brien's arm around my shoulders.

"Hurry." O'Brien glanced around. "Your magic." He swallowed. "Watch for transients."

I hurried until O'Brien passed out and slid to the asphalt. I helped him up and managed to get him into the passenger seat.

I jumped into the driver's seat and started the car. I drove out of the parking lot toward the freeway. Every pedestrian was a shadow. Could they be transients? None chased us.

With Justine safe and driving in who knows which direction, I turned my thoughts to who I needed to save next.

Oh, no!

Justine and Dylan were long gone, I'd just destroyed their SIM cards, and I had no way to find Mom.

CHAPTER 37
FLIGHT

I slapped the steering wheel in anger, sending a wave of pain through my palm. I'd raced to the freeway in hopes of catching up to Dylan and Sis, but I knew deep down I wouldn't find them.

What if finding Mom leads them to her?

It hurt me to do it, but I had to take the chance and hope that Mom would be safe. Perhaps moving into a new apartment and not telling anyone was God's way of helping her where I had failed her. I wasn't churchy like Kendra, but I took a moment to whisper a prayer. It was all I could do for my mom. At my funeral, O'Brien had mentioned there was power in prayer. I'm not going to lie, I didn't feel any power in it. I didn't feel anything—except maybe a bit more calm.

I called Luiz—they didn't know where Mom's new apartment was—but I told his dad that O'Brien's phone might be compromised. He started speaking in code, telling me where to go by talking about memories we shared. Like the time when Luiz and I bought something illegal, and on the way back, got a flat tire with no spare. A vague memory to an eavesdropper, but one that told me exactly where to go. He came up with a plan to ditch our current phones and get new burner phones. I couldn't help but wonder more about Mr. Espinoza. What secrets did he have?

O'Brien and I went by the druid cache to grab supplies. Mostly we needed a box of money. Before leaving the cache, O'Brien thought it best that we disable the BMW's GPS in case someone tracked us with it. It took some guidance from him, but I found some wires to cut. After that, we started toward our first stop.

I took I-80 east to Evanston, Wyoming. That flat tire had kept Luiz and me from ever firing off those illegal fireworks. I stopped at the local Walmart and bought a prepaid SIM card with data. I also bought a lighter. Behind Walmart, I found the dumpster with a piece of paper taped to it. Some questions were scrawled on the paper. The first question asked how old I was when I met Luiz. I answered that and the other questions until I had a list of ten digits.

Mr. Espinoza proved far too experienced with the whole anonymous-cell-phone thing.

I burned the paper with the lighter and dialed the number. I could have burned it with magic, but then I would have had to create a containment too. As overexerted as I was from casting four magic missiles, the lighter was the easiest solution.

"*Aló,*" Mr. Espinoza answered in Spanish.

"Got it," I said, and hung up.

A few seconds later, I received a text message with a link to GPS coordinates. I clicked the link and a map came up. It zoomed in on a cabin west of Bear Lake, a large lake on the Idaho border.

In case we were being followed, we drove about ten minutes east of Evanston. There, I threw out a small magic missile at an extra-large sagebrush. Hopefully, whoever was looking for us would sense the magic and think we were fleeing east.

I would have preferred to use fire light, but burning a sagebrush in July in Wyoming would burn down the whole state. I didn't erase the plant's existence. I wasn't sure if it was because it was just a plant, or because I didn't attack its spirit, but there was no pleasure in it—which left me with an insatiable craving.

We followed the new phone's GPS directions to take us northwest on side roads until we reached the main highway.

The map said it would take two hours from Evanston to the Bear Lake cabin. I drove through the darkness. The moon and the stars decorated the night sky above the mountains. But soon my eyes lapsed into tunnel vision, seeing only the part of the road illuminated by the headlights. Darkness shrouded everything else.

O'Brien stayed awake all of fifteen minutes before his fatigue took over and his breathing steadied, leaving me alone to my thoughts.

As I drove, I looked back at the life that I had hated so much. I hated the way my mother flinched at the sight of me. I hated how I was conceived. I hated John for what he'd done recently, and how he had corrupted my family. As bad as it was, I'd take it all back if it meant that everyone I cared about could be safe.

Sadly, time is not something that can be turned back—even with magic. My situation couldn't be changed in the past; I had to change it in the present. I had already started. They had sent the nightwalker after O'Brien and me, and we had survived. I had just saved Kendra by responding quicker than the bad guys had. I had also saved my sister from two gunmen and two vampires.

Erasing the existence of those who threatened us gave me a thrill which I enjoyed too much. Was erasing bad guys wrong? Maybe. But they forfeited their existence by coming after me, right? They were bringing it, not me. My church teaches not to be the one who starts the fight. Defense only. But once started, win it. That was just what I was doing, right? So why did it feel wrong?

I had to be more careful. The pleasure had nearly taken control of me. I'd have to make sure that didn't happen. I would handle its addictive nature better next time.

My thoughts drifted from my enemies to Alexis. Thinking of her brought up a kaleidoscope of emotions. I had fallen for her in just a few days, even if my infatuation had originated from unnatural causes. We had kissed twice. The second time had been during the most intimate moment of my life, a more mental than physical intimacy. Through our magical connection, we had shared the deepest parts of our minds and memories.

At least, I had thought so.

She had held back her plan to run off with the enchanted diamond, and she had walled off a portion of her mind. The mental thread connecting her to her grandfather had helped her hide her secrets. What had been hidden there? I wanted these answers. Would I get them? Not if I never saw Alexis again. I refused to believe she was a killer. She had fed again the night she betrayed me, but that didn't mean she had killed. While connected, I'd felt her empathy for humanity, which was precious to her.

You saved me. I remembered the words she had spoken just before betraying me. Had I saved her? Or had I released a monster into the unsuspecting Utah population?

Had she meant I saved her from the nightwalker or from her grandfather? Perhaps both. She abandoned me anyway, taking the stone to save herself.

I tried to imagine her grandfather and was surprised that his face came to me clearly not just from Alexis's memories, but from Caradoc's. Caradoc had met with him several times. The Vampire King stood tall and foreboding. He had pale skin and white hair, all one length that hung to just above his shoulders. Like Alexis's, his red eyes turned black when angry and black with blood-red lightning streaks when hungry. No one had beaten him in over eight hundred years, which is why he reigned as the Vampire King.

I assumed he had sent the two vampires that had attacked us in the Megaplex parking lot.

The parking lot . . .

I had missed something, but I couldn't put my finger on it.

The thoughts of Alexis were too strong, and they pulled me away before I could figure it out.

Alexis spoke clearly, emphasizing every word and never using a contraction. She walked with confidence in a way I had never seen. She was strong, and yet she had needed me. Her ability to survive was the foundation of her confidence.

Kendra had confidence, too, but her foundation was goodness. Was Alexis good too? If the thoughts we shared while connected were true, she had never killed to feed. She had always stopped before the blood loss was too great. But was that true? Or had she simply hidden the truth in the part of her mind I couldn't access?

Couldn't Alexis have saved herself from her grandfather without stabbing me in the back?

My thoughts spiraled into a jumbled mess of all my mistakes.

How had I failed to recognize the magic connection between Kendra and me? She had created it when we first kissed and then used it at the cemetery.

Why hadn't I anticipated Alexis's betrayal? I'd wasted time working out when I could have read the druid manual. Had I read on, I would have encountered the simpler healing spells. Alexis's motives went beyond what she shared. I should have been more careful. How naive could I be?

Why hadn't I asked Justine about their new apartment? Would Mom be safe because nobody knew where she'd moved? Or had one of the Vampire King's minions already found her? I couldn't explain it, but I had a feeling Mom would be safe.

Did the nightwalkers kill John? Had my decision to save my sister instead of him cost him his life?

After hours of driving and mental and emotional turmoil—and a very sore palm while the steering wheel remained unharmed—I pulled into the cabin. I parked next to Luiz's Hyundai Sonata.

My headlights lit up the front of what looked less like a cabin and more like one of the expensive mega-homes near Alexis's mansion. Gray stucco covered the exterior and white borders wrapped the windows and the three garage doors. A fenced-off gravel carport contained a ski boat on the right side of the house.

I noticed O'Brien's mangled ear as I nudged his shoulder.

"We're here," I told him.

He gathered himself and stepped out of the car a few moments after me. Maybe it was the two hours of sleep, but he could walk without assistance.

Even though it was after three in the morning, an adrenaline rush surged into me at the idea of seeing Kendra and Luiz.

CHAPTER 38
CABIN

'd forgotten how visible stars were away from the ambient light of civilization. The cabin was surrounded by dozens of others, enough that there was still a faint glow from the lights, but it was nothing like Salt Lake City. Ursa Major pointed to the North Star of Ursa Minor. The Milky Way trailed from one end of the sky to the other, dividing the universe in half. Bear Lake's mirror-like surface reflected the starry sky, making it appear as if the universe continued right through the earth. I searched for Orion but couldn't find him, probably hidden below the hills surrounding Bear Lake.

"Pop the trunk," O'Brien asked, leaning against the rear of the car. I fumbled with the electronic key to pop the trunk open.

Wow! My eyes widened.

Every inch of the trunk was filled with weapons. There were guns and grenades but there were also blades of all sorts, many of which had symbols that emanated with power. Some of the symbols held so much magic that they glowed in full color.

"John Kaloyan is always ready for a fight, and this is his car," O'Brien explained to me. "I wouldn't doubt if the trunk of every car he owns looks just like this. His life is a giant game of king of the hill, and he's been the top vampire for a long time. He keeps his other vampires weak, and if one starts getting strong, he kills them early before they pose a challenge."

Was that what he was trying to do with Alexis? Kill her before she poses a challenge? Her grandfather had basically ordered her to fight the nightwalker and die.

Luiz came out the door, followed by Kendra. They must have heard us pull in. Seeing them safe, I took deep breath, and my shoulders dropped. I hadn't even noticed how tense my muscles had been. Luiz pulled the earphones from his ears and let them hang. Despite the chirping crickets and other night sounds, I could hear the faint beat of Maná coming from his dangling earphones.

"Jake!" Kendra squealed in excitement.

She ran to me and jumped up into a hug, wrapping her arms around my neck and her legs around my waist. I managed not to fall down. Good thing I worked out a lot. The now-scabbed skin on my shoulder stretched in pain. But I didn't care. Her hair smelled of lavender, and I breathed it in as we hugged. She kissed my cheek and then dropped her feet down. She smiled at me for just a second before moving aside so Luiz could hug me. We hugged with closed fists and beat each other's backs like real men do.

Kendra grinned from ear to ear and suddenly, my chest sank, hollow with guilt. Should I tell Kendra about Alexis?

O'Brien coughed.

"Hey, guys. This is Charles O'Brien," I said.

"Mr. O'Brien." Luiz reached out his hand. Luiz's eyes darted to the half-healed wounds on the left side of O'Brien's head.

"Call me Charles." O'Brien shook his hand. The sniper glanced at me, aware that I had never asked his first name. I'd heard the nightwalker use it.

O'Brien shook Kendra's hand too.

"Why don't you help me carry all this inside?" O'Brien nodded at the weapon-filled trunk.

Luiz looked into the trunk and let out a string of expletives in Spanish. Kendra looked inside and froze.

"Oh, my heck! Someone really is after us," Kendra admitted.

The weapons in the trunk brought down the hammer of reality. I didn't tell her that she'd gotten away just in time—that someone had used magic near her house just minutes after she had left. I didn't tell her my house had been compromised and I didn't know what happened to my stepdad. I didn't tell her that we had barely arrived in time to save Sis and Dylan.

Instead, I said, "It could be *something*, instead of someone."

They nodded as if they already knew what I meant. *Huh.* I expected some questions.

I regretted dragging them into this. Not that I had chosen Kendra to be the other druid. That was just the way it happened. I felt guilty because I had wished it were her and now it was. Her involvement was outside of my control, but the involvement of Luiz and his dad wasn't. My fault or not, I blamed myself anyway as if I had dragged all three of them into this mess.

"What are we up against?" Luiz asked. That was the obvious question after my "*something*, instead of someone" comment.

"If we've chosen a good hideout, nothing," O'Brien replied.

"And if our hideout isn't good enough?" Luiz pressed.

"Well, there could be the regular assassins with guns and bullets," O'Brien stated, "or there could be creatures that make your worst nightmares look like My Little Pony."

"Wow, you've watched My Little Pony?" I interrupted.

O'Brien gave me a don't-start-with-me look.

"Which pony is your favorite? Applejack? Rarity? Rainbow Dash?" I asked, ignoring his look.

"Help me get this stuff into the house, and I'll let Jake tell you what a nightwalker's scream sounds like."

Oh, crap.

If I hadn't held the healing stone on the ride back from the druid grove, I might have collapsed in panic at the mention of its scream—like I'd collapsed in front of Alexis just before offering myself to her.

"Is that like a vampire?" Kendra asked as Charles handed her a shotgun.

"Not exactly. Vampires are different," I told her.

"Do they really sparkle in the sun?" Kendra asked.

"No!" I growled.

O'Brien tilted his head slightly at Kendra. "Why would you think they sparkle?"

I shook my head, amused at how book- and movie-challenged O'Brien was. "I bet he knows about Twilight Sparkle the pony!" I laughed.

O'Brien scowled at me but didn't respond.

Luiz eyed the weapons in the trunk like a kid in a candy store. "Grenades? Between swords? A pair of SIG P250s?"

O'Brien raised an eyebrow at Luiz and started quizzing him about the guns and grenades. Luiz knew a lot more than O'Brien expected. The ex-marine looked impressed until Luiz mentioned he learned it all from his unhealthy addiction to first-person shooters.

Luiz and Kendra weren't taking this seriously enough. To them, this was just an exciting road trip with friends. The danger wasn't real for them . . . yet. They hadn't almost lost their minds to the cold, dark abyss of the nightwalker's scream. A vampire—er, half dhampir—hadn't influenced them with her allure or controlled them with her touch. I had begged Alexis to take my blood. I glanced at Kendra and my chest tightened. I'd survived Alexis's crush-enhanced allure and touch only because she'd chosen not to drain me. I needed to make a protection stone for everyone as soon as possible. I just didn't have any crystals.

"Wait," O'Brien said as Luiz reached to remove the last of the weapons. "Let's leave some in case we have to make a run for it."

How safe were we here? We hadn't been followed and we'd ditched our cell phones for new ones, but it was always possible we could be tracked. O'Brien still wore his crystal that warned him of danger and it wasn't glowing. Still, the nightwalker had found us. The warning stone hadn't been much help then. It could happen again. If it did, where would we go? How long could we keep running?

F-o-r-e-v-e-r. If only the beasts I'd soon face were just dogs that chewed baseballs.

I entered the cabin behind Kendra and breathed in pumpkin spice. I froze. It lasted only a second. At least, I *thought* I had smelled it. I looked around for Alexis but she was nowhere to be found. Her aroma was too powerful to come and go like that. I must have imagined it. Or had I hoped for it? I hadn't admitted it to myself yet, but I hoped that I would see Alexis again, despite her betrayal. I glanced at Kendra again then lowered my eyes.

The cabin's vast front room extended forever. It had been set up like two rooms, the first area containing a few chairs around a nice wooden card table and the second area containing two couches and two love seats arranged in a rectangle. The furthest couch sat against the wall that had an arched opening just left of the couches that led into the dining room and kitchen. Another opening, also left of the couches but on the other wall, led to a hallway.

What's with all the big houses lately? I wondered.

"Jake," Mr. Espinoza greeted as he walked in from the kitchen. "I am glad you're here." He stretched his hand out and I shook it.

"Thanks for finding us this," I glanced around at the cabin, "hiding place."

Mr. Espinoza took a seat on the couch against the wall.

Luiz walked around eyeing the place. "Hey! We could go all One-Eyed Willy and set up booby traps everywhere. If anyone comes for us, we'd hear them blow themselves up."

"No!" O'Brien snapped. "You really want to wake up tired and have to navigate to the kitchen to get a drink without blowing yourself up?"

"Not me. I don't get up to drink at night," Luiz shook his head.

"The bathroom, then?" the sniper countered.

"I'm good all night," Luiz replied nonchalantly. Then he glanced at Kendra. "Isn't it usually girls that have to get up to pee at night?"

"Hey!" Kendra complained. "Are you saying it is fine for me to blow up?"

"You can blow—Ouch!" I stopped Luiz's remark with a hard smack to his arm. Luiz rubbed his arm.

"Booby traps are just a bad idea, but we can stash some weapons where we can get to them easily," O'Brien added.

Luiz loaded a shotgun and stashed it along with a few grenades behind the cushions of the nearest couch.

O'Brien sat at the card table, looking relieved to be sitting, and methodically loaded the half-dozen clips he'd pulled from the box. He'd brought in the pair of SIG P250s and two sound suppressors that sat on the table. The gloss on the wooden table reflected dull images of the guns.

Kendra brought in a short sword and two daggers lined with runes. Either guns scared her or the runes had intrigued her. The runes sure intrigued me. As I looked at the markings on the two blades, I realized how little I knew about being a druid. The book hadn't yet mentioned runes. I tried to pull up a memory from Caradoc to tell me about the runes. How were they made? How do we use them? As usual, his memories fled the moment I reached for them.

"We all need some sleep. I'll take first watch," O'Brien offered as he finished loading the last clip.

I caught myself staring at the pink scars around his partially mutilated ear and the mostly healed cuts around it that still had stitches. The hair on the recently shaved spot above the ear had grown to partially cover the two small scars that I'd mistakenly thought were from Alexis's teeth. No way should he take first watch.

I spoke up. "Actually, I slept all day long, so I can take first watch. I won't be able to fall asleep right now anyway."

O'Brien nodded gratefully. He was too tired to stay awake. He caught my eyes and glanced at the two handguns and loaded clips on the table. A long hallway exiting to the left from the oversized front room had two bedrooms and a bath on each side before turning to stairs leading to the second floor. O'Brien took the first bedroom on the right.

"I'm next. Wake me up when you need me," Mr. Espinoza instructed, then started hacking up a lung. He didn't look much better than O'Brien—terrible, actually. Driving half the night to Bear Lake had really done him in. I'd never seen Luiz's dad looking so worn down.

"¡Ay, no! Papá," Luiz cut in. "Wake me for next watch, Jacob."

"OK," I agreed.

"Do you want company?" Kendra asked. "I'm not tired, I slept in the car." I wanted to say yes, but it's hard to keep watch and focus on a girl at the same time. If we sat together alone at three in the morning, there was no way we wouldn't end up making out. A horror movie montage of all the couples who'd died while getting physical flashed through my mind.

"I couldn't do a good job keeping watch if you stayed up. Try to get some more sleep so you aren't grumpy tomorrow, OK?"

"Like I am ever grumpy!" she complained and walked over and took my hand. "I missed you." She leaned forward and gave me a quick kiss, which warmed me from my lips down while guilt rose from my gut up. "Don't pretend to die again, OK?" she added.

"OK. Next time, I won't pretend," I said solemnly.

"Hey!" She hit me in the arm. "That isn't what I meant."

I smiled at her. She didn't realize it, but I wasn't exactly joking. There was a good chance that I was going to die. There was a good chance she was going to die. We might be safe for a while, but how long could it last?

"Get some sleep!" I told Kendra.

Luiz and his dad both went upstairs.

"I'll leave you the close room, across from O'Brien," Kendra said. She strolled down the hallway in her pajama shorts and white camisole. No leather. No Christmas bow tattoo. She disappeared into the back right room.

I walked around the house, partly because the cabin was impressive and partly to keep watch.

After an hour, I grew restless. I read the druid text while keeping a magical grip around the cabin, alert for any nearby movement. I searched the text for defensive spells. The vampire protection stone had been useful, but some of the bad guys used bullets. Most of those assassinated on The Day of a Thousand Deaths had taken a bullet.

Was there a spell that could protect against bullets? I found one just a few pages after the magic missile spell—sort of. It was actually a spell to protect against "missiles," meaning arrows and such, not magic missiles. Not Mavericks, Sidewinders, or AMRAAMs, either. Yes, I'd played my share of fighter jet simulators. Anyway, in medieval times, arrows or anything launched from a catapult were called missiles. The book specifically mentioned crossbows, which proved that the book was outdated.

The spell involved enchanting clothes to prevent arrows from penetrating the cloth. It worked differently from the healing stone and the protection stone. Blocking a vampire's allure didn't take much magical energy, similar to a containment. Healing didn't use much either. It simply enabled the cells to reproduce at a rapid pace. The real energy came from food and body fat. Also, those stones used magic constantly. Stopping an arrow—or a bullet—needed far more energy, but only at impact. It also needed a separate power source so the blanket didn't shred.

Which took more energy to stop? A bullet or an arrow? A bullet moved at well over a thousand feet per second, depending on the weapon, but it had less mass than an arrow and wasn't as sharp.

The book suggested using pebbles for the spell's power source. I wondered why not a crystal at first until I read on. The particles of the pebble would provide enough energy to stop a single strike of a crossbow bolt. Most of the pebble would dissolve. I hoped the speed-to-mass ratio worked out so that a pebble still worked to stop a bullet.

Outside, I found gravel under the boat and filled a pocket. I tested it on a blanket against the wall first. I hung the blanket using thumbtacks from an unused bulletin board in the kitchen.

I cast a containment as I didn't want to announce my location to the magical world. Then I enchanted the blanket to convert the mass of each rock to the magical energy needed to stop a bullet.

The enchantment was supposedly difficult. But it was a piece of cake compared to the two I'd cast previously. It involved brute-force magic and mass-to-energy conversion. Nothing intricate, which suited me.

I grabbed one of the handguns O'Brien had left for me while I kept watch. He'd attached a silencer, so I hoped it wouldn't wake anyone. I switched off the safety and fired. The blanket only rippled, but the bullet ricocheted loudly as if it had hit steel.

I ducked, covering my head. The bullet embedded itself into the ceiling, leaving a visible hole.

Oops. I glanced around, sheepishly. Why had I expected the bullet to just stop and fall to the floor? That's what would have happened in a movie. In real life, ricocheting made much more sense. I checked the rocks. One rock had broken, but only into a couple of pieces. Not all its mass had been converted into energy. That felt off to me, so I read the spell again. It said the pebbles only had to be the size of a small button. The gravel stones were about ten times that size. A slight grin lifted the corners of my mouth. I couldn't carry around an unlimited amount of gravel stones, but I could pack enough to keep a few bullets from ripping through my flesh.

I worked on some improvements to the spell for a few hours until I took a break to watch the sunrise over Bear Lake. The world seemed at peace, completely at odds with our front room, which we'd littered with weapons to defend ourselves from the inevitable.

CHAPTER 39
NIGHTMARE

When I woke Luiz at nine, the sun had risen high enough to brighten and warm the day. Everyone else still slept. It had been a long night. The smell of the coffee Luiz brewed would likely wake the rest of them—especially O'Brien. I slipped into the first room on the left. I'd sleep for only four hours, and I didn't want to bring attention to that fact. If this many people hung around long-term, they would start to notice—unless I faked it and hid in my room some of the night.

I got into bed with my clothes on and fell asleep right away.

Alexis and I drove to the druid's grove. We started out in the car, but when we arrived, I was on the back of her motorcycle. She wore the bustier with laces up the front, showing a lot of skin even though my dream started in the daytime. But after stepping into the druid's grove, it became night.

We laughed together until we connected magically. We needed to cast some spell together, but try as we might, we couldn't make it work, even connected.

We forgot about the spell. We spent hours searching through each other's minds. We searched and learned new things about each other, then kissed and talked about what we had learned. Eventually, I found the dark, closed-off portion of her mind. I tried to talk to her about it, but she wouldn't tell me what was in there.

A memory slipped out, and my dream changed.

Alexis—perhaps only sixteen then—stood in a dark room, though she could see with far more clarity than average eyes could. The humid air dampened the stone walls. Mold grew in the mortar. Human feces stained the floor. Alexis scrunched her nose.

Shadowy figures hung from chains on the far wall. As she approached, the figures took shape. A man, woman, and three children, all Latino. They'd been stripped of their clothes and from their filth and the sores at their chained wrists, it was clear they'd been imprisoned for days.

The boy was only eight, but looked like the man. The girls were ages four and two. They were a family.

Alexis's grandfather had forced her to travel with him to Ecuador. The man had been a priest. A local vampire had sucked several of his parishioners dry, so he went all vigilante on the leech and took the liberty of removing his head.

A robed figure set a candle in a metal ring on the wall and then left.

The Vampire King stood behind Alexis, his eyes black. I recognized his white hair, pale face, and tall figure from Alexis's memories. He could not let the death of one of his vampire children go unpunished.

"Your mother has not trained you properly," the Vampire King told his granddaughter. "I brought you, Alexis, because I have decided to provide some personal tutelage."

Alexis glanced over her shoulder at her grandfather, and he bared his fangs in a wicked grin.

"Feed on the woman first. Then the children in order of age," he commanded. "I want him to see his family leave this world in the order they came into it."

Alexis fought her grandfather's control. She withstood it until he lifted his hands and gripped her bare shoulders.

He stripped her self-control away. The power of her grandfather's touch controlled her just as Alexis's hands on my cheeks had controlled me. She wished she had fed recently. After feeding, she could withstand his control. Almost.

Alexis could feel the power in him, vast and never-ending.

All emotion faded from Alexis as she turned toward the family. Her grandfather compelled her, and she would obey.

The family screamed and quivered, eyes wide as she approached. She placed a hand on the mother's cheek. The mother's face relaxed and her crying and quivering stopped.

The father cried out, then said something to his children that I couldn't quite translate. The children closed their eyes.

Without being asked, the mother tossed her hair to one side, exposing her slender neck. Her carotid artery bulged, as if swollen with blood in anticipation. Alexis's fangs extended, and she lowered her mouth to the pulsing artery. Her fangs pierced the mother's skin. Alexis pressed her lips tightly against the woman's neck as if giving her a sensual kiss. Alexis's pleasure surged as blood rushed into her mouth.

Tears poured down the husband's cheeks. It seemed impossible, but he found the courage to steady his voice enough to urge his children to keep their eyes closed.

Alexis grew strong as she fed. Feeding from the woman took time. Except "feeding" was the wrong word. The stomach was not involved. Alexis breathed the blood into her lungs and it transferred like air directly into her veins, which expanded to hold the excess blood. She held the woman up long after she would have collapsed. Alexis did not tire. Instead, the blood invigorated her. It flowed into her muscles and as they swelled, she could feel the increased tightness of her clothes. After long minutes, she released the woman's pale, empty corpse, but the chains kept her from collapsing to the ground.

Alexis moved to the eight-year-old boy. The father cried for mercy, and the boy screamed at the top of his lungs until she touched his cheek. Then he, like his mother, went still. His little body emptied and collapsed so much faster than his mother's. The other two children screamed furiously, their eyes no longer closed.

The father could bear no more and turned his head away sobbing out a frantic prayer through short uncontrolled breaths. His arm stretched up to the chains as he slumped in emotional agony.

Alexis moved to the four-year-old girl. She also stopped screaming at her touch and dropped to the floor lifelessly, more quickly than the brother had.

With every part of her body swelling with blood, Alexis felt her power surge. Her body held so much blood that her lungs remained full and she didn't need to breathe. Still, she craved more blood but her self-control flared to life. She stepped in front of the two-year-old and looked into her innocent brown eyes. Alexis moved the little girl's dark hair from her cheek then glanced back over her shoulder at her grandfather in defiance. Her eyes went black and she snarled, flashing her blood-stained fangs.

The dream shifted again.

Alexis and I sat on the couch in the cabin at Bear Lake. We connected our minds with magic. The pride she felt at never having killed a single person by feeding emanated strongly from her mind. It was her most guarded secret.

"How can you feel this way when you killed every member of that family?" I asked. She looked at me with her red, apologetic eyes but didn't answer. The Vampire King appeared behind her. He walked up and put his hands on her bare shoulders.

As if they'd been in my dream all along, Kendra, my sister, O'Brien, and Luiz all appeared, sitting around the couches arranged in a rectangle.

"Feed on them all," her grandfather commanded.

Alexis stood and stepped toward Kendra, who now hung from chains. I tried to convince Alexis to stop, but she didn't. Alexis moved aside Kendra's golden brown hair and touched her face. As I had done, Kendra begged Alexis to take her blood. When I protested, Alexis snarled her canines at me before she bit down on Kendra. She didn't stop. She drained her completely and tossed her lifeless body away. The chains caught her pale and empty corpse, and she hung from them, just as the Latina woman had.

Alexis then drained my sister, Luiz, and O'Brien, one by one, until it was my turn.

"I love you, Lexy," I said.

She looked at me with a small smile. "I love you too."

Her hands came forward and touched my cheeks. At once, I became hers. I looked into her blood red eyes.

"Please," I whispered. Only I wasn't begging for her to let me live. I was begging her to drink my life-blood as I exposed my own neck.

She looked at her grandfather, her eyes turning black in defiance. She flashed her canines at him. Would she overcome his control and fight him? She turned back to me with black eyes patterned with red lightning streaks.

Then she bit me.

CHAPTER 40
LIES

I woke up sweating and crying. Yes, crying. I managed not to scream, though. At least nobody came running into my room to check on me, so I assumed I hadn't screamed. I remembered the nightmare—well, Alexis's memory from Ecuador had been real.

I shivered uncontrollably, sick at what she had done. I had kissed the same mouth that had drained that mother and those children dry—likely the father too. My stomach twisted. If I hadn't gone without food since dinner the night before, I might have thrown up for the first time in my life.

Was it only last night that Alexis had betrayed me, taking the black diamond? O'Brien still needed that healing and protection stone. As I sat up in bed, my chest burned and my muscles flexed in rage at her. Which angered me more: that she lied about having never killed or that she left me? After the days we spent together, I had expected it to end differently. Or maybe I had just expected it not to end. I didn't know.

I slipped out of bed, breathing deeply and consciously calming my tense muscles. Pumpkin spice filled my first deep breath, causing me to cut it short. When I breathed again, the aroma was gone. Perhaps connecting to her had done something to me. Would I ever be the same again?

A nervous guilt rose up from my gut. Alexis and I had kissed—twice. What would Kendra say when she found out? Would she be hurt? Would she be angry? Of course, she'd be both. Would I lose her? I had already lost her once and that had hurt. I had also lost Alexis. Her betrayal hurt more.

I shook off the queasiness of the dream and walked into the bathroom. I stripped down and basked in the shower's warm water, wishing it could also wash away the vile dream. The magical energy flowing over my body couldn't wash it away either. I stayed in the shower until the water temperature dropped.

I got dressed and left my room.

Luiz, his dad, and Kendra sat in the kitchen around a simple pine dining table. I didn't see O'Brien. Kendra held a long knife and was fingering the runes, her eyes wide.

"Good morning," I said.

"You mean good afternoon." Kendra smiled, setting the blade down and glancing at a clock on the oven. It was after three o'clock. Had I slept six hours? I had used a lot of magic. Supposedly, that makes druids sleep longer. Or the disturbing dream had ruined my sleep.

"Where's O'Brien?" I asked.

"He went to town for supplies," Luiz responded.

"He's bringing raspberries," Kendra squealed and tapped her fingers together.

"Why would he bring raspberries?" I asked.

Luiz smiled. His eyes moved from me to Kendra. I thought I detected a hint of jealousy.

"We come here every year for Raspberry Days. It's often the same week as my birthday," Kendra answered, her voice soft and her eyes looking up and left, obviously enjoying her memories.

"What's Raspberry Days?" I asked.

She smiled like she'd been dying for me to ask.

"It's a city festival to celebrate the raspberry harvest. They have raspberry ice cream, raspberry pies, raspberry shakes. They have raspberry everything around here. There are also rodeos and parades and all kinds of activities. I've never celebrated my birthday anywhere else," she finished, happiness glistening behind her lashes as she blinked.

I didn't tell her that she'd never do that again. Why ruin her mood? I'd wait and let O'Brien do that. She only thought she was in danger because she was my girlfriend. She still had no idea I was a druid. Worse, she had no idea *she* was a druid. We hadn't had that talk yet. A talk wasn't what she needed anyway. O'Brien had Dumbledored me into figuring it out on my own. Trouble was, I wasn't sure how to get Kendra to figure it out on her own.

"So, no raspberries yet. Is there anything to eat?" I asked, obeying my growling stomach. I hadn't eaten since dinner the previous evening. I should have grabbed something at Walmart or a late-night drive-thru, but my mind had been too busy whirling.

"There's cereal but no *leche*," Luiz responded, glancing down his long nose at the cupboard.

"Darn. *Me gusta leche*," I replied with a horrible gringo accent. Luiz unleashed a loud laugh. My Spanish accent always cracked him up. His dad laughed too, but then started coughing. He'd hacked a lung out the night before, so why not hack out the other one?

I opened the cupboard, and to my surprise, found a box of Frosted Flakes—my favorite cereal. Who said everything was all bad luck all the time? Something about finding my favorite cereal, the only food item in the cupboards, in this Bear Lake cabin, made me feel remembered. Like maybe God was watching out for me. I lost myself in the box of cereal, and before I knew it, it was gone.

I threw the box away. I looked at Kendra. She'd picked up the knife again and was back to tracing the runes with the tips of her fingers. Magic visibly jumped from the runes into her fingertips—at least it was visible for me.

How was I going to Dumbledore her into realizing she was a druid? Then how was I supposed to tell her that some unknown society wanted her dead? I'd barely come to terms with it myself. Who was I kidding? I hadn't even come to terms with it yet.

Kendra stared at me. Wait. Were they all staring at me? I had eaten in silence and hadn't realized they had stopped talking and were waiting . . .

Oh.

They wanted me to start talking. They were being polite by not coming right out and asking me while eating, but now that I'd finished, their patience appeared to be waning. The scene looked rehearsed. Of course, now that I was looking at them . . .

"So, what is really going on?" Luiz asked.

All three of them eyed me expectantly.

"We should talk when O'Brien gets back," I said, not caring if I disappointed them for a little longer.

For the next hour, nobody managed a real conversation. I was grateful when the hum of the garage door came through the kitchen wall. O'Brien had taken Mr. Espinoza's car. Maybe he had decided a Hyundai Sonata would be less conspicuous than a BMW. And what if he got pulled over and they checked the trunk? O'Brien opened the garage door and stumbled in with grocery bags hanging from his arms. Luiz and I ran to help him, grabbing milk and a bag of frozen pizzas. We went out to the car and brought in the rest.

O'Brien looked much better than yesterday. After a shopping trip, he should have been tired, but he didn't collapse into a chair. His mangled ear and the scars surrounding it still attracted my eyes with a morbid desire to stare, but he moved with energy. How was he still healing so quickly without the healing stone? If I didn't know better, I would have sworn he'd worn it overnight. Did wearing the healing stone have effects that lasted after taking it off? Maybe it worked on his whole body, organs, blood flow, and more. Could that be it?

As we finished putting the groceries away, O'Brien told everyone to gather around the table. They complied obediently, anxious to finally get some answers.

Looking at the group, I was reminded of how strange it was that everyone had done what I asked last night. I'd had the same thought last night. It seemed even stranger in the light of day.

Why had Luiz and his father jumped to help me last night? Why had Kendra's parents just let her come so easily?

I didn't have answers to those questions. But they felt important, like my friends already knew something that I didn't. Of course, they knew I had faked my death. I had told them someone was trying to kill me and that Kendra was in danger. Had they simply believed? Had hearing my voice been enough for them? Dylan had sure been harder to convince. He heard my voice too, and even after he saw me, he thought I was crazy.

O'Brien seemed to be the only one who belonged here.

"Mr. Espinoza, Luiz," the ex-Marine focused on them, "this involves only Jacob and Kendra. Your help has been welcome. I regret that I was not recovered enough to avoid involving you." His words were oddly formal. "If you stay, those who are after us will not hesitate to kill you." He let that sink in. "Your presence actually makes the situation more difficult because I'll be spread too thin defending you two. Protecting Jacob and Kendra will be difficult enough. Jacob and I have barely . . . Like I said; it will be difficult enough as it is."

"What are you saying?" Mr. Espinoza cut in with frustration.

"I would like you to consider going home."

"No way!" Luiz shouted.

Mr. Espinoza remained calm and put his hand on his son. His eyes locked onto mine as if telling me to listen well. "I am willing to die to protect Jacob and Kendra," he said, his conviction evident even through his Spanish accent. "My son and I prefer to remain here."

Luiz quickly agreed.

The sniper shrugged. "OK," he replied, agreeing too easily.

I gaped at him.

"Tell me what you already know," O'Brien ordered flatly.

Mr. Espinoza nodded to Luiz.

"I was there when Jacob was shot in the leg," Luiz began. "It was weird from the start because the ambulance was on its way before he was shot. It didn't make sense. Then he died that night while I was in the waiting room.

"But Kendra kept saying he wasn't dead. She said they kept her from seeing him, and she never saw him die. Then the hospital couldn't find his body. Nobody could. But I didn't believe her until I got a call from Jacob that he needed us to get Kendra to safety because *someone* was coming after her to get to him."

Everything Luiz said was true. I had forgotten he had been right there when I was shot. I hadn't even considered that. That felt like a lifetime ago. It actually explained why Luiz would have jumped to help me when I called. But it didn't explain everything. It didn't explain why his father helped, why he went so far as to borrow a friend's cabin, or why Kendra's parents just let her go with them in the middle of the night.

"You mentioned drug dealers on the phone," O'Brien added, glancing at Luiz's father.

"Perhaps I wasn't clear," Mr. Espinoza replied. "I didn't mean that I know anything about who might be threatening Jacob, but I have had experience with bad people. I had to . . ." He paused and his lips pursed as if he were reliving the memory. "I killed a man in self-defense."

That was news to me. I didn't know Mr. Espinoza very well. He was in his early sixties, though Luiz's mom was only thirty-eight. He was amazing at chess—one of the best tournament chess players Mexico had ever had. According to Luiz, when his dad was in his early twenties, he had beaten the world number one chess master, who was vacationing in Cancun. I'd heard he grew up in a dangerous neighborhood, but to have killed a man? I wanted to ask Mr. Espinoza to elaborate on his story, but O'Brien moved on.

"What else?" O'Brien asked.

"*Nada*," Luiz responded.

"There must be something more. What else?" O'Brien pressed harder. Something felt off. Did he feel it too? He looked each of them in the eyes as if demanding they share more.

"I've known for a while that Jacob is different," Luiz finally spoke up again, eyes darting to me and then the floor.

O'Brien glanced at me questioningly. I shook my head. I hadn't told Luiz anything.

"Different how?" O'Brien asked.

"He's a freak of nature," Luiz added. "He works out and just gets stronger, and he never feels sore, and he never gets tired."

"He never gets tired?" O'Brien glanced at me as if just realizing something.

"I've never even seen him yawn," Luiz admitted.

Whoa! My eyes widened. I've always known I was a freak, but I hadn't known that about myself. I had never even thought of it. Luiz was right, I had never yawned. O'Brien eyed me with a raised eyebrow and new interest, surprised by the information.

"Is that *all?*" O'Brien asked, staring into Luiz like he should have more to say.

"It's *your* turn, *amigo,*" Luiz shot back. "You tell us what is going on!"

O'Brien didn't respond. What did he plan to tell them? He looked at me. "Jacob, can I talk to you in the other room for a moment?"

I nodded. The others should have looked annoyed as we walked away, but they didn't. Weird.

When we were alone, he said, "Why don't you ask Kendra to go for a walk? See if you can get her to use magic. Inside, the house's threshold will hide simple spells, but outside, any spell will be like a beacon, so create a containment. We can't tell your friends about magic, Jacob. I am going to tell them you witnessed a drug exchange while jogging and didn't even know it. I'm going to pretend to be a witness protection agent from the FBI working with the DEA. Same story that worked on you."

His FBI lie *had* worked on me. I felt foolish for having fallen for it. Would it work on Mr. Espinoza? After the hard life he'd lived? He had real history that I guessed Luiz didn't even know about.

"OK, but how am I supposed to let Kendra in on the real world?" Calling this new world of magic and druids and monsters the *real world* sounded funny.

"Get her to figure it out on her own," he told me. "Then spill once she is ready."

"You want me to Dumbledore her like you did to me," I concluded.

"What?" he asked, confused.

"Sorry. You need a My Little Pony reference," I grinned. "I'll *Friendship-is-Magic* her," I teased.

He tried not to react but he couldn't hide the bulging vein on his left temple.

I turned to leave, but he grabbed my arm and pulled me back to say one more thing.

"Later, we're going to have a chat about some things you've been keeping from me. Like never getting sore and never getting tired. I always knew there was more to your story than Caradoc was sharing with me." He released my arm.

I breathed deeply then nodded. In a recent dream, my biological father had said: "Even for a druid you are a freak." O'Brien clearly agreed. I could read it in his eyes, which examined me as if I were going to morph into some alien creature the second he looked away.

"Now go ask Kendra to take a walk with you."

We walked back into the room and executed our plan. O'Brien sat down with Luiz and his dad to lie to them and I asked Kendra to take a walk with me so I could tell her the truth.

I thought O'Brien and I were hiding the truth to protect them. I had it all wrong. Everyone else knew the truth, and it was me they were lying to.

CHAPTER 41
SIGHT

Bear Lake is over a hundred square miles of fresh blue water surrounded by hills. The cabin sat on one of those hills about a mile from the lake. The view from the hill couldn't be ignored, even with so many worries on my mind. A few clouds hung in the sky as if enjoying their solitude in the vast blue heavens. Trees were sparse, but where they grew, they clustered together, surrounded by bushes.

Kendra took my hand, which I didn't expect, but it felt good. At least it felt good on my hand. My gut felt guilty. Should I tell her about Alexis? No. Breaking the news that she was a druid would be hard enough without making her angry first.

A cluster of trees stood between two empty lots and a hill of bushes. I led Kendra toward it. It was nothing like the druid grove, but it was a bit of coverage anyway.

"You don't seem too mad at me," I mentioned to Kendra. "You know, for putting you through . . . everything."

"Like having to go to your funeral?" she replied. She tugged at my arm so I'd stop walking and so her blue eyes could focus on my brown ones. "You were there, weren't you?"

"Yes," I confessed.

"You wore a disguise, but I recognized you." She smiled and we started walking again.

"How do you think you recognized me?" I hadn't expected the topic to involve magic so quickly.

"I don't know," she shrugged.

"When you caught me looking at you, what happened?"

"I don't know. I just looked at you and knew. Well, I suspected it was you."

She glanced at me as we walked off the road onto a trail between the sagebrush. Her modest light blue blouse hugged her figure. Her jeans fit just right too. Her golden brown hair fell straight down, framing her smiling face. She wore leather sandals. Little flowers decorated the red polish on her big toes. She was a different kind of beautiful than I had been around recently.

"But how did you just know?" I pressed.

"I just did."

"Yes, but did you *just know* because you felt . . . something?"

"What do you mean?" She gave me a sideways look like I was weird.

She wasn't getting there on her own. Had she ever noticed when she used magic? Maybe magic was as subtle for her as a change in emotion. Why was I already worried she wasn't getting it? We'd only been outside one minute. To get me to figure out I was a druid, O'Brien had followed me for days, shot me in the leg, faked my death, and pretended to be FBI. He hadn't done that in one minute.

We entered the cluster of trees just as a small breeze fluttered through, causing the thousands of leaves to wave at us as if welcoming us inside their cover. The breeze continued for a dozen seconds before settling to a barely perceptible movement.

"I felt something when you looked at me," I told her.

"You did?" She smiled back at me softly.

"Yes, it was the same as when you kissed me."

Her smile widened and she beamed back at me. She was thinking of emotions, not magic.

"Kendra, do something for me. Close your eyes and concentrate on me. Tell me what you feel."

She looked at me, and her cheeks flushed.

"You really want me to close my eyes?" She blinked her long lashes at me.

"Yes," I nodded.

"Fine." She closed her eyes and placed a hand over them.

I wrapped the cluster of trees in a containment, using the trees as markers for its boundaries. While holding Kendra's hand, I reached for the energy around me.

Containment magic is simple and doesn't take much energy and doesn't ripple out. There is no way another magic user wouldn't sense it while holding hands with the caster. It worked. Kendra's body trembled in a slight wave that made her push her shoulders back. I was about to ask if she felt that when she spoke.

"I'm waiting." She peeked with one eye between spread fingers.

"You didn't just feel that?" I complained.

"Feel what?" She removed her hand and opened her eyes.

I sighed. It hadn't worked as I had expected. Maybe I should try something else. The high bushes under the thin-trunked quakies gave me an idea.

"Let's play a game," I told her. "I am going to hide, and I want you to do the same thing you did when you saw me at the funeral. See if you can use that to find me without looking. Like hide and seek, only keep your eyes closed after you count to ten."

"That's silly."

"Just play along. Please," I pleaded.

"OK." She laughed a little as she closed her eyes again. "You want me to count to ten?"

"Yes. Slowly."

"Fine. One . . . two . . . three . . ."

I quietly hid, choosing a bush that wasn't obviously the largest one but would conceal me if I squatted down.

". . . nine . . . and ten. Ready or not, here I come," she laughed. "Uh oh, I opened my eyes."

I wanted to tell her to keep them closed, but then she'd know where I was, making this silly effort pointless. I felt stupid. I was trying to Dumbledore her like O'Brien had done to me, but this just felt cheesy. If someone were watching, they'd be making jokes about how Kendra and I made them nauseous.

Then magic rippled inside the containment. The emotional rope flared to life, leading directly from Kendra to me. She turned, eyes closed again, and pointed directly at me. Good thing I still had a containment around us.

She opened her eyes and stepped closer.

"Found you," she said. I stood up in front of her. She blinked like she knew something just happened that she couldn't quite explain.

"Did you feel that?" I asked. "Like a rope pulling between us."

"Yes, I . . ." she started. "A rope?" I could see her mind working through her eyes. "I guess that is what I felt."

Well, maybe cheesy worked with Kendra.

"That is—" I started to say.

"Love?" she interrupted.

Oh, no! I was so not prepared for her to drop that word. Maybe cheesy wasn't working. What do I say to that? If I said yes, I was practically saying "I love you," and if I said no, I was saying "I don't love you." This was *not* going how I had planned. Her blue eyes gazed into mine expectantly.

"Uh . . ." I stammered.

She looked down at her feet, no longer willing to look me in the eyes. My reaction was not exactly what a girl hopes for when she drops the word "love" for the first time.

Was I in love with Kendra? Maybe. I had known her as my sister's best friend for years and I'd had a secret crush on her for months. A crush that I hadn't even admitted to myself until that night at Kevin's house when Sis told me she was fair game.

But since then, my life had changed drastically—much more than Kendra's had. Sure, she'd become a druid too, but she hadn't been shot. Everyone didn't think she was dead. She hadn't faced transients, nightwalkers, and vampires. Most importantly, she hadn't met Alexis. I gulped and looked down at my feet too.

"Look, Kendra," I started. "I'm sorry. There is too much going on right now. I . . ." What could I say? I needed to change the subject. "There are other . . . more important things . . ."

Kendra glanced up and back down. I shouldn't have used the words "more important."

I gave up. Forget Dumbledoring her and forget this cheesy crap.

"Kendra, you used magic," I told her bluntly.

"Magic?" She lifted her face to mine, eyes wide and questioning. "Jake, what are you talking about?"

"I'm talking about magic! See?" I stretched out both my hands with the palms up. "*Fyr leoht!*" Flame flickered to light, rising a foot high from each palm. At the same time, I pushed a wave of energy toward Kendra that she certainly would feel. She flinched at the flames. As she tried to step back from the wave of magic, her foot caught on the rising terrain, causing her to trip. She'd had one hand in her pocket, and the other reached back to stop her fall but caught on a sagebrush. She went down and hit her head on the ground. The sticks, leaves, and dirt hadn't provided much padding.

Oops. That wasn't exactly the reaction I had expected. I dropped the spell and hurried over to help her up.

"I'm sorry. Are you all right?" I asked. "Can I help you up?" I offered her my hand. Her hesitation reminded me of how Sis had pulled away and refused to look at me last night. I worried Kendra would react the same way, but after taking a breath, she reached out and took my hand, letting me pull her up.

She had dirt and sticks down the back of her jeans. I went to brush them off, but she arm-barred my hand and pushed it away.

"I've got it." She gave me a stern keep-your-hands-to-yourself look.

OK, I guess I was about to put my hand where it didn't belong, but I really had just intended to brush the dirt and leaves off. Instead, she brushed her pants off herself, looking over her shoulder to see if she got it all. I reached for a small stick in her hair and she pulled away slightly, but then begrudgingly let me remove it.

"Is your head OK?"

"I'm fine. The ground was soft." She pursed her lips. "Jacob, what just happened?" Kendra demanded.

"You know what happened." I nodded at her. "Magic."

She opened her eyes wide at me.

"Just close your eyes and feel it."

"I'm not playing that game again," she shot back.

"Right, this isn't that game," I explained. "Close your eyes and just try to feel."

"Fine." She pursed her lips before closing her eyes again.

"Kendra, you used magic on me when we kissed—"

"I did not," she cut me off, opening her eyes.

"Keep your eyes closed," I ordered. "And you *did* too. You created something between us—a rope of emotions. You used magic again to revive that connection at the funeral and again just now . . ."

"I did not," she repeated.

"Yes, you did."

"I did not," she insisted emphatically.

I decided not to act like a five-year-old by saying "did too" one more time.

"Just feel this." I used my druid detection spell. I sent a clear, green-glowing tube of magic her way. It flowed into her and she shivered and opened her eyes.

"What was that?"

"Magic. And you did too use it." OK, maybe I would act five.

"Magic isn't real, Jake." She pursed her lips.

"Don't call it magic then. Call it what you want. Maybe it is just an energy source like electricity that science hasn't discovered yet," I responded. "But we both can use it."

I kept the energy flowing into her so she wouldn't lose contact with it.

"Now close your eyes again. Take the energy I'm pushing into you and gently push back."

She closed her eyes on her own this time. That was a good sign.

"Can I touch it?" One hand reached forward. Her forearm had a deep scratch. Had the sagebrush scraped her when she fell? A drop of blood dripped down to her palm. I glanced around nervously. If a vampire were nearby . . . but the sun still ruled the sky, and except for Alexis, I didn't know anything dangerous that could walk around in the daytime.

"Not with your hand. Can you feel it with your . . . mind?" Mind wasn't the right word either but it was close enough.

"Yes," she said. "No, not my mind. My . . . my emotions."

"Push it away," I said again.

A few seconds passed before the energy stopped flowing into her. She was pushing back!

"Wow!" she cried out and rushed over to me and wrapped her arms around me. "That was amazing."

Her hug felt great. Her hair smelled like lavender. I let her hold me as long as she wanted.

"That's just the basics," I told her when she finally stepped back. "I want you to try something more. I'm going to show you how to turn your hand into a candle."

She squinted her eyes at me hesitantly. I pressed on.

"Don't worry. The spell to make fire is extremely easy," I told her. "Fire is just the result of putting a lot of energy in one place and the air will burn."

I explained the steps for casting *fyr leoht*. I told her how to gather magic in and how to focus it. I warned her against gathering too much. I told her she might need a lot of time to make it work.

"What does *fyr leoht* mean?"

"It means 'fire light' in Old English," I translated.

"Why Old English?" she asked. "Why not Latin or something?"

"I have no idea," I answered. I knew so little about the druid world. "Wait." I had an idea. I held out my palm.

"Fire light," I commanded, using the energy exactly like I would have when using Old English. A flame appeared in my palm. "I don't think the language matters." I held out my other hand, then concentrated on casting without the words. Hesitantly, a flame lifted from my hand, but it required extra concentration. "Words just help with concentration and speed." I knew what I wanted to have happen, and the words boxed up the steps. Just saying the words opened the box and made the steps happen. Without the words, I had to consciously think of each step.

I extinguished the flames and looked at Kendra.

"I'm going to teach you to cast fire light, OK?"

"OK." Her nod was barely perceptible.

I explained to her how she needed to relax and feel the magic and then cast her spell. She concentrated for some time. My first time, it had taken me hours to get a feel for magic and use it. She had used magic twice, so I had expected her to figure it out quickly, but she hadn't known she was using magic either time. She had used magic subconsciously as part of her feelings for me. She now had to consciously do it, and that was going to be different. I watched as she struggled to control magic.

"I feel the magic and I can . . . I can grab it, but I can't do anything with it," she explained.

Kendra wasn't using enough magic for me to really see the colors of it, so I couldn't see what she was doing wrong. I could feel it, but that wasn't enough. I tried to focus my eyes on the magic flows, as if willing them to open wider to see more. I pulled a small amount of magic into my eyes as if I had done it hundreds of times—except it hadn't been me who had done it a hundred times, it had been Caradoc. I wasn't ready for what happened. The world exploded into color and I could see everything—every fiber of energy in the life around me. My instincts had led me to a spell that allowed me to see more than the natural eye could.

Kendra stood in front of me, but with my new sight, she was no longer just Kendra. Her body was alive with white light inside her. Her face radiated—her hands and feet too. Like the shade of a lamp, her clothes dimmed her inner light. I gaped at the light of her spirit. Seeing her spirit seemed important to me. There was doubt in the world as to whether the spirit actually existed or whether there was just the body and the brain, but seeing Kendra's spirit proved that a person was more. Of course, I had already known spirits existed. I first had proof of the spirit when fighting the nightwalker. It had threatened both my body and my spirit, and I returned the favor, erasing both its body and spirit. When I was with Sis and Dylan, I'd annihilated the vampire and watched its spirit dissolve. My new sight just confirmed what I already knew. Perhaps it meant more because Kendra was special to me—not some creature dying from a magic missile.

With my new sight, the trees and bushes were the most vibrant greens and they had their own glow—their own spirits—that was nothing like Kendra's. Kendra was brighter than the trees, but the trees were bigger. Seeing the spirits of the foliage around me and how they flowed down their roots into the earth, I gained an understanding of why some believed that every living thing was connected to the earth—to Gaia, as it was often called—though I couldn't see Gaia or any evidence of a spirit belonging to the earth itself.

Kendra still struggled to bring fire light to life. But with this sight, I could see what she was doing wrong. She was supposed to be gathering magic and focusing the energy into heat in one small area above her palm, but that wasn't what she was doing. She could gather magic in, but she released it all around her. I explained to her what she was doing wrong, guiding her. Seeing every line of flowing magic made instructing her easier. Too bad following my suggestions wasn't easier for her. She would pull the magic in and focus it, and then she would say the words and it just wouldn't happen, but she was improving. Her attempts to focus the magic became stronger and stronger and more compressed into one place. She was so close.

"Fire light," she said, trying again.

Then it happened. A small flame, like that of a candle, flickered weakly to life in her hand. She opened her eyes and stared at it in awe.

I could barely see the fire in the kaleidoscope of colors that my new sight allowed, so I released my enhanced vision and everything returned to normal . . . well, a beautiful girl stood in front of me with a magic flame flickering above her hand. So maybe "normal" was the wrong word.

"I have felt this for a week. I didn't know it was magic," she confessed softly. Then she dropped the magic, and the flame faded out. She looked at me, and a moment passed between us. Her life had just changed drastically, and I was right next to her when it happened. It brought us closer. She hugged me again, this time caressing my neck. Then she jumped back, pushing me at arm's length.

"Jacob . . . I . . . need to tell you . . ." She stopped speaking. Her lips pursed and she appeared to be struggling internally.

"What?" I asked.

"There is . . . She . . . I'm sorry I can't tell you," her voice cracked and tears fell from her eyes.

She pulled me back into a hug, caressing my neck again. I could feel her palms on my skin. Her hair smelled of lavender, but this time, it also smelled like pumpkin spice—Alexis? I stiffened, but then it was gone. Only the lavender that normally accompanied Kendra's hair remained. I looked around anyway as I held her close, but it was just Kendra and me.

If Alexis were really here and close enough for her aroma to reach my nose, wouldn't I be able to see her?

Perhaps my nose confused the scents, I told myself. I felt like I was betraying Kendra by thinking of someone else during her hug, so I pushed all other thoughts away and focused on the girl who had her arms wrapped around my neck. I hugged back. She lifted her head and looked up at me with smiling eyes. I gulped again. I needed to tell Kendra about Alexis, but not yet.

"What were you trying to tell me?" I asked.

"So magic is real," she stated as much to herself as to me, ignoring my question. "What am I?" she asked. "A witch?"

"No," I told her, forgetting whatever it was she had been unable to share.

"Not a witch, then?" Her face beamed.

"Well, O'Brien says we're druids," I replied. "Does it matter?"

"It does if it means I won't turn green and grow hairy warts."

"Elphaba wasn't that bad. She was misunderstood."

"Oh, no! I am not Galinda, am I?"

"Not anymore," I said. "Remember, the 'Ga' is silent."

"Hey!" She hit my shoulder and we both laughed.

The sun was approaching the mountains, but we had some time. "I'll show you how to create a containment."

CHAPTER 42
NIGHTFALL

The trees' shadows had lengthened until the hill's shadow swallowed them. The sky surrendered its bright blue for a faded blue-gray as dusk neared. The approaching darkness made me uneasy. I didn't want to be outside with Kendra after dark. No, I wasn't afraid of the dark, just the creatures that come out in it. So far, O'Brien and I had vanquished a transient—I still didn't know what that was—a nightwalker, and two vampires—all creatures that could only come out at night. Of course, I'd also erased two gunmen, so the daylight wasn't exactly safe either.

"Let's get back," I said, hustling Kendra along.

We walked silently, so I considered what I'd taught Kendra. Recognizing the emotional rope. Fire light. Then containments, which she was a natural at—already better than me.

Teaching Kendra made me realize that I had no idea how magic really worked. There were rules I hadn't learned, nuances that would take years to discover. I had read most of the druid manual, but it hadn't answered all my questions. I had a chemistry question. If every atom could unleash the power of an atomic bomb, why did a full molecule, with multiple atoms, provide only enough energy to power the protection stone for a single second?

Kendra had asked me questions that I couldn't answer.

"Where does the magic come from?"

"I don't know," I answered.

"Why can we feel magic around us and others can't?"

"Why can somebody roll his tongue while someone else can't? Is it in our DNA? Is it something spiritual? Or something in our environment as we grew up?" I answered her with more questions. "I don't know."

"Are there fields of study in magic? Like in college?" she asked.

I shrugged.

She had stopped asking questions. Too bad the druid textbook didn't have the answers either. Did a more up-to-date druid manual exist? Did O'Brien have any answers?

Worse, nothing I taught Kendra offered her protection from the transients, nightwalkers, or vampires.

It only appeared to be dusk on our side of the lake because the sun had long since hidden behind the western hills. Across the water, the sun still illuminated the eastern hillside, reflecting beautifully off the massive, mirror-like lake. At any other time, Kendra and I might have been on a romantic walk, but instead, I spent the walk hoping that whoever—or whatever—was after us hadn't found us yet.

My uneasy feeling increased as we approached the door. Was something wrong?

I stopped at the cabin door and turned to Kendra. "Remember, we can't tell Luiz and his dad," I whispered to her. "O'Brien is making up a story for them, something to do with drug dealers."

She nodded.

I grabbed the doorknob and hesitated. Why did I just flex my stomach? And why was I holding my breath?

Pushing away my nerves, I opened the door and we walked inside. I expected to find everyone dead or captured. I expected blood. Instead, O'Brien, Luiz, and his dad sat talking on the couches at the far side of the oversized front room. Still, I didn't feel safe here. The feeling escalated beyond worry. My mind flashed back to the previous night when my sister and I were attacked in the parking lot. There was something about that fight that I couldn't really put my finger on. I let it go. Everyone was fine, right?

They stopped talking as we walked in. They must have been discussing the cover story O'Brien had shared with them. Since we were pretending I had taken Kendra for a walk to protect her from hearing what was going on, they'd clammed up so she wouldn't hear anything she wasn't supposed to. Except when they fell silent, they all looked at me—not Kendra—as if nervous that *I* might've overheard something. I must have just misread their looks.

I took a deep breath and could have sworn I inhaled a faint hint of pumpkin spice, but after stepping inside, the scent was gone. Kendra walked just in front of me. She stopped abruptly and my face ended up in her hair where I detected only her normal lavender shampoo. Why did my mind keep imagining Alexis's aroma? I didn't want to think of another girl while with Kendra.

Fortunately, another aroma made my stomach growl and took my mind off all things bad.

265

"Did you guys cook pizza?" I grinned.

"Yeah. We baked a pizza a while ago," Luiz said. "There's only a *pedazo* or two left but there's another pizza in the freezer."

"Sounds good." I smiled as I trekked across the family room and into the kitchen with Kendra in tow.

The chrome oven looked brand new. They'd turned it off but it still held a lot of heat. I turned up the heat to four hundred degrees. Kendra and I flirted, turning up the heat ourselves as we waited for the oven to heat and then for the pizza to cook. I cleaned up the blood from the scratch on her arm.

Twenty minutes later, the oven beeped. I don't know why I did it, but I opened the oven, used magic to keep the heat off my hand, similar to how Alexis had told me to cool myself, and reached for the pizza. The pizza sat on the oven rack with no pan. I carefully slid my hands under the pizza, palms up. I felt the metal of the oven rack on the back of my hands and the pizza crust on my palms. The heat poured into the magic, but not into my skin. I set the pizza on the granite counter and sat down on a stool.

"Oh, my heck," Kendra breathed, watching me.

"I'll have to teach you that." I decided against telling her it was the first time I'd done it. "Let's eat."

Supreme pizza wasn't my favorite, especially when it came from the freezer, but I didn't really care. I was more interested in the family-size quantity than the quality. Kendra sat on a stool next to me and only slid one slice on her plate. Alone, we ate and whispered about the possibilities of our magic. She only took one more slice. I ate the rest of the pizza and the last slice that the other guys had left over.

With our stomachs full, we went back into the double-sized family room where everyone still sat in the rectangle of couches and love seats.

"Luiz used my tablet to voice chat with Dylan and your sister," O'Brien told me, giving Luiz a scolding look. Mr. Espinoza held the tablet, playing a game of chess.

"Hey, I went through two separate proxy servers to get online," Luiz defended himself.

"But did they?" O'Brien snapped. Luiz looked down. Of course, O'Brien neglected to state the obvious—if Justine saw Luiz's request for a chat, then she was already online and logged in and nothing Luiz did or didn't do would have made a difference. They hadn't left their devices on airplane mode.

"You distract me," Mr. Espinoza commented in his thick accent and went into the kitchen.

266

"I'm going to watch my dad play chess," Luiz said as he followed his dad to the kitchen to avoid another reprimand.

"They drove south all night on I-15 and didn't get off until Anaheim," O'Brien informed me. "I suggested that they spend the day at Disneyland. Safest place on earth."

"Really? Why's that?" I asked.

"OK. It's not the safest, but it is close." O'Brien glanced at the kitchen, waved us closer to him and started whispering. "Walt Disney supposedly knew all about the druids. He had them surround Disneyland with one of the largest containments in the world, then place hundreds of smaller containments inside. It isn't a house but still has a threshold at the gates. It's difficult to do any nasty magic in there. Evil avoids it."

Wow.

"Wouldn't Disney World have a larger containment?" I whispered back, glancing at the kitchen.

"No, the druids involved went with a bunch of small ones at Disney World. Similar effect, but not quite as protected since they never got a threshold working."

"How do they power the containment?" I asked.

"They don't. People do. They just don't know it. I don't know much more. It happened long before my time."

"Checkmate," Mr. Espinoza yelled from the kitchen. He came back to the family room and handed the tablet to O'Brien. "Fork it over," he said with a thick Spanish accent.

"O'Brien bet *papá* he couldn't beat the computer," Luiz explained, his wide grin accentuating his long nose.

"No. I bet that he couldn't beat the computer at the highest level in less than eight minutes," O'Brien corrected. "I'm impressed." He pulled out two crisp fifty-dollar bills and handed them to Luiz's dad.

I caught a glance from Kendra to Luiz.

Luiz cut in, "How long are we going to hide out? Are we talking days or weeks? Kendra has drill team and I . . ." Luiz looked my way. "We have football practice starting soon."

O'Brien's face dropped. If he had an answer, he held it back.

Would we keep running forever? I had no hope of ever practicing football again, but what about Kendra? With drill team starting soon, what would she do? Luiz, Kendra, and I were also supposed to start school in just over a month. Luiz and his dad would go back for sure, but not me. Would Kendra go back? I wasn't sure. My answer was easy. I was supposedly dead and even though Teresa and her boyfriend had seen me, nobody would believe them if they claimed I was alive.

Kendra was another story though. If she just disappeared, she would be reported missing and become a permanent figure on milk cartons. When a girl like Kendra goes missing, it is big news. If she'd been last seen with Luiz and his dad, they would be blamed as kidnappers. Unless she went on the run with O'Brien and me, and we let a few people see us so the blame would go our way. Of course, then the truth of my supposed death would be outed.

Why had Kendra's parents just let her go with Luiz and his dad? Shouldn't they have wanted to protect her too? Something about this just didn't feel right.

Outside, behind the closed blinds, the darkness deepened. I breathed. *Nobody knows we're here.* But my unease escalated again. The nightwalker had found us. They'd found my sister. I would've been dead if I hadn't felt magic . . .

Oh, no!

I'd killed two men with rifles. I'd killed two vampires, neither of which could use magic. So, who had used magic? And why had that magic user remained hidden instead of attacking?

O'Brien sat in the love seat across from Kendra and me. He looked at his crystal beneath his shirt and flinched visibly in a way that reminded me of my mother, except my face wasn't the cause. After the flinch, his jaw tightened. It was the same look he had given me when he had decided to defend me to the death against the nightwalker. His warning stone lit up so bright that it glowed through his shirt. We had gone from being completely safe to inches from death in less than a second.

Evil rolled up and down my body, wiggling like larvae just below my skin. Nobody else in the family room noticed the warning stone's light. Kendra sat next to me in the love seat just chatting away about how she didn't want to be on a milk carton. Luiz, who sat on the couch with his dad, was telling her he'd make sure to look for her each time he ate at the school cafeteria. Mr. Espinoza appeared to be resting, not really listening. Maybe he was asleep.

A knock came to the door. That brought everyone to attention. I sucked in a quick breath and then stopped breathing.

"O'Brien?" Mr. Espinoza asked, suddenly alert. O'Brien nodded and Mr. Espinoza rose from the couch and walked around the card table and chairs to get the door.

What is he doing? Why is he opening the door?

I stood. "Wait," I tried to both whisper and shout.

Mr. Espinoza didn't stop or even acknowledge me. He acted all wrong. Everyone acted like this was a normal, everyday, run-of-the-mill visit. But O'Brien's warning stone and my writhing muscles screamed that we shouldn't open the door.

"Everything shall be OK." O'Brien looked at me with a blank expression I had never seen on his face before. It was obedience. It was the same blank expression I had often seen on the servants in Alexis's mansion.

"No!" I hissed between gritted teeth.

It disturbed and frustrated me that nobody listened to me. I grabbed as much magic as I could and prepared myself for what was coming through the door. Whatever it was, it wasn't going to come inside and hurt anyone. I formed a magic missile in front of my palms.

Mr. Espinoza opened the door.

CHAPTER 43
KING

Two figures in black stood on the dark porch, the light off. A tall man and a woman whose silhouette matched Alexis's enough to stop my breath. Vanilla and musk mingled and flooded the room.

"Come inside," Mr. Espinoza offered, holding the door open.

What the hell! Why had he so foolishly *invited* them inside? Was the whole never-invite-a-vampire-inside-your-house-myth true? I didn't have a freaking clue. True or not, inviting them in felt wrong.

Mr. Espinoza's face had O'Brien's same blank expression.

Oh.

Luiz's face: blank.

Kendra's: blank.

Oh, no. A harsher expletive left my tongue. A vampire had taken ownership of their minds.

How did they take control of them so fast?

The two black figures stepped inside and surveyed the room. The smaller figure walked like Alexis. Was it her? No, her face was a bit older. She was mostly dressed in all black, too, except her red earrings caught the light. Slits to her hips rose up both sides of her long black skirt—not leather. Spider outlines sewn with red thread crawled from the hem of her skirt to her mid-thighs. The taller man had perfectly white hair and pale skin. I recognized both of them from the memories I'd shared with Alexis. When Alexis had said her mother, Carina, was dead, she had left out that she'd turned. The man was the eight hundred-freaking-year-old Vampire King.

John Kaloyan held himself like a king. I'd never seen a king, but there was a power in his stance that had nothing to do with being a vampire. He knew how to be a king. He knew how to rule and control because he had done it for centuries. He had to be five inches taller than me. His cheeks had color as if he were blushing . . . or as if he had recently fed. His red irises looked painted with the blood of his latest victim. He wore the thick leather body armor of a military leader and a cape, one more like Batman's than a costume vampire's cape. It wrapped around his shoulders and flowed to the ground.

Did he plan to kill me or control me? I wasn't really excited about either. He'd used his control over Alexis to kill the priest's family in Ecuador. I would become his weapon of evil. I would help him feed. I would kill. I would be responsible for thousands of deaths over my lifetime. I wanted to cringe away from him and curl up into a ball until he left. John Kaloyan smiled at me as if he'd heard my thought. I preferred death.

I refused that fate. My heart raced and my adrenaline kicked in as I prepared to take advantage of the way he'd walked in so carelessly. I'd decided I wouldn't hesitate, and I hadn't. He couldn't run away in time. My spell was more accurate than a heat-seeking missile. I targeted the Vampire King. I poured more magic into the glowing orb than when I'd fought the nightwalker.

"*Bealustræl!*" I shouted, releasing the magic missile. My mind and body felt taxed as it left my palms, but I was stronger now. I wouldn't pass out.

Like a ball of lightning, the missile traveled over the card table and hit him in the chest. His smile turned to a grimace as the magic began to consume him. His chest lit up like a light bulb, and he staggered. His eyes went white and one hand grabbed at his throat—no, at a crystal that hung from a chain with a half-dozen others. I readied myself for the keen joy of decimating the body and soul of the Vampire King.

But abruptly, the light faded. John Kaloyan remained. He lifted his chin. His grimace became a smile, and the red returned to his eyes.

"He's as strong as your daughter promised," the Vampire King said to Carina. He had a strong voice, and when he spoke, he expected to be listened to. As one, the Vampire King and Carina began walking toward us. They passed the card table and stopped at the opening between the couch and love seat.

They looked at me.

"Be still, young druid," the Vampire King ordered.

Do not move! I heard the command as a voice in my head that sounded exactly like Alexis, but I assumed it was her mother.

The power of both commands overwhelmed me. I froze. I didn't even blink. I should've been protected from their power by my protection stone. I wanted to reach up and touch the crystal to make sure it was still there, but I couldn't move. However, I didn't need to move to feel the lack of the silver necklace and the absence of the ruby crystal.

When did I take off the protection stone?

I hadn't taken it off. I'd last seen it outside when I'd shown it to Kendra after helping her use magic. Seeing Kendra's vacant face out of the corner of my eye sent chills down my spine. Out in the trees, during our hug, she'd rubbed my neck. Dots connected in my head.

Had Kendra betrayed me like Alexis had?

Maybe it wasn't her fault. Kendra's face had gone blank before the door had even been opened. No vampire could inflict such control from outside the house. No. She had already been bewitched. Or be-vamped. Or whatever.

She had been under their influence since . . .

Oh.

No wonder her parents agreed to let her come so easily.

No way had Luiz and his dad convinced Kendra's parents to let their teenage daughter leave at midnight. That doesn't happen.

No wonder Luiz's dad insisted on coming. Luiz was my best friend, so it made sense he'd rush to my aid. His dad coming along never made sense. The Vampire King could have gotten to Luiz and his dad days ago. Had he guessed that, in a desperate moment, I would turn to my best friend? Had Luiz and his dad been under his control before I tried to contact him?

There is much you do not understand and much I cannot tell you. Alexis's words rang in my mind as if she had just spoken them again. They were never truer than now. I should have seen it. I should have been more aware of what was going on around me. I was losing. It was like I was playing chess against Luiz and he knew my every move before I made it until finally: checkmate.

My reality came crashing down on me. What about Kendra? Had she really forgiven me so easily for faking my death and putting her through my funeral? Or had she just played it cool to get close to me so she could steal my protection stone? Was all of it part of the Vampire King's plan?

I fought back against the control that held me immobile. It wasn't just their vampiness that had me, either; he and Carina could use magic, too. Most of the magic emanated from the Vampire King. He could use more magic than I could, and *I* was supposedly a freaking heavyweight. Carina's magical presence felt the same as what I had felt the previous night a second before someone shot at my head.

I still had control of my own mind, which gave me hope. Of course, my hope took a hit when others walked in behind John and Carina. First came two men and then a woman. All three had eyes as blood red as the Vampire King's. The scents in the room became indistinguishable as too many aromas clashed.

Besnick. Artan. Ivana.

Their names popped into my head as if they were spoken to me. Had I pulled them from Caradoc's memories? Maybe, but the voice in my head sounded like Alexis. Had the names come from her memories? The three vampires walked to the card table and stood around it. Besnick placed his pale hand on the table. His fingernails looked more like claws. I gulped but otherwise remained frozen in place.

After the vampires, an older couple entered—Darth Sidious and Darth Wife. I'd seen them enter my house the night before. They could have been anyone's grandparents except they carried staffs covered in runes, indicating their druid status. I'd heard that couples sometimes start to look alike with age, which was never truer than with this couple. Both had the exact same pattern of age spots on their skin. The only differences between the two were that the woman barely reached the man's chin and that her white hair extended to her waist, while his inch-high white hair stood up in a military fashion. I'd never seen anyone look so old who wasn't in a nursing home or a coffin.

I expected their names to pop into my head as the vampires' names had done, but nothing came to mind. They only took a few steps inside, just past Mr. Espinoza who still held the door open. With every other step, their staffs clacked against the wooden floor.

They're traitors, I thought. I swallowed hard. O'Brien had told me that some of the druids who had disappeared were likely alive and traitors who joined the genocide or worse: the instigators of the genocide.

Behind them, a shadow walked in. As the nightwalker stepped into the family room, the light dimmed, though it didn't go out. The light bulbs weren't putting out less light; the nightwalker's cloak and skin were consuming it. Only its gaping mouth remained visible under its hood. Its gray tongue slid along black teeth, demonstrating a hunger for flesh that I felt from across the room. The crawling under my skin increased and I had to fight to protect my mind. The obsidian-skinned shadow moved past the aged druid couple and the three vampires at the card table to stand behind Carina.

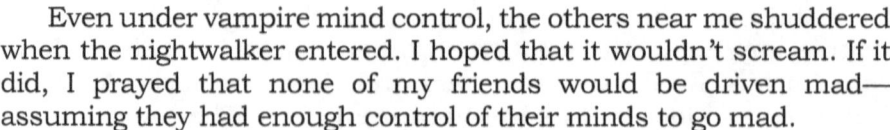

Even under vampire mind control, the others near me shuddered when the nightwalker entered. I hoped that it wouldn't scream. If it did, I prayed that none of my friends would be driven mad—assuming they had enough control of their minds to go mad.

For half a second, I thought the nightwalker would take charge, but it was clear that John Kaloyan was in charge. Except for the nightwalker, everyone looked to him and waited for his command. He had handled my magic missile with only a grimace as if I'd given him nothing more than a hard handshake. Everyone and everything seemed to be under his dominion. I had thought that nightwalkers were higher on the food chain and that I'd be able to defend myself against the Vampire King because I had erased a nightwalker. Yes, I'd been a little cocky and had no real idea of the worst things that existed in this world. Even now I couldn't even begin to fathom the extent of the Vampire King's power.

How do we get out of this alive? Nothing came to mind. I couldn't move. I couldn't cast a spell. I was nothing. I was insignificant. The Vampire King was everything.

"Charles," John Kaloyan called with a voice that demanded we listen. "I see you are alive. I find that very disappointing. I sent my best nightwalker to kill you. How unfortunate that it failed." He spoke dramatically, emphasizing every word clearly, just like Alexis. However, unlike her, he spoke with a trace of an accent. "You and Caradoc have eluded me for long enough. Where is Caradoc?" His eyes danced around the room. None of us answered.

He doesn't know what happened to Caradoc?

Alexis knew Caradoc had disappeared, so I expected that the Vampire King knew as well. Had Alexis kept this information from him? If so, why and how? If the Vampire King didn't have this knowledge, then he was fallible. Hope cracked its way into my trapped and motionless body.

"Where is he?" the Vampire King demanded, pushing power into his voice.

The desire to answer his question surged into me. I would've answered except a greater desire to remain silent overrode it.

O'Brien hesitated then spoke, his expression still blank. "I am not yours to command. You shall get no answers from me."

"It is true, then," the Vampire King surmised.

"Yes, *John*," O'Brien answered, emphasizing the Vampire King's first name.

Blackness pushed away the red in the Vampire King's eyes and his minions cringed at O'Brien's indignant use of his first name. An image of O'Brien's head being ripped off flooded into my mind, pushed there telepathically by the Vampire King's enraged impulse. But he did not act on it. His black eyes looked past O'Brien, scanning the room for someone else to unleash his wrath upon.

"I see." The Vampire King's eyes shifted toward the hallway. Suddenly, he darted unnaturally fast, stopping directly behind O'Brien. He grabbed the sniper's head with one hand and his shoulder with the other. I wanted to react, but frozen in place by an outside power, I could do nothing. Slowly, he tilted O'Brien's head to the side, exposing the sniper's neck. The Vampire King flashed his long fangs as he prepared to bite.

In those seconds, O'Brien did nothing. His face was no longer blank; it displayed contempt for the Vampire King, which made no sense.

If O'Brien was not under the king's control, then whose control was he under? Who else could have gotten to him? Who else could have gotten to Luiz and his dad and Kendra?

I guessed the answer just as a bedroom door opened. A lithe figure dressed all in black leather stepped out.

CHAPTER 44
ALEXIS

"Halt!" Alexis's voice rang through the oversized front room. She sauntered from the hall to face the Vampire King. She stared him down, unafraid and indifferent to how he held O'Brien's neck exposed. Her command, powered by her allure, pushed me. Since I was already frozen, the only thing left to halt was my breathing. So I stopped even that, desperately wanting to obey. Her grandfather stopped moving as well.

If I weren't frozen in place by her command, I would have run to Alexis and embraced her. My mind was not my own. It was hers. My chest burned with longing and betrayal—or maybe it just burned for air because I'd stopped breathing. I sucked in a much-needed breath, picking out Alexis's aroma from among the other strong vampire scents.

Alexis stood before me, as beautiful as ever, still in black but now dressed for war. Her usual bustier had been replaced by full-coverage body armor and two bandoliers crossed over her chest. A weapons belt decorated her waist. A handgun and a rune-covered blade hung from each hip, and a short sword was strapped to her back.

"These are mine." She waved her hand at us. "They obey me." She spoke with authority.

Even the Vampire King blinked at her allure.

Hope returned to me. She planned to save us. Logic suggested I let them fight and kill each other. Then I could finish off whichever remained alive. Unfortunately, that wasn't an option. We were her pawns, and if she fought, so did we. No, Alexis had betrayed me. She'd manipulated my friends. Despite the control she had over me, I imagined separating her head from her body. Even better, my addictive desire urged me to break her control and erase her.

"One so young cannot control so many," Alexis's grandfather said, as if she were still a child. "Especially one who will not feed."

"Even still, they are mine," she insisted. "And by vampire law, you are forbidden to feed on them without my permission."

"Granddaughter, you are weak." He said it like a command. "Permit me to feed," he ordered. His words dripped with vampire influence, his musky scent rising to dominate the room. Still holding O'Brien's neck exposed, he slid his tongue from one protruding fang to the other. He expected her to acquiesce.

If he'd directed his order at me, I would have begged him to feed on O'Brien. I wouldn't have stopped there, either. I would have let him feed on me and Kendra and anyone in the room—worse, I would have thanked him for it. I shoved against his influence, fighting to return to my senses. This time, it worked. His commands and allure failed to stick to me as if . . . as if the Vampire King couldn't control me because Alexis already did.

A mind cannot have two masters.

Alexis had taken control of me the moment her hands had cupped my cheeks. The protection stone had blocked her control but hadn't removed it, leaving it there, dormant at the edge of my mind where Alexis could restore it the moment the crystal left me. I hadn't noticed because Alexis hadn't used it. Until now. I could think clearly for one reason and one reason only: Alexis allowed me to—no, she wanted me to.

"I am *not* weak, grandfather." Alexis's demeanor switched to that of a ferocious mother protecting her offspring. "I have grown tall, beautiful, and powerful." Her voice quieted with those last words. She smiled a smile that pulled on the emotions of everyone in the room—including those that followed her grandfather. Only the nightwalker seemed unaffected.

My usual overprotective compulsion formed in my chest, directing itself at Alexis.

But she betrayed me! She only wants to control me. I need to erase her. I glanced around the room at the other vampires, the nightwalker, and the turncoat druids. *I needed to erase them all.*

"Lexy, my child. You have finally grown up." The Vampire King smiled widely at her, as if proud of his granddaughter's new power and confidence. But his smile didn't reach his eyes.

"These are only the beginning." Alexis swept her hand our way.

"You would create an army to challenge *me*?" His eyes flashed with insulted pride.

"Grandfather, so many have tried to dethrone you and have failed. I am not so foolish. I have no desire to rule in your stead."

"Then why have you separated yourself from me?" he demanded, his brow creased.

"I had no other way to show you the level of power I have attained," she replied. "You have been sending me on the most difficult missions—I recognized your plan to strengthen me."

"Yes." He nodded in satisfaction. "To strengthen you." The smile that didn't reach his eyes returned.

He was lying. I had been in Alexis's mind. He regretted letting his granddaughter live to grow so powerful. He had no desire to kill her himself so he had planned for others to do it. He had sent her to help Caradoc while sending the nightwalker to kill him. He had expected the nightwalker to eliminate all of us, including his own granddaughter.

"You hate the new world," Alexis continued. "You prefer to stay in the old country. I can be your princess. I can rule this new world, grandfather, answering only to you."

She pushed truth into those words, and I believed them. She really wanted to rule the vampires on this continent. This really had been a play for power and blood the whole time.

I'm such a fool. Alexis *was* the monster that O'Brien had warned me about. She was not the girl I had spent a few days with, or the girl I had magically connected with. She was just like her grandfather. She lusted after nothing but power and blood.

The Vampire King's false smile fell away. He glanced at Carina and then back at Alexis. Had this request caught him off guard? Then as if he'd just solved some grand riddle, he let one side of his mouth twist up in a grin.

"Why would I give the new world to you, Lexy?" he asked, always perfectly pronouncing each word.

"Because doing so will create a layer of power that will buffer you from those who continually try to . . . remove you."

His irises flared black, contrasting with the pale skin and white hair that hung at one length just above his shoulders. He exuded the smell of copper and blood.

"I do not need the protection of a child," he chastised, his accent just a bit more detectable.

"Quite true, grandfather," Alexis agreed. "I misspoke. Giving me the new world will only increase your power and will allow me, as your princess, to rid you of some who seek to usurp it. Everyone knows I am yours. My power only increases yours."

"Then remove that stone," he ordered.

As he spoke, he grabbed magic and shot it in tendrils toward Alexis. The glowing tendrils attached to the stone and pulled at the necklace until it stretched horizontally. I expected the chain to break and fly toward her grandfather, but it held.

Alexis didn't move or react for a long moment.

"Grandfather," she chided, placing her hand on the stone and tucking it beneath her body armor, against her skin. "I used an enchanted chain. It cannot be removed by magic."

"Are you asking me to wrap my fingers around your neck?" He laughed and glanced at Carina like he'd just shared a joke with an old friend. "Very well. I accept."

He stepped toward Lexy but stopped when she raised a hand.

"You know as well as I that the only way to prove my power is to show everyone that it is nearly equal to yours. And when I make a lifelong oath of peace to you in front of all your children, everyone will know how your power has increased."

"A lifelong oath of peace?" The Vampire King's eyes returned to red, and he tilted his head. "Yes. Perhaps that would suffice," he spoke softly. Pride flooded his countenance. "It will be so." With one white-skinned hand, the Vampire King indicated us. "You may keep what is yours, my *Princess*." He spoke the word "princess" as if it were a new title he'd granted her.

"Yes, grandfather." Alexis breathed a sigh of relief. Had her grandfather's eyes twitched with her breath?

He turned to the three vampires around the card table and spoke, "I agree that my granddaughter Alexis will rule as Princess of the new world. On All Souls' Day, she will present herself to me and repeat her oath."

While he spoke, Alexis looked me in the eyes. Something changed between us. What was it? Whatever she did, I was no longer frozen in place. I was also no longer hers. She had released me from her psychic leash.

Why did she release me?

Should I attack immediately? I hesitated. John Kaloyan had absorbed my magic missile as if it were nothing more than a bad meal that gave him indigestion. I could try again, but even if I used more magic, would it work any better? Could I gather that much energy inside me without being noticed? The two druids with powerful-looking staffs stood obediently. Surely, they'd notice if I powered up. The Vampire King could also use and likely detect magic. Besides, it appeared that we weren't going to be harmed.

The Vampire King turned back to Alexis.

"But of course, the oath must start now, Alexis." He cast his eyes challengingly at his granddaughter. "Can you really make such an oath? Have you outgrown your . . . limitation?"

"Of course, grandfather," she replied, and Mr. Espinoza moved away from the door, catching my attention. He started

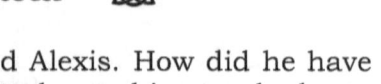

walking toward the Vampire King and Alexis. How did he have the courage, not to mention the control over his own body, to approach them? Perhaps he only planned to sit down.

"I speak to the existence that thrives around me, and I give my oath of peace that my grandfather, John Kaloyan, while I exist, in life or death, will be safe from me and from all who are in my control. Make it so by blood of life."

I felt the power in the oath—the magic. She had bound herself in a way that would forever forbid her from harming her grandfather. If he decided to kill us all, she could only watch.

Her grandfather nodded. He smiled again, only this time the smile reached the corners of his eyes. His black lashes contrasted against his pale skin. This may have worked out for him better than he had expected. He had intended to kill Alexis and instead he had obtained a loyal general.

Except why had she released me?

The oath!

She had promised he would be safe from her and from all who were in her control. Everyone in the room belonged to either Alexis or her grandfather. Except me.

She had planned this all along. This was a chess match. Only I had the players wrong. It wasn't me versus those after me; it was Alexis versus her grandfather. We were just pawns in their game. And the game wasn't over. We hadn't been checkmated. Instead, she had placed me in position to threaten the king, literally. I had him in check. The question was, how could I turn check into checkmate?

Lexy, are you here to save us? She couldn't answer but I wished we were connected again so she could. *Yes, you are,* I answered for her. Hope swelled up inside me. Could it be that she was protecting us and she wasn't here just for power?

Was she here for me?

I felt the familiar desire to protect her. The same desire I'd felt when needing to protect my sister. Any part of me that wanted to bask in the pleasure of vanquishing her disappeared. Despite my freedom from her control, I'd formed a strong emotional bond with her. It had nothing to do with magic; it just had to do with her.

At that moment, I was foolishly and dangerously in love with her—at least until, with a flash of teeth, she bit into Mr. Espinoza's neck.

CHAPTER 45
FIRST WAVE

M *ake it so by blood.*
The oath's phrase hammered into me. I dropped to my knees, clutching at my broken heart. Every idea I'd had about Alexis was wrong. I'd convinced myself she was here to save us. Foolish. She had betrayed me once already. Why was I so floored—literally—that it was happening again?

I should have attacked, but the betrayal rocked my existence. Instead, I watched Alexis drain the life from my best friend's dad. Worse, Luiz watched, completely indifferent. Ouch! My breath caught, keeping me from crying out.

Why didn't I attack? Fear. They'd kill me in seconds. There were too many of them, and they were eyeing me for having fallen to my knees. Besides, I didn't want them to know I'd been excluded from Alexis's oath.

I cared more about surviving than saving Mr. Espinoza, and I hated myself for it—for being so cowardly. More importantly, I hated Alexis. When we connected our minds, she had been so careful to share the "secret" that she never once killed by feeding, and I had believed it. How had she manipulated her memories during our connection? How had she taken control of my friends? Somehow, she had done both. She had played me like a cheap instrument and now she expected me to help rid her of her grandfather.

I stood back up. After Alexis had first taken control of me, I'd used a containment to block out magic, thoughts, emotion, scents—everything. I created that same containment around me, only I left it open at my feet so I could slowly absorb magic through the floor without alerting anyone. I didn't dare pull the magic quickly, which meant that it would take minutes to fill my reservoir. But once full, I was going to ignore Alexis's evil grandfather and take her out first. I just had to be patient.

Alexis fed and bloodied herself without remorse. I could hear her lips sucking the blood from Mr. Espinoza's neck, and I wanted to be sick. I could never look at her again without seeing her as the bloody monster she was, her fangs in my best friend's dad.

In movies, it takes a vampire a few seconds to drain their victim of blood, but in real life, it takes much longer. Ten minutes. Alexis's straight, black hair hid her face while she fed. When she paused to lick her lips, blood slathered her mouth and oozed down onto her black leather body armor. As the minutes passed, her arms flexed to hold Mr. Espinoza up. He had long since lost his ability to stand.

Finally, she let go of Mr. Espinoza, and he dropped limply to the floor. All color had left him and traveled into Alexis. Her skin flushed. Her veins bulged with stolen blood. Her body armor stretched.

While Alexis had sucked the life from Mr. Espinoza, I had sucked in magic. I could do that scared. After ten agonizing minutes of watching her drain my best friend's dad, she was full. But so was I. So full that I wasn't sure I could contain the magic. It had only been a few days since the battle with the nightwalker. Yet I was stronger now. I held more magic inside me than I had then. My target stood, lips and chin dripping blood. I just had to be patient and wait for the right moment.

"Impressive, Lexy." Her grandfather's eyes gleamed wickedly. "I see you have finally learned to finish your dinner."

"Yes," Alexis said. "I pretended to be weak long enough to keep others unsuspecting of my power."

His dark red eyes studied her.

"You may keep those two pets," the Vampire King motioned toward Luiz and me. He left out Kendra and O'Brien. "However, O'Brien's fate has already been decided."

"Yes, grandfather, I am aware," she replied. "Of course, by your own law, I must give you permission to feed on those that I control. You have my permission to feed on O'Brien." She gulped and licked some blood from her lips.

She had just given O'Brien away.

"I request one other *gift*." He smiled, emphasizing that last word as if it had some special meaning to her. He wasn't done testing his granddaughter yet. Alexis was not the only one playing this chess match, and it was his move. "I require the girl." He pointed at Kendra.

No! I wanted to scream. Could I hold back and do nothing while I watched Kendra be drained, too? I didn't think so. I built up my courage, and the need to protect Kendra returned. Once again, some unnatural force similar to magic enhanced my compulsive protectiveness.

"Grandfather . . ." Alexis protested, but the tall vampire ignored her.

"She will bear me a child, Lexy." He smiled wickedly. "I wish to have another mortal woman to give me another daughter." His words were cold. "You have grown and the nest is empty." He glanced at Lexy's mother, Carina, who stood next to him. She was no longer a dhampir. Keagan had killed and turned her into a full-fledged vampire. Would Alexis turn into a vampire when she died?

I hated the Vampire King's words. Draining Kendra would be horrible, but this eight hundred-freaking-year-old vampire forcing himself on her to make another half-vampire child was more than I could bear.

"Would you deny me this *gift*?" he continued. "What greater gift could you offer me as we celebrate this joyous agreement between us than this beautiful druid and the daughter she will birth for me?"

Alexis just stared at him. I hoped she would argue. I begged her to argue with my mind.

"Of course, grandfather," she agreed, and my hopes were dashed.

Oh, hell, no!

She had not just given my girlfriend to her grandfather. I took a breath and prepared to release my magic on Alexis when O'Brien rolled away from the Vampire King and came up on his knees holding two SIG P250s, firing at the druids and the Vampire King's three vampires. In the real world, silencers didn't actually make handguns anywhere near silent.

Had O'Brien broken free from Alexis? Or perhaps she had set him free as she had set me free, hoping one of us would dispose of her grandfather so she could take his place? Except he wasn't firing at the Vampire King.

Even though the bullets deflected from the clothes of the two elderly druids, the senior center candidates dropped to the floor. I half expected them to shout, "Help, I've fallen and I can't get up."

One of the three vampires flipped the wooden table on its side and all three slid behind it. Even though vampires could heal from bullet wounds, they preferred to avoid them.

O'Brien jumped backward onto the couch for higher ground and continued firing.

The nightwalker walked around the couch with the fluidity of death, indifferent to the bullets O'Brien unleashed its way.

My magical guns pointed at Alexis, but I had to make a decision. Save O'Brien, exact my revenge on my betrayer, or try to hit the Vampire King while he was distracted. I'd have to use all my magic to kill the nightwalker, but if I used it now, would I have time to gather enough magic to attack Alexis or the Vampire King? If I didn't survive, Alexis couldn't help my friends even if she wanted to because she couldn't fight her grandfather—she had sworn her oath. Were they any safer with her than with him? Alexis had lost. Her grandfather would blame her and kill her for O'Brien's actions.

Understanding clicked. Alexis promised not to harm her grandfather, not his minions. Since O'Brien wasn't targeting the Vampire King, Alexis still controlled him. She had ordered him to fight. She was making a stand. But . . . why jeopardize her new position as ruler of the new world? Was losing Kendra an unacceptable loss—a checkmate that ended Alexis's real game? She knew I was in love with Kendra. It wasn't possible that she was protecting Kendra for me, was it?

Just as I began organizing a magic missile to stop the nightwalker, the dark creature reached the opening between the couch and love seat and launched itself at O'Brien with unnatural speed. My magic would be too late.

Alexis, however, released her magic in time. O'Brien had used two vials to cast a similar spell at the first nightwalker.

Sunlight.

Only Alexis's sunlight formed a ball similar to my magic missile. It flashed away from her, hitting the nightwalker one step before it leaped at O'Brien. The creature flailed in pain as it hurtled itself out of control toward the sniper. Together, they rolled back over the couch and broke through the wall, landing in the kitchen.

The nightwalker screamed.

I fought a mental battle to keep my sanity from being sucked away by the cold, dark abyss. This time, I knew how to win the mental fight. Using memories that would make me fly if I had an ounce of fairy dust, I walled off the scream's murky abyss. The bulk of those memories included Kendra. Were both times I'd kissed Alexis also included? Yes, but I ignored that.

I looked around. Carina disappeared down a hallway. Besnick, Artan, and Ivana screamed in agony as the light burned their skin. The smell of their burning flesh replaced the vampire scents in the room. The Vampire King stood close to Lexy, unaffected by the sunlight. He could kill her at any moment for what she had done, but he didn't. Instead, he watched with entertained eyes. Did he think this was the Roman Colosseum? O'Brien did look like a blond version of Russell Crowe.

The sunlight Alexis created lasted a few seconds longer than the vials had. When the sunlight went out, the room darkened, leaving only the ceiling lights. I blinked as my shrunken pupils widened, trying to compensate.

The scream had no effect on Luiz and Kendra. Was Alexis responsible for that in her own twisted way? Did her control over them block the cold darkness? While I hated her for controlling them, I was grateful that Kendra and Luiz remained sane.

I could see the kitchen through a massive hole in the drywall where several two-by-fours hung awkwardly like broken bones. The obsidian nightwalker writhed, alive but badly burned. Parts of its flesh had been eaten away to the bone around the legs, crippling it. The creature spewed a mist of darkness that felt like corrupted magic on my skin. O'Brien rolled to his feet, and in a single fluid motion, he caught a large, rune-covered blade out of the air and separated the nightwalker's head from its body. I half expected him to say "Don't lose your head" with a Schwarzenegger accent, but he remained silent.

I followed the blade's trajectory back to Alexis. Luiz pulled the shotgun from the cushions of the couch nearest the card table and fired at the vampires who writhed in agony with their exposed skin burnt from the sunlight. He shot the head off Besnick before the female, Ivana, grabbed the shotgun away. So, Luiz dropped a grenade. It hit the hardwood with an audible thud, bounced, and hit again, then rolled loudly. Luiz dove behind the couch.

So far, I had done nothing. Attacked no one. Artan and Ivana fled out the front door. Apparently, vamps aren't grenade-proof. The older druid couple must have already retreated out the door because they were nowhere in sight.

"Grenade," Luiz shouted.

Finally, I acted. A mere couch wouldn't protect Kendra, Luiz, and me from the blast. I pushed Kendra down on top of Luiz and then dove on top of them. I reached my hand over and touched the couch, weaving a frantic anti-missile spell on both it and my clothing, powering it with the gravel in my pocket.

John Kaloyan stood motionless, smiling and watching. If he felt threatened by the grenade, his face didn't show it. Alexis stood next to him, the same indifference on her face.

The grenade exploded.

The shrapnel pounded against the magic-enhanced couch, too much for my spell to deflect. Shards of the wooden card table rebounded everywhere. While most embedded themselves into the ceiling and walls, plenty ricocheted toward us. My clothes stopped much of the splinter-like projectiles, but I had one hand over Kendra and Luiz's heads and the other on the couch, leaving my own head exposed. Ignoring the stinging pain in the backs of my hands and arms, I rolled off of Luiz and Kendra. As I stood up, I felt something drip from the back of my head. I reached back and touched it. Blood.

Bleeding is not something you want to do in a room filled with vampires. Alexis was full, but Artan and Ivana stepped back inside. They darted toward me with fangs bared and their black eyes, streaked with red lightning, fixed on the blood that had transferred to my hand.

Gunshots rang out.

Behind me, O'Brien stepped through the hole in the wall and fired at the vampires. With magic-enhanced accuracy, his first shot took the male vampire, Artan, in the eye, exploding out the back of his head with a spray of blood and gore. Vampire or not, a hollow point to the eye dropped it to the ground, where it thrashed in agony. As the sniper emptied his clip, the woman dodged with supernatural speed, taking a bullet to the chest but still coming in fast. O'Brien clicked a latch on his pistols, and the empty clips dropped. He dropped one gun to reach for a fresh clip.

Ivana would be on him before he reloaded. Having just saved Luiz and Kendra from the grenade, I didn't have time to form a magic missile, so I improvised. Acting on instinct, I created a rope of energy in Ivana's path and converted it into a solid, physical substance. I put the rope hip high, because in football, that is where I'd tackle someone to stop their momentum. I curved the ends of the rope down and welded them to the floor.

When Ivana hit the rope at superhuman speed, her body folded together, her hips the focal point. Her face smashed against one knee, arms and legs flailing forward just inches from O'Brien. Then my rope of energy dissolved and she fell awkwardly to the floor. I dropped to one knee, weakened by the effort. Stars glittered in front of my eyes. I hadn't understood how much it would sap my strength to convert energy to mass.

Ivana rose and hissed at me, her broken cheek healing before my eyes. Unfortunately for her, she'd paused long enough to give O'Brien a stationary target. He fired a round into the center of her neck. The bullet slipped into her skin like a dart before it hit a vertebra with a sickening crack. The hollow point exploded in a bloody mess out the back of her neck, taking a vertebra or two with it and adding to the spray of vampire blood that already dotted the room. Her head flopped to her right shoulder with a wet, scraping sound and then she crumpled lifelessly to the grenade-damaged floor.

The remaining vampire, Artan, stood back up, the hole in his eye half-healed. I couldn't see the back of his head, which was a good thing. His timing was poor, though, because I had my senses back—enough to form a magic missile. From my kneeling position, I released the orb, and in a flash of particles, Artan's existence extinguished. The pleasure of it barely tickled at my insides, disappointingly less than I'd hoped. I'd have to erase a few more creatures to reach the same level of ecstasy I'd had in the parking lot the night before.

I stood and looked around. Where were the two druids and Carina? I glanced at my friends. Luiz, weaponless but alert, hurried over to stand with O'Brien and me in the center of the couches. Kendra, also mostly herself again, crouched behind me.

So, who's next, I thought happily, *Alexis or her grandfather?* I would have chosen Alexis, but the idea of the Vampire King taking Kendra changed my mind.

I turned to the Vampire King.

"*Bealustræl!*" I yelled.

Just as I spoke, all the magic in the house disappeared, and the glowing missile dissolved in my palms.

CHAPTER 46
SECOND WAVE

"**W**ell done." John Kaloyan clapped his hands, his face showing nothing more than amusement.

Where had the magic gone? Two druids stepped into the doorway and tapped their staffs on the floor with the clack of wood on wood. Magic came from their staffs as they formed a containment around me. It wrapped around my skin, blocking me from magic. They hadn't just contained me; they'd sucked the magic from around me and from my spell.

Without access to magic, we were just regular people against the Vampire King, Alexis's mother, and two venerable druids. My jeek mind calculated the odds of survival and came up with zero. *Never tell me the odds!* I mentally shouted at my own brain. I needed to survive this, if for no other reason than to see my sister again.

A reservoir of magic glowed from inside each druid. They were filled with it. Alexis and her grandfather also glowed. Were they blocking Alexis from magic too?

Did I have some magic reserves inside me?
I gathered up what magic remained in me. I found enough for one spell, but not a strong one. What should I cast? Let's face it, I was a newbie, and I couldn't attack with anything except fire light or a magic missile.

Luiz and O'Brien had stopped attacking. If Alexis still controlled them, she must have called them off. Was she waiting for me to make the next move?

"Lexy." The Vampire King smiled viciously at his granddaughter. "Your generals have fought very well for you. Unfortunately, as you surely must know, those," he waved his pale palm at the dead vampires, "were not my generals."

His enunciation of each syllable annoyed me. Lexy's memory of when she was thirteen came to mind, in her apartment where the Vampire King's general covered her mouth with his hand. Two of the Vampire King's generals had taken her and killed her mother. What had their names been?

"Do you think I failed to smell the death on that one?" He nodded toward the body of Mr. Espinoza. "Of course, I knew your oath would still allow you to kill these." He waved his hand at the bodies of the three dead vampires. "Do you think that I would be so foolish as to bring a weak force against you? They were mere playthings who had broken my laws. I promised to forgive them if they dispatched you and your pets. It all worked out as I planned. I planned for you to kill them for me, and you have. I planned for you to hope for victory, and you have. Now I plan to destroy your hope, Lexy."

The druids stepped away from the doorway. As they did, I heard Mr. Espinoza's words repeat in my head—words he'd spoken to me after a game of chess, which seemed a lifetime ago. *Always have a second wave of attack planned. If your first wave is blocked, use your second.*

John Kaloyan might have made a good chess player because, sure enough, three nightwalkers stepped in behind the druids. They wore the same shadowy robes I imagined the Grim Reaper wore, except their robes hung slightly open, exposing obsidian skin stretched over their bones and muscles, like the first nightwalker I'd faced. Fear flooded into the room with them, and despite the containment, the fear clung to my skin.

Can I withstand the screams of three of those creatures? Can Kendra or Luiz?

If the nightwalkers weren't bad enough, two more vampires walked in.

Keagan and Dane. Their names came immediately once I saw them. Compared to these two, the vampires we had fought were peons.

I picked out another useful memory from either Alexis or Caradoc. The Vampire King refused to allow any other vampires to wear a healing stone to protect them from sunlight, so that meant the sunlight spell Alexis had used on the first nightwalker would burn these vampire generals, too. I could handle the two vamps and the three nightwalkers *if* I could solve two problems. First, I didn't have enough magic to cast an attack spell, let alone sustain a powerful one for a long time. Second, I didn't know how to cast sunlight.

"Lexy. How does it feel to be bereft of magic?" the Vampire King grinned, flashing his fangs at her. "It is time I take my gifts."

Oh, no! Kendra. O'Brien.

"You foolish child!" he mocked. His white hair swung slightly as he shook his head.

I wished for more experience. Then I thought of something. Between Kendra and me, did we have enough magic for something more powerful? Had the few hours of druid initiation I'd just given her made her aware enough to pull in a reserve of magic? I hoped so. She was shivering in a crouch close enough behind me for me to reach back and offer her my hand. She took it, brave enough to stand up even though her movement brought glances from both generals and the trio of nightwalkers.

I had good news and bad news. Good news: I could sense the magic she had inside her. Bad news: she held very little of it and was also blocked.

The emotional rope between us flared to life. That gave me an idea. I hadn't taught her to connect our minds magically, so I pushed my magic into her. Then I grabbed it from her, hoping she would feel what I had done. For a second, Kendra didn't understand. She wasn't going to figure it out. I grabbed for the magic using our emotional rope and as if on instinct, she let me in. Kendra's eyes widened at me and she breathed deeply, her mind and mine joined.

This is amazing, Kendra thought.

Kendra's memories spilled into my mind. I found her mind filled with mostly peace and happiness—the present situation not included. Her life had been as complete as it could get for her age. She'd grown up with both parents still together and with multiple brothers and sisters. She had lots of aunts and uncles and nieces and nephews—so many people loved Kendra, and she loved so many. Her life was a life that I had wanted but fate had denied me. Kendra pitied me for my thought. I didn't want any of that.

Don't move and don't say anything, I thought to her.

Even under the dire circumstances, I blushed at the depth of her crush on me. She'd felt that way for years. I'd thought it was more recent. As much as I wanted to explore her memories and experience her feelings, we had more important matters to focus on right now.

Close off your memories and listen, I thought with urgency.

I felt Alexis's mind brush against Kendra's. If my suspicions were correct, she would know I had connected magically to Kendra. I looked at Alexis, who still listened to her grandfather's rant. She returned my look and then glanced at Kendra. Her red eyes flickered to our hands, unable to hide her envy, even as her grandfather continued to reprimand her.

"I have let you live. I have given you everything you have," Alexis's grandfather spat the words carefully, despite the wrath that dripped from them.

She knows, Kendra told me.

I didn't understand why Alexis envied the connection. Had our moment in the druid grove meant as much to her as it had to me?

Uh oh. I shouldn't have thought about that. My most passionate memories with Alexis flooded into Kendra, giving her a front-row seat to a video reel of Alexis and me magically connected, our bodies wrapped tightly around each other, and our lips pressed together. I hadn't told her about Alexis and me, or what had happened between us, but she knew now. Her breath caught in her throat, and her eyes filled with tears.

Sadness, envy, betrayal, fury—Kendra's emotions slammed into my chest and crashed over me like an entire defensive line driving me down to the turf one foot from the end zone.

I'm sorry. I didn't know I'd ever see you again. She knew I'd forgotten about her for days. *Hate me later. Just stay with me for now,* I begged, pushing away my feelings for Alexis. *We have to focus to get out of this alive.* She agreed that while under the threat of the Vampire King, his two generals, three nightwalkers, and skilled geriatric druids, it was not the time to unleash her fury on me.

I showed Kendra how to poke holes in a containment, which supposedly wasn't possible. Teaching her mind-to-mind let her understand everything almost instantly. In seconds, we created thousands of pinhole openings. Too bad they only let magic out, not in.

Now for the next step. I slipped a hand into my front pocket, my fingertips resting on broken gravel. Using a few molecules, I tested the same conversion I had used to enchant the ruby and the black diamond. But I didn't send the magic anywhere; I only created it from matter. The increased power tingled against my skin, sweeping away the clingy nightwalker fear.

The bits of gravel and my clothes wouldn't be enough.

Clothes? Kendra cringed.

We need more. What else do we have? As soon as I asked, I found more molecules to use.

You're not serious? Kendra thought, practically shouting in my head.

It's a last resort, I promise.

It had better be, she thought, appalled at the thought of me taking such drastic measures.

I ignored her and moved on to the next step in my plan.

I need Alexis.

Kendra's fury flared at my thought. *We need her to connect with us and cast sunlight. I don't know that spell. Plus, we need to use our magic and hers. Just keep repeating these words in your mind: Connect with Jake.*

I stopped verbalizing my thoughts. All I had to do was think and Kendra could follow along. I watched Alexis, hoping Kendra's mental communication would work. I spared a glance for John Kaloyan, who had been gloating over Alexis and mocking her.

". . . shame that you have to die so young and so foolishly," the Vampire King told her as I wondered what parts of the conversation I had missed.

Suddenly, Alexis glanced at me. She understood.

She got the message, Kendra thought to me. *She needs a distraction.*

Glancing away from her grandfather infuriated him. His arm swung forward like a bat, smacking Alexis's cheek. Her head whipped and her body fell toward her mother who peeked out of the hallway. Her mother looked down on her indifferently.

Alexis lay there for a second, then she raised up on her hands. Her eyes moved to O'Brien, who walked to the Vampire King.

"I am yours, my king," O'Brien stated, face smooth with a serenity that was not his own.

"Please." He begged the same way I had begged when Alexis had taken control of me.

I'd grown too accustomed to my crawling skin and almost didn't notice John Kaloyan's evil swell with anticipation at taking a life.

"Lexy," her grandfather grinned down at her with mocking eyes, "your first gift has arrived." His eyes darkened, leaving red lightning streaks. His musky smell morphed into copper and blood.

Ask her what the heck she's doing, Kendra.

It's not like that. Her impressions seep through, but I can't talk to her. Besides, her control is . . . failing.

Alexis stood, but did not look at us. Her eyes remained on her grandfather. She had just commanded O'Brien to offer his blood. I thought of separating her head with her rune-covered blade. Kendra cringed at my detailed imagination, but the furious part of her approved.

The Vampire King gripped O'Brien's head and shoulders with his creepy hands, baring O'Brien's neck as he had done earlier.

The tall vampire's jaw flexed as he widened his mouth. The warning stone glowed brightly as he bit into O'Brien's neck with fangs far longer than his granddaughter's.

Kendra shivered in her mind just before her hand trembled in mine. We gulped simultaneously. Luiz cursed in Spanish but stayed back.

Alexis took one slow step. Then another. Agonizingly slowly, she walked toward me. She did not hurry or look at me. She almost paused between each step. That pause played on my nerves like fingernails on a chalkboard.

She kept her eyes on her grandfather as he leeched blood from O'Brien. Keagan and Dane eyed her slow steps warily. One nightwalker licked its black teeth, perhaps hoping for a chance to feed on our flesh.

Alexis finally stopped next to me and took my hand. With her touch, her allure almost took over, blocking out even the Vampire King's coppery odor. My connection to Kendra helped protect me from getting lost in her touch. But Alexis was not trying to control me.

Alexis reached for the magic inside me, already shared with Kendra, and the three of us . . . connected.

CHAPTER 47
DAYLIGHT

For a moment, Kendra's and Alexis's minds took over my own, leaving me disoriented. Dealing with my own thoughts, memories, and emotions was confusing enough. Now I found myself connected magically with two female minds that both flashed back and forth between feelings for me, jealousy of the other girl, and fear of our situation.

I hadn't realized that Kendra and Alexis would link to each other. I'd thought they would each only hear me. My mind rattled with the noise of the triangular connection.

Our thoughts moved at sub-second speeds.

Even held at bay, Kendra's fury that I'd forgotten her was exposed to Alexis, whose mind showed why. Alexis had erased her from my mind with her allure.

Kendra's fury unleashed as she mentally shouted at Alexis, calling her a boyfriend-stealing witch, and Alexis rhymed back viciously. I'd expected Alexis to have more restraint. Kendra's mind escalated in turn, using words I'd never expected would come from her. Neither of them could get a handle on their thoughts. They now instantly shared thoughts that neither would let reach their lips.

Stop it! You can't react to every thought! I screamed at them with my mind. *Kendra, listen! Alexis had everything she'd ever wanted. All she had to do was give you to the Vampire King. She gave up everything just now for you. You go to church every Sunday. I know you'll regret the words you're thinking—words you'd never say aloud.*

Alexis, I continued. *As the freaking Princess of the new world, you should be able to focus on the real fight here.*

Think of all the thoughts we push out of our minds—thoughts that we wish we never had. Those thoughts don't make us who we are. The thoughts we choose to keep around make us who we are. So, choose better ones.

Besides, I continued, *O'Brien's blood is slipping from him.*

Our mental conservation had taken barely a few seconds. It took them another two seconds to soften their minds against each other so we could plan. Their spite for each other only dimmed, but that was enough for our rapid thoughts to move with urgency.

We shared all our magic so any of us could use it, but we only needed Alexis to use it. Her mind opened even more to me. What I found there collided with my hatred of her like a tsunami and carried it away. But I had no time to explore it while the Vampire King continued to suck O'Brien's life away. Lexy and I would have to talk later, even if that idea infuriated Kendra.

Problem! The magic I created by converting mass to energy wouldn't transfer to Lexy. It remained with me. I didn't know what was wrong, but the answer surfaced from one of Caradoc's memories, one I had seen in my dreams. We needed to form a permanent connection, a *myndtiegan.* Remembering the dream opened up Caradoc's memory enough to show us how to do it.

A permanent *myndtiegan* wasn't something one person could *just* do to another. There was a checklist of four difficult requirements. First, each person willingly had to join magically. Check. Second, each person had to share all their magic with the other. Check. Third, each person had to willingly accept the other's magic. Check. The last requirement was the most difficult, and yet at the moment, the simplest of all: love. Check. In some rare and strange twist of fate, we already met all those requirements.

I glanced at O'Brien's body, weakening in the Vampire King's hands. We didn't have time. We needed to act now.

Wait! Lexy mentally shouted.

She tried to drop my hand, but it was too late. I had already executed the enchantment.

What have you done to us? Lexy shouted through our minds.

She only had a vague understanding of what I had just done and that it was forbidden except under special circumstances.

Don't yell at Jake! Kendra snapped back at Lexy. Her unfiltered thoughts called Lexy a pretty bad name—well, phrase—that rivaled the worst I'd ever heard on the football field. Lexy lashed back with a string of curses that a Jesus-loving girl like Kendra could have never been prepared for. Come to think of it, I wasn't prepared for it either.

Oops. No, worse than oops. Could this be undone? Uh oh. I didn't think so.

Hearing them curse at each other made me realize that I had made a huge mistake. I had permanently connected all three of us—not just Lexy and me. I hadn't meant to include Kendra, but in my inexperience, I had. I couldn't fix it now. What were the chances that I'd met the four stringent requirements for forming a permanent *myndtiegan* with two girls at the same time?

Their thoughts snowballed at each other again and Kendra's and Alexis's voices took over in my head. I urged them to stop. I tried to shame them into stopping but they ignored me, their mental talons raking into each other.

SHUT UP! I shoved the word into their minds. I sent along the image of the Vampire King sucking O'Brien's life from him right in front of us. Their minds stopped clamoring.

What have you done to us, Jake? They asked me in unison, unable to stop themselves from asking the question and exposing their fear.

I didn't have an answer. OK, I had done something bad—very bad—but the good news was that my mass-converted magic was as much Lexy's now as it was mine. The sentience in the magic no longer treated us like three individuals, but as one. A trinity of minds—like the Holy Trinity—except we were teenagers, not Gods.

At the speed of thought, I showed Lexy how to create pin-sized holes in a containment, allowing magic out. I didn't have to see the disbelief and shock on her face because it echoed through my mind. What I was doing was supposed to be impossible. Impossible or not, I could do it, and with a brief memory dump, Alexis could too. All three of us created millions of pin-sized exits in the containment around Lexy.

Let's power up! I thought to them. *O'Brien needs us to hurry!*

I started converting the molecules of the gravel in my pockets to energy. I just needed enough to get the spell started. I'd convert my own clothes and shoes next.

If Lexy had been shocked at how I had created pinholes in a containment, she was downright astounded by my ability to convert mass to pure power. It was not something that anyone had ever done though many of the great druids of the past had tried. She'd never heard of a druid that could do it. Perhaps it was Caradoc's blood. Perhaps it was because I was different in other ways. It didn't matter. I could do things no one else could.

I suddenly chuckled mentally. The Vampire King was draining O'Brien. Three nightwalkers, two vampire generals, and two druids surrounded us. The druids thought they'd cut us off from magic.

We'd gained the element of surprise.

Alexis tried doing the same mass-to-magic conversion of her clothes but failed. She tried again and failed again. But we were one and so she used me to do it. She intended me to use her own clothes before allowing me to take the more drastic measures I'd thought of. I was grateful.

Embarrassed, Kendra also volunteered her clothes. We now had gravel and three sets of clothes to power Lexy's spell. Maybe I wouldn't have to take painfully drastic measures after all.

It's time to cast the spell, I thought. *We don't need our clothes yet. Let's see how long the gravel lasts.*

It seemed like we'd been conversing in our minds for ten minutes, but barely thirty seconds had passed. The Vampire King could not have drained O'Brien yet.

"*Dæg leoht,*" Lexy whispered. It wasn't the ball of sunlight spell she'd hurled at the nightwalker. Instead, she cast a more expansive spell, one that would illuminate the entire room.

Daylight.

Magic burst through the pinholes in the containment around Lexy and became rays of daylight, lighting up the room like noonday. She'd become a human sun. As she did, I was forced to increase the speed at which I converted the gravel into energy.

As I'd expected, the spell caught everyone by surprise—especially the two vampire generals. They cringed at the daylight and covered their faces with their hands. They started toward the door, desperate for the darkness outside.

The nightwalkers screamed. The dark abyss of their shrieks collided coldly against us, but our minds were already too full. There was no room for the unnatural void. In creating our trinity of mind, we'd unknowingly created a defense against their screams. The obsidian-skinned creatures tried to cover themselves with their robes, hoping to outlast the spell. We had to outlast them.

The containments around us strengthened. Did the druids assume we'd broken down their containment? They tried to suck away the magic again, but the magic was ours. It refused them.

I felt Alexis's controlling power flare up, but it had no effect on Kendra or me. She simply sent Luiz to find a weapon, but she didn't offer him hers, so he jumped through the hole in the wall to the kitchen.

I needed to keep the vampire generals inside so I shoved magic through a pinhole and converted it to a long physical rod that I used to push the door shut before the rod's unstable matter collapsed back to pure energy. Unfortunately, Keagan made it through just before I pushed it closed. But Dane didn't.

He reached for the doorknob, but it wouldn't turn, as if someone held it closed from outside. Dane collapsed in front of the door, one hand still on the doorknob. Steam rose from his skin, especially the exposed hand.

And as for the Vampire King, well, he just stood there guzzling O'Brien's blood, his hungry eyes watching every move. *It's all just a "dinner and a show" to this creep,* I swore inwardly. But as powerful as he was, at least he hadn't entered the fray because he had such warped faith in his minions.

The trouble was, we burned through magic too quickly. The gravel in my pockets hadn't lasted more than a half-dozen seconds, so I started converting my clothes. Feeding Lexy's daylight spell took more energy than I had expected. It didn't help that I'd used a power-hungry spell to close the door either.

A wind spell would have used less energy! Lexy scolded me. *It would have shut the door faster, too.* Well, what did she expect from a rookie?

My clothes lasted only two seconds.

We started converting Lexy's clothes next. Her thick leather armor, from her shoulders to her combat boots, began glowing— at least I could see it, even though Kendra and Lexy couldn't. As the molecules of her leather clothes and body armor converted to energy and faded away, her blades, guns, and the bullets from her bandoliers clanged to the floor. Too bad Lexy hadn't been able to tap into the atoms of the knives and weapons she wore. It was the druid couple's mistake that we even had access to our clothes inside the containment. The druid text said that imagining the boundaries of a containment was often imperfect. The druids had cast imperfect ones around our bodies, making our clothes, if not Lexy's weapons, available to us.

The sunlight continued, lasting longer than the nightwalkers had expected. Hiding under their cloaks would not save them, so they changed tactics. One started toward us, but after a step, it fell to the floor and could barely crawl. The others stepped toward the door and also fell. Daylight stiffened their obsidian bodies making them brittle and hard and more like, well, obsidian.

Kendra's turn came, and embarrassed, she hesitated, but she sucked it up and urged me to convert her clothing into energy, starting with her shoes. She'd noticed that the denser the material, the longer it lasted. She had some metal on her: the zipper of her fly, her belt buckle, and the underwire of her bra. She had me continue with those, hoping not to have to use all of her clothes. Unfortunately, we used the metal up and one of the nightwalkers still crept toward us. She regretfully started on her light cotton clothing, which evaporated to energy far too quickly for her comfort.

We needed the spell to last just a few more seconds, so I converted my hair—*all* my hair.

The male druid's chin dropped and the woman's wrinkled eyes stretched wide, her lips pressed flat. I could only imagine the thoughts spinning in their antique brains. They had increased the power of the containments around our bodies, blocking us from magic, yet we used magic anyway. The containment would also block *their* magic if they attacked us. If they dropped it, we would have access to all the magic around us; if they didn't, they couldn't attack. No one came to their aid as everyone else, except the Vampire King himself, was either burned or burning.

Lexy and Kendra cringed when my hair disappeared, and reluctantly, I used up their hair too. Embarrassment and sadness pushed into me from both of them. Girls often cry when they cut their hair. We'd just done worse to Kendra and Alexis. I hurt for them, but if we lived, the crying would be worth it.

When they ran out of hair, I knew it was time. I trembled at first, but then I sucked it up and dug down deep for the will to start taking more drastic measures.

The Vampire King's eyes continued to watch, but the way his eyes thinned, I assumed he was no longer entertained.

CHAPTER 48
GIFT

It started with the very outer layer of my skin, mostly dead cells anyway. It didn't hurt, but my skin cooled despite the energy it created. I used up my first layer of skin too quickly. Alexis converted hers next. Kendra tried and failed—her body refused to comply, perhaps because she didn't share our enhanced healing abilities. So even though I knew it would hurt, I started into my skin's second layer.

Then the druids decided to attack because their imperfect containments dropped. With the energy around us available, I stopped converting my skin to magic and sighed in relief. Even so, the exposed, inner layer of my skin already registered cool, wet pain, like a scraped palm.

We pulled in magic and fed it directly to Lexy's daylight.

With three minds, we rapidly assessed the situation. Carina had known Lexy would cast daylight, so she hid in a bedroom to escape it. The nightwalkers weren't quite dead. One crawled toward us while the other two crawled toward the door. We needed the sunlight to last a few seconds more to kill them. Dane's charred body lay near the front door, like a smoldering log in a campfire. The druids held their staffs, ready to blast us with a spell augmented by the rune glowing in each.

The Vampire King dropped O'Brien, flashing his bloodied fangs as if annoyed by the direction his entertainment had taken. His eyes flashed black at Lexy and he darted straight for her.

But Kendra, Lexy, and I were one. We communicated as one. As fast as the Vampire King moved, as fast as the druids could cast their spell, our thoughts moved faster.

Kendra pulled in magic, preparing to protect us from the druid couple's attack with a containment. She waited until the last second to bring it up so Alexis's daylight spell could continue as long as possible.

Everything happened at once.

The druids pulled magic through their staffs' runes, firing lightning at us as Kendra brought up the containment. Lexy dropped her sunlight spell and my hand while I poked a hole through Kendra's containment and cast out a rope of magic, again trying to make it solid in the Vampire King's trajectory, waist high.

The druids' lightning crackled against our containment with a power that surged painfully into Kendra and me, vibrating us to the bone. I diverted some of my magic from the rope to strengthen Kendra's containment. Lexy was unaffected by the lightning because she wasn't assisting us. I didn't blame her, though.

Lexy was trying to juggle controlling O'Brien and Luiz with her mind while preparing to avoid her grandfather's charge. She ordered O'Brien to finish off the nightwalkers, but first he had to shake off his blood loss and find the strength to lift himself off the floor. She ordered Luiz to fire on the druids.

Lexy's grandfather hit the rope but did not fold in half as Ivana had. The rope collapsed back into energy, never fully becoming physical. It had been too weak because I was forced to divert most of my magic to sustain our containment. Oh, and also because I was physically in pain, both from being almost self-flayed and from the effects of the druid lightning that still blasted at us with the vibrating hum of one point twenty-one gigawatts. I collapsed to one knee again and spots flickered in front of my eyes.

My rope had slowed the Vampire King for a few milliseconds, enough that Lexy dodged when he raked his talon-like fingernails toward her bare flesh. Thank heavens Lexy hadn't inherited those nails. We'd converted her leather clothes and body armor to magic. Except for her protection stone necklace, she was stark naked. Her expanded veins bulged in dark lines from her raw and completely hairless skin.

Luiz came back from the kitchen with a handgun and opened fire on the druids, but the bullets deflected off their clothes.

Despite being partially drained of blood, O'Brien stumbled weakly to the nightwalker that crawled toward us. With the rune-covered blade, he separated the charred head from its shoulders. The head hit the wood floor with a smack, exploding into a half-dozen shards of black rock.

Kendra and I held against the lightning. Synergy must apply to magic because together we could use more power than we could alone, even with my vision blurry. When the lightning finally ended,

I ignored my dizziness and fired a magic missile at the druids. As soon as the missile launched from my palms, my vision went dark. I pressed my eyes closed and fought to remain conscious.

I hadn't meant to send the magic missile at both of them, but in my rush, I did. The crackling ball of energy split, dividing its force in half, so the attack didn't vanquish the druids. But from their pained faces, I'd hit them hard. Unfortunately for them, another magic missile split and hit them less than half a second later. Kendra had copied me exactly. They couldn't block hers so soon after mine. Her smaller missiles blasted them back. They hit hard against the wall and then dropped to the ground. Had they died? If not, at least they'd stopped hurling bolts of electricity at us.

I'd had my eyes closed. I'd seen the rest through Kendra's eyes. When I recovered enough, I opened mine.

Luiz dropped his empty gun and vaulted over the couch to O'Brien, who had collapsed to one knee. Luiz grabbed the rune-covered knife from him and with two tomahawk-like chops, finished off the other two barely crawling nightwalkers. O'Brien turned on his knees and pointed his gun at the Vampire King.

Why doesn't he fire?

Only the Vampire King remained. Lexy held her second rune-covered blade. The Vampire King held the rune-covered short sword. Lexy's weapons had fallen to the floor when we had converted her clothes to magic. Lexy's grandfather swung his blade against his own granddaughter, and though she reacted with reflexes as fast as lightning, she could only block or dodge.

Fire launched from the Vampire King, but Lexy blocked it. The fire wrapped around her containment. Lexy's grandfather jumped through the flame and swung his blade. Alexis jumped back, but not before the sharp tip sliced her under her right breast.

Bald and naked except for her black diamond necklace, with her Christmas bow tattoo exposed, she already had a cut on her left thigh. Blood dripped from both wounds, though they were already healing—a reminder that she had just fed and that the protection stone was also a healing stone.

Lexy had words—a second tattoo—below her navel, but she moved too quickly for me to read it.

With his dagger above his head, the Vampire King made a daring move, exposing his neck. Lexy didn't take advantage. She should have taken his head off.

I swore an oath not to harm him, Lexy reminded me.

She couldn't fight to win. She could only try to survive.

I need you to fight him.

In the mayhem, I'd forgotten her oath and that she'd released me before making it. That was why Luiz stood there doing nothing and O'Brien didn't shoot, despite having the gun pointed at the Vampire King.

I glanced at Kendra. She had grabbed a white throw blanket from one of the couches. It draped from where she clutched it to her chest to cover herself. She cringed as, through my eyes, she witnessed her own bare, white-skinned scalp. Through her eyes, I also saw my exposed body, hairless and raw-skinned. With her mind joined to mine, we couldn't hide our embarrassment. No time to gawk or be embarrassed. We had to help Lexy.

Could I full-on football tackle the Vampire King? I stepped toward him, but my raw skin shouted in pain at my movement. Maybe using magic from a distance was a better idea. He'd swatted away my first magic missile like a fly, so what spell would I cast? Though I had never tried it, I attempted to raise a containment around the Vampire King with just my imagination, as the druid couple had done to us. For a split second, it worked, but he stepped and spun, and I couldn't sustain it. However, I had succeeded in making him aware that we had turned the tables on him because his eyes flashed white, and I could smell fear oozing from his pores.

Moments before, the Vampire King had held the upper hand. He had three nightwalkers, two of his vampire generals, a druid couple, and himself against his granddaughter, O'Brien, and two rookie druids whom he had mistakenly thought blocked from magic. Now it was just him against me. Where had Keagan and Carina gone? I'd worry about them if they showed up.

I suddenly liked our odds for survival.

I felt Lexy try to give up her control of both O'Brien and Luiz, to free them from sharing her oath. As she suspected, it didn't work. She had been right to release me before she made her oath. Magic bound them and enforced the oath even with Alexis's control removed. If only O'Brien could be completely separated from magic.

The seal—the containment I'd used to block out everything including magic. Could I cast that on O'Brien? If no magic surrounded him to force him to keep the blood oath, could he fire?

I cast that seal around O'Brien. But there was still magic inside it, so I stole a trick from the druid couple and sucked the magic out. O'Brien blinked. It had worked.

The first muffled gunshot sounded a half-second later, hitting the king in the chest. If it affected him, I couldn't tell. The sniper fired almost a dozen times until the magazine emptied.

Lexy stepped back, her naked, dark-vein-streaked body posed in a defensive stance, ready for her grandfather's next attack.

Tattooed in a V shape below Lexy's navel were the words:

A gift from the

Vampire

King!

The word *gift* went perfectly with the Christmas bow tattoo at the base of Lexy's back.

A gift? I wondered. But then I understood. It wasn't the words. It was where her grandfather had put them.

Reading the tattoo was like a blade lancing open a festering sore. Vile memories spilled from the once-closed-off part of Lexy's mind into ours. Her grandfather hadn't just controlled her mentally; he hadn't just forced her to feed; he had owned her in every way. Besides his own horrific, incestuous abuse, he had "gifted" her many times to those who pleased him.

As if the memory were my own, the first time her grandfather gifted her flashed through my mind. She'd only been thirteen when Keagan had returned both her and her fully turned mother to the Vampire King. Keagan had requested a night with Lexy as payment for finding and returning them, and the Vampire King had agreed. I cringed at the memory.

More of her memories flooded into me, and in less than a second, I witnessed too many times her grandfather had taken her himself or gifted her to others.

Lexy's shame rolled into me like an ocean, mixing with nausea coming from Kendra, who had also experienced the same revolting memories. Kendra emptied her stomach next to me. The stench of half-digested pizza mixed with the stink of burned vampires, blood, and gunpowder. If throwing up were a possibility for me, I'd have done it too. I wanted to do something—anything—to scrape the evil out from under my skin.

I'd imagined killing my stepdad for peeping on my sister in the shower, then again for the possibility that he might've watched Kendra too. My hate and desire to kill the Vampire King for what he'd done to Lexy was a thousand times that.

My strange protective instinct kicked in, switching away from Kendra. I would protect Lexy from her grandfather at all costs.

CHAPTER 49
LAST RESORT

The Vampire King's cape billowed behind him like the wings of a vulture as he moved in on Lexy. Free to attack without defending himself from her, he swung his dagger at her face and clawed at her abdomen with his other hand. Lexy spun away, barely evading both strikes.

Even though it hadn't worked before, I readied a magic missile, looking for an open shot, when a thought from Caradoc jumped into my mind.

Nature abhors a vacuum.

Argh! I have too many freaking people in my head! I swore and received an immediate mental reprimand from Kendra, which I ignored.

What would happen to the vampire world if we killed its king? Vampires would run around wild until a new ruler was established. But a new ruler wouldn't emerge for years, and in the meantime, war would rage and innocent lives would be lost. Chaos would reign. It was the very reason Caradoc had never taken it upon himself to remove John Kaloyan from power.

I tried to ignore Caradoc's annoying wisdom. I'd seen how the Vampire King had treated Lexy. *Nothing* was going to stop me from erasing him. Protecting Lexy drove my actions above all else.

No! We save lives. Kendra agreed with Caradoc. *Keep him alive. Is there a way to control him?* Kendra asked as she recovered from expelling her dinner. With access to her thoughts, she didn't have to finish her mental words for us to understand.

Lexy's mind shared with us an image of the necklace around the Vampire King's neck. The necklace held over a dozen stones. Lexy knew little about the enchanted stones, only that many suspected they were what made him so powerful.

Kendra and Lexy started working together to form a plan.

I ignored it. I had my own plan. A simpler plan. They protested. I was going to put every drop of magic I could find in a magic missile and try to erase him again. I planned to use enough magic that I'd risk not surviving the spell.

Don't! Both Lexy and Kendra's minds shouted at the same time.

I reached for the magic and found . . . nothing.

The Vampire King had effortlessly slammed a containment around Lexy, Kendra, and me and sucked away our magic.

John Kaloyan flashed a ghastly smile. Why did the horror movie phrase, "He-e-e-e-re's Johnnie!" flash through my mind? He touched a stone hanging from his neck and raised the other hand toward O'Brien, who no longer had my seal around him. He was helpless. As if hit by a car, O'Brien flew into the far wall, his body dented the sheetrock with a loud crack. His body hung in the wall for a second before limply tumbling to the hardwood floor.

I stood, shocked. I'd thought we'd turned the tables on Lexy's grandfather. I'd been wrong. He hadn't come here doubting victory. He wouldn't have risked himself if he thought there was even the slightest chance that he wouldn't survive. He had known all along that even by himself he outgunned us. Heck, he out-*everythinged* us. We had surprised him by taking out his nightwalkers, druids, and one general, but he was still in control.

Mr. Espinoza's words flashed in my mind. *Always have a last resort. Three waves.* The Vampire King was his own last resort. The third wave.

I swore and made the decision that surprised even Alexis.

I grabbed at the molecules of my skin—all but the thinnest layer of it—and threw in a lot of cells from my muscles as well. I'd known my muscles would matter before this was over. I had plenty, and I was going to finally use them for something more important than running over kids in football pads.

After converting enough mass to energy for another magic missile, I tore an exit hole in the containment. I quivered as the widespread agony exploded like a million shards of glass cutting inside my skin and muscles.

With extreme effort, I managed to stay standing.

The Vampire King glanced at me and his eyes flickered, perhaps noticing the change in my skin and my sudden weakness.

"*Bealustræl!*" I yelled.

The magic missile formed, darting at the vampire. I'd shoved far more power into this blue-and-white orb than into the first missile. This one had cost me so much more, too, burning away masses of muscle and all but an ultra-thin membrane of skin on my arms.

The orb of energy flew into his chest, and once again, his chest began to glow.

Earlier, when he'd first walked in, the magic missile I had thrown at him had taken all his energy and all his focus for multiple seconds. If this second magic missile could give Lexy those same seconds . . . Maybe Lexy could find a way to destroy him . . . except by her oath she couldn't. Idiot! I risked everything on one missile. I was the only one that could fight him and I'd just taken myself out. I despaired.

Lexy made a decision.

No! I tried to scream out loud, but I was collapsing, my consciousness slipping—and maybe my life, too. Silent or not, my shout echoed in Lexy's mind, but she ignored it. I hit the wooden floor hard, breaking the thin membrane of skin remaining on the back of my bald head.

I'd lost consciousness too many times recently. I refused to do it again. But the blackness came anyway. I fought back hard and miraculously, I was standing again, just a few steps in front of where I'd fallen. When had I stepped forward? I wobbled with confusion and dizziness. I almost fell again, but Kendra's mind steadied me, even though she was confused, too.

My eyes fixed on Lexy, who had darted toward her grandfather with open arms. The Vampire King, still fighting off my magic missile, snarled and stuck out his long dagger. Lexy continued forward and draped her arms around his neck. One with her mind, I felt the blade slide through her as if it had pierced my chest—my heart.

Lexy hugged her grandfather as if holding herself up. His cheeks raised, changing his snarl into a smile, and his black eyes sparked red in pleasure.

"And. Thus. It. Ends!" he forced each word out, dampening her ear with his spit.

He held her a moment. His countenance softened, but his smile remained. His fangs retreated as he stroked down Lexy's bald scalp and neck with one clawed hand, then gripped her between the shoulder blades as if he was just an ordinary grandfather hugging his granddaughter, except his smile held no sweetness, no love. He couldn't hide the pleasure of finally killing his unwanted granddaughter.

The embrace lasted a few seconds as the life drifted from Lexy's body.

I felt Lexy pull on my magic. Why?

Then the Vampire King pushed her away, leaving the blade in her chest. As she fell backward, she gripped his necklace of enchanted stones and pulled it from his neck. When she landed on her back, the necklace slipped from her fingers, and the crystals clattered against the floor. One link next to the clasp was missing.

Lexy had used me to convert the link to magic and free the necklace.

His smile dropped.

My breath caught.

Lexy's dead.

I looked up as the Vampire King's pupils turned white, the rotten smell of fear clouding the room. He bent to reach like Gollum for his precious crystals, but a shotgun blast rang out painfully in my ears, the pellets slamming into the Vampire King and knocking him back a step.

Lexy's control over Luiz and O'Brien had died with her.

Luiz pumped a shell into the chamber and fired the shotgun again. He kept pumping and firing until he'd unloaded everything he had into the Vampire King. Each explosion of pellets slammed into the vampire's chest, flinging him back another step. The pellets left hundreds of bloody holes that healed noticeably slower than before.

Luiz ran out of shotgun shells, allowing the Vampire King to stagger back toward the necklace lying inches from Lexy's lifeless hand.

Kendra, no longer blocked from magic, created a breeze that blew the necklace away from the king. I tried to grab at magic, but it seemed to slip between my fingers. Where was Kendra? I couldn't see her.

I tried to lunge for the necklace, but my body didn't respond. Instead, my knees hit the floor. Why did Kendra fall to her knees, too?

Luiz went for the necklace, but the Vampire King raised his hand and Luiz stopped as if he'd hit a glass wall.

Stop him! I shouted with my mind at Kendra. Kneeling, Kendra flashed sunlight at him, just as Alexis had done, but all she could manage was a brief flash of light. Without his enchanted crystals to protect him, the light caused the Vampire King to recoil before he started toward his necklace again. Kendra couldn't slow him down for long. Not with magic this new to her. If only I could use magic—or even walk.

You have to use more magic, I urged.

Kendra stood, and somehow I stood with her. She opened herself up to more magic and sent a weak magic missile at the Vampire King. It hit him and knocked him back.

Kendra staggered backward too. She had wielded too much magic on her first day. Her head started to spin. She saw glittering spots in front of her eyes. Why did I see the same spots?

A lithe figure flashed in front of me with vampire speed, leaving a scent of vanilla. She swooped up the necklace from the floor and darted back a safe distance. Carina clasped the chain of crystals around her neck. Her eyes fixed on the Vampire King. He glared right back.

"Carina!" the Vampire King shouted her name like a curse. His eyes flashed from white to black and then back to white.

Kendra grabbed at more magic but couldn't do anything with it. Our vision blurred.

The Vampire King, now recovered from the missile, darted toward Carina, jumping indifferently over Lexy's lifeless body. His fangs and claws extended. Carina stood there waiting for him. He tried to bowl her over, but her hands struck like snakes, grabbing John Kaloyan's face while she stepped to the side. His head stopped, but his momentum swung his feet forward, lifting him from the ground. For a second, his body floated horizontally in the air until Carina slammed the Vampire King to the hardwood floor with a loud thud.

I thought she would kill him, but she didn't. I didn't understand why she held him by the face, pressed to the floor. Then I recognized the way both her hands touched his cheeks. She was asserting her vampire control on him—enthralling him. The Vampire King struggled, but Carina, enhanced by the very crystals he had once worn, overpowered him. Her eyes bored into him as he flailed his claws at her, ripping through her black dress and cutting her flesh. But the deep scratches he inflicted on her skin healed quickly.

His flailing slowed and stopped.

Lexy's mother had just tamed the Vampire King.

CHAPTER 50
BLOOD

Ignoring everyone else, I ran to Lexy. Despite dodging the bodies of dead vampires and nightwalkers, I strangely did not feel the pain of my missing skin and dissolved muscle. My pain was distant, as if in a different body.

I could no longer hear Lexy's mind in my head or feel our connection. So much blood—it had poured from her chest into a thick pool on a smooth patch of wooden floor the grenade hadn't damaged. I pulled the blade out, wincing at the hole it left just under her left breast. I cradled her head in my arms. Her naked skin, raw from converting a layer of it to magic, had paled. Her veins no longer bulged. The blood covered her like red paint on a white canvas. Her eyes had lost any trace of color. Her pumpkin spice aroma had disappeared with her life, replaced by the metallic smell of blood.

"No!" I cried, my voice oddly high. I didn't want her to die. "Save her!" I shouted at Carina, who looked at me emotionlessly.

Even though part of Kendra shared my sorrow, another part of her felt relieved by Lexy's death. I turned to glare back at her angrily. Except . . . all I found behind me was my own body lying on the hardwood floor, stripped of all but the thinnest layer of skin.

Disorientation overwhelmed me, and I looked down. The white throw blanket slipped from my grip as I nearly passed out on top of Lexy. The body I occupied was not mine. It was Kendra's. Her hand reached for the throw and covered herself back up, her modesty an instinctual reaction.

I'm in you, I thought to Kendra, but she already knew. I must have shoved Kendra's mind aside and gained majority control of her body. Now she pushed back, trying to regain control. I wasn't sure which one of us decided to look back at Lexy. I loved Lexy. Her death hurt me to the very core—even inside Kendra's body, my chest ached and a knot traveled up my throat. OK, it was Kendra's chest and throat, but I could feel the sensations as if they were my own. Or had I just felt Kendra's reaction to glancing at my body?

Kendra's jealousy of Lexy and grief at my death raged at me. But I withstood it, nudging her mind toward thoughts and experiences that proved that I also loved Kendra.

I couldn't believe that just a few minutes ago I had been ready to launch an all-out death assault on Lexy for draining Luiz's dad, for supposedly betraying me by stealing the crystal from O'Brien.

I stared at Lexy's face as I cradled her.

I'm sorry, Jake, Kendra offered.

Kendra had first met Alexis at the funeral.

She visited me at home Monday night, she added.

Monday had been my first night at Lexy's mansion. I had stayed up late working on the protection stone.

When Kendra had met Alexis, she'd thought Alexis may be the coolest girl she'd ever met. She'd even thought of making Lexy her best friend over Sis.

I didn't know it was her allure, Kendra thought. Kendra's mind was split between her anger at Alexis for erasing her from my memory and comforting me. She'd also used her influence to take control of Mom, Justine, and the jeeks.

Days later, with the protection stone, Lexy was free from her grandfather. She originally planned to run, to disappear forever. But our time together had ruined her plan—the fireworks, the grove, all of it. Lexy had fallen in love with me. In the grove, I couldn't hide that I loved her back.

Only because she made you forget me! Kendra snapped.

I hadn't just imagined Lexy's aroma here at the cabin. She'd been here. Lexy had forced Kendra to take my protection stone.

Sorry, I tried, Kendra remembered. She'd almost broken free of Lexy's allure, almost told me, while I taught her to use magic.

She needed it to free her mother from the Vampire King. She hoped that once free, her mother would take our side. And she did, Kendra thought. *Did I just defend her?* she complained.

I shifted Lexy in my arms. Her colorless eyes haunted me. My tears fell from Kendra's cheeks to Lexy's, making it seem that Lexy cried with us.

But she drained Mr. Espinoza! Kendra added, still split between anger and consoling me.

Lexy's proud claim of never having killed for blood wasn't exactly true. Lexy had killed for blood many times. However, Mr. Espinoza was the first person she had *willingly* killed for blood. Her grandfather had compelled her every other time.

311

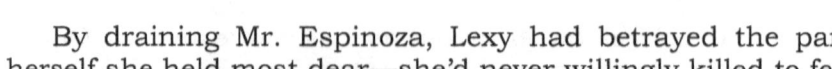

By draining Mr. Espinoza, Lexy had betrayed the part of herself she held most dear—she'd never willingly killed to feed.

Why?

For you, Kendra answered.

Lexy had hoped to save us without a battle. Mr. Espinoza's strategic mind—the one that made him a chess master—had become the missing piece. She used him to help form a plan. Her oath of peace was critical to the plan, but sealing it required blood and death. She had to kill to feed.

She'd smelled the death on Mr. Espinoza the first time they met. Why hadn't Luiz told me that his dad had lung cancer? With all his constant coughing recently, I'd known he was sick, but I hadn't figured it out.

Mr. Espinoza was already planning to stage an accident, so instead of paying for treatment, his life insurance would go to his wife and son. He hadn't gotten treatment. He was weeks from death.

Did that absolve her of draining him dry?

No, Kendra answered.

Still holding Lexy's head, I couldn't take my eyes—or Kendra's eyes—away from her face. Lexy had finally obtained her freedom, yet she'd risked her life—even given her life—to save mine, Kendra's, Luiz's, and maybe O'Brien's.

I thought she'd give me to the Vampire King, Kendra thought.

But I love you, and she loved me, I thought.

She saved me for you, Jake!

Blood still trickled from the knife wound in Lexy's chest, almost in waves, each a few seconds apart. Perhaps a spasm of her heart.

Or a heartbeat, Kendra thought. *Is she still alive?*

No. I didn't dare hope. A single heartbeat didn't mean she was alive. I had a better way to check. I pushed magic into Kendra's eyes.

Immediately my vision changed. Light came from everywhere. Everywhere except for the one place I hoped to see it most. Except for the healing stone, which still sent tendrils of magic into Lexy, her body had no light. No spirit.

Can the healing stone bring her back?

Had it been my thought, I would have cast it aside. It wasn't possible. But it was Kendra's thought. Hope took control of me completely. I dropped the magic sight as my mind raced.

Could we help out the stone? Yes. Blood. To heal, she needed blood. A large pool of blood, still wet, surrounded me—or actually Kendra—much more blood than should have come from her body. She had just breathed Mr. Espinoza's blood into her veins.

Her heart had pumped the blood of two adults onto the hardwood floor.

The throw blanket covering Kendra's body, once white, had soaked up some of it, dyeing it crimson.

We laid Lexy's bald head down in the midst of the pool of crimson liquid. We scooped blood into Kendra's hands and brought it to Lexy's mouth. Kendra's nose wrinkled at the metallic smell of blood as we tried to pour the blood into Lexy's mouth. Most of it hit her lips and spilled down her cheeks.

None of the blood had coagulated. Maybe vampire—er, half dhampir blood—didn't coagulate?

I used Kendra's bloodied hands to tilt Lexy's hairless head back and open her mouth wider before scooping a second handful of blood into her mouth. This time more of it stayed in.

Lexy's body twitched. I couldn't tell if she'd reacted to the blood or if Kendra's arms had simply brushed against her as we reached for another scoop of blood.

Luiz let out a string of swear words in Spanish and ran to the kitchen, his feet slapping on the hardwood in the silence. He came back with a dustpan, damp from a quick rinse, which he handed to me—er, to Kendra.

"Here, use this for the *chica's* blood," he said.

Scooping blood with a dustpan made Kendra dry-heave, but she'd already vomited her dinner by the grenade-tattered couch. Kendra's mind stepped back, letting me take more control, grateful to take a back seat.

I placed the dustpan tight to the hardwood floor in one hand and scooped blood into it with the other. Slowly, I—well, Kendra and I—we poured it into Lexy's mouth.

"What about Jacob?" Luiz asked, and I felt the knot form in Kendra's stomach.

"He will live," Carina cut in. "Do not touch him. Do not move his body. Do not wrap him in anything. His skin will heal." Carina spoke with an alluring forcefulness. The Vampire King's crystals increased her influence. We obeyed and believed her without question. The knot in Kendra's stomach relaxed, and once again we only worried about Lexy. We continued to pour blood from the floor back into her mouth.

"Come on, Lexy," I breathed the words with Kendra's voice.

A bubble formed at her lips. I popped it before pouring more blood. I hadn't detected her muscles move.

"Maybe it's working." Kendra voiced her hope. Kendra's mind pushed forward, taking back control of her body. She refilled the dustpan and drizzled more of the blood into Lexy's open mouth.

I know, she thought. *I shouldn't care about this boyfriend-thieving witch, but you do, so I do!* With our minds joined, she was having trouble distinguishing my feelings for Lexy from her own.

We continued the makeshift circulatory system. Blood down the throat, to the lungs, back out the blade-hole at her heart. For over ten minutes, she showed no movement.

Wait! I thought.

Was that a swallow? Kendra asked.

Were we imagining it? Perhaps it was just the weight of the blood in her mouth that forced her throat open, allowing the blood to drain into vacant space. Were we imagining the almost imperceptible waves of blood were a heartbeat? Perhaps they were just pockets of air rising from the cavity of her chest.

Then a larger surge of blood spurted from Lexy's chest as if her heart had managed one strong beat. I hoped it had, but the blood bubbled with air that rose from the opening in her chest and popped. It had just been a pocket of air. I pushed sight into my eyes. There was still no spirit.

Again, I dropped the magic sight.

My hope died with it.

CHAPTER 51
BREATH

K endra poured more blood into Lexy's mouth. But Lexy's mouth filled and overflowed. The blood no longer drained. Kendra reached her finger into Lexy's mouth and felt around. She pushed Lexy's tongue out of the way. Lexy's jaw snapped shut. Kendra jerked her hand away, but not before one fang sliced her finger.

With her mouth closed, Lexy swallowed hard. Her throat flexed as she swallowed, moving her head slightly. We watched, amazed as Kendra's finger healed. Lexy opened her mouth expectantly, and Kendra obliged, scooping blood into the dustpan and drizzling it into Lexy's open mouth.

Lexy's tongue moved. She closed her mouth and swallowed again. This time, when her mouth reopened, she drew in a deep breath, breathing in more blood than air. Her chest rose and fell, and her aroma returned with newfound strength. Kendra's stomach growled in hunger—possibly for pumpkin pie.

The desire for blood forced its way into Kendra and me. It was all we wanted. We needed it. Luiz stared as we both moved Kendra's hands to scoop up some blood and drink it—no, not drink it, breathe it. Thankfully, Kendra came to her senses before the blood reached her lips. The desire for blood was not ours. It was Lexy's. Her mind had rejoined ours.

"Lexy!" Kendra and I shouted as one, literally.

Jake. Her mind responded, but she could only focus on one thing. *Blood. I need blood.*

I couldn't resist. For the third time, I forced magic into my sight. A dim spirit pulsed from her once-empty body. Hope soared into me as Kendra pushed the sight from her eyes.

The wound below Lexy's left breast remained open, but blood stopped pumping out of it. We continued to scoop the blood into her mouth until the pool beneath her was gone and only a sticky stain covered the hardwood. Lexy breathed in the blood, pulling it directly into her lungs and from there, directly into her veins.

Lexy blinked, drawing my attention to her eyes, which had turned from black to red. Her face looked pink—a far better color than the pale white it had been a dozen minutes before.

"Welcome back, my daughter," Carina whispered. I hadn't noticed her come over and kneel next to Lexy. Strangely, the Vampire King stood next to her, and she clutched his hand as if afraid to let go.

A shot of hate lurched in my chest, but Kendra helped stifle it.

Carina moved her other hand over her daughter's face. It looked very . . . motherly . . . which contrasted with the indifference she'd shown earlier—perhaps I had misread her.

Lexy's eyes closed at her mother's touch and her mind slipped away.

"No," I said through Kendra, fearful Lexy's return to life had only been temporary. My spirit ached at the possibility that I'd lose her after filling my mind with so much hope.

"Relax, druid," Carina commanded, her words reverberating through my body. "She is a dhampir. Sleep speeds her healing."

Lexy's mind was quiet but still there. Using Kendra's lungs, I breathed a deep sigh of relief.

"Should we get her to a bed? Can we move her?"

"Yes, druid," Carina replied.

Kendra tried to lift her but failed. Kendra didn't have nearly the strength I was accustomed to. I glanced at Carina, but she had one hand occupied.

"Luiz?" We didn't need a mental connection with Luiz for him to know what we were asking. He glanced at his father's corpse, then helped us lift Lexy. We carried her to the second bedroom on the left and laid her down on the bed. Kendra and Luiz pulled the blanket and top sheet out from under her and covered her up. We—Kendra and I, not Luiz—stayed there beside her for a moment until the knot holding the white throw blanket around Kendra came loose. I looked down, again disoriented by seeing Kendra's . . . well . . . body.

Quit looking! Kendra snapped and tied the white throw blanket around herself again. Her reprimand made me feel guilty, as if I were a cheap pervert like my stepdad. Kendra's mind recoiled at the memory of my stepdad—the extent of his perversion was new to her as she hadn't explored that memory of mine yet.

I'm sorry. You're not like him, Jake. Kendra comforted me. *I didn't mean to imply you were.*

We went to Kendra's room, and I courteously moved to the back of her mind as she slipped on some clothes. Kendra cringed at the idea of getting her outfit bloody, but she didn't want to shower yet with me in her head, so she dressed anyway.

We returned to the front room and finally saw the results of the melee.

Luiz knelt next to the pale body of his father, crying. Kendra walked us over to him and knelt down beside him, putting her hand on his shoulder. I tried to give him a comforting look. It hurt to see him look at his father this way: drained of blood yet splattered with it. A thumb-sized sliver of wood—shrapnel maybe—stuck out of Mr. Espinoza's cheek. Luiz glanced up, tears streaking down his face. Of course, he was looking at Kendra, not knowing that I was there too.

For once, Luiz didn't make a joke. He just cried.

Kendra stood, leaving Luiz to grieve, and looked around. The wall between the front room and the kitchen had a nightwalker-sized hole in it. A pair of two-by-fours dangled like fractured bones. Through the hole, I could see the charred and decapitated form of a nightwalker. Dane's remains lay by the door, charred like firewood. Between where the card table had once been and the grenade-shredded couch, three more charred and decapitated nightwalker bodies lay nearby. One of them lay over Besnick's headless and shrapnel-mutilated body. Ivana and Artan's bodies littered the floor. The two old druids were still crumpled at the base of a wall. They might be alive—at least, the female druid appeared to be breathing.

The ceiling was peppered with hundreds of holes and pieces of shrapnel from the grenade. Sprays of red blood covered the walls and the ceiling. Blood splattered the floor, except where the grenade had blasted the hardwood apart. The splatter covered Mr. Espinoza's body and stretched to the huge stain where Lexy's body had been.

O'Brien now lay unconscious on the couch under the hole in the wall. The grenade had mostly spared that couch. Carina stood next to the Vampire King, who had barely moved or spoken since Carina had asserted control over him. Carina's dress, torn where the king had lashed at her as she'd taken control of him, exposed the skin of her abdomen. Her skin now appeared smooth and undamaged. She no longer held the king's hand.

Kendra and I glared at the Vampire King. The sight of him still made our blood boil. I hated him for atrocities he'd committed—mostly for forcing himself on Lexy, for forcing her to kill, and for

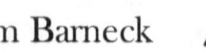

"gifting" her. He was pure evil. Sure, Carina had him contained, but I'd read once that evil contained is not evil destroyed.

Carina and her pet king stood near the door. Carina now wore two necklaces. One belonged to the Vampire King. The other was mine. She saw where Kendra's eyes were looking and immediately removed my necklace.

"I believe this is yours, Jake," Carina held it out to us. Her vanilla scent, far more powerful than Lexy's aroma now, distracted me from asking her how she knew I was in Kendra's body.

"Thank you," we said, walking over and taking it from her.

"Don't stay in that body too long, Jake. You need to get back to yours. You are still alive," Carina said.

As Kendra put on the red ruby protection stone, we looked at my body.

You'll live? Kendra's breath caught. Then she looked at my flayed body and shivered.

What's left of me will, I answered.

As Kendra fastened the necklace, Carina's aroma diminished from intoxicating to just a nice scent.

"How do . . ." we started to ask how to get back to my body, but we stopped because Kendra and I were both telling her mouth to say different words.

"I do not know." Carina's eyes flicked to my body and back to us. "I must take the Vampire King and leave now. Be warned that I cannot promise you safety," she informed me. "No one must know that I am in control of him. I must be discreet. Changes must occur slowly."

"Why are you telling us this?" we asked.

"Because, while I do not know what part the Vampire King played in the near genocide of the druids, our kind did play a part. We chose to join the fight against the druids. I cannot unmake that choice. I am not sure which faction we joined or who is in charge, but the Vampire King feared them. They will continue to give him orders and for now, we will continue to obey them. I cannot risk my control over the Vampire King to protect you. Once we leave, you must consider us to be enemies."

"Oh!" Kendra widened her eyes, and I tensed her muscles, our two minds reacting differently to her unexpected words.

"Relax, druid. We are not enemies yet." She smiled at us briefly then her stern look returned. "The Vampire King must return victoriously. He cannot be seen as weak. We need a story. The more it is based on truth, the easier the lie."

"Lexy asked to rule the new world," we suggested.

318

"Good start." Carina nodded. "My father spurned her by offering the position not only to her but to whichever general could kill her. To the victor go the spoils. He has used the tactic before, and it will be believed."

She paused as if still shaping the Vampire King's story.

I glanced at Luiz, who still cried over his father.

"Two more truths. She killed Dane and won the night. She swore her blood oath of peace. The Vampire King granted her request: Lexy will rule the new world and answer only to him. She will still have to appear on All Souls' Day as the Vampire King demanded."

"What about us? Is someone still after us?"

"Yes and no. You are hardly more than children—"

"Hey, we won today," I cut in, with Kendra's help.

"You were lucky. It was Caradoc they were after and he was not here," Carina continued. "We had orders not to kill you two. They are collecting potentials and young druids, not killing them." She let those words sink in. "I call you druid, but magic use does not make you a druid. The Vampire King took orders from someone. Hopefully they will believe you are nothing more than a petty magic user under Lexy's control."

Her red eyes shifted to my flayed and hairless body still lying on the floor. Kendra cringed.

"You are different, Jacob. You are a druid and yet you are something else—something more. Your body surviving even now proves it. I shall keep your secret. But if anyone finds out what else you are, nothing will slow the legions that will hunt you. I should kill you for what you are. I cannot believe I saved your life again." She shook her head, red earrings and black hair swaying.

"What do you mean by *again*?"

"Who do you think used magic to warn you of danger last night?" She looked at me. "It is a pity you destroyed the shooters before I could question them."

"Wait, the two guys with rifles weren't with you?"

"Of course not." She eyed me like I was a child. "I assume their leaders know you are a druid. If you are lucky, they are unaware of what else you are."

"What else am I?" I asked, then Kendra gulped, reminding me I shared her body.

Carina looked at me, raising one eyebrow at my question in a way that enhanced her resemblance to Lexy. She didn't answer my question, though.

"You and Kendra are Lexy's generals. Be her generals. Make the lie true. I will announce it. Perhaps that will give you some protection, but it will also add to your danger."

We nodded.

"I am Lexy's mother, and yet I am not. Lexy and I are rivals. Remember that. Perhaps one day, I will meet you again as a friend. Until then, you are my enemy." She grabbed the Vampire King's hand and turned toward the door.

She glanced at the charred remains of Dane that blocked the front door then gestured to the king. He kicked the unrecognizable ash form out of the way then opened the door. Together, they stepped out into the darkness.

I followed them to the door and looked out, wanting to ask her what I was one more time. I wanted to know what she knew about me. I searched the night for them, but they had already disappeared into the darkness.

CHAPTER 52
CLEANSING

Kendra wanted to go to bed, and I wanted to return to my body and heal. But Luiz, covered in blood that was mostly not his own, sat crying over his father. And the wrinkly-faced druid woman lay there breathing, able to wake up at any time. We didn't want to leave Luiz alone in his sorrow or leave the druid to wake up and kill us all in our sleep.

Should I just vanquish the druid? A part of me yearned for the ecstasy that accompanied such magic, but my desire repulsed Kendra, so I pushed it away. Besides, the druid woman lay harmlessly on the bloodied hardwood floor. Outside the heat of battle, I couldn't justify erasing her existence as self-defense. Such defenseless killing would be cold-blooded murder. Kendra agreed.

We took the two rune-covered staffs and wondered if we could use them. We didn't know if the staffs were magically tied to their owners. Once again, we were reminded how little we understood the druid world. The druid textbook contained only a brief mention of runes, nothing in depth. Maybe somewhere there was a giant library of druid texts that could explain everything. Did O'Brien know of such a place? If so, would he be willing to risk our safety to get us more books?

We took a blanket from my room and rolled the druid woman tightly inside it. We found a ski rope outside in the boat—my idea—and wrapped most of its seventy-five feet around the blanket-wrapped druid. We found a hammer and nails among the tools in the garage. With loud pounding that echoed in the nearly destroyed front room, we nailed her blanket to the floor.

Luiz looked away from his dad and gave Kendra a questioning look, still unaware I shared her body. He had stopped crying, but his eyes were red, and tears had cut clean lines through the grime on his face.

"We're trying to keep her from either getting away or using magic," we told him.

He nodded and turned back to his father. He whispered something in Spanish.

We couldn't draw a circle around the druid. Blood covered too much of the floor. We decided on gravel. It took a few trips to gather enough to circle the druid. Then we created a self-powered containment.

Should we clean up the other bodies? I asked.

Ugh! Kendra didn't want to.

As we approached the first of the four nightwalkers' severed heads, Kendra passed out—at least her mind did—leaving me awkwardly alone in her body, as if I were an intruder. For the first time all night, I didn't have someone else's thoughts and emotions floating around my head—or in this case, Kendra's head.

I didn't want Kendra or Lexy to wake up to this scene, so I started cleaning. I felt compelled to protect them from seeing it.

I found a roll of black plastic sacks in the garage next to a barrel. With a loud slap of air, I whipped a bag open. The nightwalker heads didn't just look obsidian; they were heavy and hard like obsidian. It was as if they had turned to stone in sunlight, which reminded me of three trolls and a clever little hobbit.

I slid my hands under the arms of a headless nightwalker and lifted. It moved about an inch. Would I have been strong enough before I burned away my muscles?

The first nightwalker I encountered had bowled me over, sending me flying against the Bangerter Highway sound barrier. Fighting a single nightwalker had seemed impossible then, and yet we'd just survived four of them.

Carina was right. We were lucky to be alive.

My body lay on the hardwood. It didn't look alive. OK, my chest moved up and down. Carina said it was alive. I trusted her completely. I hadn't worried about my own body, horrible as it looked. Her command held, and though a part of me knew my body was not well, Luiz and I continued to obey her. We didn't touch it.

I tried to drag a nightwalker body instead of lifting it. It didn't move.

Luiz pulled himself away from his father's corpse and helped me. He grabbed the hammer and smacked the obsidian corpse a few times until it broke in half, rage-room style.

After a few minutes, Luiz extended the hammer toward me. "Try it. It helps." He swallowed.

I took a turn. He was right. It did help.

We struggled for the better part of an hour to work the rest of the bodies into black bags and drag them into the garage. The front room looked much better without the bodies. It still looked like a grenade went off in it, because, well, one did, but it looked better.

O'Brien slept on the couch, and we decided not to move him.

We helped Luiz lift his dad's body. My chest ached for Luiz as we carried his dad to the bedroom where O'Brien had slept the night before. We left him lying peacefully on the bed and went back to the double-sized front room.

We spent the next hour cleaning what remained of the hardwood floor. Fortunately, there was a mop and bucket, so we didn't have to improvise. We emptied twelve buckets. Was it a waste of energy? The desire to protect Kendra and Lexy from seeing the destroyed room drove me.

As I worked, I wondered. Would I go home and tell everyone I was not dead? How would I explain my disappearance from the morgue? How would I explain my lack of skin? How long would it take to heal? Would I be scarred for life? Where would I live? My mother had moved out the day after my funeral. Did her apartment even have enough space for me?

Perhaps I shouldn't go home. Maybe Jacob Stevens would stay dead and I would get a new identity. Vampires were pretty good at the whole new identity thing, so Lexy might have some connections to help with that. If not, I was certain O'Brien could help.

Would a new identity be the right choice? If I tried to go home, I would become a news spectacle, and that was the last thing I wanted. I had never wanted attention. I hated how being a high school football star had changed me. I hated being so good at something I cared so little about. I had just wanted to get out of my house and away from everybody. Only, now my wishes had changed. I wished there was a way back so I could return to the life I had thought I hated.

I used to be afraid someone would find out how I was conceived. What a stupid fear. So what? It just didn't seem that bad anymore. Sis, Kendra, Lexy—they all knew already.

I even wished to go back to school and finish my senior year. The kids in my school had always given me their full support. I had thought they had only liked me because I won football games, but when we lost the state championship, they'd still supported me. I should have noticed that, but I hadn't. A lot of them went to my funeral too. They supported me even in death. A twinge of guilt rippled through my chest for calling them barnacles. I had been such a jerk.

"So . . . is someone still after us?" Luiz asked.

"I don't know. Carina wasn't sure," I responded, still not used to hearing Kendra's voice when I talked.

"What about the druid-filled blanket crêpe on the floor?" Luiz pointed.

I laughed—well, I guess I giggled like a girl because I sort of was one at the moment.

"I was going to go with taco or burrito, but she looks French."

"I'm not sure what to do with her. I'll keep watch," I offered. "You go get some sleep."

"Yeah, right!" Luiz shook his head. "You need to sleep first. You're a girl."

I didn't try to tell him it was my mind hanging out in Kendra's body. Still, he was right. Kendra's body was tired and ready to drop. I nodded in agreement.

"You need your sleep so you can grow some hair back to cover that glowing melon of yours," he laughed, pointing to Kendra's bald scalp. Luiz could be funny, so I shouldn't have been surprised, but I was. How could someone laugh after what had just happened? How could he laugh so soon after losing his dad? The answer was simple. Humor was Luiz's magic. He called on it when he needed it, and he needed it now more than ever.

"Better no hair than your hair," I jested, smiling back.

"Have you seen your *cabeza*? If you were standing in front of a window, I'd think I was looking at the moon."

I touched Kendra's bare scalp. It was perfectly smooth. Her legs too. No product on the market could give her such a close shave.

"Speaking of the moon, you sure were flashing yours around during the fight. Never pegged you as a girl who likes to fight naked. Maybe you should plan an encore and invite the whole drill team."

I imagined Kendra would have given him a hard stare, so I tried to do the same. I botched it.

"Sounds good. I'll call Andrea. She can help plan it. I'll make sure she knows it was your idea."

He blanched when I mentioned Andrea.

"You're so grumpy. You need some *sueños*," Luiz grinned.

"Agreed," I nodded. "Oh, if she wakes up," I pointed to the druid woman, "you wake me, OK? Do not let her out."

Luiz nodded.

I walked over to my own body and stood over it. I willed myself to go back but nothing happened. I tried again, imagining my spirit floating out of Kendra's body and into mine, but again it didn't work. Of course, if it had worked, Kendra's mind was sleeping. She would have fallen to the floor and hit her head.

How do I return to my body?

CHAPTER 53
AWAKENINGS

Since I was still in Kendra's body, I went to her room and lay down on her bed. I left her clothes on. Sure, I'd just seen her naked, so if I undressed her, would it matter? But with her mind sleeping, I didn't even consider going there. It was one step too close to something my stepdad would do.

I closed her eyes and willed my mind to go back to my own. Still, nothing happened. How had I left my own body? I had done it as my body lost consciousness. I didn't think Kendra would appreciate me knocking her out . . .

Oh. Duh!

I breathed slow and even, seeking sleep. As sleep came, I felt my mind—or more my spirit—pull back into my own body. Apparently, I'd experienced some type of astral projection—not exactly an out-of-body experience because I'd been in Kendra's body. I immediately regretted returning to my own body.

Pain. It was everywhere. I embraced unconsciousness immediately, but with it came the not-so-welcome dreams.

Kendra sat in my sister's room on the bed. They had been talking, but now they were glaring at each other. I'd never seen them look at each other so angrily.

"I'm sorry," Kendra said. "I just know he's not dead. I can't explain it, but he . . ."

"I can't deal with this anymore, Kendra! Just go!" Sis shouted in tears. "I have to pack anyway. We have friends from church coming to help us move in the morning."

Sis folded clothes into an open suitcase. Kendra turned and walked to the door. She stopped and turned back.

"That was him at the funeral. I just know—"

"Go!" Sis shouted.

Kendra left.

The dream changed.

Alexis stood in Luiz's front room, her hands on Mr. Espinoza's cheeks. Luiz sat blank-faced on the couch, already under her control.

"What have I found?" Alexis murmured, searching Mr. Espinoza's mind. "Your mind is . . . amazing," she said. "Your mind is the key."

She grinned and started pouring information into his mind.

"What can you do to improve my escape plan?" she asked.

The dream morphed again. It was the same dream I'd had the night before. This time, however, I wasn't just an observer; I was in it, playing the part of Alexis.

"Feed on the woman first. Then the children in order of age," the Vampire King commanded me. I wanted to refuse, but his control overwhelmed me. I obeyed, unable to challenge him.

The family from Ecuador screamed as I breathed in the blood of the mother and her two older children.

Filled with blood, I felt powerful. My body had swelled with stolen life, stretching my clothes tight. I stepped to the two-year-old girl and looked back at my grandfather in defiance. My eyes went black and I snarled, flashing my fangs. I turned back to the Vampire King.

"No," I challenged.

I turned back to the child, trying to block my grandfather's view with my body as I removed her shackles. I grabbed her and with superhuman speed, shot for the exit. But my grandfather was too quick. He cut me off, and I collided with him. The child flew from my arms, hitting the wall outside the cell and falling to the hard floor. The little girl didn't cry out—she didn't move.

My grandfather grabbed my hair and turned my head to face him.

"No," I screamed.

The Vampire King's hands gripped my bare shoulders. His touch tightened the control he had over me.

"Finish her," my grandfather shouted at me.

"No," I cried back, tears streaming from my red eyes.

He let go of my shoulder with one hand and backhanded me. I felt my cheekbone crack and my black hair fling across my face, sticking to both sweat and blood. He grabbed my shoulders again. He looked into my eyes with his own, black with fury. He held me.

326

I fought back, but he was so strong. I did the only thing I could do. I forced myself into unconsciousness.

I woke on the floor only seconds later to the father's screams. The Vampire King drained his two-year-old child in front of him. Then he dropped the lifeless girl to the ground, stepped beside her father, and exposed his neck.

He looked back at me.

"You will want to feed one day, Lexy. You will enjoy it," he shouted. Then he bit down.

The dream changed again.

I woke, unable to move. Someone . . . a man was in my room. At first, I could only see his silhouette. As he approached, I recognized him. It was just Luiz's dad—except that didn't make sense. He was dead.

I wanted to run, but my muscles wouldn't respond. He hesitated at the side of the bed, staring at me. His eyes looked wrong—black with pink streaks. Hungry—just like the Vampire King's eyes had been just before he bit into O'Brien.

I grabbed at my blanket and pulled it in front of me trying to cover up—trying to cover my bare neck where the protection stone hung. It did nothing to protect me from my own paralyzing fear. My lips quivered.

"Mr. Espinoza?" I finally managed, but it was Kendra's voice.

I twitched awake on the hardwood floor of the front room—my body screamed pain into my mind. There wasn't an inch of me that didn't hurt. It was still dark, but dawn was approaching.

I'd been chanting in my sleep. Outside, crickets chirped rhythmically, and my whisper kept their beat. *Hælan min scynn!* The words were so close to modern English that I didn't need help translating them.

Both Kendra's and Lexy's minds accompanied my own—all three of us once again thinking as one. I knew two things. First, Lexy was awake and mostly healed. Second, what I'd seen through Kendra's eyes was no dream.

The need to protect Kendra erupted inside me. I had to rise. I had to help her. As I did, the pain of my splitting membrane of skin shouted at my mind from every joint, forcing me to fall down. My flayed body had scabbed over while I slept—a single, giant epidermis-sized scab. Blood filled the cracks that formed near my joints. I fought off the pain and stood up, shuffling toward the hall.

"Luiz!" I yelled, panicked. I'd have yelled again, but pain cracked across my cheeks.

One step. Two steps. It hurt so bad. Were those my bloody footprints?

I heard Luiz's feet slapping the hardwood as he came out of the kitchen and met me in the hall.

"*¡Diablo!*" Luiz exclaimed, looking at me with wide, dark eyes.

I ignored him and forced my pained body to step toward Kendra's door.

"Kendra," I gasped. "She's in trouble." The agony of my splitting skin overwhelmed me, and I fell again. Falling hurt worse than moving. *I shouldn't be moving or falling.* I wasn't strong enough and I had barely begun to heal. However, the need to protect Kendra fought back against the pain, controlling me.

Luiz ran ahead of me, nearly colliding with Lexy as she threw her door open and stepped out. Pumpkin spice flooded the hall. She'd just woken and hadn't had time to dress, but she clenched the corner of a sheet in one fist, which still trailed behind her. Blood still marked parts of her body, but the wounds had completely healed and stubble already poked out of her scalp. The tattooed words below her navel stirred emotions inside me— guilt that I failed to kill her grandfather, sadness and empathy for what she'd had to endure.

She shared my sorrow at seeing her tattoo, a shameful reminder of what her grandfather had inflicted on her and made her do so many times. The shame exploded like the grenade, hitting my mind with emotional shrapnel. She wrapped the sheet around her body, hiding the reminder, and dashed to Kendra's door, Luiz and I trailing behind.

Lexy and I could both feel Kendra's fear. She felt our determination to protect her. Lexy flung open Kendra's door and rushed inside. I struggled to the door before I collapsed again. My feet, knees, and palms started bleeding.

"*¿Papá?*" Luiz shouted, freezing in shock.

Mr. Espinoza had his back toward us. He had one knee on the bed, leaning over Kendra, who now wore a white camisole. He held her body in an arch just above the bed. The blanket still covered her legs. His head was bent low, his face already buried in her neck.

"Halt!" Lexy ordered, holding the sheet around herself with one hand.

Mr. Espinoza's body stopped moving. He stopped feeding for a second but then continued.

Lexy tied the sheet at her shoulder, freeing both her hands so she could place them around Mr. Espinoza's head, touching his cheeks.

Grabbing the doorjamb, I managed to stand, ignoring the pain of touching anything. Then I stumbled toward them, my bloodied body barely obeying me.

"Halt!" Lexy ordered again. Only knowing that she directed the command at Mr. Espinoza and not at me allowed me to keep stumbling forward.

Mr. Espinoza dropped his arms and lifted his face from Kendra, and she collapsed back onto the bed—her mind no longer touching Lexy's or mine. I fell on the bed and grabbed Kendra, ignoring the pain of the blanket fibers on the torn, membrane-like remnants of my skin and the gruesome sight of my own arms and hands.

"No!" I cried.

She will live, Lexy spoke to my mind. *We stopped him in time. He took only enough blood to make her pass out.*

With Kendra in my arms, the two puncture marks on her neck healed right before my eyes. She was breathing fine.

With plenty of water and rest, she could be fed from again tomorrow, Lexy's unfiltered thought was only half comforting.

"¿P-p-papá?" Luiz stuttered from where he stood.

Lexy and I both looked at him. Turning my head made me wince. The breath that followed cracked the skin across my chest. Everything hurt.

"Your *papá* needs blood, Luiz," Lexy told him. "Will you—"

"No," I shouted over Lexy's words, but she ignored me.

"—give him some?" Lexy finished.

Let him. Lexy requested directly to my mind.

No! I mentally shouted back. She only planned to let Mr. Espinoza feed on his son for a pint or two, but it still felt wrong.

I am letting Luiz make the choice, she assured me. *I am not compelling him in any way.* She wasn't lying. She couldn't lie. Her mind was mine—my mind was hers.

Fine. It's his choice, I conceded.

Luiz looked from me to Lexy and back to his father, tears shining in his eyes.

"Jake? Why is *papá* alive?"

"Your father has turned," Lexy answered for me.

"No shit!" Luiz shouted back and then continued with a string of expletives in Spanish.

He's newly turned. Lexy thought to me. *I cannot control him much longer unless he gets enough blood to satisfy his hunger. I completely drained him, remember?*

I did remember, and I couldn't hide my horror. That horror rolled into Lexy, and although it hurt her, she accepted it willingly.

How did this happen?

I am not sure. He must have ingested vampire blood.

The image of Luiz kneeling over his dad jumped to the forefront of my mind. His entire body, including his face, had been splattered in blood—blood that hadn't been his. And a small piece of wood had stuck out from his cheek.

Yes. Lexy confirmed. *It is likely that enough blood entered through his mouth or the wound on his cheek.*

"Luiz, calm down," my voice grated out painfully. "Your dad either needs blood or we have to . . . uh . . . help him stay dead. What do you want to do?" I slurred each word through gritted teeth, trying to control the pain of speaking.

This is so messed up! I thought to Lexy. *I can't believe we're doing this to Luiz.*

We did not do this to Luiz. I did not turn his father last night. I was busy keeping us alive, remember.

I know. We were all trying to stay alive.

"Luiz." Lexy ignored me. "You have to decide. Do you want your father to live on as a vampire or do you want him to die?" Mr. Espinoza looked around and his hungry eyes settled on my bloodied body.

"I don't want him to be a monster," Luiz cried. "I don't want him to start killing people."

"He will not have to kill," Lexy assured him. "He can feed from many. He can live without killing. However, know this. He will change. Not completely, but he will not be the same father you remember. The choice to kill or not kill will be his."

Luiz cried and looked to me for help. He cringed at the sight of me and looked down. Mom sometimes flinched from me. My sister had recently recoiled from me. Now Luiz? Through Lexy's control, I felt his emotions. I frightened him. How hideous did my body have to be to make it the scariest thing in the room? To make it even worse than the idea of Luiz's dad being turned?

Lexy couldn't help but glance at me. I saw myself, mirrored through her eyes. Once, on YouTube, I'd seen what a burn victim looked like immediately after the fire. I'd thought nothing could look that hideous. I'd been wrong.

"We shall not choose for you, Luiz," Lexy asserted.

Luiz hesitated, then walked over to his father, muttering something in Spanish I couldn't quite hear.

"How?" Luiz asked Lexy.

"Give him your wrist."

Luiz raised his arm, then stopped. He seemed uncertain until his eyes focused on his dad's face. He raised his wrist next to his father's mouth. Once Luiz offered, Mr. Espinoza didn't hesitate to bite into his wrist. Luiz's blood dripped down his father's chin.

Lexy watched the feeding closely.

"That is enough," Lexy said after less than a minute, but Mr. Espinoza didn't respond. Lexy had to place her hands on Mr. Espinoza's cheeks again before he let go of his son's wrist. She then gave him her own wrist and he drank for a minute before she pulled away.

He needs more, Lexy communicated. I could feel her control over Mr. Espinoza slipping. He eyed me hungrily.

Suddenly, Mr. Espinoza grabbed my bleeding right hand and bit down.

"Aaaahhhh!" he screamed—the first sound he'd made—and flung my arm away with one hand and hammered it with the other, snapping the bones in my forearm.

Blisters bubbled on his lips as if he'd dipped them in boiling water.

"*¡Monstruo!*" Luiz shouted. "What did you do to him?" It took me a second to realize Luiz was calling *me* the monster, not his dad.

"I don't know," I breathed out, trying not to stretch the scab on my face as I talked. My wrist dangled from my already gruesome arm. I couldn't feel it. There was no pain. Shouldn't a broken arm hurt? Every inch of my body ached except everything below the break.

In seconds, Lexy pinned Mr. Espinoza to the wall, ordering him to stay. She then returned to me and carefully grasped my broken arm. The two holes where Mr. Espinoza's fangs had penetrated my skin had not healed instantly like they had for Kendra and Luiz—they continued to ooze blood.

Lexy touched the blood on my wrist. I heard a sizzling sound, and she yanked her hand back and winced. My blood hurt her.

What is he? Lexy wondered to herself, but I could hear her thoughts. *Sorry. What are you?* she asked me directly.

I answered by showing Lexy Carina's words. Her eyes widened. *Protector,* Lexy thought.

Then, with a quick motion, she set the broken bones in my forearm. I screamed in agony as the bones reconnected and the membranous skin where she applied pressure opened around her fingers. Lexy screamed too, wiping my blood from her hands. The pain of my broken arm, which had been absent before, flooded my already overwhelmed pain receptors and pushed everything out of my head—including Lexy and Kendra.

Sleep! Lexy shot the thought into my mind like an arrow. I felt sleep coming. I didn't understand at first how her vampire power had worked while I was wearing the protection stone. Kendra was wearing it, not me. Besides, she hadn't just used vampire power alone. She'd injected magic into her words, combining it with her allure.

My muscles relaxed. Lexy caught me and laid me next to Kendra as my eyes closed.

"Everything will be all right," Lexy whispered to me.

CHAPTER 54
ELDRA

I woke up to magic vibrating on my cheek from the soft touch of a female hand. Of course, my stomach growled like an alarm clock, so maybe that woke me and the soft hand was just a bonus.

I opened my eyes expecting to see Lexy or perhaps Kendra. Instead, Darth Wife's wrinkled face leaned over me, her long, gray hair hung to the side in a rope-like braid. I tried to jump back, but that was hard while lying in bed and feeling so weak. I thrashed backward a foot anyway. I felt a sting in my arm as an IV ripped out of my scarred skin and my nose itched from a feeding tube. A bead of blood formed on the tiny needle hole in my arm.

I grabbed the tube and pulled it, feeling it travel from my stomach up my esophagus and out. My nose stung, and except for when I sneezed, I kept my eyes on the wrinkled face in front of me. I coughed and tried to dampen my dry mouth.

Had the druid woman taken me hostage? Why were her eyes sad? Where was I? It was the room in Lexy's mansion. The large windows revealed the darkness of night.

"Relax." I heard Lexy's voice, but I couldn't hear her mind. "This is Eldra. She is harmless now."

I could feel Lexy's presence. Her emotions were dimmed but perceptible. I just couldn't read her thoughts. She felt both love and fear—both feelings directed at me. The fear was the more disconcerting emotion. It was not fear *for* me, it was fear *of* me.

I turned toward Lexy's voice. Dressed in an almost-modest, though still tight, version of her leather outfit, she was as beautiful as I remembered. Her black hair hung to her chin. She looked back at me with red eyes surrounded by full lashes and eyebrows.

How much time has passed? Why is she afraid of me? I wondered.

I didn't have time to dwell on that because the druid woman, who had blasted lightning at Kendra and me, sat next to me on the bed.

"Uh . . . why are we suddenly friends with Darth Wife?" I coughed, my throat scratchy from the tube. "We had her nice and wrapped up." Eldra's eyes were sad, not menacing.

"Yes, a druid crepe," Lexy laughed.

Eldra laughed, too. "Luiz is such a hoot."

I gaped at her. Why were she and Lexy laughing—together? And did she just say "hoot"? But the sadness returned to her eyes immediately after her laugh.

"Uh . . . why'd you let her out?" I eyed Lexy.

"Your blame is misplaced. Luiz let her out. Fortunately, he made a sound decision. She is completely friendly, Jake," Lexy assured me again. "Dane had been controlling her. His last command was for her to kill us, but his mastery over her faded after his death."

I looked at the aged druidess suspiciously. Should I trust her? Maybe she had fooled everyone. I looked at Lexy then back at the druid. Eldra wore no jewelry to help protect herself from Lexy's allure. She couldn't have fooled Lexy even if she'd wanted to. Could she? Or did this old druid know other ways?

"So, your name's Eldra, huh?"

"Well, a couple hundred years ago, it was *Young*-ra, but I became so old that I was forced to change it to *Eld*-ra." She chortled with a voice that sounded somewhere between jolly and a dying grandma's cough.

Luiz must have opened the bedroom door and heard the joke because he started laughing his head off. I cracked a grin, more at Luiz's laughing than at Eldra's joke. I touched my cheek. The grin had pulled my tight, scarred skin.

Eldra laughed at her own joke, but sadness still hid behind her eyes. While in Kendra's body, I'd helped haul away the body of her partner. Had they been more than partners? Had they been husband and wife?

"What did you let her out for?" I questioned Luiz.

"*¡Lo siento!*" Luiz apologized. "You were out—no skin and a broken wrist—Kendra was out too. Lexy and papá were taking O'Brien to the hospital. She woke up and I had to make a decision on whether she was *peligrosa* or not." He looked down, a little more serious. "I'm sorry *papá* broke your arm. I didn't mean to call you a *monstruo*."

I nodded, not sure how to respond. The memory of his dad flashed through my mind. He'd fed on Kendra, Luiz, and Lexy, and then had tried to feed off me. I looked at my arm that had been bitten. I couldn't see the bite marks. But even if they were visible, one giant, flaking scab covered my arm and would have camouflaged them. Why had my blood burned him? Maybe vampires had a serious allergy to Bombay blood type. I glanced at Alexis. What would have happened to her if she had bitten me?

"Hey, you want me to tell Kendra you're awake?" Luiz offered.

"Sure." I would have preferred waking up to Kendra's face than wrinkly old Eldra's.

Luiz hustled out the door, and I heard him yell to Kendra down the hall.

"Jacob, how do you heal so rapidly?" Eldra asked.

Lexy's eyes opened wider for a brief second. She knew the answer but remained quiet. I could feel her fear increase—her fear of me. I didn't understand why I couldn't share her thoughts anymore or why I frightened her.

I looked at my arms. I guessed she meant I healed fast because so much skin had grown back. I wouldn't have called my scarred and ugly skin healed, but I had rapidly regrown my layers of skin, even if it was hideous. I'd once crashed hard on my bike and scraped my forearm from wrist to elbow. It had scabbed up and then the scab had partially flaked off, leaving my skin white and flaky with dots of scab. Well, most of my epidermis looked like that. The rest looked wrinkly and almost-healed, like a few days after peeling off a blister. I prodded at the skin on my chest. Touching it didn't really hurt.

"I don't know," I lied.

"I'm a healer," Eldra stated. "I've never encountered anyone whose body responds to healing magic as yours does." She pointed to the black diamond I was wearing. Lexy must have lent it to me.

"What about a vampire?" I asked, indicating Lexy with the once broken, but now noticeably healed arm. Was it really still sore? Or had I just imagined a twinge where it had broken?

"Half dhampir," Lexy corrected me.

I felt a mix of exasperation and hurt feelings nudge into me. Alexis didn't like being called a vampire at all.

"OK. She's half dhampir," I restated. "She heals faster than I do."

"Of course, her kind heals quickly, but you are neither dhampir nor vampire." Eldra pursed her aging lips in thought, which deepened the many lines on her face. "Yet with Alexis's healing stone and my magic, you heal almost as fast as one. In all my years as a healer, I've never seen a regular person heal this fast even with magic. What are you, Jacob?" Her British accent wasn't thick, but it made me want to answer her as if she were royal.

"I don't know." I had asked Carina that same question. She hadn't answered me.

I had a faint memory of Lexy calling me something, but I couldn't remember what.

"No matter," Eldra stated. "Your skin has already grown back. We fed you as best we could through the NG tube and kept you hydrated with the IV. We couldn't give you enough nourishment. You're likely starving."

"I could eat a horse," I agreed.

"I've eaten horse before. It couldn't talk, but it sure was Mr. *Ed*-ible," Eldra laughed.

I looked at her like she was crazy, even though I got the ancient TV show reference. She reminded me of my scout leader when I was twelve. He also told bad jokes.

"Luiz said you took O'Brien to the hospital?" I asked.

"He's still recovering," Lexy responded. "His injuries were far worse than they seemed."

"Why the hospital?" I exclaimed. "While in a coma and dying, you kept him here, but now he needs a hospital?"

Lexy nodded.

Her silence meant O'Brien's injuries were worse than she wanted to burden me with. I considered pressing her, but didn't.

I slid my legs off the bed and found them weak. Fortunately, my body no longer weighed much. Even still, if I hadn't held onto the bed, I'd have collapsed.

My body mass had significantly decreased. I had toothpicks for arms and legs and my chest and abs, which had once controlled girls' eyes with nearly the same power as a vampire's allure, were nothing but a flat, hideous mess. Something welled up inside of me. Not pain. Something worse. I fought it off as best I could. I blinked away the moisture in my eyes before it could betray how the sight of myself affected me.

I tested my weight on my legs while holding onto the bed. After a minute, I felt stable enough. Unfortunately, I was in just my boxers. I hadn't noticed because boxers were more than I'd worn recently. I wouldn't have cared, but I didn't want anyone else to look at my hideous skin.

"Uh . . . where are my clothes?" I asked, just as Kendra walked in. She wore her hair in a boy cut. It had not grown nearly as long as Lexy's. Her lashes and eyebrows were mostly back.

She wore a light form-fitting shirt and plaid, knee-length shorts. She was still cute. Too cute for me, now.

I cringed at the thought of her looking at me this way. I sat down and pulled the blanket up to my neck.

"Jake!" Kendra's voice went up an octave. Like Lexy's, Kendra's thoughts were noticeably absent from my head, but her emotions came through. I could dimly feel both excitement and revulsion as she ran to me, hesitated for the smallest painful second, then lightly kissed my lips.

"You woke up just in time. If you'd slept a few more hours, you would have missed my birthday."

"Today is your birthday?"

"Yep!"

"Happy Birthday," I told her, trying to figure out how many days had gone by but unable to remember when everything had happened. "You're not celebrating in Bear Lake with your family?"

"Well, my family all went there," Kendra admitted, "but I already had my fill." I could feel her fear at the idea of going back to Bear Lake. It mixed with the loneliness of not accompanying her family.

"Thanks for saving me." Kendra glanced at Lexy with thin eyes, then gave me another kiss and pulled away quickly. I felt Lexy's slight hint of jealousy. Unfortunately, once Kendra pulled back, she couldn't hide the revulsion she felt at the sight of me. Should I feel bad that the sight of me repulsed her, or should I feel good that she kissed me despite it? For a second, I wished I'd just died. Except I felt her love pushing past her involuntary revulsion.

"Lexy saved you more than I did." I glanced at Lexy.

Kendra rolled her eyes as jealousy nudged my mind again, but this time from her.

"Eldra's helping our hair to grow back faster," Kendra said, changing the subject. She turned her head back and forth to show me her short boy cut. "It's nice to have eyebrows and lashes again." She raised her eyebrows twice quickly and blinked a few times to demonstrate.

"What is that stone?" I asked Kendra, pointing at an obviously enchanted diamond set in the center of a silver trinity symbol pendant that hung just below her neckline.

"Oh." She softened her eyes, apologetically. "It's a separation stone. Lexy and I both have one."

"What do they do?" I asked, but I didn't have to ask. I'd already guessed.

Kendra looked to Eldra for help, confusion and guilt seeping from her into me.

"Separation stones dim permanent connections," Eldra explained with a sigh. "You broke three separate druid laws, Jacob. You formed a permanent *myndtiegan* with both these girls. I don't know why you did it," Eldra continued with a scolding tone. "By druid law, you must be married to make a *myndtiegan* permanent, and a permanent *myndtiegan* with two girls is . . . well . . . such a *trinity* . . . it is grounds for the Druid Death."

"The Druid Death?" I asked. "You mean if the druids still existed, I'd be tried and killed?"

"No, that isn't what it means!" Eldra snapped, raising her voice. "The word 'death' means separation. The Druid Death is a spell that separates you from magic permanently, and you deserve it, too, for what you've done to these girls."

"What *I've* done?" My voice rose, ignoring my scratchy throat. "Hey, blame yourself. We did what was necessary to stay alive after you and your husband and your nightmare friends tried to kill us, remember?" I didn't react well to being snapped at for something that wasn't exactly my fault, especially by someone who shared the blame.

"Both parties should be willing to form the *myndtiegan*. I don't know how you did it but forcing a permanent *myndtiegan* is akin to . . . rrrrrr!" Eldra growled at me through clenched teeth, not saying the last word.

I knew what word she hadn't said. That word rocked my world. I'd lived with the consequences of that act my whole life. It was how I was conceived and how my mother's life had been ruined. Lexy's grandfather had also done that to her, and the way he had *gifted* her . . . Anger and shame slipped from Lexy into me, disrupting my train of thought, but her emotions were eclipsed by overwhelming sadness from Kendra. Together, their emotions kept me from unleashing a string of swear words at the old hag.

Eldra had no right to accuse me of something so vile.

"Jake," Lexy said calmly. "Do not be vexed at Eldra. The separation stones that Kendra and I are wearing belonged to Eldra and her husband. They wore them for over a hundred and fifty years. She gave them to us because they no longer need them."

"I killed . . ." Kendra faltered, tears dripping down her cheeks, "her husband."

Eldra's eyes burned with hate and she wasn't shy about directing them at Kendra. How had she been joking just seconds ago?

I understood Kendra's tears of remorse. I had killed two men. Sure, they had taken shots at me and my sister, but I killed them all the same. Even worse, I'd wiped out their existence, and that haunted me. But I didn't know them or anyone they knew. I didn't have their wife of a century and a half to answer to. How much more haunted would Kendra be because of Eldra?

"Kendra," I cut in. "*I* killed her husband. You just blasted him again before he had a chance to fall down." Hopefully, that would help her feel better.

Eldra's glare turned toward me, and I felt it as if it were the lightning that she'd shot at me. My comment might have helped Kendra, but it had enraged the old druid.

"Eldra," Lexy spoke and Eldra dropped her hateful gaze. "Just as Jake should not be vexed with you, you should not be vexed with him. Jake had my permission to form the permanent connection."

She totally just lied, I thought, blinking at her. She had tried to pull her mind away from mine when I pushed the permanent connection—the mind-share—on her. I'd acted too quickly to even give her a choice. I *had* done this against her will.

It was the only way, Lexy's thought flashed into my mind. She had her hand at her neck, touching her separation stone. She could disable it with a touch whenever she wanted to share her thoughts with me. How convenient for her.

"He had my permission, too," Kendra added, also lying as she wiped away her tears. She'd been brought along for the ride with no clue what I'd accidentally pulled her into.

Why did their lies increase my guilt? I swallowed.

Kendra and Lexy exchanged a nod. Were they bonding over defending me?

"Besides," Lexy responded, "he is not bound by druid laws. The two of them are not officially druids," she explained, gesturing toward Kendra and me. "That requires a ceremony following years of education, neither of which they have. And as tragic as it is to remind you, the druid society is no more."

Eldra's face wrinkled into a frown. "You're right, sweetheart," Eldra conceded. "Forgive me my anger. I guess I'm just set in my old ways." She grimaced and swallowed away her frown, leaving her aged lips thin and flat.

"Why don't you go check that Mr. Espinoza is still in his room?" Lexy suggested with a tiny fraction of influence in her voice. A hint of pumpkin spice filled the air. Until now, had Alexis made efforts to stifle her influence? Neither Kendra nor Eldra

wore protection stones. Lexy could control them at will, but she didn't. Why?

Influence or not, Lexy's suggestion sounded good to me. I could go for a little less of Darth Wife, even if she hadn't turned to the dark side.

Eldra nodded. "Mr. Espinoza surely needs *a bite* for dinner." Eldra tried to laugh and winked at Lexy.

I gawked at Eldra, confused by how she could switch from joking to anger to hate to sadness and back to joking all in just a few minutes.

Eldra walked to the door, then stopped. She turned to Kendra and me. Her wrinkles tightened and her lips flattened to a line. "If you are to survive, I can teach you to become true druids. We can rebuild the druid order."

Was she offering or asking for help?

Despite my less-than-pleasant first impression, Eldra's presence gave me unexpected hope. I'd assumed she was a traitor, and I was glad I'd been wrong. As amazing as Charles O'Brien had been, when it came to magic, he was a dud. Eldra, however, could teach us.

She glanced at Lexy, then back to us. "This isn't over. Do you know what you are up against?"

CHAPTER 55
CAKE

"**C**an I get dressed now?" I asked, sitting on the bed in my boxers, blanket up to my chest so Kendra and Lexy wouldn't have to stare at my white, scabby skin. Kendra's sadness switched back to revulsion.

The bed frame had been moved out from under the dagger-like chandelier and away from the silver Star of David etched into the floor. Even with the containment turned off, the pattern on the floor creeped me out.

"Can he wear clothes now?" Kendra asked.

"Yes." Alexis nodded. "The servants slipped boxers on him a few hours ago."

"Wait," I glanced from Kendra to Alexis. "I've been naked all this time."

"Well, you did not have enough skin to wear clothing," Alexis replied.

"Sorry," Kendra said with a smile, trying to recover from crying over having killed Eldra's husband.

Lexy handed Kendra some black pants to give me. I slipped the pants over part of my white, road-rash-like legs, then stood to finish pulling them up.

"Eldra said your scars will heal with time and you'll look just as good as when . . . well, you know . . ." Kendra fumbled as her cheeks turned bright red and her embarrassment brushed against my mind.

"Are you referring to when we were fighting bad guys naked?" I smiled at her, which only sustained her flushed cheeks and increased the embarrassment that flowed from her to me.

Lexy gave us both a look that said: "grow up." Her slight pang of jealousy gave her away, though. She didn't want us to grow up as much as she wanted us not to flirt in front of her.

"Your shirt," Lexy interrupted, handing it to Kendra.

She was close enough to hand me the shirt herself. Why'd she give it to Kendra? She'd done the same with the pants. I almost missed a subtle spike of fear in her as she passed my clothing to Kendra.

What's going on with you, Lexy? Why are you afraid of me? I should have voiced my question, but I didn't.

Lexy didn't answer. I took the shirt from Kendra. "Really? Does it always have to be black with you?" I asked Lexy, lamenting the black V-neck.

"Black goes perfectly with my hair. Besides, my red eyes give me all the color I need."

"You don't have to wear my clothes, I do," I reminded her. "My eyes are dark brown. I *need* colors other than black. You should try it, too."

"First, you ask for modesty and now you ask for color. I know how much your eyes enjoy how I dress, Jake." Lexy gave me a flirtatious smile. Fear and flirtation were an interesting mix of emotions rolling off her.

"Uh, um," Kendra cut in. Tension rolled off both of them as they looked at each other.

"How long did I sleep? How long exactly?" I changed the subject, as I slipped on the annoyingly black shirt.

Lexy's fear increased and seeped into me. I wished her mind were still open to me so I didn't have to ask.

"It was Saturday morning, before dawn, when we stopped Mr. Espinoza from draining your girlfriend. It is Tuesday night and well after dusk now. So it was—"

"Almost four days!" I shouted. Ninety hours. "I've never slept that long in my life." My mouth fell open. I sat back down on the bed, my legs tired. I put my head in my hands then let go because the feel of my road-rash-like hands touching my equally road-rash-like face freaked me out. The silver in the floor glinted off the light of the chandelier and caught my attention. I used it to focus.

Assuming a full night's sleep for me was four hours, I'd slept the equivalent of twenty-two nights. Eldra had used magic to help heal me too, and Alexis had lent me the healing stone. No wonder my skin had already grown back.

"The epidermis is the largest organ on your body, and it was severely damaged. You might say that you needed your beauty sleep." Lexy smiled as she said the word *beauty* as if she were mocking me—wait—she was mocking Kendra.

"It's true," Kendra laughed. "Your skin was hideous—"

"It still is," I cut in.

"Well, it was more hideous than it is now. You looked like a zombie, Jake. I . . . uh . . ." Kendra glanced at the floor, too ashamed to tell me the rest.

Lexy glanced at Kendra with a hint of disgust. "Your girlfriend has been unable to keep her food down at the sight of you," Lexy finished for her.

"My girlfriend, huh?" I said to Lexy.

I didn't like Lexy's attitude. That was the second time she'd called Kendra my girlfriend, and I didn't think it was by accident. "If she's my girlfriend, I'm confused. What does that make you?" I noticed the hint of pain in Lexy's red eyes.

She misread my look as a challenge, met it with defiance, and smiled back. Kendra looked down. The hurt Kendra felt at my question kicked me in the gut despite being dimmed.

"Kendra," I said. "I . . ." What was I supposed to say? I didn't feel any differently about her. I just had feelings for Lexy too. I clamped my mouth shut, not daring to speak for fear of saying the wrong thing.

"I know," Kendra cut in. "We know everything about each other. You, me, her." She pointed at each of us. "Eldra told me all about the *myndtíegan*. It is a permanent mind share, Jacob. The three of us will be sharing each other's thoughts for the rest of our lives, and we are supposed to live for two hundred years."

Forcing a permanent myndtíegan is akin to . . . Eldra's cutoff phrase came back to me. I told myself that I'd saved their lives and tried to push the thought aside, refusing to believe I was capable of that. But I'd made a choice that wasn't mine to make. All three of us would live with my choice for the rest of our extra-long lives.

"I'm sorry," I told both of them. "I understand that—"

"You don't understand, Jacob," Kendra cut me off.

"It is true, Jacob," Lexy chimed in. "You do not understand. You are a man with two *women* connected to you. Kendra and I are connected as well. You will never know what it is like to be forced to share our thoughts and feelings with each other."

"When are you planning to choose between us, Jake?" Kendra asked.

"Kendra!" Lexy snapped.

Oh, crap!

I hadn't thought of it like that. Now that I had to face it, the need to choose seemed obvious. Why did I need to choose now?

"I'm seventeen—at least for another week or so. You're just eighteen, Lexy, and Kendra . . . well, you are only fifteen."

"Hey, I'm sixteen," Kendra jumped back in defensively. "It's my birthday today. Like, right now! Did you forget already?"

I ignored her. Why did this decision feel impossibly complicated? Harder than fighting the Vampire King.

"I plan on being a teenager for at least two more years and then, well, I don't know."

"What are Lexy and I supposed to do for the next two years, share you?" Kendra asked.

"Kendra," Lexy said calmly. "We talked about this. It is more complex than that. He cannot simply choose—"

The door opened, and the young, auburn-haired servant walked in with food. Luiz and his dad followed them in. Had they been outside the door eavesdropping?

Thank all! I thought, relieved for the interruption and stomach aching for the food. It was steak. Two of them. Each had to be at least sixteen ounces and both rested on a pile of vegetables that rivaled the skillet meals they had made for me on multiple mornings. The servant brought the food to my bed.

"I'm starving. I haven't eaten since . . . well, since the pizza the other night." I felt weak, and I looked it. I had lost a lot of muscle. I had weighed over two hundred pounds just the other day and my skinny, road-rash-covered body couldn't be more than one hundred and sixty now. "Excuse me, what is your name?" I asked the young servant.

She glanced at Lexy and waited for her to nod before answering.

"Carolyn. My name is Carolyn," she answered.

"Carolyn," I repeated her name. "You women do an amazing job."

"Yes, Protector." She said the words like a title and nodded.

Protector. Whatever it meant, the word added fire to Lexy's fear of me.

Lexy scowled at her servant. Carolyn absorbed Lexy's silent reprimand and hurried out of the room.

Luiz and his dad stepped closer, Mr. Espinoza hesitant.

"Jacob, I apologize for breaking your arm," Mr. Espinoza told me with his thick Spanish accent.

His red eyes reminded me that he had turned.

"Don't worry about it. It's already better." I lifted my arm to show him. "Ignore the ugly skin. I did that myself. I got sick of being so good looking," I tried to joke.

I looked up at the faces in front of me. They didn't laugh. Both Kendra and Lexy still had hard faces with pursed lips. Luiz and his father just stood there as if looking for something to do.

"Did you all already eat?" I asked, but all three servants came in carrying a huge three-tiered cake covered in white buttercream and outlined with gold-colored frosting.

Kendra saw the cake, glanced at me, then sighed. She forced a smile.

"Oh, we have cake too." Kendra clapped her hands. Her smile didn't reach her eyes until the sixteen burning candles were close enough to mesmerize her like a vampire's allure. "It's the most beautiful birthday cake ever."

The thought of cake lightened her mood, and mine with it. I watched her smile. With her short, boy-cut hair, her eyes and the soft shape of her cheeks seemed so much more pronounced. How long had it been since I kissed her at Kevin's house? So much had changed since then.

Lexy's short hair made her strong cheekbones and red eyes stand out more sharply.

"Jake, do you want some cake?" Kendra asked. Her eyes betrayed her smile, which tried to hide the frustration she still felt toward me.

"I'll take some cake," I smiled back at her.

"Happy birthday to you . . ." I started to sing, and everyone except Lexy joined in on the second line.

Lexy's phone vibrated, and she pulled it from a leather clip on her hip and looked at the number. Worry rolled into my mind. She answered and listened for a few seconds. Then she reached up and tapped her separation stone. Our minds became one again. I wanted to ask her why she was afraid of me. Instead, I focused on her phone conversation.

". . . then he will want to meet you somewhere unpleasant tomorrow night." I heard Carina's voice through Lexy as I continued to sing "Happy Birthday" to Kendra. "Don't expect him to be alone. You must take your two new Generals. Yes, even Jacob. I trust he can at least walk by now."

"Yes," Alexis answered.

"Good. Reports say he is going to issue you a Blood Rule Challenge. Kill him or he will kill you. Unless," Carina paused. "Another report suggests he'll take a more complicated tactic."

I didn't need to ask whom Carina was talking about because images of Keagan flooded Lexy's mind along with a list of emotions, primarily hate, but strangely accompanied by love, empathy, and gratitude. Keagan and Lexy had a far more complicated history.

I tried to keep smiling as we finished singing. Lexy was aware that other thoughts were escaping her mind as she spoke with her mother, but chose to let them.

First, I saw my face through her eyes. Chills ran up my back, and I couldn't push away the fear that I'd look like this forever.

Second, I heard a question. *Should I ask my mom how I am going to survive being in love with a Protector?* I really wanted to know what a Protector was, but I didn't dare just ask around. Carina thought that if anyone found out, nothing would slow the legions that would hunt me. Except that wasn't what scared me. What scared me was that me being a Protector scared Alexis.

Her next thought grabbed my attention completely. It was about my mom. The nightwalkers had killed my stepdad. Mom had been arrested and charged for his murder. My choice. My fault.

Lexy wanted to tap off her separation stone, but Carina had one more message.

"We were not the only ones sent after Caradoc. There are two other groups. They'll be after you now."

The phone went dead.

I swallowed.

Kendra noticed, but tried to ignore it as everyone waited for her to blow out the candles.

Keagan was coming for Alexis. My mom was in jail. Two more groups were hunting Caradoc—now us.

I was a Protector, which scared Alexis. I guess that meant I was supposed to protect everyone. I could barely get out of bed.

Luiz handed me a slice of cake. I faked a smile and cut a bite with my fork.

Kendra's eyes were on me.

I forced out the words.

"Happy birthday, Kendra."

THE END

THANK YOU

You make it possible for me to write. Without you, my books are just words. With you, the characters and their world come to life. I hope you enjoyed this book and found it as fun and exciting to read as it was to write.

You'll know that you liked this book if you can answer yes to at least one of these questions.

- Are you excited to read the next book?
- Are you excited to tell someone about this book?
- Did this book keep you up at night reading?
- Were you anxious to get back to reading it?
- Did you enjoy the characters and the world?

If you answered yes to one of the above questions, a quick review on Amazon or Goodreads would mean a lot and help other readers find the book.

Breaking Glass, Book 2 of Trinity of Mind, is available now. Visit https://jabrambarneck.com for purchase details, or keep turning the pages to read the first chapter.

SPECIAL THANKS

I am not sure that I could possibly thank my wife, Michelle, enough. She has had to put up with me while I've been working full-time, earning my Master of Computer Science, and writing a novel, all at the same time.

I would like to thank Sarah Bylund for her excellent editing job. She helped knock off a lot of rough edges in my book. I appreciate her feedback even when some of it was tough to hear.

My proofreaders have been great. My first proofreader, my wife, is amazing. She took the time to read this novel out loud to me, and we fixed so many errors that way. Other proofreaders include Jaime Allred (my wonderful sister), Heidi Elder, LaRae Roberts, Andrew Roberts, Josh Weekes, Trisha Packer, Mark Minson, Ryan Gardner, Greg Westbrook, Paul Price, Janet Hamilton, Robert Matthews, and Vernie Chapoose.

LaRae Roberts, also my wonderful photographer, provided me with the amazing skyline of Salt Lake City at dusk for my cover.

I'd also like to thank David Wolverton for everything he taught me in my creative writing class. He always seems to motivate me and the daily writing tips he sends are a great help.

I'd like to thank Mrs. Orton, my English teacher in my senior year of high school. Despite being primarily a dance instructor, she was the best high school English teacher I ever had. Without her, I may have never studied creative writing in college.

I'd like to thank all my friends who came to Leading Edge with me from 2002 to 2004. Reading slush and trying to find that one good short story really helped teach me the importance of quality writing. The people there, like Chris and Kris Kugler, Jillena (O'Brien) Peters and Catherine (Verhaaren) Gruver made Leading Edge one of my favorite college experiences—even better than going to college football games.

I'd like to thank my favorite authors who have inspired me. Terry Brooks, Dean Koontz, David Eddings, J. R. R. Tolkien, Jim Butcher, and so many more.

I can't forget the roommates I had during my college years. Nate and Mike taught me humor, a much-needed skill in my life.

Oh. Did I mention how wonderful my wife is?

Thank you all,

J. Abram Barneck

ABOUT THE AUTHOR

J. Abram Barneck lives with his wife and kids in West Jordan, Utah. He has been writing science fiction and fantasy since he was sixteen. He grew up next to a creek with land to run on. He also grew up with a computer to game on.

He graduated from Brigham Young University with a degree in English and an emphasis in Creative Writing. He also completed a Master of Computer Science through Utah State University.

At BYU, he took the Science Fiction and Fantasy creative writing course taught by David Wolverton (David Farland). He also participated with Leading Edge Magazine for almost three years where he became the Assistant Fiction Director.

He currently works full-time as a Principal Software Engineer while continuing to write science fiction and fantasy.

For a more complete bio, please take a moment to visit his website at: http://jabrambarneck.com/about

BREAKING GLASS

TRINITY OF MIND
BOOK 2

WRITTEN BY
J. ABRAM BARNECK

CHAPTER 1
CLEAN DIRT

Eldra is forcing us to write a journal about how the Trinity of Mind affects us. She warned us that sharing thoughts at our age could get awkward and embarrassing quickly. First, it got old. Quickly. Kendra misses drill team. Again. Alexis is trying to clear her mind and hiding thoughts from us. Again. Now, the awkward and embarrassing topics arrive unexpectedly. There is so much in a girl's mind that a guy should never know. I know them now. -Jake

The car lurched to a stop, and I snapped awake. I couldn't believe I'd fallen asleep in the car despite Lexy's fast driving. Usually, I needed very little sleep. Growing back most of my epidermis sapped my energy.

I glanced toward Lexy, catching her lithe, leather-clad form exiting the car with angelic grace. I unbuckled, opened the passenger door, and nearly tripped and fell on my face. But I clung to the door and my dignity, barely staying on my feet. I was no longer the athlete I once was. Kendra snickered behind me. OK, maybe I hadn't clung to my dignity.

North Salt Lake stayed plenty warm in August, but late at night, the air reached a comfortable, cool temperature, which did nothing to hide the stench of the nearby oil refineries.

The cheap burner phone that Mr. Espinoza had lent me rang as I swung the door closed. I answered, ignoring the mental reprimand from Alexis. It was Sis. I had to answer. Kendra approved, so, two against one.

"Hey, Sis." I hoped to hear her tell me all about her days at Disneyland with Dylan. Any trip that alliterated so well had to have been magical. I needed some good news.

No such luck.

"Jake," Sis's voice sobbed through the phone. "Those . . . people. The ones who tried to kill us," Sis sniffled. "They murdered John. The police think Mom did it. They think she might have been involved in," another sob, "in your murder, too."

"I know," I felt a pang of guilt. A few days ago, I had made the difficult choice to rush after my sister and leave my stepfather unprotected. I'd make the same choice again, but that didn't absolve my guilt.

I glanced at Lexy and Kendra, who waited impatiently beneath a dim, bug-infested porch light. Neon signs glowed across the front of the building, one shaped like a pinup girl, while bass thumped from inside.

Sis and Dylan were the only two *uninvolved* people who knew that O'Brien had faked my death.

I wished Luiz hadn't told Dylan and Justine that it was safe to come back. They could have stayed at Disneyland for a few more days.

"You have to tell them, Jake," Sis pleaded. "You . . ." her voice caught. Being my sister, I'd seen her chin quiver often enough to know it quivered now.

I really wanted to help. I wanted to tell someone that Mom was innocent. Unfortunately, it was two in the morning, and there was nothing I could do at this hour. Even if it were daytime, I was supposedly dead. If I revealed that I was alive, I could become a target again. That could endanger Sis. Even if I took that chance, what could I say? That three nightwalkers and two druids killed my stepdad, John. Neither the cops nor the judge would believe the truth.

"Justine, I can't." I pressed my knuckles against my head as I squeezed the phone. "We can't tell anyone. Everyone needs to keep believing that I'm dead. If you say different, people will think you're crazy."

Lexy tapped her separation stone, and her mind joined mine. She wore a necklace with two pendants. The first, a pear-shaped black diamond pendant, was enchanted to be both a healing and a protection stone—spells Lexy and I had cast on the stone together. The second pendant, a two-carat diamond enchanted as a separation stone, sat in the center of a silver trinity symbol.

Tell her that I have already called a lawyer, she thought to me. *He will be here tomorrow.*

She tapped the separation stone again, cutting off her thoughts. I also heard a few other thoughts before she tapped off our connection—thoughts such as, *Keagan is waiting,* and, *Hurry, Jake. This is neither the time nor the place.* Other memories slipped out, ones that I'm sure she would have preferred to keep secret. It wasn't by her choice, but at only eighteen, Lexy was no stranger to the type of dancing that went on inside this building. Keagan's desire to kill Lexy provided me with something to distract my mind from such thoughts. Keagan hungered for power.

"Sis, it will be OK." I tried to assure her. "I have a rich friend. She has a lawyer coming to help Mom tomorrow. You'll be fine staying at Kendra's house tonight, right?" I asked. At Kendra's request, her parents had left their Bear Lake trip early to come home and take care of Justine.

"Kendra's not here, Jake. Do you know where she is?"

I glanced over at Kendra, who stood right next to me. She also wore a necklace with a protection stone and a separation stone, though both were mounted on one pendant. Her separation stone, a trinity symbol with a two-carat diamond in the center, differed from Lexy's only in the diamond's cut. Lexy's was princess cut while Kendra's was Asscher cut. For Kendra's protection stone, Eldra had enchanted a small Burmese ruby, Kendra's birthstone, and mounted it to the top arch of the silver trinity symbol pendant. In crystal lore, a ruby represents emotion, and Kendra excelled at emotional magic. I had a hunch that Eldra had enchanted that stone with more than just the protection spell.

"Yes, she's fine," I said, trying to avoid lying to my sister. Inside the building, the music had switched. Hopefully, Sis couldn't hear the muffled thumping of the increased bass. "Sis, I gotta go. Don't tell anyone that I'm alive, and don't mention anything weird to anyone, OK?" I hung up, not giving Sis time to argue.

Kendra didn't give me any time to shift from talk-to-sister mode to daunting-meeting-with-Keagan mode. She stepped forward under the yellow porch light, which accentuated her short, golden brown hair, and pressed a button on a card reader next to the metal door. The faint sound of a buzzer fought its way to our ears over the muffled music.

My skin, white as an albino where it didn't appear road rashed, must have looked hideous while reflecting the yellow porch light. I pulled my hoodie on and tightened it to hide my face. My skin's lack of healing left me disappointed. I looked exactly the same as when I had woken Tuesday night. It had only been twenty-eight hours since I had woken, but I had slept three more times, so I expected some progress. The healing progress had stalled. What if my skin had finished healing and the result of the damage I'd done to my deeper layers of skin had caused it to heal hideously? What if I was going to be a road rashed albino forever?

Lexy shifted her stance and elevated her chin, her long neck somehow making her more royal. She knew exactly how to own her new title as Princess of the New World.

"Positions!" she ordered verbally, with a pronounced, regal tone.

As her newly dubbed generals, Kendra and I had to maintain formal positions. Kendra stood to her front and I stood just at her rear—which, by the way, gave me the better view. Yes, Lexy wore her usual tight leather pants and bustier that left her ribbon-bow tattoo exposed on her lower back. Being a few inches shorter than Lexy and drill-team thin, Kendra wore borrowed leather pants that didn't stretch around her backside like Lexy's did. They hung loose, allowing for bunching below her pockets and at the back of her knees.

They both disabled their separation stones and our three minds became one, while my eyes still focused on their lower curves.

Oops. They caught me looking.

Seriously? Kendra didn't turn back and glare at me because she didn't have to. Her mind scolded me with both her thoughts and feelings. That didn't make much sense to me because just over a week ago, she had worn a white, string bikini with every intention of me noticing. I didn't get how she didn't want me to notice her now when she was dressed far more modestly.

Things are different now! Kendra answered my thought.

I caught a hint of guilt from her as she remembered wearing a bikini for me.

You tempted me to wear it! she accused.

Great, now she blamed me for breaking her usual modesty standards.

I didn't ask you to wear it, I reminded her.

Focus! Princess Alexis ordered, half her mind on Keagan and the other half fixated on my memory of Kendra in her white bikini juxtaposed against her own memory of Kendra demanding to wear a modest leather outfit. She formed a single thought: *Hypocrite.*

The metal door opened halfway, letting out the beating music and cutting off Kendra's mental protest. Lexy breathed in a thousand different scents from inside while ignoring the oil-refinery stench in the outside air.

I'd imagined the door would be opened by a six-foot-six bouncer with a metal chain hanging from his front pocket to his wallet, or maybe some thick-necked bodyguard with a gun on his hip. Instead, a short, white guy in slacks and a white, button-up shirt stepped into the half-open doorway. He didn't even look creepy. He looked completely normal. In fact, he looked like he'd just stepped out of church, tie removed and top button undone. He stood in front of a hallway with doors on the sides.

Lexy picked out the guy's thoughts. His brain consisted of only simple, all-business thoughts. We were as young as he'd been told we would be, but he'd been ordered to ignore that. Honestly, I felt the same way. We were young and had no business going into such an establishment, but we were also ignoring that.

"Welcome to Club Exposed." The man smiled. "Mr. K is inside." He opened the door the rest of the way, stepped aside, and gestured with his white-sleeved arm for us to enter.

"Welcome to Club Exposed." The man smiled. "Mr. K is inside." He opened the door the rest of the way, stepped aside, and gestured with his white-sleeved arm for us to enter.

Two Salt Lake City Mormons and a vampire—Half-dhampir, Lexy interjected—*walk into a strip club. What's a good punch line?*

We get caught, answered Kendra.